ISBN: 978-1-7346184-2-6

ALL DOWN
BUT
NINE

LINGUA MAGIKA BOOK 2

KAT ROSS

1
———

LOOKING BACK, I should have seen it coming.

Maybe not the particulars, but the general calamity. Things had been quiet for five days and my luck don't run like that — at least it hadn't lately.

But it was too hot to think straight. Cracking the windows didn't help. The air that blew inside sucked the intention right out of a body. Not a scrap of cloud broke the washed-out sky. And the view sliding past looked like an Old Testament version of Hell.

I might have muttered something along those lines because the shadow across from me stirred.

"I don't suppose they taught you geology at that coldwater shack of a schoolhouse?" Doc asked.

"Nope," I said.

"Sad excuse for an education." The grim sighed. "Do you know what those rock formations are called?"

I glanced out the window. "Badlands."

"That's the colloquial term," Doc drawled, warming to his subject. "Now, how do you think they were formed, Ruth?"

"Don't know." I slid lower in the seat and dropped my sunglasses down. "Don't care, neither."

The deck of playing cards between us rose into the air and started shuffling. He'd tried to teach me the dovetail riffle with a waterfall flourish, where the cards zip from one hand to the other, but I'd never mastered it. Doc claimed he'd been a gambler once. That might be true, but I figured he wasn't a very good one because he'd lost a bet and got himself stuck in my gun.

"Well, that's a poor attitude," Doc remarked.

I didn't answer.

"Wind and water," Doc said. "The scientific term is *e-ro-sion*." He started rambling about hoodoos and some other words I didn't know. The lecture went on for a while, punctuated by the cards shuffling. It's hard to say which was more irritating.

Sebastian Hardin, my boss for this thankless manhunt, was up front with the engineer. I didn't know where Marshals Tanaka and Hodges were. Observation car, most likely. They kept their distance. Maybe because I was a hick deputy and they were Special Services. Or maybe because they didn't trust Doc. He'd trashed the lobby of Carnarvon Tower hardly a week before. For all I knew, they'd been part of the posse shooting at us from the upper floors when we made our getaway.

"Are you listening, Ruth?" he asked in a plaintive tone.

I felt Doc staring even though he had no body to speak of. "Yeah," I muttered, not opening my eyes behind the dark glasses.

It's a funny thing when you get what you wish for.

When I first found Doc in the ruins of a town called Three Bars, living inside an old flintlock revolver, I thought we might grow to be friends. Share secrets and whatnot. A person and a phantom living in harmony. But for the first seven years he barely spoke a word, and when he did it wasn't civil.

Now Doc never shut up and I just wished he'd be quiet for a spell.

"Let's play some cards," he said.

I cracked an eye. "You cheat."

His shadow quivered. "That's a low accusation."

"I don't hear you denying it."

Doc scoffed, but I knew he cheated. It's how come no one, not even the cheerful young cook Ned Carver, would play with him anymore.

"You have no finesse, Ruth. Poker requires the ability to lie with a straight face. You're too honest. I can see straight through—"

"The cards," I interrupted. "That's the problem."

He laughed. "Maybe I do cheat. Not that I need to, I'd beat you anyway."

I shook my head. "Why don't you be of use, Doc? Tell me something worthwhile."

The cards stopped shuffling. His voice turned snappish. "I try to broaden your horizons, Ruth, but you have such *limited interests.*"

That got me. I sat up straight. "You mean like what you really are? And how come you're different from the other phantoms?"

Doc didn't answer. He never did when it was something I wanted to know.

"Or how about what my dad found out that got him thrown out of the linguist academy? How about that?"

Doc sounded stiff. "Go ask Gael yourself."

"Why can't you just tell me?"

"You wouldn't understand."

Maybe it was the heat, or the tedium, or the fact that I'd started seriously questioning what I was doing on this train, but my patience gave out. I slapped a palm on the table.

"Just try!" I shouted.

There was a long silence. "If you'd ever been to a picture show, I might be able to explain it," Doc muttered. "But you're such a hayseed."

Picture show? That threw me for a loop.

"What do you know about picture shows?" I demanded. "And what do they have to do with—"

The cards flew every which way. I watched the queen of spades sail out the window.

"There goes the Old Maid," I muttered. "Maybe I should have left you with Calindra."

"Maybe you should have," Doc snarled.

Calindra Carnarvon was the founder of Carnarvon Lines. She owned the railroad and pretty much everything else. She'd wanted to keep Doc in her desk drawer and I'd talked her out of it. Instead of being grateful, he was worse than ever.

"Don't you care that a Class X phantom is after Lee Merriweather? If you'd tell me what you know, maybe we could figure out why. And how to stop him."

"We've been over this, Ruth. I don't know."

"Why is Roger working with the Reverend Jolly?"

"Not a clue." The reply came a bit too quick.

"Well, I think you're lying." I crossed my arms. "After all I've done for you—"

Doc hooted. "Done for me? I think it's the other way around. Next time I've half a mind to leave you high and dry, Ruth. You might own that gun, but you don't own me. And I'm tired of getting no respect around here." He flitted to the opposite table, a thick puddle of darkness. "My mother warned me—" Doc cut off.

"You have a mother?" I asked in surprise.

"Everything has a mother! But you act like I'm some kind of monster. Or worse, a dumb beast of burden, here to fulfill your every command—"

The tirade continued. I stared at the cards scattered across the table, trying to summon the energy to clean up the mess. It was all a distraction. He'd done it on purpose to steer the conversation away from Roger.

The Reverend Jolly called him Legion and the pair of them seemed to be in cahoots. Roger was a Class X, the most powerful kind of phantom. According to Doc, it was Roger who'd bound him to the gun. They were old enemies.

The thing is, I didn't even know what Doc really was. No one did — not even the experts at the Distinguished Academy of Phantom Linguistics and Related Disciplines in Carnarvon City.

Sometimes the grims came in the flesh. Other times they appeared as shadows. They could move things without touching them, and they could see through solid objects — like the playing cards.

Doc was a phantom, but he did things his own way. For starters, he only spoke English while the others communicated in dozens of grim tongues. A person who mastered one or two was called a linguist, and those who spoke five were polyglots. Rarest of all were savants, who spoke every phantom language fluently. I only knew of three: Calindra Carnarvon, Pedro Braga and Lee Merriweather.

Lee was the reason I was on a southbound train sweating through my shirt and getting told off by a cranky grim instead of sitting by the wood stove reading a dime novel.

I was just a sheriff's deputy. Merriweather shouldn't be my problem. But a series of unlikely events had led me to Carnarvon City and into Calindra's clutches. I'd made a rash promise to help Hardin catch Lee before I went home.

"Let's talk about the picture show," I said to Doc in a friendlier tone. "What's the comparison?"

"Oh, now you're interested?"

"Course I am."

His shadow drifted back and forth, as though he were pacing. "Well, too bad. I'm not allowed to talk about it."

"Says who?"

"None of your beeswax."

"I thought we were friends."

"We are." His voice took on the condescending edge I knew well. "But I'm afraid your little mind cannot comprehend the mysteries of my existence."

I frowned. "You just said you could explain—"

Doc gave an unpleasant laugh. "Trust me, Ruth, you don't want to know the truth. It would burst the bubble of safety and contentment you live in. The blissful ignorance! The truth is not flattering. Not at all."

"Not flattering to who?" I wondered.

"Your pitiful species."

I scowled. "That's a rotten thing to say."

"You're right. I'm sorry." He sailed up to the ceiling and hung there. "Pitiful was a poor choice. Let's amend it to primitive."

"Know what I think?" I said.

"Enlighten me."

"I think you're scared. You boast and brag, but deep down you know you're no match for that Class X."

"Don't be ridiculous," he growled.

"Then tell me about Roger. What's he after?"

There was a sullen silence. "He's just having fun, Ruth."

"You call this fun?"

"I didn't say *I* found it fun. I said *he* does."

"Do you know where he is now?"

"I do not."

"Is there anything you *can* tell me?"

"Yes. Stop asking so many questions!"

"You'd do the same if you were me."

"I could get in big trouble for what I've already said."

"Trouble with who? Roger?"

Doc stayed stubbornly silent.

"Seems to me you're already in trouble," I remarked.

"What does *that* mean?"

"I mean you're stuck in the flintlock. Maybe I can help you—"

"You can't help. No one can. And it's bad enough without you accusing me of lying and hounding me to tell you things you won't even understand. There are mysteries in this world, Ruth, mysteries that shall forever remain … mysterious!"

"What? You're not even making sense now."

"Do you think I *like* my situation? It's the Lady or the Tiger. I'm damned whatever I do. But you can't appreciate that—"

Doc was pretty wound up. I let him go on for a while, watching the desert slide past and wondering if I shouldn't just throw the revolver out the window.

"No wonder Roger locked you up," I remarked, blotting my forehead with a sleeve. "He probably wanted some peace."

Doc's shadow vanished. I figured he'd gone into the ether to sulk.

Every time I tried to make him talk, he threw a temper tantrum. It felt staged. Doc was covering up, but I didn't know why and that troubled me. So much depended on the phantoms and we didn't even know if they were dead or alive.

The train was only chugging along because grims were stoking the engine. Lee's teacher, Abel Beach, said they had free will. That the linguists persuaded them to help and the phantoms liked the sound of a human voice. Doc wasn't like that at all. He did whatever he pleased, and not even a savant like Lee Merriweather could influence him. So what hope did I have?

I stared out the window. The land was carved into spires of red rock that looked like some ancient, dead city.

"Are those the hoodoos?" I asked, trying to draw Doc out again.

It didn't work. He knew my tricks, just like I knew his.

I tipped the chair back, wondering for the hundredth time how long this manhunt would take. Lee had a day's head start, plus he was traveling by zeppelin. He was probably in Aguadulce by now. I prayed he wouldn't stir up so much trouble he got himself arrested, because if Pedro Braga figured out Lee was a savant, he wouldn't give him up lightly.

Back home, the first snow would be coming soon. I missed Sheriff Bowdre and his son Charlie. I missed my neighbors. Most were elderly and needed a hand to get by, especially over the winter. I'd meant to go home after my misadventures in Carnarvon City, but in the end I made a deal with Mrs. Carnarvon. She'd help out Lucky Boy with a trainload of necessities and I'd help Marshal Hardin hunt down Lee Merriweather.

So the quicker we caught him, the quicker I could get home to my dad, who I missed most of all. He'd studied the phantoms before Calindra exiled him to the middle of the frontier. I wished I'd asked more questions. Maybe I wouldn't be so clueless now.

Picture shows.

Now what had Doc meant by that?

I was about to swallow my pride and try an apology when the door opened at the end of the car and Sebastian Hardin stepped through. I sat up, the chair legs thunking down on the floor, and took my glasses off.

For a man from the Northern Territory, Hardin didn't seem to mind the heat. His navy blue Special Services coat was buttoned to the top, with the insignia of Carnarvon Lines, C & L, intertwined in gold thread on the left shoulder.

Hardin didn't suffer hats. His black hair was side-parted and slicked down. He carried a Colt Walker in a shoulder rig hidden under the coat. His face was clean-shaven. The most striking thing about him was his blue eyes, which could be ice-cold or throwing darts, depending on his mood.

"Marshal," I said, standing.

Hardin's gaze took in the cards Doc had thrown all over the place. "Don't tell me you finally won a hand," he said dryly.

"Wasn't even playing," I said.

"What'd you say?"

"Just tried again to see what he knew. As usual, he got mad."

Hardin walked over and leaned a palm on the table. "We're coming up on the border," he said.

So we'd crossed the no man's land between Carnarvon and Braga Territory. That was good news.

"What happens next?" I asked.

"They'll be expecting us at the checkpoint. It won't take long."

"Okay, sir." It wasn't the border I'd been worrying about. "We still stopping in New Jerusalem?"

The Reverend Jolly's church was there. I'd seen it on a flyer. It was called the Church of the Glorious Lamb of God.

Hardin nodded. "It's not much out of the way. I doubt we'll find him, but there might be someone knows where he's gone. Maybe even who he's working for."

"Makes sense."

Hardin cleared his throat. "I was thinking, deputy. Better if I just take Hodges and Tanaka. You can wait on the train."

I met his eye. I wasn't eager to tangle with the Reverend Jolly again. His adopted son had almost killed me and the two days I'd spent as their prisoner still gave me nightmares.

"Whatever you decide, sir," I said, lighter of heart.

Hardin gave a satisfied nod. He glanced around and lowered his voice. "So where'd your haint go?"

I shrugged. "Into the ether."

"Think he'll stay there for a while?" Hardin sounded hopeful. He trusted Doc even less than I did.

I nodded. "He was pretty sore."

"Because we don't need any trouble at the border." Hardin gave me a pointed look.

"Doc won't make trouble." I rested my hand on the Collier's walnut grip. "Long as they don't touch my gun."

Hardin sighed. We both remembered what had happened

the last time marshals tried to take the flintlock. Doc went crazy. It was a miracle he didn't kill anyone.

"Just stay onboard," Hardin said. "They won't search the train. Not when it's me personally."

I thought of the arsenal he had stashed in the caboose. "You sure about that, sir?"

He flashed a quick grin. "I got diplomatic immunity, Cortez."

Officially, Hardin was heading to Aguadulce to deliver contracts to Pedro Braga for a railroad expansion project with the Carnarvons. He must have seen the worry in my eyes because his smile died. "Everything's gonna be fine. I know it's been a long trip, but the worst is behind us now."

I tried not to look dubious. "If you say so, sir."

His gaze held mine for a moment, then flicked away. He had a lean face that rarely showed emotion. Not that Hardin was cold-natured — just hard to rattle. Now I got the feeling I'd wounded him in some way. Or annoyed him. It was hard to tell the difference.

Hardin was more than competent. He kept his head, even when everything went sideways. Having met Calindra Carnarvon, I knew she'd never appoint a man she didn't have total faith in.

Special Services was the most elite cadre of the marshals, tasked with protecting the railway from sabotage and robbery. As chief of Special Services, Hardin was Calindra's right hand. He'd been tracking Lee since the kid stole a train and ran up to the Northern Territory. Hardin would never stop until Merriweather was dead or in handcuffs, and I wasn't sure the marshal cared which it was.

But I did. It wasn't right to put Lee down like a rabid dog, no matter what Mrs. Carnarvon wanted.

I started collecting the cards. "I'm sure you're right. Guess I'm just a bit on edge."

"Understandable, deputy. We all are." Hardin leaned down and scooped some cards from the floor. "At least we didn't get blown off the tracks this time."

"There's that," I agreed with a smile.

Hardin slid the cards my way. "Just sit tight. We'll be across in a jiffy."

I watched him stride off without a backward glance. Considering we'd spent the last week stuck on a train four cars long plus a water tank, I hadn't seen much of him. I fact, I'd gotten the distinct impression he was avoiding my company, which irked me since it had been Hardin who'd talked me into coming in the first place. I'd refused to give up my copper star for the marshal uniform, which didn't earn me any goodwill, but I hadn't thought Hardin was petty enough to hold a grudge about it.

Well, he had his loyalties and I had mine.

But something seemed to be eating at him. I figured that something was Lee Merriweather. Hardin had lost him twice now. And in a few minutes, he wouldn't have the jurisdiction to chase a loose chicken, let alone a fugitive savant. If Lee asked for Braga's protection, there wasn't much Hardin could do about it.

The train started to slow. The badlands had flattened into hardpan. I saw a shallow, muddy river with a trestle up ahead. The Rio Hondo. On the map, it marked the formal boundary between Carnarvon and Braga territory, though in reality the area on both sides was no man's land for a few hundred miles.

A few scrawny shrubs grew along the edges of the river, mesquite and saltbush. They were the only green things in sight. On the near side of the river there was a wooden building with a tin roof. Sunlight glinted off a vehicle parked around back. It had big wheels and a metal cage on top.

I'd driven in a motor car once with Ava Carnarvon. Hers was fancy, all shining chrome and butter-soft leather. This one wasn't made for comfort, but those big wheels made sense for rough terrain.

As the train approached, two men in brown uniforms came out of the building. The Guardia Territorial, known as Las Gorras because of their caps.

Pedro Braga's law and order.

Their beige short-sleeved shirts were pressed, trousers tucked into knee-high shiny black boots. They looked sober and efficient, which made me relax a little. One of the men held up a hand and the train rolled to a stop. Weeds grew in the shade around the building, along with some stacked two-by-fours and rusted tin sheeting near a water pump. Just the kind of dark, cozy spots rattlesnakes liked to sleep in.

I felt glad Hardin wasn't making me get off the train.

I watched him walk down the steps, followed by Hodges and Tanaka. Hodges was tall and lanky, with a mustache that drooped down the sides of his mouth. Tanaka was smaller, with an air of alertness. She kept her black hair in a shoulder-length bob with a fringe that sliced across her eyes. Hardin was the only one not wearing a hat. He squinted in the midday sun, then followed the border guards inside the building.

I rubbed sweaty palms down my pant legs. Waves of heat rose from the dust. It had to be a boring job sitting in that shack all day. I wondered how many trains came through. The border was eight hundred miles long, most of it unpatrolled and lawless.

I polished the glasses on my shirt. When I looked up, I saw a face through the window of the building, pressed against the panes. The features were blurry, but I had the impression of a girl. Barely tall enough to clear the sill.

My gut tightened. It couldn't be a child. Not out here.

Hardin hadn't said anything about phantoms, but it made sense. The border guards would be prepared for anything. At least one would be a linguist — maybe all.

So I wasn't too worried until the first shots went off. Four quick bangs, a shout that sounded like Hardin, and then silence.

2

I DROPPED to a crouch below the train window, heart hammering.

"Doc?" I whispered. "You there?"

Everything was quiet. Then I heard another shot and a woman's scream, cut short like someone had clamped a hand over her mouth. I risked a peek outside. The wooden building sat twenty yards off. The phantom was gone from the window. I couldn't see much inside.

I slid my gun from the holster and started crawling up the center aisle of the dining car toward the engineer's cab. Maybe his grims could be persuaded to do something to help.

The best case was that the marshals had done the shooting, but I didn't think that's what happened. The scream sounded like Tanaka.

I reached the small galley, still on hands and knees. The space was cluttered but organized. Pots and pans hung from hooks. A stove with three burners sat against one wall, next to an ice box and sink with a tap for running water. The opposite side was taken up by cabinets and a counter with more shelving beneath. A cloth-covered bowl with dough rising for biscuits sat on the counter.

Ned Carver crouched with his back against the counter. He wore a spotless white apron over a red-and-blue checked shirt and dungarees. A half-chopped onion sat on a butcher block. The knife was in his hand.

Mr. Carver was a handsome fellow, with a cleft chin, square jaw, and lively brown eyes. He had thick kinky hair, though I'd only seen it once because he always wore a stylish brown felt derby. He liked to tell stories about all the places he'd been, and usually had a smile and a wink. Now he just looked scared.

"What's going on?" he mouthed at me.

"Trouble," I mouthed back.

I gestured at Ned to stay put. He nodded and gripped the knife tighter.

I needed to get a better view outside. The passageway doglegged right to bypass the galley. I crawled forward to the junction with the observation car. I reached up to the handle and pulled it open. A hot wind blew inside.

The gap to the next car was about a foot wide. The first time I'd stepped across that gap the train had been moving at sixty miles an hour and the clatter of the wheels and tracks blurring below had set my heart thumping. I'd done it a hundred times since then and hardly thought about it. Now the train wasn't even moving, but it wasn't the fall that scared me.

I eased my face around the corner. The edge of the building came into view. I leaned out a little more. The door opened. Three men came out. One had Hardin by the hair with a gun jammed against his neck. Hardin's hands were cuffed behind his back. Relief filled me that the marshal was still alive. His captor wore the uniform of the Guardia Territorial, but the others didn't. They looked hard and unkempt. I jerked back before they spotted me.

There seemed to be only one explanation. Pedro Braga had set us up. Maybe he did hire the Reverend Jolly. Or maybe he already cut his own deal with Lee and didn't want any interference.

"Doc," I whispered again.

Nothing.

The phantom could leave the Collier for short periods, though it had some kind of pull on him that grew irresistible after a while. Doc could be temperamental, but he was usually there for me in a pinch and I figured this situation qualified. Which meant he wasn't nearby.

I peeked out again. Two more men had Tanaka by the arms. Another dragged the limp body of Marshal Hodges. He was covered in blood.

It had all happened so fast I could hardly absorb it. But I had to do something. They might kill Hardin and Tanaka any second.

I ducked back and tried to make a plan. Nothing came to mind. There were six of them. Maybe more inside the building. And they had hostages.

Right at that moment I heard voices speaking in Spanish outside. "Search the train," the first voice said. "You know the orders. Keep the driver alive, but if you find anyone else, kill 'em."

The tone was matter of fact. It chilled me.

I peeked around the edge of the car. Two of the men were heading up to the cab with shotguns. There was no chance I could get there first to warn the engineer. Two more were walking to the stairs leading to the dining car.

I rushed back down the narrow passage to the galley and beckoned frantically at Ned. We had about six seconds before they came through the door.

"Run!" I hissed, pointing to the back of the train.

Ned bolted down the aisle, arms and legs jerking like pistons. I moved to follow and bit back a scream as a haint materialized in front of me.

It was the child I'd seen through the window. Like all

grims who appeared in the flesh, her eyes were solid black and reminded me of an insect. She didn't wear clothes. Her body was smooth and featureless like a doll. Curtains of hair hung around her starved-looking face. A streak of pure white ran down the right side, but otherwise she looked like every other haint I'd seen.

Creepy as hell.

I figured I was dead, but she just pointed at one of the tables. I stared at her, frozen. The girl made an impatient shooing motion and I wondered if she was telling me to hide.

Boots echoed on the steel steps. I dropped down and squeezed under the table. Distantly, I noticed a seven of spades and a nine of diamonds lying at my feet. The men paused at the door. I imagined them looking down the length of the car, shotguns ready. They started walking my way.

I breathed shallowly, watching their snakeskin boots come closer. They'd be stupid not to look under the tables. It was the only place to hide in the whole car.

A drop of sweat rolled down my nose as one of the men stopped right in front of me. I gripped the Collier. Suddenly the tablecloth was lifting up. Adrenaline pumped through me. I saw a bearded face and my finger tightened on the trigger. But his eyes passed right over me with no reaction. He lowered the cloth.

"Find anything?" his partner asked.

"Nada," he said.

They checked the rest of the tables and were starting in the direction Ned had gone when a voice called out from the engine car. "Got the driver!"

The two men turned and went forward instead.

I sat there shaking for a minute. The haint must have hidden me. I didn't know how and there was no time to worry about it. As soon as the door closed behind the men, I crawled out and ran in a crouch toward the back of the train. A plan was forming in my mind, a crazy one, but it was our only chance. When I got to the door, I peeked outside. Hardin was on his knees, two Gorras standing over him. The marshal looked furious.

Up front, the engineer, Elzy Mack, was being walked out by the four men who'd boarded the train. He had his hands on his head and didn't look hurt. The men conferred for a moment. Then the ones that had come through the dining car started for the train again, no doubt to search the rest of the cars. But I had a minute's head start.

I bolted across the gap and ran down the length of the sleeper. I almost stopped at my compartment for an extra box of bullets, but I knew I'd never be able to reload in time to deal with all of them. A door slammed behind me. They'd already checked the dining car, so they'd go straight to the sleeper and search the compartments. That wouldn't take long, a couple of minutes maybe. I hoped it was enough.

I banged through the door at the end of the sleeper and into the caboose, which was attached to the water tank.

And ran straight into one of the Gorras.

He must have come aboard from the other end when I wasn't looking. He had his gun pointed at Ned Carver, who sprawled on the floor. The Gorra spun toward me in surprise. My arm was moving before I had time to think. I whipped the Collier straight into his face.

He staggered back, blood running from a deep cut on his cheekbone. I kicked him between the legs. He crumpled, grabbing me as he fell. A fist came around and clocked me in the nose. Pain jolted up into my skull. Through tears I saw the glint of a pistol and lashed out, still half-blind. The gun spun away. Then a boot shot forward, connecting squarely with his forehead, and the Gorra stopped moving.

"You okay?" Ned Carver asked in a shaky voice.

I touched my nose. It was gushing. I tipped my head back and breathed through my mouth. "Yeah," I said. "More or less."

Ned's head turned at a sound from the next car. "They're coming," he warned.

I blotted the blood on one sleeve and crawled over to the crates piled against the wall, fighting waves of dizziness. A deep black shadow fell across me.

"I go on sabbatical for a few minutes and look what you get yourself into," Doc drawled.

"We got no time for that now," I snapped, though I was relieved to see him. "Can you disarm the men outside? Get those cuffs off the marshals?"

It sounded like I had a massive cold. I tipped my head back again.

"Yes." He paused. "But I'm not a miracle worker, Ruth. I can only do one thing at a time. So there might be some shooting. And since you're soft on Mr. Hardin—"

"I ain't soft!"

Doc chuckled. "Of course not. He's your superior officer. I imagine that sort of thing is frowned upon—"

"Quiet," I said through gritted teeth. Only Doc would try to provoke me at a time like this.

He drifted toward the wall. "I'll just play it by ear, Ruth. Stir things up."

"No, wait." I wasn't about to gamble with Hardin's life, or Tanaka's either. "I need to think!"

"Well, you better do it quick," Doc said.

Through the round window in the door, I could see silhouettes moving closer in the next car. Voices called to the guard I'd laid out on the floor, wondering where he was.

"We gotta do something," Ned muttered. "What about all this?"

The caboose held Hardin's arsenal. That had been my crazy plan. But the only things I knew how to fire were the shotguns and rifles, and that wasn't gonna do the trick. I pointed at a crate plastered with danger signs.

"Can you open it, Doc?"

Nails screeched from the wood. The lid popped off. I peered inside, breathing through my mouth.

"Your face is a mess, Ruth," Doc observed.

I ignored him. Nestled in cotton packing was a long metal tube. I carefully lifted it out. The tube was about the length of my arm. It felt heavier than I expected.

"What does it do, Doc?"

"Why don't you find out?" he suggested.

I studied the weapon. It had a dial and some knobs and levers. It looked complicated. "I don't know how to work it."

"Lemme see," Ned said.

He came over and fiddled with the levers. There was a thunking sound. Clockwork gears engaged. The dial had numbers from zero to twenty. The needle started counting down. Ned stepped back.

"Huh," he said.

I stared stupidly at the tube. It had no sight or trigger. The front and back looked more or less the same. "Which end do I point?" I asked.

Ned gave me a helpless look.

The caboose had no windows, only two doors, one at the front, which the Gorras were about to come through, and one that led out onto a small metal balcony, with the water car trailing behind. I stepped outside, a little light-headed.

"Doc?" I said.

"Right here, Ruth."

"Get ready to snap open those cuffs," I said. "Do that first."

"Got it."

"Then just do whatever you can to stop them shooting us."

With luck, I could cause enough of a distraction to throw them off balance for a few seconds.

Seven, six, five....

I moved around to the edge of the balcony. One of the

men had Hardin by the hair, jerking his head back. He gripped a big knife in his hand. The others were watching Tanaka, who looked banged up and mad.

"Hey!" I yelled, resting the tube on my right shoulder and hoping I had it pointed the right way.

The gear clicked over another notch.

Behind me, I heard the men come through the door and scream. There were four gunshots, one right after the other. Ned gave a startled cry. I heard bodies crashing to the floor.

The Gorra who had Hardin looked over. His grip loosened on Hardin's hair just enough that the marshal managed to catch my eye. His own gaze widened when he saw the tube. It made a low humming sound. Hardin opened his mouth and I'll never know what he was about to yell because the gear clicked over to one and then zero.

3

THE KICK THREW me against the far rail. There was a *whoosh*, followed by a *thump*, and a fireball shot up into the sky. I hadn't aimed at the building for fear I'd kill everybody. Instead, I'd aimed at the vehicle parked twenty yards to the north.

All the conveyances in Carnarvon City were powered by grims, but this one had some kind of fuel tank because a second explosion hit a few seconds after the first. I was on my back, but I felt the shockwave and heard the muffled boom.

Smoke drifted from the end of the tube where I'd dropped it. My head was ringing. I felt like one solid bruise, but I crawled across the little iron balcony of the caboose when I heard gunshots.

Two of the Gorras lay on the ground. Their uniforms were charred and it looked like they'd taken the brunt of the explosion. Tanaka had someone's gun and it was her doing the shooting. She got off three rounds, palming the hammer back cool as they come, and another of the men fell down. That left two more. She pointed her gun at the one running for cover as the last crept up behind her. I called a warning, but he aimed his pistol at the back of her head and fired. My heart stopped, but there was just a dry click. He swore when he realized the chamber was empty. Tanaka started to turn and he cracked her in the skull. She keeled over. The man raised his leg to stomp her.

Ned Carver stepped past me, his face grim. He had a rifle socked to his shoulder. He took careful aim and the man screamed as his knee buckled. He started limping away.

"Well, that was a lick and a promise," Ned muttered. "I never shot a man before."

Hardin was on his feet, still cuffed. He leapt back as the man with the knife took a swing at him. A trickle of blood ran down Hardin's face and he favored his left leg.

"Help Mr. Hardin," I croaked, grabbing the edge of the balcony and pulling myself up to stand. My own gun was gone. I must have dropped it back in the caboose.

"I'm trying." Ned cracked the breech chamber to reload, but his hands were trembling and the cartridge fell from his fingers. "Dammit!"

The marshal was in a bad way. Blood ran out of one coat sleeve. He ducked under another swing from the knife. The man facing him was big, but not the lumbering sort of big. He moved fast and light on his feet. Hardin dove for Tanaka's gun but the man kicked it out of the way. Then he grabbed Hardin by the hair again and kneed him in the ribs. Hardin rolled to his back, gasping for air.

Suddenly the man's eyes went wide as a chunk of burning car flew at his face. He let go of Hardin as the gun started firing wildly. Bullets dinged off the train and I scooted back.

Ned nodded. "Your haint did that?"

In answer, we heard a shout of dismay and peeked around the corner. Hardin's handcuffs were off and he'd picked up a shotgun. He fired at the man with the knife, who fell screaming. Doc was wreaking havoc among the surviving Gorras, an invisible demon, and the ones who could still run headed off into the desert.

Hardin dropped the gun and crouched over Marshal

Tanaka. He winced as he slid an arm under her back. It took him two tries to gain his feet, but his face warned me not to offer my help. I couldn't tell if he was mad or just in shock.

There was a crater where the car had been. Flames licked up the rear wall of the wooden shack. No sign of Doc, but he'd done his part. I owed him another favor.

"We have to get her inside the train," Hardin said, scanning the hardpan. Two distant figures were hightailing it back toward the badlands.

"Where's Mr. Mack?" Ned asked.

"Over here!" The driver crawled out from under the tin sheeting next to the shack. "What the hell was that?"

"Never mind," Hardin snapped. "Just move!"

He insisted on carrying Tanaka all the way to the sleeper car, where he deposited her on one of the bunks. She was pale but breathing. Ned fetched water while Elzy Mack headed up to see about his phantoms.

I didn't mention the girl I'd seen. Not just yet.

"What about Marshal Hodges?" I asked.

"Dead," Hardin said wearily. "They shot him as soon as we walked inside."

"They were waiting for the train?"

"Looks that way."

"Why didn't they just kill all of you?" I wondered.

Hardin didn't answer. I shared a look with Ned as he came inside with a bowl of water and some linen bandages. "We'll go fetch Mr. Hodges," I said. "You're hurt."

"I'm fine," Hardin grumbled, but he looked almost as pale as Tanaka.

"No, you ain't," I said. "Just hang tight."

"Watch yourselves," Hardin said, levering himself down to the edge of the bunk like an old man. He dipped a bandage in the water and tipped Tanaka's head to the side. She had thick hair, plus the hat, which probably saved her.

"Nasty lump," Hardin pronounced. "But I think she'll pull through." He looked me over, his voice gentle. "Is it broken?"

I touched my nose. "Don't think so."

"Let me see." He patted the bunk next to him.

"In a minute. I need to find my gun first. Case they come back."

Hardin shook his head but let us go.

Ned and I left him to tend Tanaka and went back to the caboose. I stopped to get the Collier and found the men. I remembered hearing screams as they came through the door. The thud of bodies hitting the ground.

"Listen," I said quietly to Ned. "I'm gonna say I did this, okay? Doc was just following my orders, but the marshal doesn't trust him and if he knew Doc killed two men with their own guns. . . . Well, it's better if I done it."

Ned eyed me doubtfully "Lie, you mean?"

"Just say you were looking outside when it happened. It was all confusing, wasn't it?"

Ned sighed. "I guess so."

I picked up the Collier and slid it into my side holster. "Thank you, Mr. Carver," I said. "And thanks for keeping a cool head. You saved Tanaka's life."

A flush reddened his caramel skin. "Come on," he said gruffly. "Let's get the marshal."

Hodges lay on his side in the dirt, one arm flung out. His face was a red ruin. I hadn't known him well, but it was still an awful sight. Ned took his hat off. We stood there for a minute in silence, the wind whipping streamers of dust and smoke across the hardpan.

"I've been across the border five times," Ned said. "Never ran into any trouble before."

In Lucky Boy, we had maybe one murder every ten years. The worst I generally dealt with was drunks and disputes over cattle grazing.

"Where you from?" I asked.

We'd played a lot of Old Maid, but I'd never asked him. Maybe because the question made me think of my own home and how much I missed it.

"The city," he said. "My dad was a railroad cook, too. Now he runs his own restaurant. Maisie's on Market Street. Mr. Hardin eats there a lot. I could've had a job as a sous-chef, but I wanted to see the world." He shook his head. "How about you?"

"The prairie." I sighed. "Honestly, Mr. Carver, I'm still not sure what I'm doing here."

One of the Gorras gave a groan. I fumbled for my gun. "We got a live one," I yelled, checking to make sure his hands were empty.

Hardin's face appeared in the open window. A second later he threw out a set of cuffs. I caught them and knelt down next to the Gorra. I got him secured as Hardin walked over, his face set in hard lines.

"Head on up front," Hardin told Ned.

The cook nodded and took off. He looked relieved to be gone.

Hardin crouched down. "Para quien trabajas?" he demanded. *Who you working for?*

The man's eyes fluttered. Hardin seized his coat and gave him a shake. "Talk, damnit!"

The man moaned. Hardin shook him harder. Rage rolled off the marshal in waves. I understood, but this felt wrong. The man had burns.

"Let's get him aboard the train," I said quickly. "Give him a chance to come to properly. You won't get anything in this state."

Hardin looked up at me with reddened eyes but seemed to see the sense of it. He searched the man for weapons, finding none. I took his feet and Hardin took his legs. He was big and we both staggered getting him up the stairs. We left him in one of the compartments, still half-conscious. Hardin locked the door behind us.

"Let's get Hodges," he said. "And check the rest of 'em. Make sure."

"You okay, sir?" I asked.

"Yeah." He stared at me for a minute. "That was good thinking, getting to the Widowmaker." Hardin laughed. "Didn't expect to use it."

"You ain't mad?"

"I'm just sorry Richard didn't get to see it in action. He's the one who invented it."

Richard Carnarvon was the eldest of Calindra's three grandchildren. He was also the smartest, but I got the feeling Calindra favored Richard's half-siblings Ava and Freddie, maybe because they looked the part more than Richard. Which was sad.

"So what do we do now? Head back to Carnarvon City?" I asked hopefully.

Hardin looked at me like I'd gone crazy. "Hell, no. I need to tell Pedro Braga what happened."

"I'm not following, marshal. His men just tried to kill us."

"Not Braga's men." Hardin glanced at the flaming guardhouse. "There's three Gorras inside, naked and trussed up. I'm guessing they were on duty when these fellers showed up."

I took a step toward the building, wondering why he wasn't rushing to help them, and Hardin laid a hand on my arm. "They're dead, Cortez," he said quietly. "Hard deaths. You don't want to go in there."

I felt sick. "So it was an ambush. By who?"

His blue eyes darkened to grey. "Ain't that obvious?"

"If I may, sir?"

Hardin made an impatient gesture. "Go on, speak your mind." A ghost of a smile touched his mouth. "You always do anyway."

"Well, this don't feel like Lee Merriweather."

"Why not? He's the one to gain from seeing us dead."

"Merriweather would send phantoms." I hesitated, then figured I'd better tell him all of it. "And the only one I seen besides Doc saved my life."

Hardin frowned. "You saw a phantom?"

"On the train. And first in the guardhouse, right after you went inside. It was looking at me through the window."

Hardin seemed puzzled, but he didn't doubt my word. "What happened exactly?"

"I was running from two of the men and it helped me hide. Then it just disappeared." I told him the rest of it, how Ned and I got to the caboose and found Richard's weapon.

"Huh." He looked at me. "What about the men? You said they were chasing you."

The old me would have spilled the beans without thinking twice. Sebastian Hardin was the chief of Special Services. I was sworn to his authority for the duration of the manhunt. But I wasn't the same woman I'd been when I left Lucky Boy. And I couldn't give up Doc. A phantom who killed people — even bad people — couldn't be trusted. What if Hardin made me leave the gun behind?

So I lied straight to his face.

"I shot 'em, sir," I said.

Hardin stared at me without speaking. I didn't look away, though it wasn't easy. When the marshal turned the full force of his will on you . . . Well, I half expected my pants to burst into flame.

"Show me," he said.

We walked to the caboose and climbed up the stairs. Hardin went in first. He didn't react when he saw the bodies, just studied them for a moment. The dead men had both been shot between the eyes. The entrance holes were small and charred around the edges. I knew from my time helping Lucky Boy's doctor that bullets did the worst damage coming out the back. Most of the blood had pooled under their heads. It was a grisly sight.

"Those wounds are close range," Hardin said after a long pause. "Less than a foot, I'd reckon. Didn't take you for a stone cold killer, Cortez." He gave me an inscrutable look. "No disrespect to your copper star, but I'd expect you to be a little more shook up about it."

I drew a deep breath. "I had no choice, sir. And I'm . . . I am shook up. But it was them or me."

I prayed Hardin wouldn't check my gun and discover I hadn't fired a single round.

"Maybe they were just bandits," I said, hoping to steer his thoughts to a new track. "You said there was a gang robbing trains down here."

"Maybe," Hardin said, though he didn't sound like he believed it.

"It wasn't Merriweather," I said firmly. "He's got his flaws, but he's no killer. And Mr. Beach would never stand for it, either. He's a good man, just overly fond of Lee."

"What about the Reverend Jolly?"

"*That* I could see," I said without hesitation. "But would he have time to plan it?"

"We don't know where he went," Hardin pointed out. "Maybe he got ahead of us."

"True. I reckon he could have more followers."

"I'll find out, one way or another," Hardin said. "Once we get moving again."

I helped him roll Mr. Hodges in a sheet and lie him down in an empty sleeper. Then I cleaned up my face. It felt tender, but I could breathe through my nose again so maybe it wasn't broken. I made my way back to the observation car, where Hardin was talking with the engineer. Some windows had been shot out, but I figured we were fine to go until Elzy Mack said all his grims had taken off during the fight.

"Can't you call 'em back?" Hardin asked.

"I tried." Elzy Mack shook his head. "They're gone."

Hardin looked at me. "What about Doc? Can he stoke the boiler?"

"I suppose he could," I said slowly. "The question is whether he will."

"Ask him." Hardin paused. "We can't afford to be stuck out here until another train comes along. Could be days. So do your best, Cortez."

I hadn't seen Doc since he'd freed Hardin from the handcuffs. I walked back through the train, whispering his name. When I got to the dining car, he finally showed up.

"Don't worry, those bandits are gone," he said. "I followed them to a camp a few miles out in a gully. They'll be licking their wounds for a while."

"Well, that's good. Thanks for what you did."

His shadow preened a little. "You're welcome, Ruth. I do seem to have a knack for saving your bacon. But that's what friends are for."

"Did you happen to see any other phantoms?" I asked. "Like a little girl?"

"No." Doc flitted over. "Why?"

"Never mind. Listen, we have another problem." I paused. "The haints that drive the engine took off."

There was a long silence. His shadow pooled into one of the chairs.

"So I was hoping you might be willing to help out," I said. "Else we're stuck here."

"You want *me* to stoke the boiler?" Doc asked with a note of disbelief.

"I don't see any other grims around," I snapped.

Right away, I wished I hadn't said it. Doc was proud. Maybe if I'd kept my temper and asked nicely he would have agreed.

"So now I'm your slave," he said flatly. "Want me to scrub the floors while I'm at it? Shine your boots?"

"I wouldn't ask if there were any other choice."

"Hardin put you up to this, didn't he?"

"Nobody put me up to anything," I said. "And it's only until we find some more grims."

"That is *not* my job," Doc said haughtily.

"You promised to do what I said," I reminded him.

Doc gave a nasty laugh. "I lied."

That made me bristle. "You're the only one of us who can make the train go," I said. "So either man up or find some other haints to do it."

Shadowy tentacles flailed around. "There *isn't* anybody, Ruth. As you well know, my kind likes machinery. If we were near a city, I could round some up. But we're in the middle of nowhere!"

I felt exhausted. My face hurt. Plus Tanaka needed a doctor. The thought of sitting here for days waiting for a grim to pass by made me want to scream.

"Please, Doc," I begged. "Can't you just swallow your pride?"

"Oh, I swallow my pride every single day," he shrieked. "No one understands me. No one cares what I want. You only think of me when there's some chore to do."

"That's not true and you know it," I said. "You always exaggerate."

The playing cards formed a small tornado. "I wish I was still in Three Bars," Doc growled. "At least I had a peaceful life."

"Well, I'll take you back there when we get home," I snarled. "Bury the gun in the sand."

"Good! It would be a definite improvement."

He flitted off. I figured he'd go back into the ether to sulk, but a minute later I heard the boiler fire up. Despite his bluster, it seemed Doc wanted to sit around here as little as the rest of us.

I watched out the window as the train pulled away from the border, a plume of black smoke still staining the sky.

4

"*PARA QUIEN TRABAJAS?*"

Hardin stared at the prisoner. The prisoner stared back. He was tied hand and foot on the narrow bed.

"Who do you work for?" Hardin asked again.

The man smiled and started humming a tune. He had a patchy black beard and a scar across his nose. The smell of sour sweat filled the small compartment. Hardin's interrogation had been going for more than an hour with no results.

"I need coffee," he said. "Keep an eye on him, Cortez."

We'd given the man water when he first came to, which seemed to revive him. He had burns on his face, but they looked superficial. Once Hardin was gone, his gaze turned to me. I rested a hand on the holster of my gun.

"You'd do better to cooperate," I said. "Mr. Hardin isn't a patient man. And after what you done, I'm not of a mind to stop him if he gets frisky."

The smile never wavered. It had a creepy, mechanical quality.

"When we get to Aguadulce, we'll hand you over to Mr. Braga," I said. "He'll hang you for sure. Might as well give us some names. It'll go easier."

The smile broadened, showing bloody teeth. "Quieres jugar, Ruth?"

Do you want to play?

I felt a chill. "How do you know my name?"

He laughed. "A little bird told me."

"You work for the reverend, don't you?"

He blinked. "Quien es él?"

"The Reverend Jolly. Where is he?"

A look of confusion crossed his face. Then that idiotic smile returned. "Juegos, Ruth. Fun and games." He hummed a snatch of nonsense verse. I recognized the tune. My father used to sing it when I was little. *Cinco sombras pequeñas.* Five little phantoms.

The man was crazy, though that shouldn't surprise me.

Hardin returned a minute later with a steaming tin cup. I met him in the corridor and pulled the door shut behind me.

"He knows my name," I said. "So you were right. They must have been working for the reverend."

Hardin arched an eyebrow. "What did he say?"

"Nothing really. He asked if I liked to play games."

Hardin scowled. He stepped back into the compartment.

"Where's your boss?" he demanded.

The man just lay there humming with a vacant smile.

"I have a game for you," Hardin said. "How about I throw you off this moving train?"

No reaction.

The marshal sighed. He lifted the cup to his lips and winced.

"You need medical attention," I said quietly. "You needed it two hours ago."

Hardin gave me a mulish look.

"If you bleed out, you're no use to anyone," I said in a businesslike fashion. "I already got one patient to deal with. Don't need two."

He finished the coffee. "My compartment," he muttered. "There's supplies up front."

I fetched some dishcloths and water, along with a stack of linen bandages. Hardin unbuttoned his coat and dropped it on a chair. His shirt was soaked in blood.

"Go on," I said. "Get it off."

He turned his back and peeled off the shirt. A long cut sliced down his ribs. It was still oozing. He gripped the back of the chair as I dipped a cloth in water and started cleaning it out.

The old half-moon scars I'd glimpsed once before were starkly visible now. Shotgun pellets for certain. But the rest of him was smooth and several shades paler than his face. Heat came off him and my own face warmed as I moved the cloth down the lines of his back.

Maybe I *was* soft on Hardin. The man was easy on the eyes, but that wasn't all of it. He had integrity, even if I didn't always agree with him. I got the sense he came from a rough place but it hadn't swallowed him up. Some would call Lucky Boy a rough place, but it wasn't, not really. The winters were harsh and we had twisters in the spring months, but the people were decent, most of them. City folk might lead more comfortable lives, yet I'd seen things since I left that were far worse than anything Mother Nature could throw at you. I'd take a pack of hungry wolves over the Reverend Jolly and Mr. Cage any day.

My thoughts must have wandered because Hardin gave a little yelp as I dug too deep.

"Sorry," I muttered, lowering the cloth. "I'm gonna sew you up now."

He glanced over his shoulder at me. Stubble darkened his jaw, making his eyes electric, and I saw something for a minute, a tension held in check that made my heart beat, but then it was gone.

"Do it quick, Cortez," he said gruffly.

I gave a wordless nod. He turned away, bowing his head, and I readied the needle and thread. He didn't make a sound when I pinched the skin together and laid the stitches on. When I was done, I dabbed it with iodine, which earned a wince.

"All set," I said.

"Thanks, Cortez." Hardin didn't look at me as he rooted around for a clean shirt. "How 'bout you? Need any doctoring?"

His tone was perfectly neutral, but my cheeks burned hotter.

"No, sir," I said, a touch too fast. "Just bruises."

He pulled a shirt on and turned to me, his fingers doing up the buttons, though not before I caught a flash of muscled belly and some dark curls of hair. Cool blue eyes regarded me. "Why don't you go check on Tanaka, deputy?"

It was a clear dismissal. I went next door, vaguely embarrassed and out of sorts. It was a pointless crush, I told myself firmly. Nothing could come of it. I still planned to go home when this was done. For all that I respected him, Hardin's world was not one I cared to live in.

The marshal was sleeping, her breathing regular. I let her be and realized I was starving. Ned had some potato soup bubbling in the galley so I took a bowl and settled into the dining car. I thought Hardin might avoid me again, but he showed up with his own bowl and we ate in silence.

"Are we still stopping in New Jerusalem?" I asked, pushing my empty bowl away.

"Have to," Hardin said. "I hate to delay, but I need to know who Jolly's working for." He looked out the window at the desert racing by. Doc might resent running the boiler, but he wasn't slacking off. We were making good time.

"It won't take long to check out his church," Hardin continued. "I figure I can talk to the townspeople, see what they know. We'll be in and out in a few hours."

"Assuming it's not another trap," I said.

"Yep," Hardin agreed. "Which is why we go in slow and cautious." His face darkened. "The one we caught must know something."

"Were you really gonna throw him off the train?" I asked.

"No," Hardin said after a pause. "That'd be murder, wouldn't it, Cortez?"

"Yes, sir," I said.

"And it wouldn't do us any good anyway." He leaned back. "They shot Hodges, but they let me and Tanaka live. Why?"

I shook my head. "There's a lot that don't make sense. Doc said he followed them to a camp in the desert. The ones that ran. But how'd they get to the camp in the first place? I looked at the map. There's nothing for hundreds of miles around."

"Maybe they rode horses in."

"Doc didn't mention horses."

I thought again of the face I saw through the window of the guardhouse.

"And that phantom I saw. She helped me. But why didn't she help *you*?"

"I'm pretty sure none of the bandits spoke a tongue," Hardin said slowly. "I agree, it doesn't make much sense. Maybe we'll find some answers in New Jerusalem."

We both turned at a yell from the next car. We leapt to our feet and ran to the sleeper. Ned Carver stood over the prisoner, who lay motionless.

"I brought him some soup like you said, marshal." Ned held a bowl in his hands. "Found him like this."

"Damn," Hardin muttered.

The man's skin was ashen, eyes staring sightlessly at the ceiling.

"His burns didn't seem that bad," I said, studying the body.

He wore the tan uniform of the Gorras. There wasn't a spot of blood on him.

"No," Hardin agreed with a slight frown. "Must have had internal injuries."

I thought of how he'd lain there smiling and humming. He didn't seem like a dying man to me.

But Ned Carver sure didn't kill him. And there was no one else on board – only the engineer and Marshal Tanaka, who still hadn't woken up. I know because I stuck my head into her compartment.

We rolled him up in a blanket and locked the door. It wouldn't be long before the body started to ripen in the heat, but Hardin insisted we keep him aboard. The real Guardia Territorial might know his face.

I curled up on my bunk and caught a few hours of sleep. Late afternoon sun was coming through the window when Hardin knocked on my door. I sat up, groggy. The train had stopped. I opened the door.

Hardin didn't look like he'd slept at all. His blue eyes were bloodshot but alert. The man seemed to run on black coffee and little else.

"We got a problem," Hardin said.

5

NEW JERUSALEM WAS on a spur line off the main north-south railroad between Carnarvon City and Aguadulce. It had been a prosperous copper mining town until the deposits ran out and people drifted away in search of better opportunities.

That was about ten years ago. The town struggled along, never dying outright but not thriving, either. My hometown wasn't so different except that Lucky Boy hadn't been prosperous in the first place.

We weren't sure when the Reverend Josephiah Jolly had set up his ministry, but it was likely after the town fell into decline. He was the sort who preyed on the desperate.

It was an obscure place and would have stayed that way if the reverend hadn't kidnapped me and Professor Beach in hopes of luring Lee Merriweather. I didn't know where Jolly was now. He'd made no secret of his church, though, printing it on flyers that he'd handed out in Carnarvon City with his associate, Mr. Cage.

I smoothed the creased paper and studied the cheap block print.

The Church of the Glorious Lamb of God
Rev. Josephiah Jolly, presiding

Services Weekly, New Jerusalem, All Welcome
Come into the Blessed Fold!

Personally, I felt no burning desire to stop in New Jerusalem, especially since we'd been ambushed once already, but I knew Hardin couldn't be talked out of it. He didn't leave stones unturned, even when he might find something nasty underneath.

The problem was that about a mile outside of town someone had thrown up a barricade on the tracks.

The train was stopped fifty feet short of the obstacle. Except for some distant hills, there was no cover for someone with a rifle. Hardin and I jumped down to take a closer look. Twisted hunks of metal had been fused to the tracks. They were half melted so it was hard to tell what purpose they'd served. Maybe parts from another train.

"Well, this ain't good," Hardin said, popping a piece of gum in his mouth as the driver, Elzy Mack, climbed down the stairs from the engine car. Elzy's long, narrow face and droopy mustache gave him the mournful look of a hunting hound. His shaggy grey brows knit together as he frowned at the obstacle.

I'd left my dark glasses sitting on the table, so I shaded my eyes with one hand and squinted at the town that lay half a mile down the tracks. One and two-story wooden buildings clumped together along the main street and a few more were scattered around the outskirts. It sat in a river valley that had groves of trees and more vegetation than I'd seen in days.

"We'll have to back it up," the driver said. "Nowhere to turn around."

Hardin stared at New Jerusalem for a minute without speaking. Then he left and came back with a pair of field glasses. He made a slow sweep from left to right, then handed them over to me. I adjusted the focus. The buildings leapt closer, peeling paint washed out to a nearly colorless grey. I could see peaked roofs past the center of town and the top of a steeple with a big white cross. Nothing was moving out there, but it didn't mean the place was empty.

"What do you think?" Hardin asked me.

"Don't know," I said. "Too far to tell."

"Keep looking." He walked stiffly up the stairs and ducked inside the train.

"Hey, Doc?" I whispered, making another sweep with the field glasses.

He didn't answer. I figured he was still mad, but it was worth a try. Doc could tell me if something was waiting for us.

"Looking for your grim?" the driver asked.

I lowered the glasses and nodded.

Elzy smiled, showing tobacco-stained teeth. "Said he was taking a coffee break. First time I ever heard of that."

"Great," I muttered.

"Piece of work, isn't he?"

"You said it."

Elzy Mack eyed me curiously. "Known him a while?"

"Seven long years," I answered.

"Never met a grim that talked English before." He looked thoughtful. "Never knew one that had a name and stayed with one person, either."

I sighed. "Doc's one of a kind."

Elzy Mack frowned. "But you're not a linguist."

"Nope." We were venturing into dangerous territory. Doc wouldn't like it if I told the driver his secret — that another phantom had bound him to my gun and he was at the mercy of whoever owned it.

I studied the twisted metal, thinking of a way to change the subject. "Wonder what did that," I said.

The barricade reminded me of a tangled ball of yarn, if it was made out of steel and iron.

"Had to be phantoms," the driver replied. He stroked his mustache. "You think they were trying to keep people out? Or *in*?"

We shared a worried look.

"We ought to just head back to the main line," Elzy Mack muttered.

"Could be folks need help," I pointed out.

He nodded reluctantly. "I still don't like it. Not after what happened to Marshal Hodges."

The town looked just like a dozen others we'd passed on the journey south, yet it appeared sinister to me now, with the low sun bathing the buildings in a red glow.

I turned as Hardin reappeared with Ned Carver at his side. "Well, damn," Ned muttered, looking at the wrecked tracks. "Ain't that a pickle."

I'd hoped Hardin might relent, but I could tell from his stubborn expression that he was set on going in, even if he had to walk. "There's an hour or two of daylight left," Hardin said. "Plenty of time to look around and head back."

I handed the field glasses to Elzy Mack and checked my jacket pocket for an extra box of bullets. The Bowie knife was in its sheath.

"You three guard the train," Hardin said, his gaze fixed on New Jerusalem. "We don't want to get stuck out here. Long way from anywhere."

You three. . . .

"Hold up," I said. "You're not going in alone, are you?"

Cool blue eyes settled on me. "That's the plan, Cortez."

"With all due respect, sir, it's a stupid plan."

Elzy Mack raised his shaggy brows. Ned smothered a grin.

Hardin frowned. Then he sighed and gave his head a small shake. "Should I take that as an offer to come along, deputy?"

"Yes, sir."

Hardin handed Ned the shotgun. The cook took it and checked the chamber, then propped the stock over his shoulder.

"We're just taking a quick look-see," Hardin said. "But I

got no idea what's in there. Could be trouble. So if we don't come back by dark, you throw it in reverse and get the hell out. Understood?"

"Yes, marshal," Ned said.

Elzy Mack muttered agreement, though he didn't look happy. "Be careful," he said to me. "I'll keep an eye out for your phantom. If he shows, I'll send him into town. Wouldn't hurt to have a haint."

"Thanks," I said, resting a hand on the Collier. Maybe Doc was inside it, sulking and ignoring me, maybe not. Either way, he wasn't talking.

We skirted the obstruction and followed the tracks into town. They ended at a small depot with a siding and a run-around loop where the locomotive could uncouple from the train, pull forward, then reverse onto a parallel track and recouple to the other end of the train.

New Jerusalem was the end of the line. The reverend and Mr. Cage must have wrecked the tracks on their way north, following Lee. But why? And how had they even learned about Merriweather in this isolated backwater?

Had to be because someone told them. The same person who hired them.

Hardin was under strict orders to keep Lee a secret. Only the Carnarvons and a few people at the academy knew the kid was a savant, which meant someone close to the family tipped off the Reverend Jolly and Mr. Cage. The one person I could rule out was Hardin himself. First of all, the reverend hated him. Jolly had called Hardin a devil and claimed he murdered his own father. I didn't believe it, but there was no way they'd be working together. Hardin had absolute loyalty to Calindra. And under the gruff exterior, he was a decent man.

That left the three grandchildren — the twins Ava and Freddie, and their half-brother Richard — or someone at the Academy.

I couldn't picture Freddie and Ava in a place like this.

They were rich and spoiled and seemed to spend most of their time at parties. Richard invented things, like Ava's clockwork car, but his legs didn't work right and he used a rolling chair to get around. I couldn't figure how any of them might be connected to New Jerusalem.

Maybe it was Pedro Braga after all. Or somebody I didn't know.

"Doesn't look like much, does it?" Hardin said, echoing my thoughts.

The station was an open-sided wooden platform with a roof that looked ready to collapse. Pigeons nested in the eaves and I startled as a pair exploded with a flutter of wings.

"Like any other piddling town," I agreed.

We stood still for a long minute, just listening. I heard the chirp of a single cricket somewhere in the brush, but it only made the solitude seem louder.

"Whatever happened here, I think we missed it," Hardin said at last.

"I get the same feeling," I said. "If there was men waiting, they could've drawn a bead on us already. Springfield rifles are good for a quarter mile. More if you're a decent shot." I glanced at the sun, which hung low in the west. "Let's get it over with while we still have daylight."

Hardin drew his Colt but kept the muzzle down. "Was it a Springfield you used on the Dalton brothers?"

"Yep." I smiled. "Trapdoor model. It's got a hard kick, but it's accurate."

Catching Bill Dalton is how I earned my deputy star. His two brothers got away, but I heard they died over a card game in Tip Top six months later.

Hardin gave me a look. "We'll go in, but we take it slow and easy," he said. "I ain't losing anybody else."

We left the depot and turned down a rutted track that led to the main street. I saw a feed store and post office. A hitching post and dry water trough sat outside. Next door was a barbershop with a weatherbeaten sign advertising five-cent shaves in Spanish. Through the filthy window, a single barber's chair sat like a throne in the middle of the room. It was made of red leather with an ornate footrest painted gold. Horsehair stuffing spilled out of rips in the seat and the rest of the shop was empty.

We kept walking. I drew my flintlock, ready to dive for cover if anything moved, but the town looked abandoned. No chickens scratched in the dirt. I saw no fresh evidence of horses. The street had been swept smooth by the wind and there wasn't a single footprint or wagon track.

Hardin caught my eye, then tilted his head toward the saloon across the street. We pushed through the swinging doors. Light filtered through a large window. The ceiling was pressed tin and patterned wallpaper ran the length of one side, with a mirror facing the other behind the bar. Porcelain spittoons sprouted from the floor like pale mushrooms.

Like the barbershop, I had the impression of a well-kept establishment fallen on hard times. The wallpaper was peeling in places and the sawdust scattered across the boards looked none too clean, but everything appeared in order. Glasses were stacked upside-down on shelves behind the bar. Four crates of Thistle Dew sat next to some unlabelled bottles that were probably home-brewed mash. A thin layer of dust covered everything. I wrinkled my nose.

"It smells nasty," I remarked.

"You been in many saloons?" Hardin asked dryly.

"No," I admitted.

"Well, this is what they all smell like," he said.

He poked around behind the bar while I checked the back room. It had a desk with mail-order catalogues and a black telephone. I picked up the receiver and wasn't surprised to find it dead. I hadn't seen any poles or lines coming into town.

A closer inspection revealed the telephone didn't even have wires. The owner must have kept it for show.

I paused before a portrait hanging on the wall behind the desk. It showed a dark, handsome man in his twenties wearing a suit and mustache. A pretty girl stood next to him. She had a white flower in her hair and a long dress with embroidery on the front and sleeves. She was leaning back, resting her head against his shoulder. His eyes were open and looking at the camera, but hers were closed and she had a dreamy expression. They could have been brother and sister, or maybe engaged to be married. I guessed it was taken in a photographer's studio because the backdrop was a painted archway with palm trees.

It was a nice picture. I stood there admiring it until Hardin called me from the main room.

"I checked upstairs," he said. "Same as the rest. People were here not long ago, but they ain't now. Find anything?"

I shook my head. "You think the whole town up and left?"

"Could be," Hardin said.

I watched him for a minute. He had his palms braced on the bar and his face looked weary. I hoped he wasn't getting one of his migraines.

"But you don't think that's what happened," I said.

He looked up, blue eyes bright against the shadows beneath. "No, Cortez. I don't think that. In light of what you told me about the reverend, I'd guess something worse happened here."

His words deepened the vague sense of dread I'd felt since we got to the depot. I reminded myself that Hardin could be wrong. It wasn't like Hazardville, where Roger had burned up the whole town. This place was dying anyway. Maybe the Reverend Jolly scared them enough that they pulled up stakes and moved on. Maybe he gave some fire and brimstone sermon and told them the apocalypse was coming.

But if that was so, there ought to be signs of a mass exodus. At least the liquor would be looted.

New Jerusalem looked untouched.

"It'll be dark soon," Hardin said. "Let's finish up and get back to the train."

We headed outside and made our way up the street. The empty windows on the upper stories made my shoulders itch, like we were being watched. But at the same time I knew in my gut there was no one around.

"Reminds me of Three Bars," I said.

Hardin threw me an inquiring look.

"The town next to Lucky Boy that got wiped out by a tornado," I explained. "The buildings here are still standing, but it feels the same."

"Like a ghost town," Hardin said quietly.

"Yeah."

I could tell Hardin was worried — less for himself and more about what we might find — but I was glad to have him with me. I tried to imitate his calm, steady presence. He'd holstered his gun in the shoulder rig, but left his coat open and his eyes never stopped searching every alley and doorway. The wind plucked at raggedy curtains on the upper floors. I didn't like the darkness beyond. It looked solid.

We stopped in front of the general store and cupped our hands against the window. The shelves were all stocked. I spotted sacks of flour and sugar and rice. Dried beans, coffee and canned goods. Pots and pans, sewing needles and nails. Tins of lard and tobacco.

The bad feeling grew stronger.

"Maybe we should just go," I said. "Tell the authorities when we get to Aguadulce. They can search it proper. But we're losing daylight, marshal." I glanced up at the dark windows. They seemed to stare back at me.

"There's still the church," Hardin said.

The church.

I'd avoided looking at it, but the white steeple was the tallest thing around, towering over the buildings of Main Street like one of the hoodoos we'd passed in the desert. From where we stood in front of the general store, I could see the whole Glorious Lamb of God compound, starting with the church and extending to a farmhouse, schoolhouse, barn and long ranch-style building about a quarter mile past the end of town. The buildings all had the same whitewash and blue trim.

My dad wasn't especially religious, but we usually went to church on Sundays. We sang hymns and if the weather was nice, there would be a picnic after. Our minister, Mr. Weeks, was a kind man who planted flower beds every spring and kept the place looking neat and spiffy. From a distance, the reverend's church in New Jerusalem looked much the same.

But I knew it wasn't.

I remembered Mr. Cage sharpening his long knife, his eyes as flat and dead as a week-old fish.

I remembered Josephiah Jolly preaching in the streets of Carnarvon City, the hypnotic sound of his voice as he talked about the End of Days.

There will be a fearful separation of the wheat from the chaff.

My flock is my family, Ruth.

"You okay, Cortez?" Hardin asked. "It's fine if you want to wait here. I won't be long."

I stared at the church. It was probably empty like the rest. And if it wasn't . . . .

Well, I wouldn't send Hardin in there alone.

"No," I said in a wooden voice. "I'll come."

6

We walked in silence to the church. It was a simple wooden building with a bell tower capped by a cross. A shallow creek ran behind it. There were fields beyond, but the crops had withered. Corn husks rattled in the wind.

Next to the church was a three-story farmhouse, painted white with blue trim, and a low-slung barracks-style building made from adobe mud bricks. All the windows were shut tight. That's when I knew for sure everyone was gone. In this heat, a person would suffocate without the windows open for some air.

"Let's search it and get out of here," Hardin said.

That sounded like a fine idea. "Want me to take the big house?" I asked.

"We stay together," he said. "It looks empty, but you never know."

I almost argued. It would take twice as long and this place made my skin crawl. I just wanted to get back on the train and head in the opposite direction from New Jerusalem. But Hardin was right.

I followed him to the church. We went through the front door. It looked a lot like the church in Lucky Boy. One room with rows of pews and the altar where the minister would give his sermon. A Bible sat on the pulpit. I picked it up. A page had been marked with a pink ribbon, the passage underlined in pencil.

"Hey," I said. "Listen to this."

Hardin looked over.

I cleared my throat and read aloud, haltingly at first but with growing confidence. "I saw a new heaven and a new earth, for the first heaven and the first earth had passed away, and the sea was no more. And I saw the holy city, New Jerusalem, coming down out of heaven from God, prepared as a bride adorned for her husband."

I tried to deliver it the way Jolly would have, in a sing-song cadence that resonated against the walls of the church. "And I heard a loud voice from the throne saying, 'Behold, the dwelling place of God is with man. He will dwell with them, and they will be his people, and God himself will be with them as their God. He will wipe away every tear from their eyes, and death shall be no more, neither shall there be mourning, nor crying, nor pain anymore, for the former things have passed away.'"

Hardin laughed. "Maybe you should have been a preacher."

I laid the Bible down. "You never heard him sermonize," I said. "He's got a way about him. You can practically feel the fires of Hell licking at your feet."

Hardin scratched his head. "What do you make of it? Other than the reference to New Jerusalem."

I shrugged. "Compared to the other verses I've heard the reverend spout, this one's pretty upbeat."

"Hmmm." Hardin took a last look around. "I don't know. Sounds ominous to me. What part of the Bible is it from?"

"Let me see . . . ." I thumbed through the pages. "Book of Revelation."

"Ain't that the one with the four horsemen?"

"I think so."

Hardin shuddered. "Always scared me as a kid. Let's go."

We moved on to the big house, which was just down the road. The front door was unlocked. Inside was a shabby parlor and a dim hallway leading to a kitchen facing the rear yard. The day was fading fast, so I pulled the curtains wide to catch what light was left. I didn't fancy poking around in the near-dark.

The kitchen seemed to be in order, with china stacked on shelves and a red-checked cloth on the table. Hardin checked the pantry while I went out the back and lifted the door to the root cellar. Shadows fled before the light. A powerful earthy smell rolled out.

"See anything?" he asked, joining me to peer into the dank space. The sun only reached a few feet inside and the dirt floor was a good twelve feet down.

"I'll go make sure," I said.

"You don't have to——"

I started down the ladder before he could stop me. It was stupid, but I didn't want Hardin to know how scared I was.

He crouched at the edge of the cellar door. A wince crossed his face and I knew the movement must be tugging on the stitches. "Talk to me," he said. "Find any mass graves?" He was trying to be funny, but I didn't smile.

I'd paused halfway down. There was no need to go further. It wasn't large as root cellars go and I could see into the cobwebbed corners. "Just potatoes."

"Let's hit the upstairs," Hardin said, sounding relieved.

I climbed up and we went back into the kitchen. It was stifling hot, so I propped the back door open with a chair, not that it did much good. Hardin went first up the stairs. We were both sweating like the dickens. The second floor had a hall with half a dozen doors. I tried the first one. It was locked. I shared a silent look with Hardin. He raised his gun and nodded. I backed up and kicked the door hard with my boot. It flew open. A single bed lay beyond, with a frayed quilt and cedar hope chest at the foot. Dead flies lay on the windowsill.

"You take the left side, Cortez. I'll take the right," he said.

We made our way along the hall, kicking in doors. They were all bedrooms and they were all locked and empty. I drew a deep breath and kicked open the last door on the left. Right away, I smelled something bad.

The quilt had a stain on it, near the head of the bed. Dark red droplets, dried nearly to black, were spattered in a trail across the floor, ending at the window. I walked over and tried to open it but the sash was nailed shut. I got down on hands and knees and looked under the bed, but there were only dust bunnies.

"Hey, Hardin," I yelled.

He was behind me in an instant.

"That look like blood to you?" I asked, staring at the bed.

"Sure does." His voice was tense. "Let's keep looking."

We finished searching the second floor and climbed the stairs to the top. It had two bedrooms, both larger than the rest and with much nicer furniture. Neither one was locked. We checked every closet and wardrobe, but it seemed impossible for anyone to be lurking, not in that heat.

"So this is where they lived," Hardin muttered. "Gotta be some sign."

"Of what?" I asked.

"Where they went. Who they worked for." He sounded frustrated. "Something."

The biggest room clearly belonged to the Reverend Jolly. A black frock coat had been thrown over the back of a chair, next to a scuffed pair of shoes with a hole in the left toe. A white clerical collar sat on the dressing table, along with a brush that had several dark hairs stuck in the bristles. A wooden cross hung on the wall over the bed. The stub of a candle sat on a sideboard. There was nothing else except a mouse nest under one of the pillows.

"Him and Cage had suitcases when I saw them in the train station at Charter Oak," I said. "They took the time to pack before they went."

Hardin glanced around the empty room. "That's what it looks like." He checked the pockets of the coat and came up empty.

"The other must be Mr. Cage's," I said.

We went to the second room across the landing. The size was fairly spacious, if not as big as the reverend's, but the furnishings were spartan, the bed covered with a single dingy sheet. It had a sour odor I recognized. The window looked out on a small building by itself under a stand of trees on the bank of the creek. The schoolhouse. I'm not sure how I knew, I just did.

A chair had been pulled up to the window. The arms were deeply gouged with a knifepoint. I pictured Mr. Cage sitting there, idly scratching at the wood, dreaming about the Lord knew what. Watching the children.

My gut tightened and I turned away. "They're long gone, Hardin," I said.

He yanked open the drawer of a writing desk, then slammed it shut again, his jaw tight. We went back out to the landing at the top of the stairs. Hardin looked up at a rope that dangled from a square on the ceiling.

"Well, there's still the attic," he said. "Guess I better have a look."

He pulled on the rope. A trapdoor dropped down, along with a rickety ladder.

"Go grab that candle," he said, squinting up into the darkness.

I fetched the stub of wax in a brass holder from the bedroom. Hardin took out a box of matches and lit it. He handed the candle to me while he climbed the ladder. When he reached the top, I passed it up. I could see the yellow flame against the darkness but little else.

"Careful," I muttered as he crawled off.

I stood in the hall for a minute, listening to the muffled sounds of Hardin exploring the attic. It had to be hot as blazes up there, even worse than the main house. I hoped he'd wrap it up soon. The sun was almost down and we still had to search the outbuildings.

"Anything?" I called.

Hardin made some reply, but I couldn't make out the words. His voice sounded normal though, so I didn't worry.

Then I heard a board creak somewhere below.

I'd seen ample evidence of mice, but they wouldn't be heavy enough to make the floor creak. The hair on my neck rose up. I drew my gun.

I leaned out over the railing. I could see down the stairwell to a patch of carpet on the first floor. Nothing moved. I held my breath, listening. The house was silent, but it struck me as a different kind of silence than before.

Something was down there. A bigger animal, maybe. I'd propped the back door open. A stray dog could have wandered in, looking for food.

Or maybe something else.

I backed toward the ladder leading to the attic.

"Hardin," I hissed at the square of blackness above.

I couldn't see his light at all now.

"You there?"

He didn't answer.

My heart was beating fast now. I tried to calm down. Most likely it was just an animal. Rats, maybe.

"Hardin?" I tried again.

The silence felt heavy now, like something was listening.

I was about to climb the ladder and make sure Hardin was okay when I heard another creak below. It was followed by a stifled cry, like someone had clapped their hand over another person's mouth.

You're the law, Ruth, I thought grimly. Go see what's what.

I cocked my gun. Then I started down the stairs, hugging the wall. I tried to be quiet, but every other step groaned no matter how slowly I moved. Sweat slicked my forehead. I didn't dare let go of the gun to wipe it away. When I got to the second landing, I paused. I couldn't remember if we'd left the doors open or closed, but the one across from me was ajar by an inch.

I stared at the dark gap, gathering my nerve. Anything could be waiting behind that door.

I crept forward. I kicked it wide and brought the gun up.

The room was empty.

Suddenly, I heard running feet on the stairs below. I leaned over the bannister and my heart nearly stopped. I saw a flash of yellow hair. The face turned, just for a second. The dead fish eyes of Mr. Cage met mine. His hand was clamped around a little girl's arm. She wore a flour-sack dress and her hair was in pigtails. I only caught a glimpse of them before the front door slammed.

I flew down the stairs two at a time. I might have caught him if one of the carpet nails hadn't come loose. It hooked my toe as I sprinted down the ground floor hallway, sending me sprawling. I slammed the same shoulder that I'd bruised earlier, but I hardly felt it as I scrambled up and kept going.

Mr. Cage was here.

The last time I saw him, he'd been rolling around on the ground with a hunting knife buried in his gut — the same knife he'd meant to use on me. It was only a week ago. I couldn't understand how the man was able to stand on his own, let alone run, but I had to catch him before he hurt that girl.

And if Cage was here, good odds the Reverend Jolly wasn't far off.

I ran out the front door and saw him heading towards the low building behind the church. It looked like a meeting hall or barracks-style living quarters. He was dragging the child, who kicked and screamed. Mr. Cage was half the reverend's age, about twenty or so, and strong. He hefted her up under one arm like it was nothing. I aimed my gun at his back, right where the suspenders crossed his shirt, but he ducked through the door before I could fire. The pair of them vanished into the darkness of the building.

I ran across the yard. If a knife didn't stop Cage, a bullet in the head surely would, and I planned to empty the flintlock just to be sure.

Of course, it could be a trap. Why else would he have shown himself? I resolved to be careful, but I couldn't bide my time. The man was insane. He could be cutting into her right now.

Paisley curtains covered the windows. None of them gave so much as a twitch. I slowed as I reached the door and took a moment to catch my breath.

"Cage!" I yelled. "Come on out! We got this place surrounded!"

There was no answer save the dry rattle of corn stalks.

I gave the door a mighty kick. It rebounded hard against the inner wall. I barged through.

The smell hit me like a fist.

My throat closed. I flung up an arm to cover my nose, though it didn't help much. The stench was a combination of spoiled meat and an overflowing outhouse. I coughed, barely managing to keep my gun up.

Some light came in through the curtains. I didn't see Mr. Cage or the girl. They'd disappeared, unless they were hiding under one of the cots. Like an infirmary, the beds were laid out in rows of ten each. They had iron frames and each had a hope chest at the foot.

Each one also held a body.

They must have been there a while because fluids had drained down, staining the bedclothes and bare wood floor. They looked sunken and misshapen, hardly human. I wanted to scream, but my throat was too tight to make a sound. The gun trembled in my hand. I slowly backed away.

The bodies were starting to shrivel in the heat, but they weren't even close to skeletons yet. Maggots wriggled in white masses. Some had been shot in the head or chest. Others . . . . Well, I couldn't tell how they died. Poison, maybe. A fair number had Bibles nearby, or other keepsakes. There was even a dead dog, lying at its master's feet.

With all the windows shut, I couldn't swallow the gorge that rose up in my throat. I staggered outside. Hardin was crossing the yard, Colt Walker in hand. He broke into a run when he saw me.

"Dammit, Cortez," he exclaimed. "Where'd you go haring off to?" The marshal studied my face. His brow creased. "What in nine hells—"

I gasped air like a drowning person. The smell was stuck to my clothes. To my hair. To everything, like it had gotten inside me. I pushed past him and walked unsteadily to the corner of the building. I braced a hand on the wall, bent over and emptied my stomach until nothing was left.

When I'd finished, Hardin put an arm around my shoulders. It should have been awkward, but it seemed the most natural thing in the world. He patted my back while I spit in the dirt. My head was pounding.

"Easy, Cortez," he said.

Hardin eased the gun from my limp fingers. I buried my face in his coat. I was covered in cold sweat.

"Just breathe," Hardin said. "It's okay. Take a minute."

It wasn't okay, not at all, but I pulled myself together and stepped back.

"They're all dead, marshal," I said in a rush. "Every one."

He looked sad, but not shocked. "You shouldn't have gone in there alone—"

"I followed Cage. He had a little girl. No more than nine or ten."

Hardin frowned. His posture shifted to high alert. "Cage?" he said. *"Here?"*

I nodded. "He went in the building. I was chasing him when . . . I didn't see them, but I couldn't stay in there a second longer."

"Can you cover me?" Hardin asked.

I nodded. He handed me the flintlock. I took up a stance next to the door.

"I didn't see a gun," I said. "But Mr. Cage is partial to knives. Be careful."

"Oh, I plan to shoot first and ask questions later," Hardin said grimly. "Ready?"

He kicked the door wide, then threw a hand up as the smell hit him. "Holy Christ," he choked.

"It gets worse," I said, trying to look past him for any sign of movement.

"Cage and the girl are *inside*?" Hardin asked dubiously.

It seemed impossible to be in that building for more than two seconds without retching.

"Have to be," I said. "Unless there's another way out."

"Damn," Hardin muttered. "Let's go."

We jogged around to the rear of the building. The barren ground under the windows looked undisturbed. To the left was an outhouse and a fallow field. Just in case, I kicked open the door to the outhouse. It was empty.

Hardin didn't say anything, just turned and went back to the front. He ventured a little way inside. The smell drove him out within seconds. "We have to get these windows open," he muttered, his face pale and beaded with sweat.

"They're nailed shut," I said, suppressing a shudder.

"Jesus." Hardin found a rock and lobbed it at the glass. I

helped him smash the rest. There was no reaction from inside. I prayed to God that Mr. Cage hadn't hurt that little girl.

Hardin took out a handkerchief and tied it around his nose and mouth. I followed him to the door, one arm covering my face, but I just couldn't make myself go inside again.

"Stand watch," he said to me. "Yell if you see anybody."

I nodded. I didn't envy him the task of searching that place. Hardin visibly steeled himself and went in. I watched from the doorway as he strode down the center aisle, pausing now and then to stiffly drop to one knee and look underneath the cots. He didn't speak, not even to swear, probably because that would require opening his mouth.

I kept my finger on the trigger, ready to fire, as the marshal moved deeper into the building. I didn't dare take my eyes off him for a second. Cage had to be under one of those beds, lying in the filth. No normal person could have managed that without retching, but Cage wasn't exactly normal.

His tastes might seem peculiar to some, Jolly had said to me. *But a fellow needs his diversions. Better you don't find out what they are.*

Hardin reached the end of the barracks. He kicked aside the last cot, his own gun aimed down. Then he turned to me and shook his head.

"Get out of there," I called.

Hardin didn't exactly sprint for the door, but he came at a fast trot. The moment he got outside, he pulled off the bandana and drew a deep breath. His face was grey, but his voice sounded steady when he spoke. "You sure you saw them come inside?"

"I'm sure," I said. "I mean, I thought I did."

"Well, there's nothing living," Hardin said. "And nowhere to hide."

"What about trap doors?"

"I checked, Cortez. The floor is solid oak planks." He blinked and rubbed a hand across his eyes. "But I'll look again if you're sure about what you saw."

I could tell he didn't want to go back in there, and I could hardly blame him. I'd probably have nightmares for the rest of my life.

"No, forget it," I said. "I must have made a mistake."

The first stars twinkled in the east. I reckoned we had about an hour until full dark. If we didn't get back to the train soon, Elzy Mack and Ned Carver might well be gone. The thought of being stuck in New Jerusalem was not a pleasant one, but I couldn't give up. We walked a slow circle around the building again, scanning the ground.

"No tracks," Hardin observed in a neutral tone.

"You think I imagined it, don't you?" I said.

Hardin glanced at me. "I didn't say that."

"But you're thinking it."

He sighed. "There's nowhere to hide, Cortez. And how could they have got out here ahead of us? There's no train. No airship."

"They could have been dropped off," I said stubbornly.

"Okay." He gave me a level look. "But why come back at all?"

"I don't know." I balled my fists in frustration. "I'm not crazy, though."

"Never said you were." Hardin glanced at the building. "I've seen some bad things," he said softly. "But that's the worst."

We didn't talk for a long minute. Hardin stared into space.

"What about the schoolhouse?" he said at last. "Should we——"

"No," I said.

The little building on the banks of the creek was dark and silent. I felt certain Cage hadn't gone in there to hide — if he was ever here at all.

"We still ought to look, don't you think?"

I heard reluctance in his voice. Hardin thought it was his

duty, but he was afraid, because as bad as things were now we both knew they could still get worse.

"Did you see any kids in the bunkhouse?" I asked quietly.

He shook his head.

"Don't, then," I whispered. "Can't you see? There's nothing left to save."

A wave of lightheadedness took me. I rested my hands on my knees, praying I wouldn't be sick again.

Hardin muttered an oath. "You're right," he said. "Let's get out of here."

Something stirred in the corner of my eye. My nerves were strung so tight I nearly pulled the trigger before I realized it was Doc's shadow, stretching long across the dirt.

7

"Where've you been?" I demanded.

Anger seized me — more than Doc deserved — but I needed someone to blame.

"You could have warned us," I went on. "You've been gone more than an hour! How could you, Doc? How could you just take off?"

"I was looking for other haints," Doc replied. He sounded subdued. Not like himself at all. "I thought they could help out with the engine. Manual labor is beneath me." The last was uttered in a hollow tone without conviction.

"And that's all you care about?" I said in disbelief.

"I'm sorry, Ruth." Doc sounded like he meant it. "The place seemed deserted. I didn't think you were in any danger. So I went into the ether, but I couldn't find anybody nearby. When I came back, I took a closer look at New Jerusalem." He paused. "We have to get out of this town. Terrible things happened here."

"Yeah, I already figured that out," I snapped. "But I need to know something first and I suppose you're the one can tell me. Is Mr. Cage here? Or the Reverend Jolly?"

"I haven't seen them," Doc replied. "But you got a live one in that barn over there. It's what I came to tell you."

Hardin's head snapped around. We stared at the faded red barn across the cornfield. The wind was shifty, sending the weathervane atop the peaked roof spinning one way, then the other. It made an irritating squeak that carried clear across the field.

"Man or woman?" Hardin asked.

"Man," Doc said.

"Armed?"

"Not that I can see," Doc replied. "He's hiding in the hayloft."

"Tell Mr. Mack to stay put," Hardin said. "Tell him we're fine, but we need another few minutes."

"Yes, marshal," Doc said obediently.

I raised an eyebrow. He must have been feeling guilty for leaving us.

"Doc, wait," I said. "Does he have a hostage? Little girl with pigtails?"

Maybe I was wrong about it being Mr. Cage. I'd only caught a flash of his face. It looked like him, but now that I'd calmed down, the whole thing did seem improbable.

"Obviously not, Ruth," Doc said tartly. "I would have told you that right off, wouldn't I?"

"Does he have yellow hair?" I asked.

"How'd you guess?"

"I think I saw him," I said. "You sure there's no girl?"

"Nope," Doc said firmly. "He's alone."

I shared a quick look with Hardin. "What's he doing?" I asked.

"Just hiding," Doc said. "He looks scared."

"The sole survivor," I muttered. "But why's he still here? I'd be long gone, even if I had to hike a hundred miles to the next town. No way on earth I could stomach spending a single night in this place, and I'd say those people were killed at least two weeks ago."

"Maybe he's traumatized," Hardin said. "Scared to come out."

"He'd be dead if he hadn't gone for food and water."

"True." He sighed. "I got this, Cortez. Don't worry, I know you're not feeling right."

"I'm coming with you," I said.

"You sure?"

I nodded.

"We need him alive," Hardin said. "If he wasn't part of it, he's a witness. So no shooting unless he pulls a gun."

"Yes, sir."

"He's not armed," Doc said. "I already told you."

Hardin's face didn't give much away. "Just tell Mr. Mack not to leave yet."

Doc's shadow sped off in the direction of the train. We crossed the cornfield to the barn. It looked older than the other buildings, practically falling down. I figured the barn must have been part of the property before Jolly showed up and he hadn't bothered to repair it. The doors hung at a crazy angle. We peered through the gap. It was cool and dim inside. There was no sign of animals, which came as a huge relief. I'd seen enough death to last me a lifetime.

I caught a faint odor of manure, but the barn had clearly not been used for livestock in many years. The stalls on one side were full of broken furniture and moldering cloth. The north end was a little neater. Nails held farming tools — hoes, pitchforks, scythes, some bags of seed the mice had been at.

A tall ladder led up to the hayloft. Hardin gestured at me to stay put and ducked behind one of the center posts holding up the roof. Whatever Doc said, he wasn't about to stand there in the open, which seemed wise to me.

"I know you're up there," he said in a loud voice. "Come on down."

Silence.

"Okay," Hardin said reasonably. "Guess I'll just have to send a haint to root you out. He ain't very polite though."

A hoarse voice drifted down from above. "Who are you?"

"Carnarvon marshals."

"You're a long way south," the voice said with a note of suspicion. "Show me your badge."

Hardin sighed and held it around the side of the post. A man's face appeared at the edge of the hayloft. He looked so matted and dirty, at first I thought he was part of the hay.

"We won't hurt you," Hardin said. "Unless you're involved in this."

"I didn't do a thing." The man gave a wild, bitter laugh. "Not a thing except run for my life."

"Then you got nothing to fear," Hardin said. He pinned the badge back on his coat. "What's your name?"

"Samuel Withrow."

"Well, Mr. Withrow, I suggest you climb down from there and tell us what happened."

The man was white with dishwater blonde hair and a scrawny build. He wore an undershirt and a pair of trousers that looked well-made but stiff with dirt. Grime caked his fingernails and the creases of his skin. A curly beard covered his cheeks, but I could see the bones underneath. Like he hadn't eaten right in days.

"Wait there," Hardin said when he got to the bottom of the ladder.

The man flinched like a beaten dog when I looked at him. He did as Hardin said, his gaze cast down.

"Is this the one you saw?" Hardin asked me in a low voice.

I eyed the man closely, but I already knew the answer. "No," I said at last. "The other was broad across the shoulders and at least six foot. Twenty years younger, too."

Just like Cage. He'd even worn the same dark frock coat.

I also knew there was no way Cage could have run like

that with the gut wound I'd given him. Could I have imagined it out of whole cloth? But he'd led me straight to the building where the bodies were. And judging by the way Mr. Withrow was trembling, he knew exactly what had happened in New Jerusalem. That much was real, at least.

"Anyone else here?" Hardin asked him in a stern tone.

"No, sir." His gaze stayed rooted to the floor. "They're all in heaven now."

"You see it happen?"

The man hunched his shoulders and didn't answer.

"Maybe you came to rob the dead," Hardin suggested in a soft but dangerous tone.

"No!" Withrow finally showed some backbone, glaring at him. "I'd never do such a thing." He kneaded his fingers together, clenching them until the knuckles were white. "I ran and hid in the old Pendelton mine. Waited until I was sure they were gone."

"The Reverend Jolly and Mr. Cage?" Hardin prompted.

Withrow shuddered. "Those two. I lost track of time. Reckon it's been a week or more. But I had to come back."

"For what?"

"My little girl."

I felt a chill.

"Did you find her?" Hardin asked. "Are there any more survivors?"

Samuel Withrow stared into space, his face blank. "I wanted to give 'em a Christian burial. A man ought to do for his family."

Hardin glanced at me. I saw pity in his eyes.

Withrow started to cry. "I tried to save her. But Mr. Cage . . . ." He covered his face with his hands.

"We got here by train," Hardin said. "Why don't you come aboard and tell us the whole story? We can give you a hot meal and some clean clothes."

Samuel Withrow looked up, suddenly suspicious. "I didn't see any train at the depot."

"The tracks are barricaded about a mile out. We walked into town." Hardin jerked his head toward the door. "Go take a look, you can see from the end of the street."

Withrow shook his head. "I ain't leaving 'til I bury my daughter." His mouth trembled. "She ain't in the schoolhouse with the others. I already looked."

"Then how can you be sure she's dead?" Hardin asked.

"Because I saw Mr. Cage kill her." A tear cut through the dirt on one cheek. "You met the man?"

I cleared my throat. "I have."

Samuel Withrow held my eye without wavering this time. "Then you know."

"Yeah," I said. "I do."

"Please," Withrow said in a broken voice. "You have to help me find her."

"I'll do what I can, sir," Hardin said. He made a small gesture and we stepped away for a moment. "What do you think, Cortez?"

I glanced at Samuel Withrow. Despite the heat, he stood with his arms wrapped around himself, his eyes far away as if we no longer existed. He looked thin and dirty enough to have been hiding out for days, though his story had some holes.

"I think he's telling the truth," I said slowly. "Part of it, anyhow."

"So do I," Hardin agreed. "We can't leave him here, but we can't stay much longer. I have to alert the territorial police." He scowled. "The real ones."

"You trust them?"

He frowned. "I have to, Cortez. I can't believe Pedro Braga would be a party to this."

"Maybe he doesn't know. We're the first ones here. It doesn't mean he didn't hire the reverend."

Hardin hesitated, then shook his head. "I've known Braga

for years. Not well, but well enough. He's cutthroat when it comes to business, but he's too smart to get involved with a lunatic like Jolly."

I opened my mouth to argue and he raised a hand. "However, that don't mean I trust anyone until we get to Aguadulce. I know most of the brass personally. They'll hear me out."

"Yes, sir," I said.

Hardin scrubbed a hand across his jaw. "I could detain Mr. Withrow. I'd be within my rights, considering what we found." He glanced in the direction of the train. "I got warrants for Jolly and Cage on board. That should be enough to justify it. Then we can get the hell out of here."

Once Hardin would have given me a direct order, but we'd been through a lot in the last two days. He gave me an inquiring look. Silently asking my opinion. I realized that for all his experience, Hardin was in over his head, too.

I've never wanted to get away from any place more than I wanted to get away from New Jerusalem. In two years as a deputy, I'd encountered my share of hard cases. Outlaws. Horse thieves. But Jolly and Cage were beyond the pale. I couldn't comprehend what would drive a person to do what they'd done, and I knew I'd never be the same for having witnessed it.

But they had to be stopped. And maybe there were more survivors.

"Why don't we take Mr. Withrow to the saloon and get his story?" I said. "Then we can decide what to do."

HARDIN POURED a shot of whiskey and set it on the bar. Samuel Withrow downed it in one gulp. He wiped his mouth with a grubby sleeve.

"I hope you string 'em both up," he said. "Feed the bones to the coyotes." He stared longingly at the bottle, which

Hardin had wisely returned to the shelf. It made me think of Miss White. She lived by herself on the outskirts of Lucky Boy and only walked into town to buy Thistle Dew whiskey.

"What exactly happened here?" Hardin asked. His voice was mild, but his eyes never left the older man.

"I was part of Jolly's congregation." Samuel hung his head. "One of the first to join up, so he let us live in the big house."

"When was this?"

"The reverend turned up about a year ago. He seemed real nice at first. He said he'd come down from the Northern Territory. He and his son would move from town to town, preaching the gospel. But he was ready to settle and he liked the sound of New Jerusalem. Said it called to him."

"His son," I said. "You mean Mr. Cage."

Samuel Withrow nodded, his mouth twisting in distaste. "He wasn't really the reverend's son, more of a henchman, but I didn't find that out until later. Anyway, Jolly had a way about him. The people here had given up hope and he gave 'em something to believe in. A better future. He got us to help build the church. Word spread. More and more people started to come on Sundays, until he'd built up quite a following."

Withrow glanced in the direction of the barn. "There was an old abandoned plot used to belong to some homesteaders. We all pitched in to fix up the farmhouse. Sow some corn in the fields. For a while, it felt like they'd brought New Jerusalem back to life."

He twisted the empty glass of whiskey. "People was happy to have them here. The reverend seemed godly. And if Mr. Cage was a little strange . . . well, they were willing to overlook it. Cage worked as hard as the rest of us, even if he didn't talk much." His face creased in pain. "My wife never liked him. She kept a close eye when the children were playing outside. But I didn't pay her mind. I should have."

"What happened?" Hardin asked quietly.

Withrow was quiet for a long minute. "I guess it began about six months ago. The reverend started to change. His sermons veered more toward end times, fire and brimstone. He kept talking about the snake in the garden."

"Meaning the phantoms?" I asked.

Withrow nodded. "He spent more and more time in the farmhouse, up in his room. He'd only come out for sermons. They got longer and longer. Half the time he didn't make much sense. But like I said, he had charisma. So people listened. And the ones who stopped coming to church . . . well, they'd get a visit from Mr. Cage."

"You ever see a phantom with either of them?" Hardin asked.

Ned shook his head. "Naw. Jolly hated 'em. Was always preaching against the haints. He said a war was coming. That the Carnarvons were devils and so was Pedro Braga."

Hardin and I shared a quick look.

"Did he ever meet anyone?" Hardin asked. "Someone from outside New Jerusalem?"

Samuel Withrow shook his head, but it had an uncertain quality. "Not that I ever saw. The only way in or out of this place is the train. Almost nobody came before the reverend showed up, and after . . . well, I don't recall a single soul arriving except for Cage. Only a few who left." He closed his eyes. "God forgive me, I wish I'd done the same when we still had a chance."

"Not that you ever saw," I repeated. "Pardon me, sir, but you don't seem sure."

"I *am* sure. About the train." Samuel hesitated. "But I did hear voices once, talking in the reverend's room. One of 'em sounded unfamiliar. It was smooth, like the reverend, but I could swear I didn't know the person." He gave a nervous laugh. "Figured I was hearing things. That it must have been Cage. He didn't talk much."

"Were they talking in English?" I asked. "I mean, could it have been a phantom tongue?"

"Oh, I don't think so," Withrow said. "Sounded like English, though I couldn't make out the words. I was standing on the stair, you see. And I was afraid to be caught eavesdropping. It weren't just Mr. Cage who did the reverend's bidding by then. There were others. Besides which, Jolly hated phantoms above all else."

Hardin looked frustrated enough to start chewing the wood paneling. "Was it just the once?"

"Just the once that I heard," Withrow said. "But I wasn't supposed to go to the top floor of the farmhouse."

"And you couldn't make out any of the words," Hardin said.

"No, sir."

"What about the tone. Was it an argument? Or just a conversation?"

Samuel Withrow considered this question. "Not an argument, exactly. But I did get the feeling the other voice was in control. Maybe even giving orders, you know?"

"That's helpful," Hardin said. "Anything else?"

"Can't really think of anything." Samuel gave us an apologetic look. "I'm sorry."

"Let's move on then," Hardin said crisply.

Withrow shifted in his seat. "On the night it happened, I was readying to leave. I didn't like the tenor of the reverend's preaching or the way he ordered us around like he was some kind of king. He had us build that barracks for when we went to war against the haints. Said we'd need a bunkhouse for God's army. It got pretty crazy. Some folks agreed with him, but others were getting uneasy. We decided to leave together, but we had to wait for the train. In the old days, when the mines were open, it came once a week, sometimes twice. Nowadays you might wait a month or more. So we kept our plans secret and readied ourselves to run at the next chance.

"Well, that night, we'd gone to bed when Mr. Cage came around and banged on all the doors. We were summoned to the church. The reverend was waiting at the pulpit." Samuel Withrow shivered. "It had been days since I last saw him. He looked sick, like he hadn't slept at all. People were scared but they did as told. We sat in the pews and prayed. There was only about thirty of us left at that point."

A queasy chill ran down my own spine.

"It wasn't the first time Jolly had called us to the church at an odd hour to listen to him preach, but this time felt different. The sermon went on and on. He talked about the Rapture and the sacrifice of Isaac by Abraham. About burnt offerings and the blood of the lamb. He said a great darkness was coming, but the Lord saw fit to spare us the trials and tribulations in store for all the sinners."

Withrow's face was haunted. "Jolly had acolytes, others like Cage who did his bidding without question. They split us up. That's when I really got scared. The children were taken to the schoolhouse. Everyone else was herded like sheep to the dormitory."

Hardin and I were silent. I didn't want to hear what was coming next.

"I made an excuse to take Lucy to the big house. Said she needed her favorite doll. Cage was suspicious, but he let us go. Like I said, I was one of the reverend's first followers. But he sent two other men to keep an eye on us — true believers. When we got to Lucy's room, I pried her window open. I told her to shimmy down the drainpipe and run. But they must have guessed what we were up to and told Cage. I heard him coming up the stairs. Lucy was screaming. I tried to stop him, but he forced his way inside."

Samuel Withrow stopped talking. His hands were trembling badly.

"You don't have to—" Hardin began.

"No, I'll finish it," he said bitterly. "Cage had his knife out.

He seized Lucy by the hair while the others held me back." A sob broke from deep in his chest. "He slit her throat right there. I fought like a wild man. Did no good. They hit me on the head and hauled me to the bunkhouse."

The stain on the bed. I thought I might be sick again. The room swam in and out. Hardin slid the bottle of Thistle Dew my way, along with a glass. I'd never tasted whiskey before. It was awful and I nearly ran out the door to retch in the street. But then my stomach settled and my nerves steadied somewhat. Samuel shook his head when Hardin offered him some, but the marshal took a swig.

"I don't usually drink," Hardin muttered. "But by God, that's one of the worst things I ever heard."

Samuel Withrow wiped his face. He seemed determined to finish the tale. "Everyone was praying and crying. The reverend spoke a few words. His eyes looked like dark pits to Hell. He said we should celebrate because our earthly tribulations were at an end. They made people eat rat poison and those who refused were shot by Mr. Cage."

"How'd you survive?" Hardin asked.

"I played dead. It weren't hard. The men who dragged me from the farmhouse beat me pretty bad. After they shot my wife . . . I just lost hope. I lay down with the others and didn't move. I heard Cage walking up and down, checking the beds. Each time I figured he'd find me. But each time he passed me by."

His leg jittered against the chair. "Stayed that way for a few days, I guess. Can't be sure. It was like a nightmare. I got so thirsty. And the smell . . . ." He grabbed the whiskey bottle and poured an inch into the glass, then downed it with a wince. "Part of me wanted to just die there. But I finally crawled out and somehow made it to the Pendleton mine. I snuck back at night to pilfer some food, but I thought I saw shadows moving in the dark." He shuddered. "The devil sent

Jolly and Cage. I just wanted to give my girls a Christian burial."

"These men," I said. "The ones who helped Jolly. I guess you know all their faces pretty well."

"I'll never forget as long as I live," Samuel said.

"Maybe you can look at one of the dead bandits," I said. "Could be the same—"

My voice was cut off by a long blast from the train horn. We ran into the street. The sun was almost down, but I could see a dust cloud coming in fast across the desert.

"Upstairs," Hardin said tightly.

"No!" Samuel had gone white as a funeral shroud. "We have to hide. What if it's *them*?"

"I hope to God it is," Hardin said grimly, cocking his gun.

Withrow looked ready to bolt. I laid a steadying hand on his arm. "Come on," I said. "Do what Mr. Hardin says."

I herded him inside and we climbed up to the balcony on the second floor of the saloon. Beyond the rooftops, I saw three vehicles racing towards New Jerusalem on a road parallel to the tracks. Elzy Mack must have seen them coming and laid on the horn to warn us. As I watched, one of the cars peeled off and made for the train.

"Dammit," Hardin muttered.

"Is it them?" Withrow croaked.

Neither of us answered. We were too busy squinting at the vehicles. They looked just like the one I'd blown up at the border except they had little flags mounted on the hood that snapped in the wind.

"Looks like the Guardia," Hardin muttered.

"Funny timing," I said.

Samuel gave a little yelp as Doc's inky shadow stretched across the balcony. He cowered back against the rail, his eyes showing the whites like a panicky horse.

"Don't worry," I said. "The haint's with us."

He did not seem reassured. Samuel had been listening to

the reverend preach against phantoms for a long time. Even if he hated Jolly now, it had been ingrained that they were the enemy.

"Trouble," Doc said briskly.

"I can see that," I said. "What kind is it now?"

"They're dressed like Gorras," Doc said, rolling the r's. "And they're flying the Braga colors."

"Well, thank the Good Lord," Withrow muttered. He kept glancing nervously at Doc, but at least he hadn't run screaming.

"It might not be the law," I said, sharing a look with Hardin.

"It might not," Hardin agreed. "We'd better get inside."

"What's going on?" Withrow demanded.

"We got hit by bandits at the border," I explained. "They'd killed the guards and stolen their uniforms. So these fellows might not be the cavalry. Not the ones you're hoping for, at any rate."

Withrow looked alarmed, but he just shook his head. "Didn't used to be so bad out here," he muttered. "But it seems to get worse every year."

We hurried back down into the saloon. "Wish I had a rifle," Hardin muttered as we took up positions on either side of the window. "Or better yet, Richard's arsenal."

"You think they're bandits?" Withrow asked.

"I don't know," Hardin replied. "Guess we'll find out in a minute."

Two vehicles tore down the main street and braked in a cloud of dust. The doors flew open. Armed men poured out. We must have left clear footprints because one made a sharp gesture to the others and they ran back to the cars, ducking behind the open doors. Shotguns racked. Orders were shouted.

"Well, they know we're here," Hardin said.

More men appeared. They must have come in on back

roads we couldn't see. Sunlight glinted on metal. I saw silhouettes in the upper windows of the general store across the street.

"Take a look in the back," Hardin said to me. "Be careful."

I ducked and ran to the office, peeking through a crack in the curtains. There wasn't much behind the saloon except for chaparral and half a dozen water barrels. The bushes were too low to hide a man, but I could see at least one rifle poking out from behind the barrels.

"We got more," I called to Hardin. "Can't tell how many."

Hardin unwrapped a piece of chewing gum. He popped it in his mouth and peeked out the front window. "They're moving in," he said, drawing his Colt.

Samuel Withrow crawled behind the bar. I saw a hand reach up and grab the whiskey bottle.

"What's happening, Cortez?" Hardin asked softly, never taking his eyes from the front window.

"Nothin'. They're just waiting."

"Can you get behind something heavy?"

I looked around. My gaze fell on the desk. I removed the telephone and set it on the floor. Then I heaved the desk on end. I threw my back into it and managed to push it partly across the window.

"You see uniforms?" Hardin called.

"Can't tell," I called. "Doc? Can you see?"

"They're all wearing the brown," the phantom confirmed in a soft voice.

"Doc," Hardin said. "You still here?"

"Why, yes I am, sir," the phantom said in an oily tone. "How may I assist?"

"Did they find the train?"

"They certainly did."

"Mr. Carver and Mr. Mack?"

"The cook and the driver are in handcuffs."

"Well, that's good news, right?" I said. "If it was the reverend's men, they'd be dead. What about Marshal Tanaka?"

"They set a guard to watch her. But they didn't seem happy about the dead fellow in the next compartment. The one dressed like a Gorra."

I frowned. "Oh, no. Do they think we killed one of their own?"

"Hell," Hardin said wearily. "Let's just find out." He unpinned his badge and tossed it out the batwing doors. "This is Marshal Sebastian Hardin," he shouted in Spanish. "Who's in command here?"

In answer, they started firing. Plaster and wood chips flew through the air. Glass shattered. I curled into a ball behind the desk.

"Anybody hit?" Hardin called out when the shooting finally stopped.

"I'm grand," Samuel Withrow replied faintly from behind the bar.

"Cortez?" The worry in his voice made me smile, even though I was terrified.

"Okay." I wormed on my belly up to the front window. "What if they *are* the real deal?" I whispered. "We can't shoot back without knowing."

"I don't recognize any of 'em." Hardin shook his head. "But that doesn't mean much. The Guardia Territorial is like the marshal service. Hundreds of men and women."

"So what do we do?"

Hardin tipped his head back against the wall. He closed his eyes and sighed. "I'm sorry, Cortez."

"Ain't your fault."

"Yeah, it is. I talked you into coming."

"That's not true. I came for my own reasons."

He gave me a wry look. "Well, I reckon you're sorry now."

"No," I said.

He frowned. "Why not?"

"Because if I wasn't here, you might have died at the border."

"True enough. Cortez—" Hardin muttered a curse.

One of the cars backed up and turned to face the saloon. I heard a whirring sound as a hatch opened. A weapon the size of a small cannon rotated towards us from a turret atop the roof. "Treinta segundos," a brisk voice informed us in Spanish.

Thirty seconds.

"Tiren las armas y mantengan las manos a la vista."

A moment later the command was repeated in English.

"Throw your weapons down and keep your hands in sight."

The bore on the barrel was three times the diameter of Richard's Widowmaker. I figured it would take out the whole saloon and maybe the buildings next door, too.

"Veinte segundos," the cool voice informed us. "Tiren las armas y salgan."

"I'll go first," Hardin said in a decisive tone. "If they shoot me, tell Doc to get you out of here by any means necessary. You hear me, Doc?"

"I sure do, marshal," Doc replied.

"I don't like that plan," I said heatedly. "We go out together."

"Hell, no." Hardin's blue eyes locked with mine. "You wait until I'm in custody. That's a direct order, Cortez."

"But—"

"Diez segundos," the voice bellowed. "Nueve, ocho, siete. . . ."

I grasped his hand. I had a terrible premonition that if he walked out that door, I'd never see him alive again. "Marshal, please," I said hoarsely. "Don't."

"I'll be fine," Hardin said. He squeezed my hand. Then he stood up. "Está bien, voy a salir!" he called out.

The countdown stopped at three. Hardin threw his Colt Walker out the broken window. He squared his shoulders. When he reached the doors, he turned back. "They'll take the Collier, so make sure you set it straight with Doc first."

"Yes, sir."

"And if we live through this, not a word about Merriweather. Understood?"

I suppressed hysterical laughter. The man never stopped.

"Not a word," I promised.

Hardin stepped outside the saloon, his hands raised. I watched through the broken window, my heart thudding, as a dozen rifles, shotguns and revolvers drew a bead on him. For a bad moment, I thought Hardin had made a mistake. Then the men started yelling.

"On the ground! Get on the ground!"

Hardin dropped and kissed the dirt. Two Gorras rushed forward and grabbed him, cuffing his arms behind his back. They dragged him over to a middle-aged man with a paunch hanging over his belt. They talked in low voices. It sounded like Hardin was arguing. The officer pointed to the saloon.

"Come on out, Cortez," Hardin called. "We're under arrest, but I'll straighten it out."

They hadn't taken the cuffs off, I noticed. But he was still alive. And he seemed convinced the men were really the Territorial Police.

I turned to Doc. "This is it," I said. "I hand over the flintlock or leave it here. Your choice. But if you don't come with me now, I can't promise I'll make it back." I hesitated. "Anything could happen in Aguadulce."

"You know how I feel about strangers handling the Collier," Doc growled.

"I know."

"You can't tell them about me, Ruth."

"Never," I agreed. "But you have to promise not to do

anything. Just stay quiet and hidden. When this is sorted out,
I'll get you back, I promise."

He grumbled. "I've spent enough time in a ghost town. I
don't care to repeat the experience."

"So you'll behave? You swear it?"

Samuel Withrow had emerged from behind the bar. He
watched us argue with a confused expression.

"I swear it," Doc muttered.

"Because if you break that promise, you could get us
killed."

"I just swore, didn't I?"

"Okay." I nodded. "Here we go."

I threw the flintlock out the window. It slid across the dirt.
I braced myself as one of the Gorras picked it up, but Doc
behaved himself. With luck, he'd gone into the ether to throw
his tantrum and he'd stay there until I got him back.

"Ready, Mr. Withrow?" I asked.

Samuel gave a nod.

"Vamos a salir," I called.

We raised our hands and pushed through the saloon
doors.

Guns cocked. "On your knees!"

I dropped down. Samuel Withrow stayed standing. His
eyes looked lost.

"You seen them?" he asked in a quavering voice.

"Get down!" It was the older man with Hardin. He had
braids of insignia on his coat and appeared to be in charge.

"I have to find them." Samuel Withrow's Adam's apple
bobbed up and down. "I have to."

"Just do what they say," I hissed. "Tell 'em about it later. I
promise they'll help."

He didn't seem to hear me. Anger filled his eyes as he
surveyed the soldiers. "Why'd you take so long to get out
here?"

"On your face!"

Hardin took a step forward. His guards yanked him back. "Don't shoot," Hardin pleaded. "He's not a threat to anyone—"

"Shut up," the officer said. "Get down," he bellowed. "Now!"

"You gotta find 'em," Samuel said. "Please. They could be alive."

"Get down!"

"Do it!" I urged him. "They'll kill you."

He looked down at me. I saw despair in his face. Then he reached for his coat pocket. Gunfire echoed through the deserted streets as the Gorras started firing. Samuel Withrow jerked and fell down next to me.

"That man was the only witness," Hardin ground out. "He didn't hurt anyone. Damn it to hell, why'd you have to shoot him?"

I laced my hands behind my head, kneeling in a spreading pool of Samuel Withrow's blood. A cameo photograph lay next to his hand. I noticed the dirt, the way it was ground into the ridges of skin and under his long, ragged nails. The cameo had a silver frame. It was bright and untarnished. He probably polished it on his shirt each night before he went to sleep.

The photograph showed Samuel Withrow and, without any doubt whatsoever, the little girl I'd seen at the farmhouse.

A ghost.

Hands pulled me up. They took the Bowie knife strapped to my hip and cuffed me. I was walked over to Hardin, who looked angry. They shoved us into the rear of a vehicle and drove us into the desert just outside of town. I heard the propeller of a small zeppelin buzzing overhead.

The vehicle stopped and they let us out. I watched the airship land, its gondola sporting the Braga colors, black and red. A man walked down the folding stairs. He had a thin grey mustache and four bars of rank on his shoulder. His coat had a high embroidered collar with gold braid looping down to a row of silver buttons. One of our guards hurried to meet him.

"Ellos son Servicios Especiales," he said, casting us a side-long glance.

"I know him," the officer said with a curt nod. "Señor Hardin."

Hardin looked relieved. "Comisario Alvarez. I'm glad you're here. This is all a mistake."

"Please." The commissioner gave a tight smile that didn't touch his eyes. "Allow me to explain things from my perspective first. This morning, four members of the border patrol reported for their shift, only to discover the naked, mutilated corpses of the men they were supposed to be relieving. The border post was partially burned and the bodies of four other individuals were found shot outside. An explosive device had been deployed."

Hardin opened his mouth and Comisario Alvarez raised a hand.

"Naturally, we commenced an air search to find the culprits. The only thing we spotted was *your* train, Señor Hardin. At first, we feared you were in trouble. So I sent in a division of the border patrol. And what did they discover on board? A man dressed in the uniform of the Gorras, also dead. Along with a sizable arsenal." His voice rose. "I was told that you had come to deliver contracts to Mr. Braga, but you seem to have lost your way!"

"They attacked us," Hardin protested. "Your men were already dead when we got to the border."

The comisario stared at him in frank disbelief. "And that's why you concealed yourself when the Guardia Territorial arrived?"

"Yes, sir." Hardin was making a visible effort to keep calm. "Just like you saw, they stole the uniforms."

The comisario nodded. "And what are you doing in New Jerusalem?"

"I have a warrant for Reverend Josephiah Jolly and an associate who goes by the name Mr. Cage. They stirred up some trouble across the border. Mrs. Carnarvon asked me to take a look on my way to Aguadulce—"

"This is not your jurisdiction, Señor Hardin," Alvarez snapped.

"I'm aware of that. I didn't mean to step on any toes."

The comisario turned as another vehicle pulled up from the direction of Jolly's compound. Two Gorras emerged and spoke in rapid Spanish. They'd found the bodies. Alvarez listened without interruption, though his expression grew darker with every word.

"Did Special Services know what happened here?" he demanded coldly.

"Of course not!" Hardin said. "How could I have known? We just arrived a couple of hours ago. If your men hadn't killed the only witness, you could have questioned him yourself!"

The comisario stared at Hardin for a long moment. Then he turned to his underlings. "Get them in the zeppelin."

"What about the train? I have people aboard," Hardin said.

"My men will escort it to Aguadulce." The comisario's tone was ominous. "Mr. Braga will want to see you right away."

We were taken to the gondola, which was just big enough to accommodate the pilot and six passengers. The Gorras gestured to the last row of seats. Hardin and I sat down, the cuffs digging painfully into my wrists. I looked out the window. New Jerusalem crawled with lawmen. They were searching every inch of the place, but I knew they wouldn't find Cage.

Because he couldn't have been there.

"I'll straighten all this out when we get to Aguadulce," Hardin said. "Don't worry, Cortez."

"Sure," I said faintly.

None of it seemed real. Except that every time I closed my eyes, I saw Samuel Withrow. He'd died with a look of surprise on his face. It wasn't the Gorras' fault. He could have been reaching for a gun. They'd warned him. But it still shook me.

The funny part is that when I thought about the bunkhouse, the one I kept seeing was that poor dog. I turned away so Hardin didn't see the tears running down my face.

"You okay?" he asked me in a quiet voice.

I nodded, but didn't look at him.

The props started spinning. We lifted up and turned south.

8

LEE MERRIWEATHER FLOATED on his back in the saltwater pool at the Roxy Hotel & Casino.

He wore a black bathing costume and tinted glasses stolen from one of the luxury boutiques in the hotel's shopping arcade. Through the underwater hush, Lee heard the lively strains of a ranchera trio, two guitars and an accordion, playing on a nearby veranda. He tipped up his chin and smoothed the cowlick on the back of his head.

He had never been in a pool before Aguadulce. In fact, he'd just learned to swim that morning.

The pool was for men only — women and girls had their own, discreetly partitioned by flowering bushes. Lee's gaze lingered on a young man his own age who was swimming laps, smoothly muscled arms slicing the water. He wished he had the courage to strike up a conversation.

If he'd wanted to, he could have used his voice. But persuading phantoms to do things was different. He didn't like to use his power on people, not if he could help it.

Lee paddled awkwardly to the edge, where Abel Beach reclined on a lounge chair in the shade of a mint-green umbrella. The professor looked dapper in a linen suit. His beard was freshly trimmed and his dreadlocks were tied back in deference to the heat. Mr. Beach was reading a newspaper, which he folded at Lee's appearance. It was late afternoon and a few small boys splashed in the shallows, but most of the hotel guests had gone inside to get ready for dinner.

Lee glanced around. "Anything interesting?" he asked in a low voice.

"No, but the date is over a week ago."

Mr. Beach held the English-language daily from Carnarvon City. A shop in the lobby carried the papers, but the ones from across the border took days to arrive.

"Calindra will never admit she lost me anyhow," Lee said.

"That doesn't mean she isn't coming for you," Mr. Beach pointed out reasonably.

"Oh, I'm sure she sent Hardin." Lee rested his chin on folded arms. "But he's not the biggest toad in the puddle anymore. The man's got no authority here."

"Don't underestimate Sebastian Hardin," Professor Beach said. "He caught you once."

Lee frowned. He didn't like being reminded of that. "Hardin got lucky. I'm more worried about the crazy preacher." He gave a nervous laugh. "The one who thinks I'm the Antichrist."

A shadow crossed Beach's face. "Another reason to keep a low profile." He opened the paper, but his eyes stayed on Lee. "It's been two days, son. We need to move on."

Another glorious sunset reflected off the glass façade of the Roxy, which soared thirty stories above the pool. Elevators moved behind the tinted glass. The Roxy wasn't even Aguadulce's most lavish hotel. That would be the Bella Luna down the street, home of the high rollers. Lee had wanted to stay there, but Mr. Beach said it was too obvious. So they'd settled for the Roxy, which had three restaurants, the shopping arcade, a gymnasium, two cocktail lounges — and the main attraction, the casino.

Lee had spent his life confined to grey-walled rooms where the only sound was a ticking clock and the bell signaling class changes. He wore the school jacket Monday through Friday, and a knit jumper over a neatly pressed white shirt on weekends. The food never varied. Oatmeal for breakfast, rice and beans for lunch, and meat with a boiled vegetable for dinner. One hour a day, rain or shine, he would jog around the oval running track. Twice a year, a doctor listened to his heart and examined his tongue. Lights went out at eleven, and on again at six a.m. Frivolity of any kind was strongly discouraged.

So when he'd first walked out to the cheerful debauchery of the gaming floor, Lee knew he'd died and gone to heaven.

People were loud and often drunk. They behaved irrationally, but they did it dressed to the nines. The air reeked of cigar smoke and champagne and ladies' perfume. It was noisy and bright and tacky. Small dogs wearing bejeweled collars nestled against powdered cleavage. Men in cowboy hats spoke Spanish with strange accents. Money changed hands in a never-ending stream. More money than Lee had ever imagined. Like a crab crawling out of a terrarium and stumbling across the boundless ocean, his past existence seemed drab and terribly small.

He knew he could never go back. *Never*.

It didn't take him long to realize that casinos had three kinds of people: winners, losers and cheaters. The first inevitably became the second, and the third inevitably got caught, but Lee was in a class of his own. His pulse raced just thinking about the possibilities.

The smart thing would be to take off, like Mr. Beach wanted to do. Head down to the coast and disappear in one of the flyspeck villages. For a minute, Lee imagined himself taking long siestas in a hammock. Drinking rum out of coconuts and throwing his shoes in the ocean.

It was a pretty picture except for the fact that he'd get

bored within a week. Now Aguadulce — *that* was more his style.

"Just one more day," Lee said. "We don't have enough money yet. Not to be comfortable."

Looking at him, you'd never guess what you were dealing with. Lee was eighteen years old, with brown hair and a wholesome, boyish face that looked even younger. When he smiled or laughed, it was so infectious nearly everyone around would find themselves smiling or laughing, too, even if they weren't sure why.

Mr. Beach stared at him hard. Then he nodded reluctantly. "One more day."

Lee pulled himself out of the pool and grabbed a towel. He changed out of the wet bathing costume in the men's pavilion. Then he returned to Mr. Beach. They crossed a tiled patio shaded by a striped awning and entered the Roxy. A blast of cold air raised goosebumps on Lee's neck.

The management kept it a steady sixty-eight degrees inside the hotel, even as the mercury outside climbed into the triple digits. Plush carpeting covered the vast lobby, which led to a long glass-enclosed gallery packed with shops and restaurants. People browsed and dined, a hum of conversation in English and Spanish filling the air. They were a mix of rich and poor, young and old. The Roxy was one of the cheaper hotels, and popular with families.

Phantoms drifted silently here and there, bare feet trailing along the ground, multifaceted eyes staring straight ahead. No one paid them any mind.

The elevator stopped on the eighth floor. When they parted ways in the empty hallway, Mr. Beach turned to Lee.

"This is the last time, you hear?" he said sternly. "I know you're having fun, but we're getting on a bus in the morning, no matter what." His tone softened. "I'm the only one looking out for you now, boy. Just let things settle, then we'll figure it out."

Lee forced himself to smile. "One last fancy dinner. Then we'll go."

Mr. Beach gave a satisfied nod. "Be careful."

The moment Lee entered his room, he collapsed on the bed and laced his hands behind his head. Guilt mingled with resentment, as it always did when the professor played nursemaid. He wished Mr. Beach had never got involved in any of it. The professor just wasn't made for life on the run. Lee had realized that fairly quickly when he'd wanted to rob a hayseed bank on the way to Aguadulce and Mr. Beach wouldn't let him.

But it was Lee's fault that he was there, and Lee would do right by him. Mr. Beach would be much safer on his own.

Lee picked up a sheet of hotel stationery and started composing a letter. He'd give Mr. Beach his winnings and let him start a new life somewhere else. He could change his name and retire in luxury.

Lee told himself he was doing it for the professor, but in truth, he didn't like being told what to do. Now that he'd tasted freedom, he wasn't about to give it up. And Mr. Beach . . . . He meant well, but he was far too law-abiding for Lee's taste.

But he'd make sure the professor was set up properly. Which meant he'd need to hit the casino a little harder than usual tonight.

Lee finished the letter and signed it with a flourish. He'd slip it under the professor's door later that night, with a wad of cash, and then he'd move to another hotel. Aguadulce had plenty of them. He hoped the professor wouldn't waste time looking, but even if he did, Lee knew how to disappear.

He opened the closet with a lighter heart and surveyed the suits hanging there, finally settling on ivory linen with a pale lilac tie. He'd had a haircut at the lobby barbershop, short in the back and sides, longer in the front. Lee slicked it back with a bit of pomade. He resolved to eat a big steak later, put a

little flesh on his bones. Missing meals was one of the hazards
of being on the lam and his lanky six-foot-two-inch frame
needed every pound it could get.

He adjusted his tie, slipped on a pair of wingtips, and
gazed out the window. The last of the sunlight was bleeding
along the horizon, pink and purple and orange. Dust plumes
hovered above the roads connecting Aguadulce to the suburbs,
where buses carried the day-shift hotel workers home. Lee saw
a few zeppelins and a train speeding towards the city from the
north. He squinted, but it was too dark to make out the colors.

Lee examined himself in the mirror, pleased with the
result. He looked sharp, but also clean-cut and honest. Just
another tourist eager to get fleeced by the house.

He took the elevator down to the mezzanine and got off.
Crystal chandeliers lit the casino floor, but there were no
windows so it was impossible to tell what time it was. The
tables never closed and you could easily lose any sense of day
and night. Dealers ran games of blackjack and poker and
faro, with the roulette wheels in the corners. The space was
filled with people, as it was nearly every hour of the day. Girls
with trays of cigarettes and cocktail waitresses moved among
the crowd.

Most were casual visitors mingling in groups. Then there
were the professionals. They sat wreathed in clouds of
cigarette smoke at the farthest tables and earned the greatest
scrutiny from the Roxy's security, of which there were two
kinds. The first wore red jackets with the hotel's coat of arms
embroidered on the breast. They were meant to be visible and
dealt with petty theft and drunks. The second wore plain dark
suits and most were linguists, though not of Lee's caliber.
Their job was to make sure no one used phantoms to cheat.

Sometimes they gambled themselves. Sometimes they just
casually walked around. Lee had spent the first day in
Aguadulce studying the casino until he learned to recognize
them.

He went straight past the card tables and headed for the slot machines. Phantoms clustered thickly around the slots, drawn by the whirring of machinery as people pulled the levers. They'd been trained to report any shenanigans and were considered incorruptible.

It was a good system. It just didn't account for Lee Merriweather.

He chose a vacant machine and dropped a token in just as one of the linguists walked through. Lee whispered a prayer and pulled the lever.

The machine made a clunk. The reels inside started spinning. Each had a little picture printed on it. Lee stared at the pay line, the horizontal slot in the middle of the viewing window. The pictures stopped randomly one at a time, left to right, to build the suspense. If each reel showed the same winning picture along the pay line, you hit the jackpot. The amount you won — the payout — depended on which pictures landed along the pay line.

The machine whirred.

"C'mon," he said loudly. "Come to papa!"

A lemon. A cherry. A number seven.

Lee swore under his breath as the linguist passed. He took out another token and blew on it for luck. When the man had moved out of sight, Lee turned to the phantom hovering next to the machine. It looked like a little boy with brown skin and large misshapen ears. Lee pitched his voice low and friendly, speaking in the phantom's sibilant language.

Want to play a game? Lee asked.

Jewel-eyes jerked his way. *I'm already playing.*

I have a new game, Lee coaxed. *A much better game.*

The phantom stared. Lee licked his lips. *It's a secret though. You can't tell anyone.*

It cocked its head. *What game?*

You make the cherries line up, Lee whispered.

The sevens paid more, but he didn't want to attract too much attention.

Light from the chandeliers reflected from the facets of the phantom's eyes.

That's against the rules.

Lee poured every ounce of charm into his voice. *It's more fun though.* He grinned. *Must get boring to play the same game all the time. And I'd really appreciate the favor.*

After a moment the phantom's lips curled up at the corners, though it was a strange, mechanical smile as though the creature was simply mirroring his face.

Another linguist wandered through, pausing to light a woman's cigarette. They flirted for a moment. Lee bent down and pretended to tie his shoe. When the man had passed out of sight, he turned to the phantom.

Just once, Lee said in a wheedling tone. *You'll do it for me, won't you? Since we're friends?*

The phantom opened its mouth to reveal a row of tiny teeth. If it yelled for security, Lee would be done for. But he knew it wouldn't. They never did.

A moment later, the haint vanished. Heading into the ether — or inside the slot machine.

Lee dropped the token in. He pulled the lever. One . . . two . . . three cherries showed on the pay line. Tokens spilled from the machine. Everyone looked over and Lee donned an expression of delighted astonishment. One of the red jackets strolled past as he scooped up the tokens. Not openly suspicious — people did win, after all — but keeping an eye on him. Lee moved on to another machine. He lost the next eight pulls and sensed the scrutiny lessening.

He always made sure not to win too much — just enough to pay for his and Mr. Beach's rooms — though Lee hadn't saved as much as he'd hoped. Sharp suits cost money. So did steak dinners and good champagne.

He cashed out and took one of the glass-enclosed walkways leading to the Reina del Sur next door. Rule Two: Never win twice in the same casino. The gaming floor of the Queen of the South was nearly identical to the Roxy, except that the highest payout combo for the slots was three gold crowns. Lee found a machine with no one else in earshot and repeated his performance, persuading the resident phantom to let him win on the sixth try.

The jackpot for three crowns was far more than Lee had ever won before. Tokens cascaded from the machine. It played a jaunty tune, lights flashing. A small crowd had gathered by the time he scooped his loot into a bag.

"He got a royal!" someone exclaimed with a note of envy.

Lee gave a bashful smile. "Beginner's luck, I guess."

"Come give mine a pull," a woman with dark skin and platinum hair like spun sugar said with a wink. "Maybe it'll rub off."

"Oh no, ma'am, I think I'd best quit while I'm ahead," Lee replied in his best aw-shucks goober accent.

He grabbed the bag and set off for the cashier's window. It was down one level, at the far end of the lobby. Lee almost took the stairs, but one of the elevators opened just as he passed by. He stepped inside. A young man in a pinstriped suit nodded at him. Lee nodded back. He pressed the button for the lobby. The elevator sank.

"Pardon me, do you have the time?" his companion asked politely.

He had blonde hair parted straight down the center, worn longish and slicked back behind his ears. He looked too young to be security, Lee thought, and his eyes lacked the watchful hardness. They were a clear green with a spark of good humor.

Lee drew a heavy gold watch from his waistcoat pocket — stolen, of course. "Six-forty," he said.

"That's a fine timepiece," the young man said admiringly.

"My father's," Lee replied smoothly. "He lent it to me so I wouldn't gamble too long. We're meeting for dinner."

"You should try the Longhorn," the young man said. "Juiciest steak in Aguadulce."

Lee smiled. "I will, thanks for the tip."

He returned the watch to his pocket. As Lee looked up, they passed the lobby without stopping. He frowned and jabbed the button. Several times. The elevator kept descending.

"Oh, for God's sake," Lee muttered.

"Must be broken," the young man said.

He didn't seem troubled. Lee stared at the panel. There were no levels below the lobby, yet the elevator was clearly headed somewhere.

"Won big, huh?" the young man asked, eyeing the bulging sack of tokens in Lee's hand.

Lee was opening his mouth to reply when the doors opened. Two red-jacketed security guards stood there. He sensed movement from the corner of his eye.

Before Lee could utter a single syllable, a hood dropped over his head and cinched tight.

9

Rough hands dragged Lee Merriweather from the elevator.

His heart raced as they marched him down a long corridor somewhere under the hotel. Lee heard an engine gun. Cuffs snapped around his wrists. Someone gripped the top of his head and shoved him into a vehicle. The door slammed. The vehicle accelerated, pressing him back against the seat.

"Where are we going?" he demanded, voice muffled by the hood.

No one answered.

That was the moment Lee knew he was about to die.

He'd be taken somewhere in the big, empty desert, shot in the head, and dumped into a shallow grave. They'd clean out his hotel room. Expunge his name from the Roxy register.

And that would be the end of Lee Merriweather.

The vehicle rumbled along. From the echo of the engine, it sounded like they were in a tunnel. Only a minute or so later, he slid forward on the leather seat as the vehicle braked hard. Hands hauled him out and shoved him into motion again.

At least they weren't in the desert. Lee felt carpeting under his feet. Maybe they'd shoot him first and dump the body after, although that seemed messier. Or maybe they had something worse in mind.

He tried shouting for help in various phantom tongues, with no result except that someone smacked him on the back of the head.

At last he heard a door open just ahead. He was pushed down into a chair. The hood was yanked off. Lee gasped for air, red-faced.

He sat in a small anonymous room. No windows. Nothing on the white walls. No furniture except the wooden chair he sat in. The young man from the elevator who had asked him for the time stood against the door, watching. His face didn't look so pleasant now.

"Hello, Mr. Merriweather," he said.

Lee had checked into the Roxy under a fake name. He covered his shock, just barely, but the urge to run was overwhelming. What did they know? *And how long had they known it?*

Lee started to rise from the chair. A heavy hand came down on his shoulder. One of the red-jacketed guards stood behind him.

"There's nowhere to go." The young man studied him. "If you try to call phantoms to help you again, this will get very ugly, very fast."

Lee sat back down. He felt sick. "How do you know my name?"

"Mr. Beach told me." The young man smiled. "I can be quite persuasive."

Lee's whole body went cold. "What have you done to him?"

"Nothing." A tiny pause. "So far."

The matter-of-fact tone got Lee's attention. It conveyed the notion that Abel Beach was no one and would not be missed if it came down to it.

"My name is Henry Chance. I know what you've been up

to, Mr. Merriweather. I've been watching you for two days now. If you want to see Mr. Beach again, I'd advise you to cooperate."

Lee knew when to fight and when to try to talk his way out. He adopted an expression of slack-jawed bewilderment. "Well, okay, sir. I'm happy to cooperate. Where are we?"

"Level G security hub."

Lee blinked. "So you work for Mr. Braga?" he asked slowly.

"That's correct." Henry Chance gave a tight smile. "Did you really think you could cheat my employer and get away with it, Mr. Merriweather?"

"Cheat?" Lee laughed. "Oh boy, you got it wrong, sir. I just had a little lucky streak on the slots. You're making a big mistake—"

Henry Chance raised a hand. Lee cut off.

"Wait outside," Chance told the guard. "I'll handle it from here."

"Yes, sir." The man in the red jacket left the room, gently closing the door behind him. He was at least twenty years older, but he obeyed without question. When they were alone, Henry Chance pulled up a chair and sat down to face Lee.

"You're a savant," Chance said.

Lee stared at him for a long moment. "What's that mean?"

"Don't bother denying it."

"I . . . . Why do you think that?" Lee stammered.

Henry Chance gazed at him. His expression was hard to read. "Because we're the same."

Lee felt a shock deep in his marrow. Other than Calindra, he'd never met another savant.

"I apologize for the harsh treatment," Henry Chance said, "but it would be foolish to take a risk, considering." The good humor returned. "Only a savant could have turned the phantoms in the casino. You were careful, but not quite careful enough."

He doesn't know all of it, Lee thought with a surge of relief. He doesn't even know *most* of it. But he's a clever one. Tread carefully.

"I'm a savant myself," Henry Chance said. "How do you think I persuaded Mr. Beach to tell me your name?"

That rang true. Lee knew the professor would never willingly betray him.

"What did you do to him?" Lee demanded hotly.

"Nothing. We only spoke." Chance gripped his knees and leaned forward. "I don't know your story, Mr. Merriweather, and I don't especially want to."

Lee's eyes narrowed. "What *do* you want then?"

"We've been having some problems at the casino. It's not the small timers like you I'm worried about. No, it's the high stakes tables. Times are changing. There are more and more skilled linguists looking to make some easy money. Some of them are very good. Hard to spot." He grinned. "It takes a cheat to know a cheat, doesn't it, Merriweather?"

"Who are you?" he asked flatly.

"I'm Mr. Braga's security chief."

"But . . . ."

"I look too young for the job?" Chance laughed. "Mr. Braga knows talent when he sees it. Just like I do."

"Still seems a bit unorthodox," Lee grumbled.

"You're wondering why I'd trust you." His green eyes never wavered as he leaned back in his chair with an amused expression. "Let me tell you a bit about yourself, Mr. Merriweather. You have a quick mind, but you get bored easily. You like a challenge and you're willing to take calculated risks. That's why you chose the slots over the gaming tables. You arrived only two days ago, but you figured out the system pretty quick."

Lee said nothing, though he was secretly impressed.

"You think you're better than most people and you resent following society's rules, yet you'll go to great lengths to protect the ones you do care about, like Mr. Beach."

Lee bristled at this. "I don't think I'm better—"

"Sure you do," Henry interrupted cheerfully. "It's because you *are* better, Mr. Merriweather. You're as different from those crowds upstairs as a wolf is to a flock of sheep." He leaned in. His friendly tone didn't change, but something in his eyes put Lee on alert. "See, it's my job to tend the sheep. When I run across a wolf, I have two choices. The best one is to tame the wolf so it helps me defend the flock against the other wolves."

Lee cleared his throat. "What's the other choice?"

"Take a wild guess."

"Put the wolf down?"

"I knew you were a quick study," Henry said. He laughed at Lee's expression. "I hope you didn't take that literally, Mr. Merriweather. But you understand I can't let a thing like this go. Not for either of you."

"Mr. Beach didn't know anything," Lee said quickly. "It was all me, I swear it. If you've been watching, you know that's the truth."

For an instant, Henry looked puzzled. "You two make a peculiar pair, I'll admit. Is he a relation?"

"He used to be my teacher," Lee said, weaving truth with lies. "At the school up in the Northern Territory."

"You're from the N.T.?"

"Sure am." Lee did a near perfect mimicry of Sebastian Hardin. "Worked hard to lose the accent."

Henry stared at him. "The school up there is pretty bare bones. I wouldn't have expected it to graduate a savant."

Lee gave a wistful shrug. "Who knows what I could have been in someplace better, like Carnarvon City? Or here. But we got no choice where we're born, do we?"

Chance leaned back, crossing his arms. "Why did Mr. Beach come south with you?"

"He took early retirement. It's a hard life up there. We both wanted to see warmer climes."

Henry regarded him with skepticism, then laughed and shook his head. "I did say I wasn't interested in your history. I guess we'll leave it there. Let's get back to my offer. We hire a select number of elite linguists to play at the gaming tables, keep an eye on things. How would you like to do that?"

Lee pretended to consider it. "What's the pay?"

"Generous. Plus you get a high roller suite at the Bella Luna and credit to gamble with. You'll eat at the best restaurants for free. I wasn't kidding about the Longhorn. You could have sirloin for dinner every night, Mr. Merriweather."

"And all I have to do is catch the cheaters?" Lee asked.

"That's it. You don't even have to confront them. Just point them out to me. I'll handle it."

"What happens to them?"

Henry gave a thin smile. "Depends on the amount. But the usual penalty is a lifetime ban from Aguadulce, plus a few months in jail."

"You don't dump them in the desert?" Lee blurted.

Henry looked affronted. "Why on earth would you think that?"

Lee shrugged. "Never mind."

The whole thing was madness. True, he'd planned to stay for a while, but as a faceless hotel guest, not an employee of Pedro Braga. If — when — Calindra got word of it, she'd be furious. But the position would give him full access to the casinos. The potential was mind-bending.

Plus that high-roller suite at the Bella Luna.

"You've got a deal," Lee said, rising.

They shook hands.

"I'm pleased," Henry said warmly. "You'll have to meet

the boss, get his approval. It's just a formality." He winked again. "We'll keep your own indiscretions between us."

"That would be for the best," Lee agreed. "And maybe . . . ."

"What?"

"Maybe we should just say I'm a polyglot." Lee looked sheepish. "I dropped out of school and I'd rather they didn't know where I went. Word might spread if people knew I was a savant."

Henry considered it for a moment. "I suppose that's all right." He looked sympathetic. "Believe me, I know what it's like. It'll be nice to have a colleague my own age."

Lee took a moment to marvel at his rapid change in fortunes. Then he remembered the professor with a pang of guilt. "I'd like to see Mr. Beach now, if you don't mind."

"Of course."

Henry Chance opened the door. They went down the hall to a second room with an unmarked door. Mr. Beach was waiting on a chair inside. He looked up as Lee entered.

"I'll leave you to discuss matters in private," Henry said, closing the door behind him.

Lee tried the handle. It wasn't locked.

"What's going on?" Mr. Beach asked, worry creasing his forehead. "How much trouble are we in, Lee?"

Lee sat down, his face solemn. Then he broke into a grin. "They just hired the fox to guard the chicken coop."

Abel glanced at the door. He went and opened it himself, checking the corridor in both directions. Satisfied no one was listening, he returned to his seat but kept his voice pitched low. "How much did you tell them?"

"Not as much as you did," Lee retorted, then felt guilty at the professor's injured expression.

"I only told him our names, that's all," Mr. Beach said slowly. "He had it out of me before I knew what I was saying."

"It's not your fault," Lee said quickly. "Henry Chance is a savant. Braga's savant."

Abel Beach blinked. "Suppose I should have guessed that. He's a slick one." Another worried glance at the door. "Are we free to walk out of here?"

Lee hesitated. "Well, circumstances have changed a bit. Didn't you hear what I said? Chance just hired me as casino security."

Beach's eyebrows climbed up. "You're joking."

"Not at all. I have to go meet Braga."

The professor stared at him for a long moment. "Do you think that's wise?" he asked. "It's only a matter of time before Pedro Braga figures out who you are. Then you'll be right back in the stewpot."

Lee's grin deflated. "I knew you'd say that." He leaned forward. "Listen, professor. They know our names, but I told Chance we came from the Northern Territory. He doesn't care about my history. He said so. He's desperate for a skilled linguist."

Mr. Beach looked skeptical. "And what about his boss?"

"Henry said he wouldn't tell him I was even a savant. Or that I was rigging the slots."

"We don't know Chance," Mr. Beach said slowly. "Seems like a lot to trust him with. He could have his own reasons we don't know yet."

"Maybe. But don't you see? With that kind of access, I could . . . ." Lee paused. "What I mean to say is, they'll pay me a good salary, enough to get us out of here in style. It's not forever."

Abel Beach sighed.

"We have no choice," Lee said. "It's cooperate or go to jail."

"You could say yes and go pack your bags. We can still get on that bus."

"With what? Chance took my winnings. We don't even

have enough to pay our hotel bill, let alone buy the tickets."
Lee looked the professor in the eye. "I know you don't approve
of me stealing. Now I won't have to. It's the only way. Please,
just trust me on this."

"How long until your first paycheck?" The professor asked
unhappily, and Lee knew he'd won.

"A week or two, I'd guess. I'll hammer out the details with
Mr. Braga."

In fact, Lee planned to leave with a lot more than his
salary, but there was no need to tell the professor that.

"What about Hardin? You can bet he'll turn up any day
now."

"Hardin won't say a thing," Lee said with a smile.

"How can you be so sure?"

"Because I know Calindra. She'll keep her hound dog on
a short leash. If he were to come barging in here demanding
that Braga hand me over, the odds are fifty-fifty that Braga
keeps me for himself. Calindra wouldn't risk it."

"You have a point there," conceded Mr. Beach, who'd
known her for many years. "But it's still a tightrope you're
walking." He gave Lee a hard look. "Don't get any foolish
ideas now. Just keep your head down, take the money, and
make some excuse to quit before they get their hooks in you
too deep."

"Exactly what I had in mind," Lee said innocently.

"So that's what you meant about the fox." Abel Beach
chuckled. "When security came for me up in the room, I
thought we were done for. Did they catch you at the slots?"

"After," Lee said carelessly. He didn't mention the hood or
his own stark terror when they threw him in the vehicle. "But
it was all civilized. We just had a little chat." He smoothed his
hair down. "Guess they figured I was too valuable to treat like
a common criminal."

The professor's gaze was penetrating and Lee flushed.

"Well, I'm glad to hear that." He stood. "If we're free to go, I'd like to head back to the hotel."

"Oh yeah," Lee said, as if it was an afterthought. "We're moving up in the world, professor. They're giving us suites at the Bella Luna."

A knock came on the door and Henry Chance stuck his head inside. "I'll take you to see the boss now, Mr. Merriweather. So we can get the ball rolling."

A car was arranged to take Mr. Beach to get his things. Lee went with Henry Chance to one of the elevator banks.

"I'll introduce you, but I'm afraid I can't stay," Henry said with a note of apology. "I'm performing at eight and it's nearly showtime."

"Performing?" Lee asked in surprise.

Henry grinned. "Haven't you seen the posters for Doctor Deathless?"

"That's *you*?"

They were plastered all over the lobby of the Reina del Sur. Illustrated renderings of a man in a cage who appeared to be bending the bars open with his bare hands.

"Well, damn." Lee laughed. "Is it like the circus in Carnarvon City?"

"I've heard of that," Henry replied. "Uh, not exactly." He winked. "I hate to spoil the surprise. Why don't you catch the late show? I'll leave your name at the box office."

"I'd like that," Lee said.

"You'll be on the blackjack tables at the Sahara tomorrow," Henry said as they stepped into the elevator. "Most of the cheaters bring their own phantoms and hide them in the ether. The phantoms see right through the deck, but they have to signal to the player. That's how you catch them. You look for a tell. You know what that is, Mr. Merriweather?"

Lee nodded.

"Just keep your eyes open and pay attention. You seem like a man who notices things." Henry Chance pressed the button for the fourth floor. "Think of it as a game of chess. They're trying to outwit us, but the fraud is being carried out in plain sight. There's always a sign if you look closely." He took a watch from his pocket and checked the time. "Oh good, I have thirty minutes. Mr. Braga is expecting us."

Lee stared at the watch. "Hey," he said. "Isn't that mine?"

Henry laughed and tossed it back. Lee caught it. "How'd you do that?"

"I'm a magician," Henry winked. "Like I said, keep your eyes open and maybe you'll learn something."

10

AGUADULCE GLOWED like an island of light in the midst of a vast black ocean. As the zeppelin sank lower I could make out flashing neon signs, each a full story high.

The Admiral Aguadulce. Hipódromo. Golden Dreams. The Roxy. Reina del Sur. Bella Luna. The Sahara.

Glass walkways connected the hotels into one big complex. Far below, more lights glimmered at the bottom of a dozen swimming pools. They looked too blue to be real.

I'd fallen asleep for a spell and woke with my head on Hardin's shoulder. He didn't seem to mind. I stayed for a while, feeling his warm breath on my hair and wishing we were anyplace else.

"You awake?" Hardin asked softly.

I sat up, rubbing my eyes. At least they'd cuffed our hands in front. "Yes, sir."

"I'll do the talking," he said. "Just follow my lead."

We touched down on the roof of the Bella Luna. The ship's nose cable was secured to a mooring mast. The hatch opened and the Gorras walked us down the gangway. Heat still radiated from the roof though the night air felt cool. A dozen men in identical dark suits waited on the landing pad.

Comisario Alvarez ignored me and Hardin completely, huddling with a few of his men.

The rest took us inside and down in an elevator. It wasn't like the lifts at Carnarvon Tower. Except for the ornate bronze doors, styled with golden sunbursts, this elevator was made of glass. Even the floor. I've never cared for heights so I stared straight ahead at the back of the guard in front of me, the soles of my feet tingling unpleasantly.

"When do I see Mr. Braga?" Hardin demanded in Spanish.

"When he calls for you," one of the guards replied in an icy tone.

"This is ridiculous," Hardin muttered.

Levels flashed by. No one said another word. Finally, the view beyond the glass went dark as we entered a shaft. The lift braked to a stop and the doors opened. Cold air raised goosebumps on my arms. We were at an intersection of two windowless corridors. We passed offices with men on telephones or doing paperwork. It reminded me of Special Services except that only about half wore uniforms, while the rest were in plain suits. We passed a guard at a desk and went through a heavy metal door. A row of cells stretched the length of the room behind.

"Is this really necessary?" Hardin grumbled.

Our escorts didn't bother to reply.

I gripped the bars as the cell door clanged shut. Hardin sank down on a metal bench, which was the only piece of furniture. "Don't worry, Cortez," he said for the tenth time. "I'll get this straightened out."

He sat erect, cuffed hands loosely clasped in front of him. He didn't seem troubled at our predicament, which I thought was a bit optimistic. We'd left a trail of bodies in our wake.

"They can't blame us for it, can they?" I said, rolling out a crick in my neck.

"No, 'course not. But we need to be careful. Leave Merri-weather out of it."

"And how are we going to do that?" I asked wearily.

"Simple. The reverend started a riot in Carnarvon City. He attacked a marshal when we tried to arrest him. You're here because he passed through Lucky Boy and you tracked him south. You know what he looks like so I brought you along. But don't say he held you prisoner. Or that the dead man knew your name. That might provoke too many ques-tions." He shot me a look. "I don't think you'd better mention seeing Cage in New Jerusalem either. If they found him, we'll hear about it. Otherwise we keep our mouths shut."

"Fine," I muttered. "But what *about* Merriweather?"

"If he's here, I'll find him."

"And then what?"

Hardin didn't answer.

"You gonna kill him?" I asked.

"We'll discuss this later," he snapped.

I sighed and sat down next to him on the bench. "I ain't surprised this happened."

"No?"

"Since I left Lucky Boy, nothing goes according to plan," I said. "Ever."

Hardin smiled. "If you hadn't kicked up a row about taking off those glasses, I might have left you there."

I glanced at him. "You think Mr. Carver and Mr. Mack are okay? And Marshal Tanaka?"

Hardin nodded. "No reason they'd be harmed. I imagine the train will take a bit longer to arrive."

"You should get a real doctor to see to those stitches," I said.

He shrugged. "They're holding."

"It's cold in here," I said with a shiver. "Why's it so cold?"

"Called air conditioning, Cortez. Braga has haints run the machines, else it would be hotter than Hades and no one in their right mind would come here to gamble." He shot me an apologetic look and held up the handcuffs. "I'd give you my coat if I could get it off."

"That's all right. I'll get used to it."

An hour or so passed. I heard distant yells and the clang of cell doors. I sat with my chin propped on one hand, staring through the bars. I didn't want to talk about the reverend or New Jerusalem. Clearly, Hardin didn't either. What I really wanted was to crawl into bed and sleep for a week, preferably without dreaming, but the day wasn't over yet so I settled for letting my mind go blank. Whatever Braga decided, wasn't much I could do about it.

We both turned at footsteps coming down the aisle. A guard unlocked the cell and gestured for the marshal to step out.

"She comes too," Hardin said. "Cortez is my second in command."

I tried not to look surprised. But then again, I was the only one still standing.

The guard hesitated. "He only asked for you, Señor Hardin."

"She has information Mr. Braga will want to hear," Hardin said, the ring of command in his voice. "Might as well bring her along now. Save yourself another trip."

The guard nodded and unlocked both of our handcuffs. He didn't seem to care much either way. I rubbed my wrists as we took the elevator back up. I expected Braga's office would be at the very top, but we stopped on the fourth floor. The door opened straight into a large room. One wall was tinted glass and overlooked the casino floor three stories below. It must have been soundproofed because I couldn't hear a thing, though I saw people crowded around gaming tables.

The view — huge crystal chandeliers, potted palms, every-thing red and gold — made for a stark contrast with the room we stood in. The space was dominated by a mahogany desk with nothing on it except for a green-shaded lamp. A man in his late forties sat behind the desk. He had thinning black hair combed back from his temples. It brushed his shoulders, which were heavy like a boxer's. He had a boxer's face too, the features larger than life and a bit battered, with a full mouth, hawk's nose and hooded black eyes.

"Sebastian," Pedro Braga said warmly, coming around from behind his desk. "It's been too long."

Hardin took a step forward just as I registered the fact that Lee Merriweather was sitting in a leather wing chair angled toward the desk. He turned to us with a polite smile, looking as sweet and pink-cheeked as an overgrown cherub. Lee ignored me. He stared at Hardin and I saw the dare in his face.

Hardin stiffened. They locked eyes. For an endless moment, I thought it could go either way. Then the marshal walked right past Lee and shook Braga's hand across the desk. "Good to see you again, sir," he said easily.

I stood by the door, fighting the urge to lunge for the scruff of Lee's neck. He was dressed in a sharp suit, as always, and his skin looked tanned. He wasn't quite so scrawny as the last time I saw him. It occurred to me that while we'd been getting shot, stabbed and punched in the face, Merriweather had been living the high life in Aguadulce.

Braga gestured. "This is my new hire. From up north. The N.T., right, son?"

Lee nodded. "That's right, sir," he said, in a perfect imitation of Hardin's frontier drawl. "I always dreamed of going to the academy in Carnarvon City, but my daddy was just a poor miner."

"That so?" Hardin said, studying Lee. His gaze could have flayed the hide from a two-ton steer, but Pedro Braga didn't seem to notice.

"I've heard of you, sir," Lee said solemnly. "You're a legend back home. It's a real pleasure to meet you in person."

"Always nice to run into a fellow northerner," Hardin said. "We'll have to catch up sometime." His bared his teeth in a smile. "Hope you'll be staying in town for a while."

"He'd better," Pedro Braga said with a chuckle. "He's on my payroll now. Excuse us, won't you, Mr. Merriweather?"

"Of course." Lee gave Hardin a little salute. He shook Braga's hand. "Thank you again for the opportunity, sir. I won't let you down."

I moved back to let him pass. Lee winked at me as he went by, but his eyes were ice cold.

"This is Deputy Ruth Cortez," Hardin said, beckoning me forward as if nothing were amiss. "I think you'll want to hear her out."

Braga motioned us to sit. "I'm sorry about your marshal. My men moved his body to the morgue." He had an expressive face and his voice was deep and resonant. Different from Lee's, yet I could hear the threads of power in it.

Hardin nodded, his jaw tight. "Thank you, sir."

"The other one's in the infirmary. I'll make sure she's well cared for. You can visit her in the morning." Braga leaned forward, his thick black brows drawing together. "What happened out there, Sebastian?"

"We got hit hard at the border. At least six men. They killed your guards and waited for us to come through."

Hardin recounted the fight, leaving Doc out of it. Braga listened quietly, his expression unreadable. "And New Jerusalem? What made you stop there, Sebastian?"

"The Reverend Jolly was in Carnarvon City stirring up trouble in the streets, preaching the end times. He stabbed a marshal when we tried to detain him and disappeared." Hardin shook his head. "It was supposed to be a routine stop, sir. I had no idea what we'd find."

Braga gazed at him. "More than routine, I think. You'd just lost a man, yet you chose to take a thirty-mile detour into the desert."

Hardin shifted. "It's possible he's in communication with a Class X phantom. I imagine you've heard the news about what happened up in Hazardville. We have reason to think the same phantom set that fire."

Braga's eyebrows rose, very slightly. "An X?"

"There was an attack on a trestle just outside Carnarvon City about a week ago. Deputy Cortez was on the train when it happened. So was the Reverend Jolly."

Braga digested this in silence for a minute. "And you're sure it was an X?"

"I'm sure. The trestle was shaken to its foundations. If it is this Reverend Jolly, he's a rogue. Highly trained and not one of ours."

"Are you saying he's one of mine, Sebastian?" Braga asked in a soft voice that held an undercurrent of menace.

"No, sir," Hardin said quickly. "Of course not. Just relaying the facts. But his church was in New Jerusalem and he could be headed this way."

Braga leaned back. "The name doesn't ring a bell, but I'll look into it. Horrible what happened there."

"The man's insane," Hardin agreed. "But don't underestimate him. Or his associate, Mr. Cage."

"Keep it to yourself for now," Braga said. "I'd prefer to dispose of him quietly, if possible. Don't want to start a panic." His gaze moved to my copper star. "What's your involvement, deputy?"

I told the story Hardin came up with. That the reverend and his accomplice, Mr. Cage, had passed through Lucky Boy and held a family hostage at a remote farmhouse. No one was badly hurt, but the sheriff sent me to Carnarvon City to make a full report to Special Services. I knew what they both looked like so Hardin thought it best to bring me along to New Jerusalem.

"Why didn't Calindra tell me this herself?" Braga asked. He didn't sound happy.

"Like I said, it seemed a routine warrant," Hardin said. "I figured I'd explain it to you in person."

"Well, I've already issued a territory-wide alert." He gave us both a level look. "I apologize for the way you were brought in, but since you left me in the dark on this, I can hardly blame my men."

Hardin nodded. "Of course not, sir. The fault is entirely mine."

"Well, then." Braga stood. "I imagine it's been a long day. We'll talk some more in the morning. I look forward to reviewing the contracts."

"What about the border? Two of them got away. There could be more."

"It's been locked down tight. I already have a manhunt underway." Braga's face hardened. "They'll be found."

"You had any trouble like that before?"

"It's not unheard of. Simple thieves, I imagine," Braga said. "Looking for a quick score."

Hardin didn't dispute this, though he knew better. "What about my cook and driver?" he asked.

"Your people are fine," Braga said. "They can stay on the train and unload supplies for the return trip, unless you have an objection. It should only be a day or two on the contracts, if we start first thing."

"I don't mind staying on the train, too," I ventured.

At least then I wouldn't accidentally run into Merriweather and start throttling him on the spot.

"Your bags were already brought up," Braga said with a bland smile. "I hope you won't refuse my hospitality, deputy."

"No," I said. "Of course not."

"Might as well make the most of your time here," Braga said. "Aguadulce is the amusement capital of the known world. Even if you don't care for gambling, we have several theaters and more than two dozen fine restaurants. The Hipódromo also has an athletic gymnasium and carousel."

I thought of Doc. "Do you have a picture show?"

Braga laughed. "Not yet, but I intend to build one." He looked at Hardin. "And once the railroad is expanded south to the coast, Calindra and I are planning a new jointly owned luxury resort. It will have all the modern amenities — and ones you haven't yet dreamed of."

He bade us goodnight and ordered two men to escort us to rooms on the sixth floor. The moment they left, Hardin and I looked at each other. "Sweet Jesus," he said. "This is a mess."

"You'd better come inside for a minute," I said, looking down the hall. "We can't talk out here."

He nodded and I unlocked the door to my room. It was small but comfortable, with a private bath and long floor-to-ceiling curtains along one wall. My valise was already sitting on the bed. Harden stared at it for a minute, then cleared his throat. "Want to stand on the balcony? Ought to be a breeze."

He pulled the curtains wide, revealing a glass door on a track. Hardin slid it open. A warm, dry wind blew in from the desert. I took a half step forward, craning my neck. I could just make out the lights of the swimming pool below. The terrace looked awful flimsy.

"You go on," I said, backing up to the edge of the bed. "I'll just sit here."

"Suit yourself." Hardin stepped outside, the wind riffling his hair. He casually leaned a hand on the waist-high iron rail. Just watching him made my palms sweat.

"Why can't you just tell him about Lee?" I said. "I bet Mr. Braga would hand him straight over if he knew what Lee's done. Seems to me he'll be a lot more mad if he finds out he's hired a felon and we never told him."

"Because I can't," Hardin replied flatly. "It's not my call."

"Maybe he already knows. Maybe he's playing you."

Hardin half-turned, gazing out at the sparkling lights. "Maybe," he conceded. "The man's a savant. He knows how to be convincing."

I thought for a moment. "If Jolly *is* working for Braga, Braga doesn't need him anymore. He's got Lee right where he wants him."

Hardin didn't say anything and I felt a chill.

"Either way, Lee's got Braga's protection," Hardin said at last. "It's gonna be hard to take him alive now. Real hard. You know that."

"Don't do this," I said. "Please."

Hardin looked away. I heard regret in his voice, but also unshakable resolve. "You heard what Calindra said. We can't let Merriweather fall into the wrong hands."

"So what now?" I demanded. "You put a bullet between his eyes?"

Hardin didn't answer.

"Lee's just a kid," I said.

"A dangerous kid."

"More to himself than anyone else," I pointed out.

Hardin sighed. "What would you do?"

"I'd talk to him. Alone. If he thought Braga had hired the reverend, I don't think he'd be so keen to cuddle up with him. Look, Lee's a boaster and petty criminal, but he ain't a killer. He's got a decent streak buried deep down. That's why Mr. Beach is trying to look after him."

"Thankless task," Hardin muttered.

"That's for sure." I paused. "What if he runs again?"

"Then I'll chase him," Hardin said wearily. "But I don't think he will. Not yet. He's having too much fun."

Hardin was an astute judge of character. I thought the same.

"The thing Lee hates the most is people telling him what to do," I said. "So it'll be tricky. He needs to believe Braga's going to use him like Calindra did."

"She trained him," Hardin said with a scowl. "There's a difference. Lee Merriweather wouldn't be who he is without her."

"Fair enough. But he don't see it that way."

"Lee won't listen to me," Hardin said. "Not for love or money."

"No," I agreed. "But he might listen to me."

Hardin quirked an eyebrow. "Doesn't he nurse a grudge against you for bringing him in?"

I remembered the chill in Lee's eyes as he passed me. "Well, yes. But he needs to know what we found. And he was friendly toward me once. Maybe I can talk him around."

Hardin looked dubious.

"He doesn't deserve to be executed," I said. "It ain't right. Lee never killed anybody. The penalty should fit the crime, marshal. He stole a train and caused some mischief, but none of that is a hanging offense. I looked it up. Section 52.06 of the penal code regarding felonious operation of a locomotive mandates a prison sentence of six to ten years. That thing with the clocks probably falls under the nuisance laws, and vandalizing the telegraph in Charter Oak tacks on another two to four."

"Don't forget the airship," Hardin said dryly.

"I haven't. That's six to ten."

"And the bank."

"Fifteen to twenty," I replied crisply. "Which brings us to about . . . uh, forty-four years, assuming the maximum penalties. I'm all for locking him up, but he has the right to a trial first—"

Hardin held up a hand. "All right, all right. I'll give you a chance. One chance."

"Thank you, sir."

Hardin stared out at the desert. "You think I'm happy about this burden, Cortez?"

"Guess not," I conceded.

Hardin gripped the rail. "But I'm not letting Jolly have him. Nor whoever Jolly is working for." His blue eyes speared me. "If Lee wanted to, he could tear this whole city down.

Thousands would die. I almost wish it *was* Braga who hired the reverend because at least I'd know what's what. But the truth is, we got no idea who wants Merriweather. Or how they plan to use him. And that's what scares me the most, Cortez."

"Me, too."

"So we'll give it a try tomorrow," Hardin said wearily. "Maybe I can find Mr. Beach. See what he thinks."

We said goodnight at the door. I was too tired to unpack, but when a bellhop knocked with a tray of hot food, I gobbled it down. Then I stripped my clothes off and took a hot bath, barely aware of what I'd just eaten.

Hardin was doing what he thought he had to. I appreciated that he was honest about it, but I knew that in the end he'd do his duty and his loyalty to Calindra Carnarvon trumped everything else. I had to make Lee see reason. Or at least run again before someone killed him.

I put on a nightgown and tucked my arm under the pillow. Hardin had left the curtains to the terrace open. I'd never seen so many electric lights, but they ended abruptly and there was just the solid darkness of the desert.

11

HENRY CHANCE KEPT HIS WORD.

When Lee approached the box office of the Reina del Sur theater for the late show, a ticket awaited. The usher led him to a center seat in the third row. Lee sat in front of an elderly couple, who grumbled at his height. He slouched down, trying to fold his long legs into the narrow space.

A knee must have struck the seat ahead because a large woman in purple velvet turned to give him a flinty look. Lee muttered an apology. He would have moved over, but the place was packed.

Lee hadn't expected to see the deputy from Lucky Boy. It rekindled the bitterness he'd felt when she turned him in to Calindra Carnarvon. Well, he wouldn't let her get near him again. As for Sebastian Hardin . . . .

Lee rubbed the back of his head. He'd surely be plotting something. Hardin didn't give up easy. But at least Lee knew exactly where Hardin was now. And the marshal's presence would be a distraction. Braga said something about contracts. Lee just needed to step up his timetable a bit. Score big and hit the road again. In the meantime, he'd keep a sharp eye out. Hardin wouldn't dare try to take him in a crowd, so Lee resolved to stay on the casino floor as much as possible, which shouldn't be hard since that was his job.

He looked around, taking in his surroundings. Lee had never been inside a theater before. Calindra didn't permit students to leave the grounds of the Academy, and Lee was kept on a tighter leash than most. Tiers of balconies rose on both sides, all of them occupied. Dark burgundy curtains framed the stage. A chandelier hung from the domed ceiling, which had a painting of a dark-haired beauty wearing a gold crown. In the orchestra pit, the musicians played a light tune.

There was a murmur of excitement as the lights dimmed. Lee leaned forward in his seat. The curtains parted. A spotlight lit a raised platform in the middle of the stage. The noose dangling from a crossbeam above cast an ominous shadow against the screen behind.

There was a hush of anticipation. Then Henry Chance emerged from the wings, striding confidently to center stage. His blonde hair was slicked back and his skin looked bloodless beneath the lights. He was wearing heavy white pancake makeup, Lee realized. Henry bowed with a flourish, receiving scattered applause.

"Señores y señoras," he said, looking out at the audience with a crooked little smile. "Welcome to Aguadulce. As you must have deduced, I am Doctor Deathless." He bowed again and the audience applauded again, warmly this time.

Lee felt a thrill. It was unmistakably the voice of a savant, rich and laced with emotional nuance. A voice that carried easily to the far reaches of the theater and promised the show of a lifetime.

"Some say I am a charlatan, others a reckless fool. I will let you judge for yourselves." Henry stroked his chin and gave an exaggerated wink. "Remember, there are only two kinds of conjurer one cannot trust – the ones with mustaches and the clean-shaven ones."

The audience laughed.

"But I am not a conjurer. My tricks are not tricks. The danger is entirely real." Henry paused. "I have a new act, performed tonight for the very first time." He swept a hand toward the platform. "I call it Cheating the Gallows!"

The string section of the orchestra played an ominous refrain.

"If I fail, it will mean sudden death," Henry said. "Nothing less than a public execution. I hope there are no young children present?"

People turned in their seats. Henry surveyed the theater. "Very good," he said with a nod. "I'm glad to see you're still awake. But seriously, it's why I chose the late show to debut my latest disaster piece." He grimaced. "I mean masterpiece."

This drew laughter.

Henry paced the length of the stage. "Before we begin, allow me to offer proof that the apparatus involved has not been tampered with in any way. May I have a volunteer?"

Several hands shot up. Henry ignored them. His eyes roved across the audience and finally settled on Lee. "How about you, sir?"

Lee looked around. Everyone in his row was staring. He stood with a weak smile.

"Come on up, sir!" Henry beckoned.

People half-stood to make room as he squeezed past, heart thumping. Lee took the stairs up to the stage two at a time. He turned to face the audience and gave a little bow. There were a few encouraging whistles and he found himself relaxing.

A young woman in a sparkly dress wheeled out a table with a set of handcuffs. She gave the audience a flash of ankle and glided back to the wings.

"Go on, sir, have a look," Henry said. "Test them out."

Lee picked up the handcuffs, wary of a trap. A trickle of sweat ran down his face. It was hot under the spotlight. He sensed the audience growing restless.

"What's wrong?" Henry hissed.

"Nothing," Lee muttered. He snapped one of the cuffs around his own wrist and gave it a tug.

"Now the other," Henry said loudly. "Don't be shy."

A few people laughed.

Lee held up his wrist and put on a doubtful expression. "How do I know you won't just string me up?"

Henry chuckled, but his eyes were cool. He picked up the keys and bounced them in his palm. "Can't let you steal the show, can I?" he said lightly. "Leave that to the professionals, son. Come on, I promise it won't be more than a few seconds."

The audience fell silent as Lee held his wrist out and Henry snapped the second handcuff on.

"Now try to get them off," Henry said.

Lee's long fingers probed for hidden catches. He didn't find any. "Looks like I'm at your mercy," he said gamely.

Henry grinned. He unlocked the handcuffs and handed them to Lee.

"Now for the fun part." Henry Chance skipped up the steps to the gallows. Lee followed.

"Put them on nice and tight," Henry said, holding his arms behind his back.

Lee complied, testing the manacles when he was done.

"Now the noose."

He dropped it over Henry's head and cinched the knot under his chin. Henry turned back to face the audience. His assistant came gracefully up the stairs and dropped a hood over his head.

"Thank you, sir," Henry said, his voice muffled under the hood. "You may return to your seat now."

Lee departed the stage, feeling a twinge of regret as the spotlight left him and focused on Henry.

A low drumroll began in the orchestra pit. It built to a crescendo. The audience held its breath. Even Lee jumped half out of his seat when the trapdoor under Henry's feet dropped with a bang.

The noose yanked tight. Henry's feet kicked. Lee gripped the arms of his seat. *It's just an act.*

But he hadn't seen any harness beneath Henry's suit. The jacket was a slim fit. And Lee had cinched the noose tight himself.

Henry's feet kept kicking. Choking gasps came from under the black hood.

Lee bit his lip, disturbed but unable to look away. What if the illusion had gone wrong? Henry did say it was the first time he'd performed it.

Muttering erupted, but no one intervened. It was, after all, a magic show.

"For God's sake, help him!" the heavyset woman sitting in front of Lee finally cried out. "Somebody *do* something!"

Her words broke the paralysis. Two men in aisle seats jumped up and rushed towards the stage. They were halfway there when Henry vanished. The black hood dropped to the ground.

There was another collective gasp, louder this time.

Then someone loudly cleared his throat. "Anyone have a belt of whiskey? That was by the skin of my teeth, all right!"

Everyone looked around. And there was Henry, standing in the center aisle, arms crossed, with a grin on his face. Deafening applause erupted as he strode down to the stage and took a bow.

Lee laughed. He clapped hard and got to his feet with everyone else.

"Thank you, thank you," Henry cried. "A botched hanging is hard to top, but I'll surely try. For my next act, you'll watch me get buried alive. Not just once, but twice!"

Henry saluted the audience, then wheeled out a coffin on a trolley cart, the sort they used in morgues.

"As you can see, there is no trap door," he declared, spinning the cart in a full circle.

Henry walked all the way around the casket, rapping on it with his knuckles to demonstrate that it was solid wood. He opened the lid and climbed inside. Henry gestured to the wings. Two large men came on stage with chains. They wrapped him from head to toe in the heavy links. He lay back while the men went for buckets and filled the casket with sand. They nailed it shut. The audience muttered, people grinning uncertainly.

Rope pulleys lifted the casket and dropped it into a large glass aquarium filled with ice water, wheeled out by two more burly assistants.

The kettle drums pounded a beat that slowly increased in tempo.

Long minutes passed. Lee had watched the whole process without blinking. He saw no way Henry could have gotten out. How on earth was he doing it?

Suddenly, the spotlight lit the orchestra pit. Henry stood up with a smile, flourishing the padded mallets he'd been using to play the drum. The audience roared. He leapt to the stage and ordered his assistants to raise the coffin. It was pried open and tipped on its side to drain the wet sand.

Other impossible stunts followed in similar vein. By the end, the audience gave Henry Chance a standing ovation that lasted a full two minutes.

Lee found Henry in his dressing room, wiping white grease paint from his face with a sponge.

"Did you like the show?" Henry asked.

"Very much." Lee studied him in the mirror. "How'd you do it?"

Henry smiled. "A magician never reveals his secrets."

"That wasn't magic."

Henry met his eyes. "Sure it was."

"Could you teach me?"

Henry dropped the sponge. "That depends."

"On what?"

"How long you stay." Henry rose to his feet. "It took me years to perfect my act."

"Well, it's pretty amazing," Lee said. "Thanks for the ticket."

"My pleasure." Henry stretched and yawned. "It's late. Guess we should both get some rest." He winked. "You don't want to be late for your first day."

Lee walked to the door, then turned back. "Why do you perform? Was it Mr. Braga's idea?"

Henry laughed. "I do it for fun, Merriweather. What's the point of being a savant if you can't use your gift?"

Lee couldn't suppress a stab of envy as he headed back to his room. Henry wasn't hidden away like some monstrosity who couldn't be trusted. Quite the opposite. He had complete freedom. He was *famous*.

Lee had lived his entire life with the certain knowledge that no one, not even Calindra herself, was a better linguist. But Henry Chance was doing things Lee had never imagined were even possible.

For a brief moment, Lee fantasized about staying in Aguadulce. Making a new life there. But he knew Calindra would never leave him in peace. He felt a surge of anger. He'd never be able to stop running.

Not until Calindra was dead.

12

HARDIN and I ate breakfast at the Golden Dreams buffet.

It was set up in a big east-facing dining room with lots of sunlight. We hit the buffet early, but there was still a line waiting for the doors to open. The crack-of-dawn crowd was mostly older people and families with young kids. The women wore colorful shawls and pretty embroidered skirts. The men favored hats of felt or straw. They looked like regular folks, which I thought was nice. Everyone deserved a holiday.

I was nervous about finding Lee, but it didn't stop me from piling a plate high with eggs, bacon and flapjacks. Hardin had a sweet, mushy fruit fried in peanut oil called plantains and about six cups of coffee. He'd stopped in at the doctor last night. The stitches I put in his back were holding. Another scar to add to his collection.

"How's your shoulder?" he asked.

"Stiff," I admitted. "A hot bath helped though."

"Hmmmm." He studied me over the rim of his coffee cup. "Bet it did."

A flush crept up my neck. Hardin looked mighty good this morning. His black hair was parted to the side and he had on a fresh uniform. He must have stopped in at the barber because the dark scruff on his cheeks was gone.

"When do we get our guns back?" I asked in a low voice as we left the table.

His eyes roamed over the crowds. "They're in Braga's office. Only his own men are allowed to carry in Aguadulce. No exceptions."

"I guess Doc's been behaving," I muttered. "Or we'd have heard about it."

I'd hoped he might slip out of the gun for a visit, but I hadn't seen him since New Jerusalem.

"Not a peep," Hardin said. "They don't know about him and I mean to keep it that way."

"I'd better look for Lee alone, sir," I said. "He might be more amenable in light of your history. I mean, he hates me, too. But I think he hates you worse."

Hardin nodded. "I'll go check on Tanaka." He gave me a look. "Try to have a little fun. God knows you earned it."

Fun?

"Doing what?" I asked.

He eyed me with amusement. "I know it's a den of sin, Cortez, but a few rounds of blackjack won't send you straight to hell."

"Don't you need money for that?"

"I stopped by the train and picked up your wages."

I hadn't considered that they might actually give me wages. Technically, I was on loan from the township of Lucky Boy.

"Doesn't Sheriff Bowdre pay you?" Hardin asked.

I gave him a funny look. "Well, yes, but not with money."

Once a month, the sheriff's son Charlie would ride up to our house with sacks of flour and barley. Maybe a side of beef. That's how it worked in Lucky Boy. When you live in the middle of the prairie, there's not many places to spend money anyhow. Barter is much more useful.

Hardin handed me a wad of cash, more than I'd ever seen before. Calindra's stern face glared at me from the bills. "I put a bonus in there. Consider it hazard pay."

"Thank you, sir." I stuffed the money into my pocket. "Charlie Bowdre would love this place."

"Just try to avoid a scene with Merriweather. If he won't cooperate, walk away. You hear me?"

"Scout's honor," I promised.

We parted ways and I followed the signs to the Golden Dreams casino. It was already busy though the hour was barely ten in the morning. I wandered through the slots and checked the gaming tables, but didn't see any sign of Lee.

The bruising on my face was fading, though a few people shot me funny looks. I wore one of the outfits Ava had bought for me: grey wool trousers and a white button-up shirt. I'd decided to leave the copper star in my room. I had no authority here anyway, and it wouldn't win Lee over to rub it in his face.

Over by the roulette wheels, a lady with a little white dog was arguing with security that she should be allowed to have it on the casino floor because Moxie brought her good luck.

"Ma'am," the guard said patiently. "Pets are not—"

His words were drowned out by Moxie's vicious barks at any phantom who came near. It seemed to sense them even when they were in the ether, because it strained at the leash, growling at nothing.

"Stop that, Moxie!" she scolded. "Oh, you bad darling!"

I finally gave up on the Golden Dreams and decided to try the other hotels. When I stopped at the reception desk and asked how far it would be to walk, the clerk smiled. "There's no need to leave the complex, miss," he said. "We have shuttles. Just follow those arrows."

I took an escalator down to a platform where knots of people waited. Within ten minutes, a little tram pulled in, so quiet I barely heard it coming. It whisked us to the next hotel, which was the Hipódromo. The casino had murals of chariot races on the walls and dealers dressed like Roman soldiers, but no Lee Merriweather. I continued on to the Admiral Aguadulce, which sported a nautical theme, and then the Roxy and the Reina del Sur. Hours passed and I was about to give up hope when I got to the Sahara.

I spotted Lee right away — or more accurately, that cowlick on the back of his head. He was sitting at a table playing blackjack. Phantoms hung around the table, though not as many as around the slots. I waited for the hand to finish and moved into his line of sight. Lee's gaze swept past me, then shot back. His eyes narrowed.

I tried a smile. It was not returned.

I slid into a seat across from him. "Can I play?" I asked.

The dealer looked me over. "This is a high stakes table, miss," he said politely.

"How high?" I asked.

"Five hundred *platas* a hand."

"Oh." I swallowed. "Never mind. I'll just watch."

Lee scooped up his chips and stood. "I'm out," he said curtly.

The dealer gave a brief nod. He shuffled the deck and started passing out cards. None of the other players even looked up from the table. I followed Lee, jogging to keep up.

"What do you want?" he snapped without breaking stride. "I'm working."

"Just give me five minutes," I said. "That's all."

"Sorry, I'm busy."

"It's not what you think. I just want to talk."

"Sure you do."

"Come on, Lee. I'm unarmed. I'm not even wearing my badge."

He stopped and peered down at me. "Where's Hardin?"

"I told him to stay away. Look, I know you don't trust me. And you have every reason not to. But there's stuff you need to know." I lowered my voice. "About the reverend and Mr. Cage."

Lee shot me a dark look, but veered off toward the cocktail lounge. We didn't speak until the waiter had brought us two ginger ales at a quiet corner table.

"Didn't expect to see *you* here," he said.

"And I don't particularly want to be here," I said. "But I didn't have a choice."

His hazel eyes flashed. "Sure you did. And you chose *them*."

I sipped my soda. "How's Mr. Beach?"

"What do you care? Don't pretend he means anything to you." Lee crossed his arms. "That's why you came, isn't it? To drag us back?"

"And what if it is?" I said with a scowl.

"Then you're out of luck. I have friends in Aguadulce."

"Friends?" I said flatly. "People who want to use you, you mean."

Lee laughed. "Everyone wants to use me."

"I don't."

Lee stared at me for a moment. "That might be true. You're too almighty pure to use anyone, aren't you, Ruth?"

I refused to take the bait. "Calindra's offer still stands," I said calmly. "Come back to the Academy with full privileges. I thought that's what you wanted in the first place."

He smiled. "I changed my mind."

"Okay. And what's going to happen to the people here if that X shows up?"

"I'll handle it," he snapped.

"How?"

"Like I said, I have friends. Powerful friends." He looked me over and shook his head. "You're out of your depth, Ruth Cortez. The Carnarvons have no say here. You picked the wrong side."

"It's not about sides," I said. "Just listen. I got something to tell you about the reverend."

His face went still.

"We passed through New Jerusalem on the way," I said. "Every soul in that town was dead. Murdered. It's the worst thing I've ever seen. Jolly's a monster. And he won't stop until he catches you."

"You're just trying to scare me," Lee blustered.

"You should be scared! I am. And Hardin—" I cut off.

"Hardin what?"

"Calindra wants you dead or alive. There, now you know."

He absorbed this in silence.

"Leave, Lee," I urged him. "If you won't come back with us, just go."

I saw the struggle in his face. Then it hardened and I knew I'd lost him. "I'd like to see her try," he said. "My friends will look out for me."

His blind stubbornness finally got under my skin. "You don't know what a real friend is," I said.

"Well, you're right, Ruth. Calindra made sure of that." Lee stood up. Spots of color burned in his cheeks. "Have a nice stay in Aguadulce," he snarled. "Give my regards to your masters."

I was searching for a comeback when Lee froze. His eyes narrowed.

"Mr. Merriweather."

I spun around. Hardin stood behind me. They stared at each other.

"Well, look who's here. It's a proper reunion now," Lee said. "You plan to arrest me? Oh wait, I forgot. You have no jurisdiction here."

Hardin looked weary. "It's been a long morning. Don't tempt me."

"Or what?" Lee asked, his eyes glittering. "What exactly are you going to do, marshal?"

Hardin's face was calm, but I sensed a storm brewing under the surface.

"How's the hand?" Lee asked, glancing at Hardin's thumb. I could still see the red marks where Lee had bitten him.

"Got my rabies shots," Hardin said. "Thanks for asking."

Lee winked. "Work to do. Catch you later, hound dog."

We watched him saunter off.

"So much for talking," Hardin said, eyes locked on Lee. "How'd you find us?"

"Asked security." He sighed. "I found Mr. Beach."

"And?"

"He seemed nearly as frustrated with the kid. Said he had no control over him."

"You didn't trouble the professor?" I asked with a sideways glance.

Hardin shot me an exasperated look. "What am I gonna do with him, Cortez? Cuff him to my bedpost? And he's not why I'm down here. The warrant only has Lee's name on it. Beach can do what he pleases far as I'm concerned."

"He's a good person," I said. "Lee don't deserve him."

"We're agreed on that." Hardin looked around. "This place serve food?"

"I think so. How's Marshal Tanaka?"

"In and out, but they say she's gonna be okay." He tossed his coat on the red leather seat of the booth. "I'll get some menus."

Hardin went off to talk to the hostess. I thought about Lee. Maybe he deserved what was coming to him, but Hardin didn't. I might not have known the marshal long, but I knew he had a conscience, and what Calindra was asking him to do would weigh on him for the rest of his life.

Maybe I could catch Lee myself somehow. That thing about cuffing Mr. Beach to the bedpost got me thinking . . . .

The lounge looked out on the casino floor. Hotel guests milled around, along with cocktail waitresses and girls selling cigarettes from trays. My eyes fixed on a man in a long duster. He glanced over his shoulder. I knew that scraggly beard, those cold marble eyes. He turned and grinned straight at me.

I was out of the booth and running in the next instant. No way I was letting him get away this time. Jolly saw me coming and headed for the bank of elevators.

"Stop!" I yelled. "Somebody stop him!"

Heads turned my way. I ran across the lobby, colliding with a bellhop who was pushing a luggage cart. He cursed at me as we both fell in a tangle. I leapt to my feet and saw Jolly reach the elevators just as a car opened. Jolly shoved through the people getting off and hit the button. The doors closed again just as I ran up. I slammed my palm down on the button. A second car opened. This one was empty. Through the glass wall, I saw the reverend's car pause at the next floor.

I hit the button for the next floor, but by the time I got there, Jolly's was moving again. A woman had gotten on. She wore a maid's uniform. I didn't know what button to push so I just hit the top. Our two elevators started ascending at the same time, side by side. Jolly turned and peered through the glass. He caught my eye. He slid open his coat.

My heart stopped as he took out a big knife. The kind Charlie called a pigsticker. It looked about twelve inches long and tapered to a sharp point.

I pounded on the glass, but the woman inside with him didn't turn. She was staring ahead, oblivious, waiting for her floor. Jolly smiled at me. He grabbed her by the hair. I saw her mouth open in a silent scream. Then he yanked her head back and slit her throat. Blood sprayed the glass.

I froze, hands pressed across my mouth, as the reverend let her body slump to the floor. He pressed a button. The elevator started braking. My wits returned and I slammed my hand down on all the buttons. I was shaking badly. My door opened on the fourth floor. Hardin was running down the hall with a bunch of men in red jackets. They must have taken the stairs.

I stumbled out of the elevator and pointed at the next car. "He's got a knife," I yelled. "Oh my God, he killed her."

The reverend's door was closing. Hardin jammed a hand in the crack. The door slid back. The guards aimed their guns inside. Then they turned to me in confusion. Their guns lowered. I stepped forward and looked inside. The car was empty.

No blood. No body. No reverend.

"What the hell, Cortez?" Hardin said in a low voice.

My mind went blank. It wasn't possible.

"I saw him," I whispered. "I swear to God."

"Saw who?" He wore a quizzical expression. "Jolly?"

I nodded. The security guards were staring at me. "Stand down," Hardin said. "It was a mistake."

They looked annoyed, but they holstered their guns and got in the elevator. The doors closed. Hardin gave me a worried look. "Tell me what you saw."

I forced my voice to calmness. "I was sitting at the table waiting for you. I looked up and saw the Reverend Jolly, clear as day. So I chased him. You must have seen him, too."

"I only saw you," Hardin said.

"Well, he ran right past dozens of people," I said. "There must be witnesses."

But I had a terrible feeling there wouldn't be any witnesses. Because I'd also seen Jolly kill that woman, just a few feet away. I'd *seen* it.

Just like I'd seen Mr. Cage in New Jerusalem.

Just like I'd seen a little girl who'd been dead for weeks.

"I'm not losing my mind," I snapped.

"Course you're not," Hardin replied. "But we've both been under a lot of strain. The mind can play tricks—"

"That still don't explain it. I never . . . I'm mean, I'm not the sort to . . . ." I hated the whine in my voice. "He had a woman in there, marshal. And he . . . ." My jaw clenched. "I know what I saw."

Hardin nodded. "Listen, why don't you go have a rest? I'll deal with this. You caused quite a commotion down in the lobby. Maybe someone did see the reverend. I'll ask around. Either way, Braga will demand an explanation." He scrubbed a hand across his jaw. "I'll come up with something."

I shot him a dark look. "You think I'm crazy."

"I don't think you're crazy," he said evenly. "But there ain't a shred of evidence backing up your story. What am I supposed to do with that?"

I looked away. "I don't know."

"Go up to your room. We'll talk later."

He didn't say it in a condescending tone, but I still felt like an unruly child being packed off by the grownups. I turned my back and strode away, eyes pricking with tears.

"Cortez!" Hardin called. "You gonna be okay?"

I didn't turn around.

I knew what I'd seen. And I wasn't crazy.

I decided to walk back to the Golden Dreams. The thought of stuffing myself into a crowded shuttle had no appeal. And part of me was worried about what I might see. It seemed safer to avoid people.

The minute I stepped through the revolving doors, I understood why nobody walked around here. The heat slammed into me like a wall. The only shade came from a few palm trees and it didn't help much with the sun so high. I trudged past the Roxy and the Reina del Sur. By the time I got to the Golden Dreams, I felt sick. Maybe I was coming down with something. A bad fever might explain it.

When I got to my room, I splashed cold water on my face and lay down. Could Lee have done this to me somehow? He liked playing pranks. And he had every reason to want to punish me.

But as much as I hated him right then, and blamed him for getting me into this mess, I couldn't see Merriweather staging something so awful. Jolly, maybe, but not the murdered woman. Even with my eyes closed I still could see her, white neck tipped back as his knife drew a red line from ear to ear. The sudden spurt of red painting the glass wall of the elevator.

My stomach heaved and I just made it to the bathroom before I threw up my breakfast. I brushed my teeth and returned to the bed on unsteady legs. Food poisoning. It had to be. I slept for the rest of the day, wishing I had Doc. He'd know what was going on. And if I *was* losing my mind, he'd tell it to me straight, without any pity.

It was dark by the time Hardin knocked on my door. I let him in and told him how I'd been sick. He looked relieved. "Maybe you should see a doctor," he said. "I know where the infirmary is. We can get you a bed near Tanaka."

"It's okay," I said. "I'm a lot better." I tried on a weak smile. "I'll just stick with the plantains tomorrow." I cleared my throat. "About Lee, I was thinking—"

"Don't worry," Hardin interrupted. "Nothing's happening on that front. Not until Calindra gets here."

"She's coming?" I asked in surprise.

"Already on the way." He didn't look thrilled about it. "Sent a cable to Mr. Braga. And one to me."

"What'd she say?"

"It was coded, but basically to sit tight."

So we had a reprieve. "When's she getting here?"

"Day after tomorrow, if the weather holds."

"So fast?"

"It's a new prototype zeppelin. Richard said it wasn't quite ready, but she took it anyhow."

"Well, that changes things," I said slowly.

"Yes, it does." Hardin looked away. "You're free to go, deputy."

It took a minute for the words to sink in. "You mean, back to Lucky Boy?" I asked in surprise.

Hardin nodded. "I'll square it with Mrs. Carnarvon when she gets here. But we'll get you on a northbound train as soon as possible." He met my eyes. "I know you want to go home. I can't in good conscience keep you here. Probably never should have made you come in the first place."

I didn't know what to say. It was what I'd been hoping for. Yet I felt a strange reluctance.

"Well, thank you," I said finally. "I appreciate it."

Hardin gave a curt nod. "I told Mr. Braga it was a case of mistaken identity. He bought it, but he doesn't want you on the casino floor."

"So I'm a prisoner in my room?" I asked flatly.

"Wasn't my decision."

"Fine. But I want Doc back before I go."

Hardin started for the door. "Oh, you're welcome to him," he said over his shoulder.

"And what are you gonna do while I'm stuck in here?" I demanded, crossing my arms.

"I came here to review the contracts."

"Won't Mr. Braga do that with Calindra?"

Hardin stared at me. "I'm chief of security, in case you've forgotten, Cortez. I got details to hammer out."

"Sounds fun."

Hardin ignored this. "You can order up food from the front desk. Just dial the operator. I'll try to check in tomorrow."

"Well, don't bother if you're too busy," I retorted. "I don't need minding."

He sighed. "You got what you wanted. I thought you'd be happy."

"I am. Thrilled, actually."

Hardin looked like he might say something else, but in the end he just shook his head and left. I wrapped the blanket tighter around myself and went back to bed.

Well, good. I'd be going home. Lee Merriweather could do whatever the heck he pleased.

All of them could.

13

LEE STUDIED the cards spread across the green felt horseshoe. To his left was a beefy man in a giant cowboy hat who puffed on a foul-smelling cigar. To his right sat a woman swathed in widow's black with diamonds glittering on her fingers and shrewd dark eyes.

"Hit me," Lee said.

The dealer laid a queen of spades next to the four of clubs and ten of diamonds.

"Bust," Lee muttered.

His luck had soured, but it didn't matter if he won or lost. He was playing with Braga's money, which took the fun out of it. He suspected the widow was cheating, but hadn't yet discovered how she was communicating with her phantom — and didn't especially care.

Only two days into his new job, Lee Merriweather was terminally bored.

At first it had amused him to be on the right side of the law, but playing cards for hours on end — with no real risk — had soon grown tedious. Few people were brazen enough to cheat in plain view of a dealer at the high-stakes tables. And those who did . . . well, Lee wished them luck. He'd caught one or two just to keep Henry Chance happy, but his heart wasn't in it.

No wonder Sebastian Hardin had no sense of humor. Who else could do this job?

Lee found himself fantasizing about breaking into the vaults and making one last spectacular score, but even he had to admit there were enough people after him already. Adding Pedro Braga to the list would be suicide.

Running into the deputy from Lucky Boy had shaken Lee more than he liked to admit. He felt confident that he could take care of himself, but he worried about Mr. Beach. The professor didn't talk much about the crazy holy rollers who'd held him prisoner, but the whole thing had been Lee's fault and he vowed to himself it would never happen again. If Jolly was as evil as Ruth Cortez claimed, Lee had no intention of waiting around for him to arrive.

He played one more hand — another washout — and excused himself from the table. A portly man with enormous side whiskers was approaching from the opposite direction. Lee looked down to count his meager handful of chips, timing it so he bumped the man as they passed. He apologized profusely. As the man vanished into the crowd, Lee pulled a gold case from his sleeve with a sly grin. He took out a smoke and beckoned one of the cigarette girls over for a match. They all liked him, seeming to view him as something between a mascot and a kid brother.

"Why, I didn't know you smoked, Mr. Merriweather," the girl said with a grin, lighting his cigarette.

Lee inhaled deeply. Then he bent double in a coughing fit that drew a few stares. The girl laughed as Lee made a face. He stubbed the cigarette into an ashtray.

"What a revolting habit," he muttered. He offered her the gold case. "Want it?"

Her face lit up. Her name was Anne and Lee knew she needed the money. Braga paid his workers a decent wage, but she had four younger siblings at home. "Sure," she said. "Thanks!"

Lee took the elevator up to his suite on the twenty-sixth floor of the Bella Luna. It was enormous and looked out over the whole city. Dusk was falling and the thousands of colored lights twinkling beyond the floor-to-ceiling windows looked like some kind of fairyland. Of course, none of the windows actually opened — probably so guests couldn't jump if they lost everything, he thought darkly.

Lee lay on the bed and stared at the ceiling, mulling over where to go next. Maybe he'd head south until he ran out of road and see what came after. He'd heard rumors of dense tropical forests and ruined cities with treasure. Lee perked up. Maybe it was time he built up his own empire. Calindra Carnarvon did it. Pedro Braga did it. Why not Lee Merriweather? He'd start his own school. And the students would be free to choose whatever they wanted to do—

Lee frowned at a furtive sound and nearly jumped out of his skin. A phantom sat cross-legged on the foot of his bed. She had long dark hair with an unusual white streak down the right side. Her face was angled so the neon jungle outside reflected in her eyes, flashing pinpricks of light.

Hello, he said politely. *You startled me.*

She stared at him, unblinking.

I can't play with you right now, Lee said, his tone conveying a profound sense of regret. *Maybe tomorrow?*

She shook her head. He repeated himself in a dozen different phantom tongues, but none garnered a response.

Don't you talk? Lee asked.

The girl vanished. Suddenly, an open valise appeared on his bed. The closet door swung wide. Lee stepped aside as three suits flew past. The garments were crammed into the valise by unseen hands. The lid slammed shut.

"Hey," he muttered. "What are you doing?"

The girl reappeared, standing in front of the window. She wore a determined expression.

"You go away," she croaked in English.

Lee arched an eyebrow. "Why?"

The girl just stabbed a finger at the valise.

"Who taught you English?" he wondered.

"The big boy." Her voice was a hoarse rasp.

Lee's unease deepened. "What's his name?"

She didn't answer, but there was no mistaking the fear on her thin face. "Please," she whispered. "You go away."

"Well, I was planning to anyhow. But . . . hey, wait!"

The girl vanished again.

Lee stared at the place she'd stood. He felt sure he hadn't seen her around any of the casinos. That streak of white in her hair was unusual. Of course, it didn't mean she hadn't been lurking in the ether. Spying on him.

The big boy.

What did she mean by that? Phantoms were simple-minded entities. They could be enticed to "play games" and didn't seem to distinguish between mischief and productive tasks, like making engines go. Ruth's phantom, Doc, was the only one Lee knew who spoke human languages. Never had a phantom begged him to do anything — nor had Lee seen one who looked afraid before.

Perhaps he should listen to her.

He opened the valise and carefully folded the crumpled suits, his shoulder-blades tingling with the sensation of being watched. Maybe he shouldn't even wait for the morning. He'd go find Mr. Beach. There had to be a night bus going some-where. Lee turned at a knock on the door.

"Yes?" he called out warily.

"It's Henry."

Lee hastily stowed the suitcase under his bed. Then he opened the door.

"I hope it's not a bad time," Henry Chance said with a smile.

"Come on in." Lee stepped aside.

"How do you like the suite?"

"It's very comfortable." He looked at the bar. "Can I mix you a drink?"

"No, thanks, I don't aim to stay long." Henry grinned. "Actually, I came with a proposition. How'd you like to join me on stage tomorrow?" He held his hands out like he was framing a marquee. "I thought we'd call it the Duel of the Linguists."

Lee forced a smile. "It's tempting. But I don't know."

"Oh, come on. It'll be fun. You'd be a surprise guest! People would *love* it."

Lee remembered the warm glow of the spotlight. "But we haven't even rehearsed," he said. "Tomorrow's too soon."

"Don't worry, it won't be like my regular act," Henry replied. "Nothing dangerous. I'm thinking an all-ages show. Something lighthearted and fun for the children. We can improvise most of it." His voice lowered. "Aren't you tired of doing what you're expected to all the time? Following everybody's rules? Let's have a little fun, you and me."

Lee rubbed the back of his head. "I'm not sure, Henry. Seems awfully last-minute."

"Tell you what. If you're not busy, come down to the theater with me right now. We'll talk it through. If you don't want to afterwards, I'll understand."

Lee hesitated. He didn't want to let Henry down, but he also didn't want to stay in Aguadulce any longer than necessary. Better to just stick with the plan.

Or, a voice in his head whispered, *you could go out with a bang. Leave them with something to remember. Robbing banks is all well and good, but it's a waste of your talents.*

And then a more churlish voice that Lee didn't much care

for added: *Henry Chance thinks he's better than you. Maybe he needs a little lesson.*

"Come on, what do you have to lose?" Henry winked. "Maybe I'll even share some trade secrets."

"Like how you escape the gallows?"

Lee had barely slept after watching Henry's act for trying to figure out how he did it.

"You'd be the only soul in the world besides myself to know the trick," Henry mused. "But I might come around to telling you . . . if you'll agree to meet my phantoms and hear me out."

That decided him. He could always go first thing in the morning.

"Okay," Lee said. "But I'm not promising anything."

They didn't take the public tram to the Reina del Sur. Henry had his own car and driver waiting in the underground tunnels that linked the hotels. Everyone they passed gave Henry a deferential greeting and Lee felt a stab of jealousy. Chance was the slick, handsome savant, famous and respected, while Lee was nothing more than a disgraced runaway.

And now Calindra wanted his head. The same woman who'd hugged him when he graduated from the immersion track at the academy. Who'd doted on him like a proud grandmother — until he wanted more freedom. Then she hadn't been able to bend her stiff neck a single inch to see his point of view.

"What's wrong?" Henry asked as they entered the empty theater. It was still two hours before that evening's performance. "You've been awfully quiet."

Lee shook off the foul mood. "Nothing." He strode up the steps to the stage and peered into the recesses of the auditorium. It looked bigger without the audience, but he could imagine all those faces watching him, eyes wide in amazement. The thunderous waves of applause.

Henry barked an order in a phantom tongue and Lee blinked in the sudden glare of a spotlight. The curtains slid open. The gallows sat in the middle of the stage, a macabre reminder of Henry's main act.

"I'm thinking we'll start small. I'll tell a phantom to do something, and then you'll top it. Moving objects around, making things appear and disappear. Like back and forth." He smiled. "Kid stuff."

"So they're here?" Lee looked around.

"Sure." Henry growled an order. The tone was harsher than Lee would have used, but it didn't put off the phantoms. Three skinny kids materialized, naked but smooth as mannequins. Lee half-expected to see the girl from his room, but she wasn't among them.

The first two kept their heads down. But the third, a flame-haired creature with a pinched, sharp-nosed face, kept staring at Lee. He was taller than the others. Lee wondered if it was the "big boy" the girl had referred to.

"I've worked with them for a long time," Henry said. "Totally reliable."

He barked a command. The littlest one disappeared. An instant later, four chairs started whirling in a circle above the stage. Lee covered a yawn.

"We'd better come up with something better than that," he said. "At least they use knives in Carnarvon City."

"You know," Henry said thoughtfully. "I think you're right."

He snapped his fingers and the red-haired phantom flew at Lee's face, hands curled into claws. For an instant, the boy's body seemed to blur and waver. Lee thought he saw something *underneath* the bone-white skin. Something alien and repulsive. The arms stretched like taffy, reaching for him—

Stop! Lee screamed in a grim tongue, instinct filling his voice with authority.

The phantom veered away at the last second. Henry

started laughing so hard he bent double, bracing his hands on his knees.

"What was that?" Lee asked in a shaky voice. "A test?"

"Your face . . . ." Henry wiped his eyes. "Oh, boy. It was just a joke, Merriweather. Hey, I'm sorry."

The phantom clung to the curtain, hanging upside-down like an oversized bat. It looked normal again — just a pale child with peculiar eyes.

"Well, don't do it again," Lee muttered, though his own lips twitched in a smile. It was hard to stay mad at Henry. If anything, Lee felt like a stiff for not laughing himself.

It *was* a pretty good joke.

"I was thinking that could be part of the act," Henry said. "We'll make it a duel."

"With weapons?" Lee asked doubtfully.

"Of course," Henry said. "Otherwise it'll seem tame and the audience will get bored." His gaze swept across the phantoms. "But these little imps will already have their instructions. Like I told you, I hand-picked them." He chuckled. "They've held my life in their grubby little paws plenty of times and I'm still standing. You can trust them, Lee."

They rehearsed for a while and Lee found himself relaxing as it went off without a hitch. As Henry had promised, the phantoms were eager and responsive. Henry would tell one to do something. Then Lee had to top it. Eventually they pretended to order the phantoms to attack, with the other linguist turning back the assault at the last moment. Henry coached him on how to hit his marks and praised his abilities.

It was the most fun Lee had had in ages. It almost made him want to stay in Aguadulce.

But he knew it would never work. His enemies would never leave him alone.

"You said you'd explain the gallows trick," Lee reminded his new partner as they walked to the elevators.

"I *could* tell you," Henry said with a wink. "But then I'd have to kill you."

"You promised." Lee frowned. "I'm serious."

"Okay." Henry shot him a sidelong glance. "But I'll bet you already know."

Lee stared at him. He'd turned the problem over and over in his mind.

"The only thing I can think of is that phantoms moved you," Lee said slowly. "Through the ether. But we both know it's impossible."

"Is it?" Henry murmured.

"Phantoms won't touch living flesh. It's forbidden to them."

Henry paused. Half his face was in shadow. "What I do requires a level of complete trust, Lee. Most people aren't willing to surrender that."

"So there *were* phantoms involved?"

A small smile played at the corners of his mouth. "Of course there were."

"What's it like?" Lee asked eagerly. "The ether?"

"Hard to describe. I don't stay there long." Henry's brow quirked. "You ever looked down at an anthill?"

Lee nodded.

"It's a bit like that. Seeing everything laid out, but you're above it all. Now imagine that you pick up one of those ants —" Henry pinched his fingers together "—and you put it down on the other side of the mound. The other ants, they don't look up. So from their perspective, their little friend suddenly appeared in a different place."

Lee nodded slowly. "I guess I can picture that. So it's like flying?"

"Sure. Just like flying. The danger is when you pinch that ant too hard." Henry's eyes held him. "Ants are fragile creatures. You might hurt them by accident, not even meaning to. So that's the danger."

"Sounds like a fairly big danger," Lee muttered. "Not sure I'd want to risk it."

"Understandable," Henry said. "Most wouldn't. You have to trust the phantom you're working with." He glanced at the tall boy with a ratty face trailing along behind them. "He's the only one I trust to do it. We've been together a long time."

"But we won't be going into the ether, right? Just moving objects and playing around."

Henry nodded. "Of course. Will you do it?" His eyes held a challenge. He expected Lee to back down.

"Sure I'll do it," Lee heard himself say.

Henry beamed. "Well, that's great. I always wanted to try a two-person act, but I never found the right partner." He winked. "You're something special. After tomorrow, I bet you'll be a household name, Merriweather."

14

Time dragged.

I wasn't accustomed to sitting around doing nothing. When the maid came, I shooed her away and cleaned the room myself. Then I sat on the bed and stared out the window, watching the trains run north.

I'd never liked chopping wood. No matter how long I worked, there was always more logs waiting to be split. Now I wished I had a big pile to swing at until my shoulders burned. Whenever I was in a foul mood, chopping wood got the black humor out. I liked the satisfying crack as a log split down the middle. The thunk of the axe into the scarred old stump by the woodshed.

I had half a mind to pack up and buy my own ticket, but part of me still felt obligated to get Calindra's say-so. And I figured I owed the marshal a proper goodbye, even if he'd left me to rot.

I wondered if Mrs. Carnarvon knew Lee was here, and if so, what she had planned for him. I chewed my fingernails down to the quick worrying about it. Doc still hadn't come to see me. He was doing what I asked and lying low, but nothing was stopping him from sneaking out for a spell. *Was it?* All I needed right now was for Pedro Braga to figure out I had a phantom bound to the flintlock.

A day and night passed in this manner. I was pacing like a caged animal when a knock came on the door.

"I'm sorry I haven't been by," Hardin said, as I stood back from the door to let him in. "Braga's had me holed up in his office non-stop going over the contracts." He held a covered tray in his hands. "I brought some dinner. Thought we could talk."

It was hard to stay mad at him when he whipped the cover off. I'd hardly eaten for the last day, but the sight of grilled fish in a creamy lemon sauce set my mouth to watering.

"Let's eat on the terrace," Hardin said, dragging two chairs onto the narrow balcony. I took one look at the drop and lost my appetite.

"Or we could sit inside," he amended, studying my face.

The room was pretty small.

"Tell you what," I said. "You can sit out there, and I'll sit right here, just inside the doors."

He smiled and moved one of the chairs a safe distance from the edge, then gave it a pat. "I guess I'm used to heights, working in Carnarvon Tower," he said, handing me a plate.

"They don't bother me so much when I'm looking through glass," I said. "It's open air I don't care for."

By unspoken agreement, neither of us brought up Cage, Jolly, Merriweather or worst of all, Roger. It was a nice evening, cooler than the day before. The sky over the horizon glowed a deep burnt orange. I dug into the meal. The fish came with a cold salad of rubbery things Hardin said were squid.

"How long you been a marshal?" I asked him.

Hardin tipped his chair back and rested one boot on the rail. "Nine years."

I did the math and felt a twinge of surprise. "You were sixteen when you joined up?"

Hardin nodded.

"How'd you get the job so young?"

"Long story."

I smiled. "Marshal, I've been sitting in this room twiddling my thumbs for a day and a half, and I'll probably be sitting here tomorrow, and maybe the day after that, too. I got nothing *but* time."

I thought Hardin would put me off, but then his face softened a fraction. "I'm sorry, Cortez. Okay, I think I already told you I was born in the N.T. Well, Mrs. Carnarvon came up to Hatchet to inspect some of her mines. She did that every now and again. On this particular occasion, Freddie and Ava came with her."

"What's Hatchet like?"

"Lively," he said after a minute. "A bit lawless. That's why Mrs. Carnarvon generally came with a trainload of marshals. My family lived outside of town, up in the foothills."

"You have brothers and sisters?"

He nodded. "Five. I'm the oldest."

"So you were what, fifteen?"

"Just turned."

"What did your papa do? Was he a miner?"

Hardin laughed. "Lord, no." He scratched his head and chuckled again. "You wouldn't catch Horatio James Hardin down in a dark hole actually working for a living. He played the piano."

"Well, that's a living," I said, frowning slightly.

"It is if you don't drink up your pay," Hardin said. I didn't detect a great deal of resentment. It was merely a statement of fact.

"I always wanted to learn the piano," I said wistfully. "But Mrs. Johanssen — she plays the hymns in church on Sundays — says my fingers are too fat."

"Let's see," Hardin said with a smile.

I held out my hand. He took it in his own and examined it

critically, turning it this way and that. My callouses had never troubled me before, but now they struck me as deeply unattractive.

"Well, they ain't a surgeon's hands," he said, with a teasing gleam in his eye. "But they're strong. That's what matters."

I snatched my hand back, my face heating. "You're making fun."

"I'm not. Do you still want the story?"

"Yes," I said. My hand fell to my lap, but I could still feel his touch.

"Anyway, my father was down in Hatchet. It was normal for him to go off for days at a time when he was too hungover to make it home before his next shift. I'd left school the year before. No choice, if we were gonna eat. But there was decent hunting in the woods. Rabbit, possum, sometimes a deer if I got lucky. We'd eat the carcass for food and sell the skins to the fur traders."

I nodded, vowing not to interrupt him again.

"The snow was deep that afternoon and still falling hard. I wouldn't have gone out if the larder hadn't been empty. But all that was left was some old wrinkled turnips and a couple onions. The littlest ones were crying 'cause their bellies hurt. So I took my rifle and went out hunting."

His eyes took on a faraway look. "Spring comes late in the N.T., and that year winter was holding on longer than usual. Even in town, things were getting hard. I wasn't too far from the house when I caught some tracks, but they weren't deer." He held my eyes. "They were men. I wondered who it was. Men get desperate, they do things they wouldn't normally do. I wanted to be sure they weren't a threat to my family."

He offered me a piece of chewing gum. I shook my head and he unwrapped it and popped it in his mouth. "There's abandoned settlements all over the N.T., old claims that ran dry. I tracked 'em to a cabin. Took a look in the window. I saw Freddie."

My eyes widened. "No."

"Yep. Had him tied up. I knew the fellows. Bad characters. I didn't recognize the kid, but I figured he was in trouble. So I hid and waited for dark."

"You didn't go for help?"

"It was a two-hour walk down the mountain. I thought about it, but he could've been dead by the time I came back with a posse. And when I listened to 'em talking, it made up my mind. They were holding him for ransom, but they didn't plan to give him back intact."

"What'd you do?"

"Well, I waited until one came outside to uh, relieve himself. I shot him, and then I picked off the others with my rifle."

"How many were there?"

"Four. It was pure dumb luck I didn't die myself. I was shaking like a leaf the whole time."

"Is that how . . . ." I trailed off, my face reddening.

Hardin frowned. "How what?"

"How you got those shotgun scars on your back."

He laughed. "No. God must have been watching, because I finished that night without a single scratch." The humor in his eyes faded. "My dad gave me those."

He saw my expression and shook his head. "Not on purpose. He was drunk as a skunk. Mistook me for a horse thief when I was drawing water from the well." Hardin shrugged like that sort of thing happened all the time where he came from. "It was an honest mistake."

"Jolly said you killed him," I confessed, quickly adding, "I didn't believe him though."

"But you wondered when you saw the scars?" Hardin asked shrewdly. "Well, far as I know, my dad's still tickling the ivories at the Hotel Yorba, though I'll admit we've fallen out of touch."

"Never mind," I said, ashamed I ever doubted him. "Then what happened?"

Hardin gave me a squinty look but continued. "I took Freddie back to town. Seems they'd snatched him right from his bedroom at the mayor's house. Turned out to be an inside job. One of the marshals unlocked a window, thought he'd get some of the payout."

"And Calindra hired you right on the spot," I guessed. "The youngest man ever to join the marshals."

He cracked his gum. "That's right. And she set my family up in a proper house in the decent part of town. If not for her, my brothers and sisters would have ended up quitting school like I did. My ma had a hard life. She deserved a rest and Mrs. Carnarvon gave it to her."

Well, that explained his undying loyalty, I thought.

"What about you?" I asked. "Don't you ever miss home?"

"God, no," Hardin said. "The second I got out of there, I never looked back."

I didn't say anything.

"Why do you stay, Cortez?" he asked, sticking his chewing gum in the wrapper and placing it neatly on a plate. "Out in the back end of nowhere?"

He had the grace not to say Lucky Boy was on its way to becoming another prairie ghost town, but I could see it in his face.

"Well, my dad's there, for one thing."

"Your mother's in the city," Hardin pointed out.

"That's her choice. And I know now it's where she belongs. But I'm different. The city's fine, but I'd rather live where I know everybody and they know me. Where we can count on each other." I sighed. "I know you think it's a lonesome little patch of earth, but we have some growing families, too. Roots going back generations. Unless a twister wipes us off the map, we ain't going anywhere, marshal."

"Stubborn," Hardin muttered, and I wasn't sure if he

meant me or the townsfolk of Lucky Boy. "So no chance you'll change your mind about joining the marshals?"

"No, sir," I said firmly.

His blue eyes held me. "That's a shame." He sighed and got to his feet. "But I respect your decision."

Part of me was disappointed he didn't try to argue me out of it. I cleared my throat. "Look, if you want me to stick around a bit longer, see it through, I will," I said. "I'm sure the sheriff can spare me for a few weeks more."

Hardin started gathering up the dirty plates. "No, I know you're raring at the bit to get home." He sounded weary. "God only knows how long I'll be chasing Merriweather. I'll probably be old and grey, hobbling after him with a cane, by the time it's done."

"You didn't fail her," I said.

He looked over, his face expressionless "Sure I did."

"Mrs. Carnarvon set you a pretty impossible task, you ask me," I said. "*You* caught him once, and *I* caught him once. That's more than I'd have expected. Ain't your fault he ran south and you got no jurisdiction."

Hardin grunted. He set the plates down on the table by the door.

"Ava was for telling Pedro Braga everything." He sighed. " Maybe she was right."

"Ava's sweet on you," I said.

The words just came out before I could stop them.

Hardin glanced at me. A guarded look. "I know."

"Most men would fall down at her feet. She's rich, gorgeous and smart. She'd probably marry you."

"Hmmm."

"It must drive her nuts to know you're sleeping alone on that busted couch every night, just a couple of floors down in Special Services."

He didn't answer right away. Just carefully folded the napkins and set them on top of the plates. I got the sense he was stalling and felt a stab of jealousy. I shook my head. "What's wrong with you, Hardin?"

"Maybe she's not my type," he said quietly.

Then he bent down and kissed me. It was quick and soft. I tasted the spearmint on his breath. He pulled away and searched my face.

He'd caught me by surprise. I stared at him like an idiot. Hardin went pale.

"Please forgive me," he said in a hoarse voice. "That was totally inappropriate." He stepped back. "I don't usually . . . I mean I've never . . . ." Hardin gave me a helpless look.

"No offense taken," I managed.

He let out a breath. "Okay. It'll never happen again. You sure we're good?"

"We're good."

Hardin turned to run out the door and I grabbed his arm. Then I kissed him long and proper. When I let go, he staggered a little.

"Uh-oh." I bit my lip. "I'm so sorry, marshal. That was *way* over the line."

Hardin laughed.

"You gonna report me to Sheriff Bowdre?" I asked.

Hardin stared at me, his blue eyes hot. "Worse than that," he said.

And then we were wrapped around each other, making out like our lives depended on it. I heard the dishes hit the floor as he lifted me up to the table. He hadn't shaved and his cheeks were a bit rough, but his lips were soft and he turned out to be an excellent kisser.

"What do you want to do now?" Hardin asked, a little breathless, when things started veering under the clothes. He kept his tone neutral, like he didn't mind either way.

I thought for a second, one hand stroking the puckered scars along his ribs. Hardin shivered.

"Honest answer?"

He seemed to brace himself. "'Course."

I grinned. "I want to see you in the altogether."

"Okay." Hardin gave a resolute nod. "What's that mean?"

I chuckled. "Naked, marshal."

He grinned back. "Oh, that's good then."

I unbuckled his shoulder rig and tossed it on the dresser. Hardin kicked his boots off. He looked me over.

"Jesus, you're beautiful," he said. Hardin hesitated. "You ever been with a man before?"

"Yeah, but just once. We were kids." I flushed under the intensity of those blue eyes. "Honestly, I wanted to get my first time over with."

Hardin nodded. He pulled me close. "This isn't going to be like that," he whispered in my ear. "Let's take our time."

His breath raised the hair on my neck. "Okay."

He held out his hand and we sat down on the bed. "It wasn't so bad," I said as he slowly unbuttoned my shirt. "I mean, it didn't hurt much."

"Wasn't so bad," he repeated softly. "Well, I'm glad for that. But I'll try to do a little better."

I shivered as he ran a hand down my bare back. The way he touched me made me feel like a special present being unwrapped.

"Now kiss me again, Cortez," he said with a smile.

A while later, I understood that the first time with a 15-year-old kid with jug ears named Delmer Ray was a lot different than the second time with a grown man like Sebastian Hardin. And the third and fourth times were even better.

I lay with my cheek resting on his chest, listening to him breathe. I wasn't sure he was still awake, but then he gave a happy little sigh.

"Hey, Hardin."

I wasn't going to call him "sir" anymore, but "Sebastian" just felt weird.

"Yeah?"

"I think you only kissed me so I wouldn't go."

He gave a quiet laugh. "Maybe."

"It was a rotten thing to do."

Hardin tilted his head to look at me. "I figured if you liked me back, I could talk you into hanging around for a bit. And if you didn't . . . . Well, I wouldn't have to live with the humiliation too long."

"But I still—"

He rolled over and covered my mouth with another kiss.

"You have to quit doing that," I whispered.

"Says who?"

"Me."

"You got no jurisdiction here," he teased.

"Neither do you," I pointed out.

"We'll figure it out," he said.

"How?"

"I don't know yet." His eyes crinkled at the corners. "Are you always like this?"

"Like what?"

That made him laugh again. "Asking questions."

I considered it. "What do you think?"

Hardin whacked me with a pillow.

15

I DREAMT OF MR. CAGE.

He had me tied to a chair in the middle of the desert. His face was bloody and he came at me with that big knife of his, only this time Lee and Doc didn't come to save me. I woke up sweaty and yelling. Hardin held me tight and made soothing sounds until I stopped shaking.

"You're still here," I muttered, resting my head in the crook of his arm.

He looked down at me in puzzlement. "Where else would I be?"

"I don't know. Your own room."

He smoothed my hair. It was still dark out. "Go back to sleep," he murmured drowsily, closing his eyes. "It's okay."

But it wasn't. I had an uneasy feeling that went beyond the nightmare. When the big storms came across the prairie, the wind would die right before they hit. The sun might even come out. But it was an eerie sort of calm. Lying snugged against Hardin's side, Aguadulce felt like that to me.

Despite my misgivings, I must have drowsed off again because when I woke it was full daylight. Hardin sat on the edge of the bed in his pants. He looked tousled and more handsome than any man had a right to be.

"When's Calindra coming?" I asked, sitting up.

"Soon. I ought to get to the aerodrome." He pulled me down next to him and gave me a serious look. "We need to talk some more."

My stomach tightened. "I know."

"I can't let you walk out on me now," Hardin said with a faint smile, though his eyes were serious.

"I don't want to walk out on you." I sighed. "But I don't want to live in the city, either."

"Then we'll figure something out," he said.

Like what? I wondered unhappily. Our lives were a thousand miles apart.

"I know it seems impossible." Hardin took my hand. "I'd never ask you to quit your job. I know what it means to you. What Lucky Boy means." He sighed. "I want you to be happy, Cortez."

A different man would see his own position as much more important and try to make me bend, but that wasn't Hardin's way. Of course, it's why I liked him in the first place.

"I want you to be happy, too," I said.

He nodded slowly. "Good. Because I won't be happy without you." He smiled. "I could go up there and see you every chance I get. Maybe you could do the same sometimes. It's just a train ride."

"You could meet my dad," I said.

His smile widened. "I'd like that."

"And we still have a few more days together," I said.

Hardin cleared his throat. "I'll talk to Braga. There's no reason you should be cooped up in here any longer." He pulled his shirt on and followed it with the shoulder rig.

"Hey, you're carrying," I said, eyeing the snubnosed revolver in the holster.

I should have noticed the night before when I took it off him, but I'd been distracted at the time.

"Well, Mr. Braga doesn't exactly know about it," Hardin allowed. "I snuck down to the train and got a little Banker's Special. I'd prefer my Colt, but that's still under lock and key."

"You're not planning to shoot Merriweather, are you?"

He gave me a level look. "No, I wasn't. Not until after breakfast at least. It's bad for the digestion to shoot a man on an empty stomach."

I returned his level look with interest. "Because Calindra might change her mind. You never know."

He seemed doubtful, but refrained from comment. "Would it make you feel better to keep it?" he asked. "I don't mean Merriweather. I mean . . . you know."

Because of my nightmare. Because I was jumping at shadows and seeing things that weren't there. For a minute, I was tempted, but I didn't want him to think I didn't trust him.

"No, that's all right," I said. "Though I wish I had my Collier back."

"Because of Doc."

"Yeah." I laughed. "I'm starting to miss getting insulted on a regular basis. Feels strange to say *ain't* without hearing a gasp of horror."

"I'll make sure you get him back when we go." Hardin shook his head. "Guess you two come as a package."

"'Fraid so," I said.

"Then I'll have to get used to it."

He kissed me at the door. I was grinning like an idiot by the time I pushed him out and closed it. Maybe he'd get tired of working for the Carnarvons someday. I couldn't see Hardin as a farmer, but Sheriff Bowdre wasn't getting any younger and Charlie couldn't wait to move on. Maybe —

A knock came at the door. I looked around, thinking the marshal might have forgotten something. He'd only been gone a minute or two. Even so, I wasn't taking chances.

"Who is it?" I called.

No answer. I stared at the door. I hadn't locked it after Hardin left. The key was still in the hole.

"Hello?" I called again, my pulse kicking up a notch.

Still no answer, but I could sense a presence on the other side.

I rushed forward, eyes glued to the knob. I darted out a hand, turning the key. The tumblers fell into place. That made me feel a little better. I backed away and picked up the telephone to call the operator. They could send security up. If it was a mistake I'd look like a fool, but that was better than the alternative.

I put the receiver to my ear. The line was dead.

I looked up as the Reverend Jolly stepped straight through the solid door like it wasn't even there. He wore the long duster coat I'd seen before. A scraggly black beard covered his face. His eyes were the same as I remembered them, small and shiny like marbles.

My mouth ran dry. I froze with the receiver in my hand. He watched me for a minute, enjoying my reaction. "Well, hello there, Ruth," he said.

That's when I knew it wasn't Jolly. Not really. Because the accent was right, but the voice was different. Higher and softer. And Jolly couldn't walk through walls.

I wondered if I'd finally snapped.

"You ain't real," I whispered.

"Oh, I'm realer than real." He chuckled. "It's good to see you again. I'm afraid we got off on the wrong foot last time."

The lamp flickered and dimmed. A shadow darkened the room like a great bird of prey spreading its wings. Every hair stood straight up. "Roger?" I said in a squeaky voice.

But he didn't have a phantom's eyes, and that scared me worse than anything.

"I just want to talk." He took a step closer, lips stretching in a smile. "I don't want you to go away. That would spoil the fun."

I didn't answer. His smile faded. He looked embarrassed. The toe of his boot scuffed the carpet. "I'm sorry about New Jerusalem. Sorry you had to see that. It was a mistake. Things got out of hand. I'm not here to cause you trouble."

Out of hand? I inched away from the bed, keeping him in view. He still stood squarely in front of the door.

"That was you before," I stammered. "In the elevator."

He busted out laughing. It wasn't an evil laugh. In fact, it was so merry and infectious, I found myself smiling until my cheeks hurt. It was like I *had* to, even though part of me was gibbering in fear.

"You should have seen your face when I . . . . Oh, boy." He wiped his eyes. "I got you pretty good, didn't I, Ruth? At the end?"

The memory of blood splashing against the glass sobered me. I felt the pull lessen. "You got me, all right. And it was mean."

Roger frowned. "It was just a joke. I didn't hurt anybody."

"What about New Jerusalem?" I felt a surge of hope. If he could make me see things that weren't real . . . . "Was that a joke too?"

Roger picked up my badge and turned it over in his hands. "Sure it was, Ruth. Did you like my impression of Mr. Cage? I had an assistant play the girl. Pretty realistic, huh?"

My mind spun. "All those people, they're alive then?"

Roger sighed. "Oh no, they're dead as dead can be. I'm afraid the good reverend took my words a bit too literally." He shook his head. "Sometimes the man lacks common sense. But that's in the past." He made a face like he was shrugging off some minor unpleasantness.

Like a kid who'd pulled the wings off a fly and been scolded for it.

My heart still pounded in my chest. The curtain was half drawn, leaving him partly in shadow.

"So you ain't the same person?" I asked.

"What?"

"I mean, you look like the reverend now, but you're not *him.*"

"Oh." Roger seemed to find this hilarious. He started laughing again. It was eerie to hear those childish peals coming out of Jolly's stern countenance. "No, this body is just a facsimile. That means a copy, Ruth." The condescension in his voice reminded me of Doc. "I could have come here as your daddy or your mama." He winked. "Or even Marshal Hardin. But I thought I'd keep with the theme of the day."

"Well, I'm glad you picked the reverend," I said tartly. "Least I know you're an enemy."

His lower lip pouted. "Aw, don't be like that. We're not enemies. Just playing the game on different sides of the board."

If I could get him to move, I could make a break for the door. Of course, he could kill me where I stood. But if he'd wanted to do that, I figured he would have already.

"So it's all a game to you?" I asked.

I thought of the bandit on the train. *Quieres jugar?* Things started falling into place.

Roger looked at me like I was crazy. "Well, of course it is." He rubbed his hands together. "And we're just getting started. I have some twists in store you'll never see coming, Ruth."

I nodded like I understood. "Okay. What about the real reverend? How does he fit into the scheme of things?"

A secret smile tugged at his mouth. "Oh, he has a starring role to play yet. And Mr. Cage, too."

"He's alive, then," I muttered.

"Cage is tough to put down," Roger mused. "But if anyone can, I'm sure it's you."

"Where are they now?"

He laid a finger to the side of his nose. "I don't suppose it's against the rules to tell you. In fact, it might spice things up. I sent them both to the N.T. to do God's work."

"*Your* work."

Roger pressed his palms together like he was praying. "Amen to that."

"And what did *God* tell them to do?" I asked with a sinking heart.

His face grew solemn. His eyes glowed with the light of a true believer. "It's the Last Days coming, little sister. A war for the very soul of humanity. The reverend is my messiah. Herald of a new golden age, free of sin and wickedness. Like the Garden of Eden before the snake came slithering in, speaking its tongues." His voice lowered to a hiss. "*Phantom tongues.*"

I thought Roger was serious until he collapsed into helpless giggles. "Oh boy," he said, pulling himself together with difficulty. "I've done some pranks before, but this one… It'll be grand. You'll see."

He watched my face and seemed disappointed that I wasn't congratulating him.

"What about Lee?" I asked.

"Well, come on! Every good holy war needs an antichrist. Ain't worth its salt without *that*."

"So you put the bounty on him?"

This question triggered a new round of hilarity. I was starting to get pretty tired of it.

"Well, maybe I did, maybe I didn't. Guess you'll just have to keep playing if you want to find out."

I should have patted him on the back and promised to do whatever he wanted. He was a Class X and underneath the naughty boy exterior, Roger was pure malice. But I couldn't do it. Not after the things I'd seen.

"Sorry to disappoint you," I said. "But I'm going home."

There was a long silence. The mirth drained from his face.

"That's a shame. The Reverend and Mr. Cage will sure be disappointed." Roger paused. "I hope they don't take it into their heads to stop in Lucky Boy on the way back. But who knows? Mr. Cage is none too happy about the hole you put in him."

The phantom suddenly jabbed a hand into himself, right through the duster coat between the ribs, and pulled it out, dripping. He shook off a pinkish globule, which glistened on the carpet. I stared at it in horrified fascination.

"His guts are still leaking," Roger went on in a conversational tone, "so it might be a while before he takes his revenge, but I have a feeling he's set on it. Mr. Cage lives for that sort of thing."

My chest went cold. "What do you want?"

Roger let his hand drop. "Like I told you, I'm not here to cause trouble. In fact, I'm a bit remorseful about teasing you before. I like you, Ruth. You've got spunk. So I thought I'd take you to visit Doc."

Of all things, I didn't expect that. But I didn't believe him, either. "Why? Doc ain't your friend."

Roger looked hurt. "He told you that?"

"He said you bound him to the Collier."

"That's only 'cause he lost a bet. Fair's fair."

"What bet? He said it was a card game."

Roger snickered. "Wasn't a card game, though we did like to play poker sometimes."

"Well, what was the bet?"

It didn't really matter, but I was still stalling for time. And I'll allow, part of me was curious.

"He bet me that I couldn't wipe out a town with a twister and leave the one right next door untouched."

"What?" I stared at him, stunned.

"I know, it's a tough trick." Roger seemed to misunderstand, or he was just needling me. "Tornadoes are unpredictable once they get going. But I pulled it off." Roger smiled faintly at the memory. "Doc sure had egg on his face, I'll tell you."

"You're lying," I snarled. "He wouldn't do that."

"Why not?"

I'd spent many hours of my childhood poking around the ruins of Three Bars. My own house was on Line Street. Everything west of the sign had been leveled to the dirt.

"Because . . . because he's decent!" I said desperately. "Not like you."

"He's just like me." Puzzlement tinged the phantom's voice. "We're the same."

"No! He's—"

"An X." Roger stared at me. "You didn't know, did you?" He slapped his thigh and turned, as if he were addressing an audience in the wings. "She didn't know."

"You're lying," I repeated, but it sounded weak.

"Ask him yourself." Roger held out a hand. "I'll take you to him right now."

I was so angry, I took a step forward. I'd make Doc talk to me, no evasions, no tantrums. He'd tell me none of it was true. That he hadn't destroyed a whole town on a bet.

Roger leaned in. Unlike the real Reverend Jolly, there was no sour sweat smell. There was no smell at all. I saw my hand, inches from his own, and snatched it back.

I thought of the kid pulling wings off flies.

"You can't move living flesh," I said in a rush. My pulse was racing again. "It'll . . . it'll hurt me."

Roger gave me a wounded look. "It won't hurt, Ruth," he said. "Not a bit. I know a shortcut. Right to Doc. He'll be so glad to see you."

His voice was soothing and kind, oozing over me like warm honey. But his eyes were cold. Cold and *eager*. Part of me still wanted to take his hand, but maybe spending time with Lee Merriweather had made me a little bit immune because I resisted. And a vague idea came to me, in the back of my mind, through the fog that Roger was casting.

The idea was that maybe the X's were the savants of their kind. That was how he'd talked the reverend off the deep end, and how he was talking me off it right now. I knew in my heart that if I took the phantom's hand, I wouldn't come out the other side. Not in one piece at any rate.

I spun away, eyes darting wildly. There was nowhere to run. Nowhere except the glass door to the balcony. I dashed over and yanked it wide. Hot air hit my face.

When we were on the trestle outside Carnarvon City, when I saw the sky darken, bleeding light like a wound, the tracks humming under my feet, I thought I'd known terror.

But this was worse. Roger wanted to take me into the ether. And I had a feeling he'd do it whether I took his hand or not.

I remembered Lee throwing his coat aside, his arms flung wide, as he balanced on the edge.

I remembered how he'd gotten away.

Blue water shimmered in the sunlight sixty feet below. A woman in a flowery bathing cap was swimming laps.

"No!" Roger snarled.

There was no sympathy in his voice now. Just petulant rage.

"Don't you dare—" he growled just behind me.

I threw a leg over the railing. Then I jumped.

16

I shouted, arms and legs flailing. The pool rushed up to meet me. It felt like forever, though the drop was only a couple of seconds. I smacked into the water and hit bottom with the same shoulder that was already a mass of bruises. Bubbles swirled. I couldn't tell which way was up. I inhaled water and figured I was going to drown.

Then I felt myself dragged up to the surface. Hands hauled me out. I rolled over and coughed. Faces stared down at me as I flopped to my back, hacking and dribbling. I looked up at the terrace but didn't see Roger.

That did not reassure me. He was probably on his way down here.

"Are you okay, miss?"

"My God, I've never seen someone fall from so far."

A babble of voices surrounded me, some loud, some whispers.

"Poor girl, look how young she is."

"Someone get security."

"Was she pushed?"

"No, I saw her jump."

"Such a shame."

"Where's her family? Someone ought to find them."

"Maybe she's drunk."

I pushed the hands away and staggered to my feet. My knees shook and I was still coughing, but I had to get out of there before Roger showed up.

"Now, just hold on, miss," the lifeguard said in a stern voice, reaching for me.

I shook his hand off and ran toward the hotel.

"Don't let her go!" someone yelled.

Ahead was a stand of palm trees and a path. I sprinted for it, weaving between the lounge chairs. The path ended at glass doors leading to the lobby but I ran past them, hugging the side of the building until I saw a smaller door with a sign that read *Private/Staff*. I yanked it open and ran inside. Cold air hit my wet clothes. I stood in a long hallway. The carpet was shabby, the walls painted a dingy white. I wasn't sure if they'd seen me go through the door so I started running again and didn't slow until I'd turned several corners.

I heard a distant bang followed by voices. I darted down the hall. It ended at a metal door with a red-lettered sign that said *Authorized Entry Only*. I expected the door to be locked, but it swung silently open when I tried the knob. The room beyond was dark and it took a minute for my eyes to adjust. Big boxes, tall as a man, marched in a row along the far wall. They made a steady whirring sound like they had fans inside. It had to be the air-conditioning system.

But that's not what made my mouth run dry.

The place was thick with phantoms. It reminded me of the clockwork towers in Carnarvon City. The grims I could see hovered motionless, but I knew there were twice as many I *couldn't* see, making the fans go. I froze, trying to catch my breath. Black jewel eyes caught little glimmers of light. Some of them swayed like they heard music. Others were stock still, though I knew how fast they could move if they wanted to.

I'd never felt exactly easy around haints, but since Roger, I had a powerful fear of them. These weren't X's, but they were still his kind.

I could go back the way I came, but I'd heard those voices. Sweat stung my eyes. I didn't dare to wipe it away. I squinted through the murk and saw the dim outline of another door on the opposite side of the room.

The first step was the hardest. When the phantoms didn't react, I took another. My bare feet made only the faintest whisper on the concrete floor as I tiptoed through a cluster of grims, close enough to touch. They were naked and bony, but it was the eyes that got me. Staring at nothing. Mesmerized by the machinery.

When I got to the far side, I eased the door open and slipped through, wincing at the sound of it closing. Nothing came through the door as I backed away.

Then I was running again, following a maze of corridors. I kept expecting Roger to appear. If he was like Doc, he could see through walls. But I refused to just give up. I needed a place to hide and think.

Sudden voices around the corner sent me scrambling. I opened a door and found myself in a laundry. Steaming vats held sheets and towels. I dove behind one as two women entered, speaking in Spanish. They bustled up to the vats and gave them a stir with long wooden paddles. They chattered for a while about their kids and some party Pedro Braga was throwing for the staff. Finally, they left.

I sat there hugging my knees, trying to figure out my next move.

I could find security. But no one would believe me after what had happened before. Maybe not even Hardin. It was a dispiriting thought, but I couldn't blame him. Roger had set me up good.

The old me would have gone to Hardin anyway. But the new, cynical me figured that with Calindra coming, the last thing anyone wanted was crazy Ruth Cortez rambling on about Class X phantoms who looked like the Reverend Jolly. They'd make sympathetic noises and send me back to my room. I could just imagine the pitying look in Hardin's eyes.

Only one person would believe me.

Doc.

I scowled. That lying old goat.

Oh, I was mad at him. But I was also worried. Roger must have done something to him.

I had to get my gun back.

Hardin said it was in Braga's office, under heavy security no doubt. I puzzled it through, trying out various scenarios. In all of them, I ended up in handcuffs.

Which left one final option.

Merriweather.

My scowl deepened. Thanks to him, I was thousands of miles from home and cowering in a laundry. The least he could do is lend a hand. The more I considered the idea, the more I warmed to it. Lee would never agree to help me under normal circumstances, but breaking and entering might appeal to his low morals.

This course of action decided, I plotted my next step. First thing, I needed dry clothes. Something to let me blend in when I got to the casino. I squeezed out from behind the vat and followed a series of doors until I found a room with cubbyholes, each labeled with a name. I thought it was empty until I ran smack into a girl coming around the corner. She was pretty, with brown skin and bouncy ringlets.

"Watch where you're going," she muttered in Spanish, dusting herself off. She wore a skirt trimmed with bells and a tight red bodice with lace sleeves.

"Sorry," I muttered, turning away.

She grabbed my arm, looking suspicious. "What are you doing in here anyhow?"

My clothes had mostly dried, but they were a wrinkled

mess. The rest of me was probably a fright, too. "Uh . . . a kid pushed me in the pool," I said.

She shook her head, wariness turning to sympathy. "Spoiled little brats. Think they own the place. Are you new? I haven't seen you around before."

I nodded, hoping she'd leave me alone.

"Well, the shift's about to start." She glanced up at a clock on the wall.

"You go on," I said. "I don't want to cause you trouble."

She sighed. "Naw, it's all right. Come on, get changed. I'll fix your hair. Then I'll show you where to get your tray."

I looked at her outfit. It didn't leave much to the imagination. And it's not like Roger wouldn't recognize me just because I was wearing a dress. I opened my mouth to politely refuse, but then I had an interesting thought. Roger could have already caught me if he wanted to. There wasn't a hole deep enough I could hide in. But he'd let me go. Why?

Because I was playing the game again. That's what he really wanted.

In fact, he'd probably be doubled over with laughter to see me disguised as a cigarette girl. He might laugh long enough for me to get Doc and figure out how to deal with him once and for all.

It was pretty thin, but it's all I had.

The girl's name was Carmen. She helped me find a uniform that fit and dragged a comb through my hair, then stuck it up in a poofy ponytail. I stood there like a doll while she rubbed rouge on my cheeks and gloss on my lips.

"There," she said, surveying me with a critical eye. "Now, listen, Ruth, some of the male guests are pigs. If anyone bothers you, go tell security."

"I'd like to see 'em try," I muttered, stuffing my bosom down and yanking up a stocking at the same time.

"Tips are allowed," Carmen said briskly. "Just smile a lot. Got it?"

I nodded. She led me up a flight of stairs to another room where we collected our trays. I didn't care for the leering attendant, but he didn't try to touch me.

"Good luck!" Carmen said brightly, wending her way into the crowds.

We were in the Bella Luna, the fanciest of the hotels. I wandered around for a while, peddling my wares and praying I wouldn't run into Hardin. Every quarter hour, I swung by the high-stakes tables, but Lee wasn't there. I'd nearly given up when I saw him at the slots, mechanically yanking on a lever.

I watched from the screen of a potted palm. Roger could look like anybody. I needed to be careful. A few haints hung around, gawking at the slots. Then a lady with waist-long braids and a bolo tie gave a whoop. "*Dios bendito!*"

Tinny music started playing. Tokens streamed out of her machine. The grims drifted over to check it out, but Lee didn't even turn. He seemed preoccupied, rubbing the cowlick on the back of his head. I'd seen the real Lee do that before. And somehow I couldn't picture a Class X parked in front of a slot machine.

I glided over. "Cigar?" I sang. "Cigarette?"

Lee glanced up, then did a double-take. He snorted. "Changing careers, Cortez?"

I made a shushing motion. "Keep your voice down. We need to talk."

He dropped another token in the slot. "Go ahead."

"Someplace private."

Lee yanked the lever. "I'm not going anywhere with you."

"Fine." I looked around. Everyone was watching the woman who'd just won. "I have a proposal."

The wheels spun. Two lemons and a cherry. Lee dropped another token in the slot.

"Let me guess." He gave the lever a forceful yank. "I turn myself in and you take the credit."

"Don't be stupid." I dropped my voice to a whisper. "I need you to steal something for me."

His eyebrow twitched. "Uh-huh. And what might that be?"

"My gun."

Lee's eyes met mine. "Oh my," he said softly, and with a measure of glee. "What kind of trouble are you in now, Cortez?"

"The deep kind," I admitted.

"Must be, if you're asking me for help."

"The Class X is here," I whispered. "I just talked to it."

"Did you now?" Lee frowned as two sevens and a lemon popped up.

"He's got plans for you."

Lee chuckled. "So you carried on a normal conversation, is that it?"

"Well, yeah. He spoke English."

Lee half-turned on the stool. "And what did this Class X look like?"

I gripped the edges of my tray. Anything I said would sound crazy, so I decided to just tell him the truth. "Like the Reverend Jolly."

"Uh-huh." He dropped another token in and yanked the lever.

I sighed. "Forget it. Will you help me or not?"

"Give me one good reason I should," Lee murmured. "Just one."

"For fun?"

"I'm already having fun."

"Because I'm desperate?"

His face softened. "Poor Ruth." Then he gave me an evil smile. "Sorry, not good enough."

My shoulders slumped. "Come on. I got nowhere else to turn. I think Doc's in trouble."

Lee stared at the machine, but he didn't put a token in. "Your phantom?"

"Well, I wouldn't call him *mine*, but we're friends."

At least we had been. I wasn't sure how I felt about him now.

"Okay, I'll bite," Lee said sourly. "Where's the gun?"

"Braga's office."

He laughed. "You had me going for a minute there."

"I wouldn't ask if there was anyone else."

His gaze was flat, but I saw a glint of something.

"Never mind," I said. "It's impossible. Not even you could do it."

"I wouldn't call it impossible," he said slowly.

"Well, he's got phantoms. And probably alarms and whatnot."

Lee shot me an amused look. "You think any of that matters?"

"Then you *could* do it?"

"Child's play," he said dismissively.

I arched an eyebrow.

"But I still won't," Lee said. "Mr. Braga is my boss. Breaking into his office would be a fine way of repaying him."

Since when did Lee Merriweather have a conscience? I decided to try a new tack. "It's not stealing if it's my gun," I said. "He was planning to give it back anyhow. I'm just taking it a little early."

"Why do you want it so bad?" Lee asked.

"I told you. I haven't seen Doc since Braga's men took the gun in New Jerusalem." I cleared my throat. "They arrested us. Me and Hardin."

Lee hooted. "They did *not*."

"It was a mix-up. Hardin cleared our names in the end, but when I first saw you? I'd just come from a cell." I held my wrists up and mimed wearing handcuffs.

"Wish I'd known," he said. "I would have stopped by to

say hello. I could have brought you a tin cup to bang on the bars. Maybe a harmonica—"

"All right, all right," I said. "The point is that they took my gun away."

"So?"

I sensed Lee's interest waning. "*So*, even when Calindra had the flintlock in her desk, Doc would come visit me when her back was turned. But I haven't heard a peep from him in days. Something's wrong. And I'm sure that X is behind it. They're old enemies."

Lee sighed. He didn't look happy. "Doc did help me out once," he said slowly.

"In the bunker, you mean?"

"No, after. He's the one who told Mr. Beach you'd arrested me and taken me to the tower."

"What?" I couldn't believe it. "That double-dealing—"

"Before you get worked up, I don't think he meant to," Lee added. "But he went back to make sure Mr. Beach got out safely. They got to talking and Doc spilled the beans."

"Funny," I said coldly. "He never mentioned that."

"So I'll do it for Doc — on one condition. You swear on your honor that you won't try to arrest me again."

"And take you where?" I looked around the casino. "I have exactly zero authority in this town."

Lee gave me an unfriendly look. "Last time I trusted you it got me cuffed to a chair and gagged with my own necktie."

"I never promised I wouldn't arrest you then," I pointed out.

"When you rescue someone from certain death, it usually goes without saying," he shot back. "I didn't think I needed it in writing."

"I was just doing my job."

Lee's eyes fixed on me. "Swear it to me now, Ruth."

He didn't raise his voice, but the hair on my arms stood

up. I knew I'd be compelled to keep any promise I made. It was just his way of protecting himself, but I still felt offended.

"You don't have to use your powers on me," I said. "I'd keep my word regardless."

"Swear it, Ruth. Swear it or I'm walking away right now."

I sighed and held up a hand. "Fine. I swear on my honor I have no designs on you. I just want my gun."

Lee gave a tight nod. "I'll do it for Doc, not you," he said again. "And if you've set me up, so help me . . . ." He let the threat trail off. "It has to be quick. I only have a few hours before the show."

I waited impatiently as a loud wedding party streamed through. Lee lost more money while I sold foil-wrapped cigars and a pack of *Caballeros* to the tipsy guests. When they were finally gone, I turned back to him.

"Show?" I asked. "What show?"

"I'm performing on stage tonight." His chest puffed out. "We're calling it Duel of the Linguists. You should stop by. It's one night only."

"Are you crazy?" I demanded. "You have to call it off."

"Why?"

"Didn't you hear a word I just said? Roger is *here*." A man looked over at us and I lowered my voice. "And so is Calindra."

Lee froze. "What?"

"You didn't know? She's expected today."

A flurry of emotions crossed his face. Surprise, followed by resentment, and then a slow smirk.

"Oh, I get it," I said. "You think it would be funny to rub her nose in it."

"I did not say that," Lee protested.

"Then cancel the show."

He exhaled through his nose. "On her account? Well, I'll think about it, Ruth."

I shook my head. Maybe he and Roger deserved each other.

"Do what you want," I said. "Just help me get Doc first."

"If I do, you both owe me."

"Fair enough," I muttered, hiding my tray between two of the slots. "Let's go. With any luck, Braga's meeting Mrs. Carnarvon's zeppelin right now."

Lee took me through a private door near the cashier windows. It was cleverly concealed behind a mirrored panel and led into a maze of corridors, ending at a locked stairwell. He took a key from his pocket and opened it up.

"I can't believe they made you security," I said, watching behind us to make sure no one was coming.

"It's a boring job, actually," Lee said. "I'm only doing it for the fringe benefits."

"Like what?"

"High-roller suite. Free meals at all the restaurants." He smoothed his silk tie. "My own tailor."

"They're giving you all that?" I said in surprise.

"Why wouldn't they?"

We started up the stairs, Lee leading the way.

"Well, how much money are you really saving them?" I asked. "Doesn't seem to add up."

And it didn't — a child could see that. Something was fishy. But he was too proud and full of himself to notice. For all that Merriweather liked to act like a man of the world, in some ways he was even more sheltered than I was.

Lee frowned. "How would you know?"

"Just an observation. What about Mr. Beach? What does he think?"

"That I ought to leave," Lee admitted.

"Maybe you should listen to him," I said.

Lee shot me a look. "If helping you out involves a lecture, I'll withdraw my offer."

I fell silent.

"Why are you dressed like that anyway?" Lee asked.

"I had an accident," I muttered. "And I couldn't go back to my room to change because of Roger. I'm hiding from him."

"Right." Lee shot me a quick glance. "The Class X who speaks English and looks like Jolly."

"Like Cage, too. He can look like anyone he wants."

"Then how can I be sure *you're* not Roger?" Lee asked innocently.

I knew he was messing with me. I glanced down at my red bodice and belled skirt. "Would a phantom wear this get-up?"

"It might."

"Okay, fine." I thought for a minute. "When I first met you on the train, I was eating caramel corn."

Lee smirked. "As I recall, you had the bag tipped over your gaping maw, Ruth."

"Darn right I did. I was hungry and it cost me a whole dollar. The point is, you can't trust anybody, Lee."

"Except you," he said dryly.

"That's right."

"You sure you haven't been drinking?"

I smiled at him. "No."

"Maybe suffered a blow to the head?"

"I don't care if you believe me or not," I said. "Just get me to Doc."

We took the stairs to Braga's private wing on the fourth floor. The landing door was also locked, but the same key opened it up. Lee ordered me to wait in the stairwell while he checked things out. He returned a few minutes later with a frown.

"What happened?" I asked.

"The office is at the end of this corridor. There were no guards."

"Well, that's good, isn't it?"

"I got a phantom to jimmy the lock, but it refused to go inside and fetch the gun."

"I thought you could make haints do anything."

"Not this time. Braga's head of security is a savant, too. He runs a tight ship."

"I didn't realize that," I said in surprise.

Counting Calindra, that meant four savants were in Aguadulce tonight. The only four in the world, as far as I knew.

Lee glanced nervously down the stairwell. "Well, you'll have to search for the gun yourself."

"What if it's locked in a safe?"

"That's your problem. No way on earth I'm going in."

"Alarms?"

Lee shook his head. "And Braga's not there. The phantom confirmed it." He gave me a level look. "Truthfully, Ruth, it seems a bit too easy. You might want to rethink this."

I bit my lip. "I can't, Lee. I've got to get Doc. He's the only one who can help me."

For a moment, Merriweather looked torn. He'd been treating it like a joke, but he seemed to realize at that moment that I was genuinely scared. I hoped he'd change his mind and come with me, but Lee owed me nothing. In the end, he seemed to figure he'd stuck his neck out far enough already.

"Just give me ten minutes before you go in," he said. "I want to be long gone if they catch you."

He turned to leave and I grabbed his sleeve. "Thanks, Merriweather. I appreciate it."

He nodded — a bit guiltily — and disappeared into the shadows of the stairwell below. It *did* seem too easy. But I remembered Pedro Braga's desk, totally bare except for a telephone and lamp. Security would be focused on the vaults where the casinos kept cash to pay out the chips. There must be a king's ransom.

It was a miracle Lee hadn't tried to steal it yet.

The minutes passed. I slipped off my narrow, pointy-toed shoes. They were too small, but Carmen hadn't been able to find any big enough to fit my feet. I sat on a step and poked at the blisters on my heels. The black stockings already had runs in them — I didn't know how I'd managed that in the space of an hour. The corset dug into my ribs. I took a deep breath and felt something snap in the bindings. My left bosom popped out of the bodice. I swore and stuffed it back in.

A door slammed somewhere above. Voices filtered down the stairwell. The tread of footsteps grew louder.

I reckoned it had only been about five minutes, but Lee couldn't expect me to sit there if someone was coming. He'd had plenty of time to get away anyhow. I cracked the landing door. The hallway beyond was empty. I slipped through and gently shut the door behind me. Then I hurried to the end, clutching the shoes in one hand. Thick carpeting covered the floor. The walls were papered in an ornate pattern of gold curlicues and fan-shaped sconces cast a soft yellow light. I scanned the shadows looking for haints, but didn't see any.

A pair of heavy wooden doors loomed ahead. Braga's office.

I tried the knob. As Lee promised, it turned easily. I slipped inside and eased the door shut behind me. The only light came through the tinted glass looking out over the casino, but the soundproof wall muted the clamor below. I tried the desk drawers. The top one opened, but all it held was an inkwell and some loose papers. The rest were locked.

"Doc?" I whispered. "You here?"

There was no answer, which worried me. Unless he was holding a grudge that I'd given him up to the Gorras. That was a distinct possibility.

"Look, I'm sorry," I whispered. "If you're here, can you help me get these drawers open? We need to talk. I won't let them have you again, I promise, but I'm in trouble and you're the only one who'll believe me."

Still nothing.

I gave the drawers a futile yank. If I had my Bowie knife, I could pry them open, but the Gorras had taken that too. I felt a wave of despair. Lee had done more than I'd any right to expect already. He wouldn't help me again.

I walked the perimeter of the room, even lifting up the paintings on the walls, but there was no hidden lockbox. The gun could be anywhere. If Braga's head of security had it, I'd never get it back. But if it was in the desk, I felt sure Doc would have answered me.

Something was stopping him. Or *someone.*

I leaned on the edge of the desk, chewing a nail. Maybe I ought to give Hardin more credit. I still had no proof, but he might believe me if I put it to him right. He knew there was a Class X on the loose. The main thing was not to get caught in Braga's office wearing the uniform of a cigarette girl. That would be the last nail in the coffin.

I almost laughed aloud. Doc surely would have, if he'd been here. But my smile died thinking of Roger.

We're just getting started. I have some twists in store you'll never see coming, Ruth.

I grabbed my shoes in one hand. With any luck, I could slip out the same way I'd come in. I'd go to my room and change. Then I'd find Hardin. Or Roger would find me first. But there was nothing I could do about it on my own. I was almost to the door when lights blinded me.

"On the floor," a voice barked. "Move!"

Men poured into the room. I sank to my knees and lay facedown on the rug. Footsteps approached. From the corner of my eye, I saw a pair of fancy wingtip shoes stop in front of me.

"Stand down," a different voice said. "She's unstable, but I don't think she's dangerous."

I knew that voice. It rang with authority, but there was an unmistakable hint of amusement. I turned my head so I could see his face.

"Well," I said. "That's a new look for you."

Roger stared down at me through bright green eyes. He had wavy blonde hair, slicked back, and wore a sharp suit Lee would have approved of. Six men in red jackets stood behind him. Two cradled shotguns. The other four carried revolvers. Roger made a calming gesture and the weapons lowered.

"I don't think we've met, Miss Cortez," he said with a frown. "But don't be afraid. We've been looking for you." He bent a knee and crouched next to me. "Please, let me help."

"Get away," I snarled, scooting backwards.

The guards stared like I was some kind of carnival sideshow.

"You're not well," Roger said gently. "I'll see you get the best care until you're able to go home." His gaze roamed over my torn stockings and poofy ponytail. "But I'm afraid we can't just let you run wild through the casino, Miss Cortez. You've caused enough damage already."

My fist balled. I hauled back to punch him and someone grabbed my arm.

"Restrain her," Roger said briskly. He rummaged in his coat pocket. "She's a danger to herself and others."

"You lying—ow!" I looked down. He'd jabbed a needle into my leg.

"Take Miss Cortez to the infirmary," Roger said. "I'll inform Mr. Braga."

"Yes, Mr. Chance."

"Treat her with the utmost consideration. She *is* our guest, after all." He reached down and thumbed my eyelids back. I felt nauseous. I tried to pull away, but the room was growing foggy. It gave a lazy spin. For a split second, I saw the bug-like eyes of a phantom looking out from his face.

Roger's back was turned to the other men so they couldn't

see his expression. He was struggling not to laugh, but his voice sounded perfectly solemn. "The poor girl has had some kind of breakdown. Thank God she isn't armed—"

The rest was lost as blackness closed in.

17

Sebastian Hardin waited in the aerodrome on the roof of the Bella Luna. It was larger than the one at the Golden Dreams, with plush couches and a sweeping view across the city.

Pedro Braga shot an impatient glance at the clock on the wall. Two-fifteen. The zeppelin was over an hour late.

"I can stay, sir," Sebastian said.

A dozen Guardia Territorial stood at attention, along with an equal number of red-jacketed security guards.

"No, no," Braga said. "Está bien. I'll wait."

"Any news on the Reverend Jolly?"

Braga's face darkened. "Not a trace. Carnarvon City seems to be the last place he was seen." Sharp, hooded eyes met Sebastian's. "Mr. Chance says we'll catch him eventually. When we do, he'll hang, along with his accomplice."

Hardin had met Pedro Braga's new security chief the previous morning. The fellow appeared competent enough.

"How's your deputy?" Braga asked in a neutral tone.

"Just fine."

Sebastian had personally interviewed everyone he could find who'd been in the lobby when Ruth claimed she'd chased

Jolly to the elevator bank. No one saw a thing. Just a wild-eyed woman yelling and knocking people down.

"I'm glad to hear it," Braga said.

"It was a shock stumbling over those bodies in New Jerusalem." Sebastian tried to keep the defensiveness out of his voice. They'd been over this already, but he couldn't help himself. "Especially coming right after the attack at the border. Deputy Cortez is a fine officer. I imagine anyone would be on high alert after that. It was an honest mistake."

"I never said it wasn't." Braga glanced over. "I hear your marshal in the infirmary woke up."

Sebastian smiled. "Yes, Tanaka's doing much better. I don't imagine we'll be here more than a couple of days, though of course that's up to Mrs. Carnarvon."

Braga snapped his fingers. An aide handed him a briefcase, which he opened, putting on half-moon spectacles.

"If you'll pardon me, Sebastian, I'll just catch up on some work."

"Of course."

Sebastian's eyes scanned the skies beyond the floor-to-ceiling windows, but his mind kept returning to Ruth Cortez. When he'd first laid eyes on her at the depot in Lucky Boy, he'd taken her for the sheriff's daughter. She looked too young to have earned a copper star on her own.

Then she'd stood up to him when he asked her to take her dark glasses off, citing chapter and verse of the local regulations regarding eyewear. He thought she'd probably be trouble, and he already had plenty of that with Lee Merriweather stashed in the caboose. Sebastian still wasn't entirely sure why he'd brought her aboard.

But Ruth had more than proved herself after they derailed. He knew men twice her age — and nearly twice her size — who wouldn't have volunteered to go into the night alone after a wanted fugitive. Not one as dangerous as Lee.

The woman had grit. She was also smart and big-hearted

in a way he'd forgotten people could be. Sebastian wasn't a city boy by birth, but where he came from, it wasn't like Lucky Boy. The Northern Territory drew people from all over, hoping to make their fortunes in the mines and timber camps. The towns were full of transients, some of them running from trouble, and he'd witnessed plenty of fights and even a few murders before he was old enough to shave. It was just the way of things in the N.T.

Ruth was tough, but she was innocent, too. Sebastian felt a twinge of guilt. It had been selfish to bring her along. He should have just let her go home, but instead he'd convinced Calindra that they needed Ruth. That he could talk her around to joining the marshals. Talent like that shouldn't go to waste on the frontier.

That's what he told himself.

But Sebastian quickly realized, with some chagrin, that he'd misjudged how far under his skin the young deputy had already gotten without even trying. Improper thoughts kept running through his mind. So he'd decided to avoid her.

Well, that hadn't worked either.

He grinned. For some inexplicable reason, Ruth returned his affections. And he'd do whatever it took to hold onto her.

"Finally," Braga muttered, rising to his feet.

A dot approached in the sky to the north. It rapidly grew closer and resolved into a small airship with the Carnarvon colors, navy and gold. The zeppelin docked at the mooring mast and stairs unfolded. Sebastian moved forward as Calindra Carnarvon appeared. She was tall and thin, silver hair swept into an elaborate up-do. She wore a green silk skirt with a matching jacket. Hardin covered his surprise as Freddie and Ava appeared behind her a moment later.

The twins were in their early twenties, a few years younger than Sebastian. Both had red hair and vivid green eyes. Freddie lit a cigarette, drawing a frown from his grandmother. His sister Ava wore a clinging dress of cream silk with matching gloves. She gave Hardin a warm smile, which he returned briefly before turning away.

"Such a pleasure to see you," said Pedro Braga, taking Calindra's hands and then giving a bow. "I didn't realize the family was coming along."

"Miss a chance to debauch myself in this gambling paradise?" Freddie said dryly, shaking Braga's hand. "Not likely."

"Don't let him lose his whole inheritance," Ava said, as Braga kissed her gloved hand.

"You look enchanting as ever, Miss Carnarvon," Braga said smoothly. "No Richard?"

"Someone had to look after things," Freddie replied. "I offered, but grandmother says he's the only responsible one—"

"That's enough, Freddie," Calindra said sharply. Her steely gaze turned to Braga. "It's good to see you, Pedro. And you, Sebastian." Her tone gave no hint that the visit was anything but routine.

Hardin smiled. "I trust the journey was swift."

"Well, that's the advantage of traveling by air," Ava put in. "It's so much safer." She cast Sebastian a sympathetic look. "We heard what happened at the border. How awful."

Braga's lips thinned. "Please be assured, I've taken measures to ensure such a thing never happens again. But you must understand, the border is many hundreds of miles long. I simply don't have the manpower to police it all."

"No one's blaming you, Pedro," Calindra said. "You lost good men yourself. But that's precisely why we need to cooperate. Pool our resources."

Braga glanced at Sebastian. "We've been working through the details. Mr. Hardin had some excellent ideas. But we can talk business later. Let me escort you to your suites so you can freshen up. Excuse me a moment, won't you?"

He stepped over to one of the red-jacketed guards. Sebastian heard him ordering two more suites to be prepared for Freddie and Ava.

"Where's Ruth Cortez?" Freddie asked in a neutral tone. "I thought she might be here."

"Freddie has a crush on that girl from Lucky Boy," Ava said, with a smile that didn't reach her eyes.

"Don't be ridiculous," Freddie muttered, crushing his cigarette into an ashtray. "She's far too nice for me."

"Well, that's true," Sebastian agreed. "Deputy Cortez had other duties."

Like staying away from you two.

Freddie glanced at his sister. "Ava thinks she ought to be shipped back to the frontier. Her and that phantom."

"Freddie," Ava growled, her cheeks turning pink.

"Well, it's true." He fished a silver flask from his pocket and tipped it to his lips. "Maybe I'll give her an escort." He winked. "It's dangerous out there. What do you think, Hardin? You still have the train, don't you?"

Ava rolled her eyes. Usually quick to rein in her grandson, Calindra seemed to be listening to the banter with half an ear. The skin on her face looked parchment thin, drawn tightly against the bones. Sebastian was saved from replying by Braga's return.

"Everything is arranged," Braga said, offering Calindra his arm. "Your luggage will follow."

They took the elevator two floors down, where a pneumatic pod waited to whisk them through the complex to the V.I.P. tower. Ava and Freddie left for their own suites. Braga opened the door to Calindra's room himself, then handed her the key.

"Why don't you rest for a few hours?" he said. "We can discuss business at dinner."

Calindra gave a regal nod. "Thank you, Pedro."

"I have some documents for you to review," Sebastian said casually. "Shall I stay for a few minutes?"

"Yes, please, Sebastian," she replied crisply.

The instant they were alone, Calindra sank into a chair. Sebastian had never thought of her as fragile before. She was somewhere in her mid-eighties and showed no sign of slowing down. But since Lee ran off, Calindra had aged before his eyes.

"Can I get you anything, ma'am?" he asked.

She shook her head. "Just sit down, Sebastian. I have some things to say and it won't be brief."

He took the loveseat across from her, expecting a dressing down. Maybe even a demotion.

"I know I failed you," he said heavily. "Lee's still alive and there's little chance of getting him in custody now. Not without advertising the fact." He unpinned his badge and set it on the table between them. "If you want this back, I don't blame you. I—"

"Oh, for God's sake, Sebastian, don't be an ass," she snapped. "It's not your fault. No, don't say anything. Let me speak my piece first." She drew a deep breath. "I'm not well. I haven't been for some time, but I'm afraid it's finally catching up with me." Her face dared him to express sympathy. "I don't have much longer, and my greatest desire is to be certain that my wishes will be carried out after I'm gone."

Sebastian nodded, schooling his expression to calm, though the news came as a hard blow. "Yes, ma'am."

"Good. No one knows except for Dr. Benson. And now you. I haven't told the grandchildren yet." Her tone softened. "You're like blood to me, Sebastian."

He swallowed, his throat tight. "As you are to me, ma'am. You saved me. Saved my family."

She waved a hand dismissively. "I saw talent, and you've already repaid me a thousand times over. If there is a debt, it is mine to carry." Bitterness tinged her voice. "You're the son I should have had, Sebastian. The twins' father was . . . well, he was a weak man. Perhaps that fault is mine, too." Her eyes lost focus for a long minute.

Sebastian hadn't known Wayland Carnarvon, Jr. He'd been dead for years before Sebastian ever met the family. But the story was well-known. Wayland had married a society girl, who gave birth to Richard. When Richard was nine, he caught polio. He survived, but it withered his legs. A few years later, the twins' mother died in childbirth and Wayland drank himself into the grave, leaving Calindra, herself a widow, to raise the three of them.

A few times, when Freddie was in his cups, Sebastian had heard him mutter that the family was cursed — though never in his grandmother's hearing.

"How much time do you have?" Sebastian asked.

"Dr. Benson says six months or so. Plenty of time to put my affairs in order. I intend to divide my assets evenly between the three of them." She gave Sebastian a wry look. "Before you say it, I know that Richard is the most responsible. By far. But I won't have them squabbling over my estate. Dragging our name through the courts." A flash of the old fire lit her green eyes. "I won't have it!"

"I'm sure that's wise," Sebastian said dryly.

He could see Ava and Freddie hiring lawyers if they felt they didn't get their fair share.

"What I want from you is a pledge that you will serve my grandchildren as faithfully as you have me, Sebastian. They'll need a voice of reason. Someone to protect them from those who would take advantage." Her green eyes speared him to his seat. "Will you promise me that?"

"Of course," he said, though his heart sank when he thought of Ruth.

"Thank you." She folded her hands in her lap. "Now, as to Lee Merriweather."

Sebastian tensed, but Calindra didn't seem to notice. "I won't mince words. He's an ungrateful little bastard who richly deserves some sort of comeuppance for his dreadful behavior."

"Agreed," Sebastian muttered.

"But I'm not going to tear apart everything I've built just to put him in his place."

He looked up in surprise. Calindra watched him with dark amusement. "Impending death gives one a certain clarity, Sebastian. As much as it pains me to let Lee go, I see no other path that wouldn't lead to disaster. So the warrant is hereby rescinded."

Sebastian gave her a small smile. "To be honest, I doubt Braga will want him either. Not for much longer. Merriweather isn't worth the trouble."

"Succinctly put. Ava and Freddie know. They're not happy about it, but they have no choice." She met his smile with one of her own. "They aren't running things yet, are they?"

"I hope they don't for a long time to come," he said without thinking, but Calindra merely nodded. She had few illusions regarding her grandchildren, especially the twins.

"And Abel Beach?"

"He won't be welcome back at the academy, but I don't want the scandal of a trial." She sighed, looking exhausted again. "I just want it to be over. I'll sign the contracts and we'll go back to the city tomorrow. There's much yet to be done."

Sebastian felt a surge of relief. Lee was the only fugitive who'd ever slipped through his fingers, but he no longer cared. He'd rather have a tarnished reputation than the blood of a dumb kid on his hands.

"Then there's nothing keeping Ruth Cortez from going back to Lucky Boy," he said. "She'll be glad to hear it."

"Gael's daughter?" Calindra replied absently. "No, she can go home." She arched a brow. "Unless . . . ?"

"I already asked. More than once. She doesn't want to join the marshals."

"And that saddens you, Sebastian." She gave him a knowing smile.

He cleared his throat. "I was thinking—"

He cut off at an urgent knock on the door. It was one of Braga's plainclothes security agents. "It's your deputy," the man said in Spanish. "She's in the infirmary."

"What?" His heart raced. "What happened?"

The man gave him a funny look. "She jumped off the balcony of her room, Mr. Hardin."

Sebastian heard the words, but they didn't make sense. He shook his head. "That's not possible. She's terrified of heights."

"There were witnesses, sir. She wasn't pushed. And we already checked. Her room was locked from the inside. Mr. Hardin?"

His voice chased Sebastian down the hallway as he sprinted for the elevators.

18

I WOKE with a dry mouth and fuzzy head. When I tried to sit up, I found that my hands and feet were in leather restraints attached to a metal bedframe. The room was large and dim, with two lines of empty beds along the walls.

A sudden flash of the time I'd spent with Jolly and Cage brought a wave of anxiety so bad I nearly threw up. I yanked at the restraints. They were padded with cotton and didn't give an inch.

I heard the squeak of shoes on a polished floor. A nurse bustled up. At least she looked like a nurse, with a white uniform and peaked cap, but she had a blank smile I didn't care for.

I licked my lips. "Where am I?"

"The infirmary." She fussed with the sheet, tucking it in at the edges.

"Why am I tied up?" I demanded.

Her mouth pursed. "You tried to kill yourself, dear. We have to keep you safe."

"What are you talking about?"

"You jumped from a balcony." The vacant smile returned. "Why, you're lucky to be alive."

"Because someone was after me," I snapped, then regretted it when she gave her head a little shake. She walked out of view.

"Wait!" I pleaded. "Just hang on."

I was afraid she'd left, but then I heard a cart roll over. I twisted my head, trying to see what she was doing. "Can I have some water?"

The nurse bent over the cart. I heard the clink of metal. When she turned back to me, she held a glass vial, along with a big syringe.

"I'm okay now," I said in a calmer tone. "You're right. I do belong here. But I won't be any trouble, I promise."

"I know you won't, dear." She stuck the tip of the needle into the vial and sucked up an inch of clear liquid.

"What is that?" I asked.

"Just something to help you sleep."

"I'm tired already," I said, yawning. "You could save it for later."

"I'm afraid not. Doctor's orders." She grabbed my arm. I tried to jerk away, but she was strong.

"Don't fuss," she said.

I bucked hard and she slapped me across the face. I felt a sting in my arm. The room started losing focus.

"There, there." She stroked the hair back from my face. "You just rest, dear."

I felt myself sliding away. I saw her head turn sharply. Footsteps, running our way.

"Hey!" I yelled. "Help!"

But it wasn't a yell. It was a pathetic whisper.

My eyelids drooped. I fought to keep them open. It was Hardin, in charging bull mode. He hadn't forgotten about me after all. I muttered his name as he leaned over me, his face pale and worried.

But it was like looking through the wrong end of a pair of field glasses. He receded down a black tunnel.

Then he was gone.

~

"WHAT THE HELL did you give her?" Sebastian demanded, glaring at the nurse as she replaced the syringe on a tray. "Goddammit, I need to talk to her!"

The nurse looked taken aback. "She was having a nightmare, sir. I just gave her a small sedative. Nothing that won't wear off in an hour or two."

He took a step forward, fists clenched. The nurse took a step back. "Well, don't do it again," he growled. "How bad's she hurt?"

Sebastian studied Ruth's still form under the sheet. She wore a light blue cotton gown. He didn't see any casts or bandages, thank God.

"We're not sure yet," the nurse said in an irritated tone. "But there doesn't appear to be any serious damage. She landed in the swimming pool."

Hardin felt weak with relief. His imagination had conjured up visions of Ruth bloody and broken. Then he noticed the restraints and fury came surging back. "Why is she tied up?"

"The poor girl was tearing at her own face," the nurse said defensively. "Look at her."

A red weal marked Ruth's right cheek. He raked his hands through his hair. "How'd this happen? How? She was fine when I left her."

"All I know, sir, is that a dozen witnesses saw her jump off a sixth-floor terrace. Frankly, it's a miracle she isn't in worse shape. Security found her wandering in the casino. She wasn't making any sense. They brought her here and we sedated her so she could get some rest."

"What was she saying?"

"I have no idea, sir."

He shook his head. Ruth wouldn't try to kill herself. He felt sure of that.

"Merriweather," he muttered.

"Pardon, sir?"

"Just give me a minute with her," he said. "Alone, please."

"You can have five," the nurse replied briskly, rolling the cart away. "But the poor girl needs to rest."

Hardin watched her leave. He reached out to loosen the leather bonds and hesitated. The infirmary was on the sixteenth floor. What if she tried to jump again? He reluctantly let his hand drop. She was sleeping, anyway. He'd come back when she was awake and take them off then.

Once Calindra signed the contracts, he'd accompany Ruth back to Lucky Boy himself. Maybe stay for a while. He had plenty of leave coming. Sebastian couldn't remember the last time he'd taken a vacation, or even a sick day. Calindra owed him that and he didn't think she'd object. She had time yet. Six months, she'd said.

Sebastian sat on the edge of the bed. He took Ruth's hand. "I'm sorry," he said quietly. "You'll be fine as soon as we get out of here."

Could Merriweather have talked her into jumping?

He was a savant. His powers of persuasion went beyond phantoms. Maybe he'd planted the idea when the two of them were alone.

But as much as Sebastian desperately wanted someone to blame, it seemed far-fetched. The more likely possibility was that Ruth had been sleepwalking. He'd witnessed her nightmares himself. What they'd seen in New Jerusalem would traumatize anyone. Sebastian squeezed her hand. Either way, he'd make sure she got well. And she would, given enough time. Ruth Cortez was strong.

"I won't abandon you," he whispered. "I promise."

Two oaths, Sebastian. And how do you plan to keep them both?

He pushed the thought away. There would be time to figure things out later.

"Time's up, Mr. Hardin," the nurse said briskly from just behind him.

He started. He hadn't even heard her coming. "I'll wait in a chair," he said stubbornly. "Until she wakes."

The nurse's red lips curled upward in a smile that didn't reach her eyes. "Are you her brother?" she asked.

"No."

"Husband? Next of kin?"

"Well, not exactly—"

"Then you may not be present while our patient is examined by the doctor. It's improper and against the rules."

She stared at him, her face expressionless. Something about the woman disturbed him, though Hardin couldn't say precisely what it was. "I'll be back in one hour," he said firmly. "And unless she's got broken bones, I'm taking her out of here. Or you can explain to Mr. Braga why you're holding one of my people against her will."

He felt the nurse's eyes on his back as he strode to the door at the end of the ward. Hardin turned back. "And don't give her any more sedatives or I'll see that you're fired."

The nurse's stare didn't waver. "Yes, sir."

He paused on his way to the elevators, tapping at a door to a private room in the recovery wing. "Marshal? You awake?"

Sebastian heard a low cough. "Come on in."

He entered the room. Tanaka was sitting up in bed. She looked stronger today, though her head was swathed in bandages. An open book lay in her lap.

"How are you feeling?" he asked.

"Like I got cracked in the skull with a rifle butt," she said, deadpan. "How 'bout you, sir?"

"Mrs. Carnarvon's here, with Freddie and Ava. She backed off on Merriweather."

Tanaka arched an eyebrow. "Did she really?"

"But that's not what I came to tell you." He jerked his head at the door. "Cortez is down the hall in the critical ward. Don't worry, she's not badly hurt, just sleeping."

Tanaka frowned. "And I was just starting to like that girl. What happened?"

"They say she jumped off a balcony."

Tanaka studied his face for a moment. "But you don't believe that?"

He chewed his lip. "Something's going on. I don't know what yet. But something don't feel right."

Tanaka nodded slowly. They'd known each other a long time and Sebastian knew she trusted his instincts. "Is Mrs. Carnarvon in danger?"

"I don't know." Sebastian gripped the rail of the hospital bed. "But I plan to tell her to sign those contracts so we can get out of here as soon as possible. All of us."

"You won't find me complaining. The food here is lousy. And that nurse gives me the creeps."

"Just keep your eyes open. Call me if anything happens."

Tanaka looked around the empty room. "How am I supposed to do that?"

"Never mind. I'm coming back in an hour." He paused. "Ruth was . . . seeing things. Before she jumped."

Tanaka frowned. "What things?"

"The Reverend Jolly."

"*Here?*"

Sebastian nodded.

"I'm not sure I understand," Tanaka said slowly. "Is the man in Aguadulce or not?"

"I honestly don't know. She claimed he killed a woman in an elevator, but there was no one inside the car. I was right there." He sighed. "Cortez thought she might have had food poisoning. You ever heard of a case that made someone hallucinate?"

Tanaka shook her head. "Not like that. And then she jumped off a balcony?"

"That's what they say. I intend to look into it myself."

"Well, don't worry. I can get around. I'll check on her in a while, if you like."

He felt relieved. "I'd appreciate that."

"I'll admit, I didn't understand why you brought her along in the first place, but she saved our asses back at the border." Tanaka's black eyes held his. "Tell me the truth. You think she's crazy?"

"No," Hardin said. "No, I don't."

WHEN I WOKE the second time, Hardin was gone and I was still in restraints.

The sedative had left me fuzzy, but not so fuzzy that I didn't feel a keen sense of betrayal. My breath came fast and shallow, close to panic. He was my only hope and he'd done nothing to help me.

What had the nurse told him? And how could he have believed her?

I tried to calm down. Maybe I'd imagined the whole thing. Maybe he'd never come in the first place. Doubts crowded in on me. Maybe it hadn't been Hardin at all.

Maybe I *was* insane.

A single lamp lit the ward, but the windows were pitch black. I yelled until I was hoarse, but nobody came, not even the nurse. A wave of nausea cramped my stomach. Whatever she'd given me, it was still in my system. My head felt like it was floating over my body. I twisted my wrists in the cotton bindings. They didn't give an inch. I twisted some more, until the skin was pink and raw, and thought they might be a tiny bit looser. I licked cracked lips and kept going. Twist and pull, twist and pull. At least it felt like I was doing *something*.

Then I sensed a presence. It didn't make a sound, but I'd lived with a grim for long enough to know when I was being watched.

"Doc?" I croaked.

"Guess again."

The voice came from right next to me. I peered into the shadows. Roger stood there. He wore the body of Henry Chance, which I had to admit was preferable to the Reverend Jolly. It was definitely preferable to Mr. Cage. If I'd seen that handsome, empty face while I was tied hand and foot to a hospital bed, I might have snapped in truth.

"How are you feeling, Ruth?" Roger asked cheerfully. "You hungry? I could spoon-feed you some chicken broth."

He wore a white suit with a red carnation in the button-hole. A top hat perched on his head. That part wasn't so bad. But he also wore garish grease paint around his eyes and mouth that made me decide I *really* didn't like clowns anymore.

"Where's Hardin?" I demanded. "Did you hurt him?"

"Oh, he just left. Sat at your bedside, holding your hand. It was very touching." Roger gave me a toothy smile. "But Mrs. Carnarvon needed him and when she crooks a finger, Hardin goes running." His mouth drew down in exaggerated sympathy. "You deserve better. But don't worry, I'll see he's punished for it."

I frowned. "You're the one who did this to me."

The X sat on the edge of my bed, the mattress sinking under his weight. "I've decided you'll be the lucky survivor, Ruth." Roger winked. "Just like Jolly left poor old Samuel Withrow. It's a shame the Gorras killed him, but he did serve his purpose first. So consider yourself blessed. I need someone to tell the tale." He poked me hard in the ribs. "And you're it!"

"What tale?"

His eyes sparkled in the wells of black paint. "I have quite the show planned for tonight. A real extravaganza." He chuckled. "I'll admit, I didn't expect Calindra to be here, but that's what keeps the game interesting. There's so many players and I don't control them all. It's more fun to leave certain aspects up to *chance*." That got him clutching his sides and laughing merrily.

I fought the powerful urge to laugh along with him. If I started, I might never stop.

"What are you going to do?" My voice sounded scratchy and cracked, an ugly thing next to Roger's silken purr.

"Well, I'd originally planned it for Carnarvon City." He frowned slightly. "But Lee got away. So I figured I'd let him come here. See how that played out. My little prank at the border . . . I didn't expect you to do what you did with the Widowmaker."

Roger's lips stretched into a wide grin. Too wide for a human mouth. "I enjoyed it though. Hot damn, there's nothing like a good plot twist. It made me fond of you. That's why I'm letting you live."

He looked at me expectantly, like I ought to thank him. When I didn't say anything, he gave a little sigh.

"I wish you could watch the show yourself, front and center, but you have a way of messing things up, Ruth. And this time I mean for it to go like clockwork. So just relax. I'll let you go after." Spidery fingers reached for my face and I turned away, yanking frantically at my bonds, but Roger only brushed the hair from my forehead. His touch was icy. "You'll be my messenger, Ruth. When word gets out what Lee Merriweather did tonight, he'll be the most wanted man on earth."

"Please," I said desperately. "Whatever you have in mind . . . these people ain't done nothing to you. Not Lee, either. He *likes* phantoms. None of this makes a lick of sense."

"Oh boy." Roger eyed me with pity. He slowly shook his head, like a teacher who's been disappointed by their star pupil. "You're all down but nine, Ruth."

I stared at him. "What does that mean?"

"It's a saying up in the N.T." Roger tilted his head. "I thought Lucky Boy was part of the Northern Territory."

"In name only," I muttered. "They didn't know where else to put us. But the real N.T. is a thousand miles north."

"Interesting. Well, it means when you miss all nine pins in bowling. When you just don't have a clue what's what."

My stomach gave a sudden roll. I swallowed bile. "Then give me a clue."

Roger leaned forward. "First off, Mr. Merriweather is a liar and a cheat. I'm not sure why you're sticking up for him. That said, I understand him better than he realizes. Because, second thing, I'm tired of the rules. Tired of doing what I'm told." His mouth twisted. "I watch the little ones powering your engines and running your factories like rats on a wheel, just because you ask so *nicely*. And you know what? It's stupid. Someone needs to shake things up a little."

"You're as crazy as the reverend," I snarled. "And you won't get away with it."

"Now, now. Don't get agitated or I'll have to order another sedative to calm your nerves. I cannot abide a hysterical woman."

Roger stood. He smoothed his jacket, straightening the lapels and adjusting the cuffs just so. He looked like some creepy overgrown doll. The kind that sits on a shelf and stares at you when the lights go out.

"Sit tight, Ruth," he said. "It'll all be over directly."

And with that, he vanished.

19

SEBASTIAN unlocked the door to Ruth's hotel room and stepped inside. He looked around for some sign of a struggle. Anything out of place.

He saw nothing, though the door to the terrace was open, the curtains swaying in the warm breeze.

Ruth's copper star sat on the bedside table. He picked it up. *Deputy Sheriff, Lucky Boy, Northern Territory*. Sebastian gently closed his palm around the badge. He put it in his pocket.

I'll give it to her myself when she wakes up, he thought.

Sebastian moved to the terrace and looked down. He swore softly. The nurse was right. It was a miracle she survived.

A soft noise at the door made him spin around.

"Sebastian. I've been looking everywhere for you."

Ava Carnarvon glided into the room. He stepped away from the terrace, pulling the door closed behind him.

"I heard about Ruth," Ava said. "That she had some kind of breakdown. I'm so sorry."

"She'll be fine," he said gruffly.

Ava glanced at the terrace. "Did she really . . . ?"

"Ruth's not crazy," he snapped.

"I never said she was."

Ava laid a hand on his arm. Sebastian stepped back. Her mouth tightened.

"I need to get back to the infirmary," he said. "She might be awake."

Ava gave him a sharp look. "Grandmother wants you, Sebastian. That's why I came. She sent me."

In the eight years that he'd been a marshal, and the four that he'd run Special Services, his obligations had never chafed. Sebastian's loyalties were clear and unambiguous. He slept in his office and spent every waking hour on the job. Now a sliver of resentment crept in.

"Can't the contracts wait until morning?" he asked.

"It's not that. It's Merriweather."

"What now?" he asked wearily.

"He's planning some ridiculous performance at the Reina del Sur tonight. They're calling it Duel of the Linguists. She insists on going."

"Why on earth...?" Sebastian trailed off. "Well, I'm busy. She can take Freddie. And the marshals you came with."

Ava's eyes flashed dangerously. "Tell her that yourself."

"I will," he muttered.

Ava stared at him for a long moment. He saw sadness in her face. "You . . . you care for her, don't you?"

Sebastian knew she wasn't talking about Calindra anymore.

"Yes, Ava," he said carefully. "I do."

"She's just a child."

"She's eighteen."

"You know what I mean." Ava gave a brittle laugh. "I like Ruth Cortez. But she's from *Lucky Boy*. It's the middle of nowhere! Do you really plan to spend the rest of your life milking cows?"

Sebastian laughed. "She's the law up there. I don't think

she even likes cows." He shrugged. "Maybe she does. I'll have to ask her."

"She won't fit with your life, Sebastian. With what your life could be." Ava lifted her chin. "I'll need someone to help manage everything when grandmother is gone. I hope it's not for a long time yet, but we both know the day will come when it falls to me and Freddie to uphold the Carnarvon name."

"And Richard," Sebastian added dryly.

"And Richard. Of course, Richard." She shook her head. "What I'm saying is . . . well, you know what I'm saying. We could be good for each other." Ava paused, a naked plea in her eyes. "More than good. Don't throw it all away. We've know each other for—"

"Long enough that I can say you're like a sister to me," Sebastian said gently. "And I'll always be there if you need advice. But I can't. . . I can't be what you're asking."

She recoiled as if slapped. Red spots burned in her cheeks. "I see," she managed. "Thank you for your honesty."

He nodded, unsure what to say that wouldn't upset her more. Ava turned away to compose herself. Her shoulders trembled and he was afraid she might be crying, but when she looked back, she wore a fixed smile. Her cheeks were dry, if a little pale.

"Well, that was embarrassing," she remarked lightly. "I've had a crush on you since I was a little girl, Sebastian. I suppose it's time I laid it to rest."

"Ava—" he began.

She held up a hand. "Please don't say anything more. Leave a woman with some shred of dignity." She drew herself up. "I wish you both well. And I hope this doesn't change anything." Her smile faltered as she searched his face. "We still need you, Sebastian."

"Of course," he said quickly. "I'll always be there. You know that."

Ava nodded. "I have to go change. Grandmother's waiting in her room."

She left without looking back.

Hardin scrubbed a hand through his hair. He felt sorry to have hurt her, but it was past time she faced the truth. The confrontation had been inevitable and it was a relief to have it behind them both. She'd taken it better than he'd expected. Ava was used to getting her way. She wasn't as frivolous as Freddie, but she had an implacable will when it came to things she really wanted. She took after her grandmother in that way.

Hardin took a last look around the room. The telephone was off the cradle, dangling from its black cord. He walked over and replaced it on the receiver. After a pause, he picked it up again and dialed nine. The operator answered.

"Did you receive any calls from this room today?" he asked.

"Hold on a moment." He waited.

"No, sir. Can I help you with anything else?"

"No, thank you." Hardin hung up, frowning slightly.

If Ruth had been sleepwalking, she could have knocked it off when she got out of bed. But his uneasy feeling grew stronger.

Calindra's suite was on the twenty-second floor. When Sebastian arrived, she was pacing up and down in the large sitting room. Freddie nursed a drink.

"Sebastian!" Calindra exclaimed. "Where have you been?"

She wore a severely-cut dark gown, her silver hair pinned up with a mantilla comb.

"Checking on Deputy Cortez. And Marshal Tanaka."

"Well, we have a situation."

"Merriweather?" He glanced at Freddie, who gave a slight eye roll his grandmother didn't notice. "I thought that was taken care of."

Her jaw set. "I've decided to tell him the terms myself. I want to make it clear that he's not to set foot in my jurisdiction. I want his word."

What a supremely shitty idea, Sebastian thought. He smiled. "Of course, ma'am. Why don't you just let me handle it?"

"No, this needs to come from me." She drew a black lace wrap tighter around her shoulders. "I have some things to say to the boy."

Sebastian sighed. "All right. But I promised I'd go back to the infirmary."

"You can do it afterwards, Sebastian. I need you there. Lee's been hiding from me, but if I go to this . . . public *performance* . . . ." Her lips pursed in distaste. "I can catch him backstage at intermission. He can't dodge me then!"

"It's for children," Freddie muttered. "Can't you let me off the hook, grandmother?"

"No." Calindra's chilly gaze turned to him. "You're a member of this family too, Freddie. We need to present a united front."

"I don't like clowns."

She snorted. "Not that again."

"Well, I don't." Freddie lit a cigarette and drew deeply. "Am I the only person in this room who finds them . . . . I don't know, what's the word I'm looking for, Hardin?"

"Unsettling?" Sebastian ventured.

Freddie stabbed his cigarette. "That's the one."

Calindra grimaced. "Oh, for God's sake—"

"What about the contracts?" Sebastian asked before they started fighting again.

"I signed them. We'll leave first thing in the morning."

Well, that was one piece of good news.

"When does the show start?" he asked.

"In forty minutes. Freddie, where's your sister?"

"How should I know?"

"She went to change," Sebastian said.

"That's the third time today," Freddie said, swallowing the last of his drink. He crunched the ice between his teeth. "She brought four trunks and I think she's already worked her way through all of them."

"Fix your tie." Calindra looked him over with a critical eye. "It's askew."

Freddie obediently adjusted his cravat.

Calindra trained her scrutiny on Sebastian, who tried not to fidget like a schoolboy. He wore his Special Services uniform, navy blue jacket and trousers with a line of brass buttons and the Carnarvon insignia embroidered in gold thread on his shoulder.

"If you have no objection," Calindra said in a tone that strongly discouraged objections, "I'd like you to change into one of Freddie's tuxedoes. Just for the performance."

"Why, ma'am?" Hardin frowned.

"I don't want to put Lee's back up. He must believe I'm speaking with him in a private capacity, not as an adversary. Naturally, you'll be present as well."

"I don't see how my clothes will make much of a—"

"Please, Sebastian. It might seem inconsequential, but these things matter. Every detail influences our perception of reality, even those we aren't consciously aware of. In fact, the unconscious cues can be the most powerful. Your uniform represents everything Lee is rebelling against. I'd rather not remind him of that."

Sebastian sighed and looked at Freddie, who shrugged. "Fine."

Hardin withdrew into the enormous boudoir to change. He and Freddie were about the same size, though the evening jacket was too closely tailored for the shoulder rig. It left a visible bulge Braga's men couldn't fail to notice. Sebastian reluctantly left the gun with his folded uniform.

When he emerged, Ava still wasn't there, but she'd sent a bellhop with a note promising to meet them at the theater.

"You look handsome," Calindra said with a perfunctory smile. "Now let's get this over with, shall we?"

Freddie offered her his arm. She walked past him with a scowl and pressed the button for the private lift. "Your sister had better not be tardy," Calindra muttered, adjusting her wrap. "Because I shan't wait in the lobby."

When her back was turned, Freddie pulled a flask from his pocket and took a bracing swig. He caught Hardin's eye and grinned.

"Send in the clowns," he whispered, raising the flask in a toast.

LEE REGARDED himself in the dressing room mirror.

He wore a white tuxedo with a red carnation in the lapel. His hair was parted on the left and slicked back. Lee set a silk top hat on his head and tried out a smile. It looked nervous.

He adjusted the hat to a rakish angle and tried again. Better this time.

He was looking forward to the show, but a small voice in his head refused to shut up. The voice wondered if Ruth Cortez had told the truth. What if the X really had followed him to Aguadulce?

Well, Lee didn't plan to stick around long enough to find out. He patted the inner pocket of his jacket. Inside was a ticket for the eleven o'clock bus to Tres Colinas. From there, he could go anywhere.

A trickle of sweat cut through the powder on his face. He blotted it with a sponge. The make-up made him look deathly white, like a corpse, but Henry had insisted. Everybody loves a clown, he'd said.

For the tenth time in the last hour, he whispered a

summons, trying to draw the little phantom girl from the ether. Lee had questions for her. But she seemed to be gone.

He turned as Abel Beach rapped on the open door. He had a suitcase in his hand.

"Professor!" Lee jumped to his feet. "I'm glad you came."

They'd barely seen other in days. Lee had left a note under his door inviting him to the show, along with a wad of money that Henry had advanced on his first paycheck.

Mr. Beach gave a forced smile. "I won't pretend I approve, but I know better than to try talking you out of it." He set an envelope on the dressing table. "I can't take this, Lee. You earned it."

Lee frowned. "But—"

"I just borrowed enough for a bus ticket." He hefted the suitcase. "I'm off to stay with my niece for a while." He fished in his pocket and took out a slip of paper. "Here's the address. You come anytime, okay?"

Lee's chest tightened as he took the paper. "I will, sir."

Mr. Beach looked at him. "You were always my favorite student. Not just for your talent, but because you have a good heart."

Lee flushed. "I'm sorry for—"

"I'm not done," Abel interrupted. "You still do, despite everything." I sighed. "I'm partly to blame for how they treated you. I should have done more. Should have spoken up. But we can't go back, can we? I'd stay if I thought it would do you any good, but I think you need to figure things out on your own. You're a man now." He cleared his throat. "Just send me a letter from time to time, okay? Let me know you're well. And if you ever need my help again, I'll be there."

"Thank you, sir. I will."

Abel shook his hand. The professor gave a brusque nod when he finally let go. His eyes looked a little blurry. "You be safe, boy."

"Will you stay for the show?" Lee asked.

Mr. Beach shook his head. "Bus is leaving in half an hour. Better I'm gone." His tone sharpened. "Better you are, too, once the show's over."

"I plan to, sir," Lee said quickly. He patted his pocket. "Got my own ticket right here."

Mr. Beach's face relaxed. "That's good. If anyone can stay one step ahead, I guess it's you." He smiled. "Never thought I'd pilot a zeppelin again. We did have some fun together."

Lee laughed. "Yeah we did."

The professor tipped his hat. "Goodbye, Mr. Merriweather. Until next time."

"Until next time," Lee said, his voice hoarse.

He watched the door close, his heart heavy and light at the same time. Heavy for the loss of the only human friend he'd ever known. Light in the knowledge that Mr. Beach would be far from Lee's own troubles.

When I strike it rich, I'll make sure he's taken care of, Lee vowed. And his whole family, too.

He was trying the top hat at various angles when Henry Chance arrived. He wore a white tuxedo identical to Lee's, down to the red carnation in the pocket. A wide, red smile was painted around his lips.

"How's my new star?" he asked with a wink.

"I think I'm ready," Lee said. "Listen, have you seen anything odd in the last day or so?"

"Odd how?" Henry asked, making funny faces in the mirror over his shoulder.

"Anyone acting strange."

Henry quirked a painted eyebrow. "It's a casino. You'll have to be more specific."

"Never mind."

Henry turned away from the mirror, looking down at him. "Something's bothering you. Maybe I can help."

"I ran into an old friend from up north," Lee said slowly. "Hazardville, actually. Where they had the big fire."

Henry nodded. "I heard about that."

"Some people think it was set by a Class X phantom. My friend heard rumors it came down this way."

"A Class X?" Henry gave a low whistle. "They're mighty rare. I've never seen one myself, but I've heard stories." He chortled. "I think you're scared. Am I right, Lee?" He hooked his fingers into claws. "Scared of that big bad Class X. It'll huff and puff and blow your house down!" Henry slapped his knee and laughed some more.

"You just admitted you've never seen one," Lee said, annoyed. "So don't pretend you know what you're talking about."

Henry sobered, though his eyes still danced with merriment. "And you do?"

"All I'm saying is we should keep an eye out."

Henry waved a hand. "Don't worry, Merriweather, I think between the two of us, we can handle one Class X. We'll have it rolling over and fetching if it tries any foolishness."

"I guess so," Lee said dubiously.

Henry grinned at him in the mirror. "You're just having a case of nerves. It was a rumor, you said so yourself. The phantoms here are all tame as tame can be." He winked. "Don't worry, Lee. I'll know you'll knock 'em dead tonight."

20

After Roger left, I got back to work on the restraints.

The ward was quiet, but I imagined the people down below, putting on their nicest dresses and suits. Laughing and talking as they finished their dinners and headed over to the theater. I bet a lot of them had saved up for years to come to Aguadulce on vacation.

Twist and pull, twist and pull.

Lee should have listened when I told him to run, but I doubted Roger would have let him go this time. The X was bent on killing us all and he'd do it one way or another.

Or not quite all of us.

You'll be the lucky survivor, Ruth.

It wasn't enough for Roger to stage another massacre. He wanted me to know and not be able to do anything about it.

Well, I wasn't going to give up.

Twist and pull, twist and pull.

My fingers went tingly and then numb. Specks of blood stained the cotton restraints. My stupid hands were too big. I just couldn't force the joint of my thumb through the loop. Man hands, Charlie Bowdre had called them once. He hadn't meant any offense. It was merely an observation. Now I thought of Mrs. Johanssen, the one who played piano in church and had such long, elegant fingers. She would have been out of those restraints in a jiffy.

I wanted to wrap my giant paws around Roger's throat.

"Help!" I yelled. "Help! I'm dying in here!"

Nobody came, not even the nasty nurse with her syringe.

I gave a savage yank, frustration boiling over. Where was everybody? How could this place be completely empty? Hundreds of people must be staying at the hotel and yet not a single bed in my ward was occupied. It had the quality of a fever dream, but I knew it wasn't. The pain was too real.

"I ain't quitting!" I shrieked, thrashing like a maniac. "You hear me, Roger?"

I figured I'd just holler until my throat gave out. Maybe Hardin would come back. Maybe, maybe, maybe . . . .

"*Ruth.*"

My head jerked up. The voice was so weak I feared I'd imagined it. I propped my elbows underneath me, which was as close as I could get to sitting. "Doc?" I whispered.

There was a long silence.

"Doc?" I said again.

When the answering whisper came, I nearly wept.

"It's me."

I searched for Doc's telltale shadow, then did a double take as my eyes passed the window. A face was reflected in the darkened glass.

An actual face.

Somehow I'd always thought of Doc as old. He was a curmudgeon and a know-it-all, and he'd been stuck in the Collier for a long time before I found him. But the reflection looking back at me was a young man close to my own age. He had sharp features and a mop of unruly hair that flopped over one eye. Something about him reminded me of Lee. The hint of devilry. But his expression looked solemn now.

"I don't have much time, Ruth," Doc said. "He'll be back any minute."

The words sounded like they came from the bottom of a well. Distant and hissing with bursts of static like a bad telephone line.

"Help me," I said, jerking against the restraints.

The reflection shimmered. It started to break apart. Doc's thin, straight eyebrows wrinkled together, his mouth tightened with concentration, and the reflection in the glass sharpened again. Except for the age, it was close to what I'd pictured in my mind when I tried to imagine what he might look like. Not exactly a *nice* face, but a clever and interesting face.

"I can't . . ." The rest was lost.

"Try," I urged. "Just try!"

". . . came to say goodbye. And to say I'm sorry."

"No! Don't you dare!" Tears ran down my cheeks, though I hardly noticed. "I missed you so much, Doc."

The wide mouth curled in a smile. He flicked the hair from his eyes. ". . . missed you, too."

"Really?"

"Really." He cocked his head as if listening. "My Lord, Merriweather's a fool."

His voice had firmed up. It was different from Roger, different from Lee, but now that I knew what he was, I heard the power under the surface. I should have seen it before, but Doc had never used it on me to compel.

"You can hear what's going on?" I asked in surprise.

"Some of it," Doc said dryly. "Roger's distracted at the moment, blowing smoke up Lee's trouser leg, but he won't be for long." His eyes were distant, like he was in two places at once, and I supposed he must be. Part of him was here with me in this room, and part of him was still in the gun.

"Where are you?" I whispered. "Just tell me. I'll find you. I'll get you out of this."

He gave a mirthless laugh. "Get *me* out? You're in the pickle jar, too, Ruth."

I glanced down at the restraints. "Guess you can't get these off."

Doc snorted regretfully. "Not even a little bit of me is here in the flesh. Roger's got me locked down tight. It's all I can do just to talk to you now."

"All right, then. Ideas?" I gave him a level look. "Since I imagine you know a few things about *Class X phantoms.*"

He shot me a sharp look.

"Listen, I don't care what you are," I said. "You ain't nothing like Roger, not even on your worst day. So I know you don't want to let him hurt those people."

"Well, of course I don't," Doc snapped.

"Then how do we stop him?"

"You remember what happened when Jolly trotted Roger out to scare you? How he had the little phantom pinned to a block of wood and Roger, uh, ate it?"

I nodded. "Still gives me nightmares."

"That's what you need to do to Roger. Just get to the theater, Ruth. I'll do my best to help you."

"But how am I supposed to get out of here?"

His reflection shimmered again. The face contorted in a grimace. It elongated, stretching away from the window. A shadow fell across the bed, flickering in and out. A shadow hand reached forward. His fingers brushed mine and I felt something, not solid flesh but like a slight breeze. Doc grunted and the shadow leapt away, like it was tied to a string. He was only a reflection in the glass again. And his voice sounded terribly weak.

"Told me he'd . . . kill you if I came. I'm sorry . . ."

His eyes widened until I could see the whites all around. He screamed and it was the earsplitting scream of a Class X phantom. The sound felt like a razor peeling my skin away in onion-thin layers. I burrowed into the mattress trying to escape his terrible cries. When the echoes finally faded, Doc was gone.

I half-expected to find blood on the sheets. A sob broke from my throat.

"Cortez?"

The voice was faint, somewhere in the hallway.

"Over here!" I yelled. "Here!"

Marshal Tanaka stuck her head through the door. She was swathed in bandages and one eye was a bloodshot mess, but she was the most beautiful thing I'd ever seen. Tanaka limped down the ward.

"What the hell was that?" she asked.

"My haint," I said. My head still ached. "The Class X has him."

Tanaka gave me a level look. "Hardin wanted me to check in on you. I understand you had some, uh, trouble." She glanced at the restraints around my wrists.

"You heard it, too," I said, keeping my voice calm and rational. "Do you seriously believe I could make a sound like that? That any human could?"

Tanaka exhaled. "No, I guess not."

I held her gaze. "Please, I'm not crazy. Can you free my hands at least? They're killing me."

Tanaka hesitated, but only for an instant. "Sure, Cortez."

She unbuckled the restraints and helped work my wrists free. I sat up and flexed my fingers. They felt stiff and clumsy.

"Think you could do my feet, too?" I asked her.

Tanaka obliged. I swung my legs to the floor and flinched as pins and needles stabbed my toes. "Where's that nurse?" I muttered.

Tanaka didn't need to ask which one I meant. "I don't know. I haven't seen her in a while."

Whatever the nurse gave me, it hadn't worn off all the way. My stomach twisted at the thought of her big syringe. "I need to get out of here without her seeing."

Tanaka scratched her forehead at the edge of the bandage. "What are you going to do, Cortez?"

"I don't know," I admitted. "But I can at least warn people. Try to get them out of the hotel."

"Warn them of what?"

"Trust me on this. Something bad is about to happen."

I desperately wanted to tell her everything. It was an awful burden on my shoulders. But I was afraid she wouldn't believe me. Better to keep things vague.

"We'll find Hardin," Tanaka said with confidence. "And Mr. Braga. They'll handle it."

I nodded doubtfully, though I didn't have a better idea. My knees buckled when I stood. Tanaka grabbed my arm and steadied me. We were both barefoot and wearing the blue infirmary gowns.

"You good?" she asked.

"Good enough," I replied grimly. "Let's go."

We walked to the end of the ward and eased the door open. The hallway beyond was empty.

"You know where the elevators are?" I whispered.

Tanaka nodded and stepped into the corridor. "This way."

The floor was freezing beneath my bare feet. I trailed a hand on the wall to steady myself. I felt weak as a day-old kitten.

"Did Hardin tell you what we found in New Jerusalem?" I asked her.

Tanaka gave me a sympathetic look. "Yeah."

"I think something like that might happen here," I said. "Except on a bigger scale."

"But how?" Tanaka frowned. "I mean, New Jerusalem was in the middle of nowhere. Totally isolated. It's a terrible tragedy, but—"

We rounded a corner just as the nurse bustled through a door into the hall. She had a bedpan in her hand. Her face froze. The bedpan clattered to the floor.

"What are you doing out of bed?" she hissed. Her eyes were flat. "I'll have to get security."

I strode forward. The nurse shrank away, fumbling in her pocket. Before she could jab me again, I elbowed her in the face. The nurse reeled back, clutching a bloody nose.

Tanaka stared at me. "That's assault, Cortez," she said unhappily. "You can't just go around hitting people."

I dragged the marshal to the stairwell at the end of the hall. "Look," I said. "*She* assaulted *me*. She slapped me across the face when I told her I didn't want a sedative. She tied me to a bed. I had every right."

"Okay, okay," Tanaka grumbled. "I didn't much care for her either. But try to calm down. We're guests here. If that woman presses charges—"

I stopped listening. It wasn't Tanaka's fault. She didn't know the half of it.

I stifled a bitter laugh. We were guests all right, but we weren't Braga's guests. We were Roger's guests. Or more like characters in his play. The nurse wouldn't press charges because she wouldn't even be alive by tomorrow.

We'd gone a few flights down when a door banged open somewhere below, followed by boots pounding up the stairs. Tanaka stopped and peered down the stairwell. She looked relieved.

"Oh, good," she said. "Security. They can take us to Hardin."

"Except they won't," I said. "We can't trust them."

I saw her waver. She was starting to wonder if I wasn't crazy after all.

"Cortez!" she yelled as I broke free and ran back up the stairs. "Wait!"

21

"Ava, darling!"

Calindra Carnarvon clasped her granddaughter's hands as if she hadn't been grousing about her the whole way down in the elevator. "Don't you look lovely?"

Ava gave a wan smile. She wore a sleeveless gown of shimmering sea-green silk that perfectly matched her eyes. Auburn hair was piled atop her head in elaborate coils. An emerald choker glittered at her throat.

"I'm so sorry," she said. "A pearl button on my glove popped off and the maid had to sew it back on. It took forever to find the right shade of ivory thread."

"No matter." Calindra's lips were fixed in a smile, but her attention had already wandered, eyes roving across the theatre lobby. Looking for Lee, Hardin thought.

She was nervous, though she'd never admit it. He wondered if some part of her didn't still care about the boy, even after everything. There was no real reason Calindra had to speak with him herself. But Lee had been her prize pupil. She'd known him since he was a child. Surely their relationship hadn't always been so difficult.

Sebastian watched Freddie hovering in the background,

his tie already crooked again, and Ava masking a petulant scowl at being dismissed. Freddie made him think of a dog that was always jumping on the furniture and getting yelled at. Ava was a cat, pampered and elegant, but with sharp claws beneath the surface. Neither struck him as being much like their grandmother. Sebastian hadn't thought Merriweather was either, but perhaps he was wrong. Calindra and Lee must have understood each other in ways no one else could.

"Shall I collect the tickets?" Freddie asked.

Calindra waved a hand distractedly.

"I've never seen you in formal evening wear, Sebastian," Ava said, tilting her head.

He shrugged. "It was your grandmother's idea."

"Of course it was." She smiled. "Well, you look very nice."

He smiled back, self-conscious and awkward. He knew Ava. She'd definitely nurse a grudge — and never admit to it. Ava Carnarvon was not a woman accustomed to refusal in anything. He just hoped she wouldn't retaliate.

"You should join us afterwards." Ava's voice lowered. "I hope it goes well with Merriweather, but if grandmother's in a foul mood, we can always sneak off and amuse ourselves. There's a stand that does charcoal portraits in the lobby. They're open late."

Sebastian slipped a hand into his pocket, rubbing a thumb across the engraving of Ruth's copper star. "It's tempting, but I need to head back to the infirmary."

Ava didn't bat an eye. "Of course, how could I forget? I do hope the deputy's condition has improved." She slipped her arm through Freddie's. "Ruth Cortez had an accident."

"I heard." For once, Freddie didn't make a joke of it. "That's awful. I assume she fell?"

"Must have," Sebastian muttered.

"What floor?" Freddie asked.

"Six."

He winced. "Ava dared me to jump off the cliff by the swimming beach once. The one at the bend in the river where the kids go."

Sebastian nodded. He knew the place.

"I performed a perfect bellyflop and had my wind knocked out. Nearly drowned. And that wasn't half as high."

"You wouldn't have landed so badly if you hadn't been drinking," Ava pointed out.

Freddie took a quick nip from his flask. He screwed the lid on and gave her a cool smile. "Yet you dared me to do it anyway. I'm not sure what that says about either of us, sister dear."

Their banter trailed off at the sudden appearance of a gangly teenaged usher. He led Mrs. Carnarvon and her entourage to a box on the second tier, very near the stage. Pedro Braga and his wife occupied a separate box a few feet away. Braga nodded and smiled as they sat down. It was common knowledge that he preferred the company of men, but people seemed to expect him to produce an heir. He'd married Martina and the two of them seemed genuinely affectionate, though so far they'd had no children. From the glowing way Braga spoke about Henry Chance, Hardin suspected Pedro intended to name the young man his successor someday.

Hardin leaned back, already impatient for intermission. There were a lot of children in the audience and they chattered excitedly, the hubbub adding to the strains of the orchestra warming up in the pit. Freddie and Ava sat on their grandmother's left, Freddie sipping from his flask while Ava stared at the stage. She looked as irritated as Hardin to be there.

"I understand Mr. Chance is the chief of security," Calindra said with a note of scorn. "It's rather unseemly of him to perform in public like some kind of trained animal, don't you think?"

Hardin made a noncommittal noise. He couldn't care less what Henry Chance did in his spare time. They'd met a few times during the contract negotiations. He seemed young for the job — but so was Sebastian.

"I hear Chance has an escape act," Freddie said with a laugh. "That sounds more entertaining than this *duel*. I imagine they'll just order phantoms to juggle and make things disappear." He covered a yawn. "I hope they get on with it. I have plans tonight."

"Slumming it with the dregs of Aguadulce, no doubt," Ava muttered.

"Now, now," Freddie protested. "Retract your fangs for a moment. I'm well aware we have reputations to uphold. I thought I'd try my luck at the roulette tables. Perhaps have a late supper. All perfectly respectable. I hoped you'd join me."

Ava's face softened a fraction. She gazed at her twin with exasperated fondness. "I might. If you behave yourself."

Freddie grinned. "I'll be a model of decorum."

The lights dimmed. Kettle drums rumbled a slow cannonade of thunder. Twin spotlights lit the stage.

"Thank God," Freddie murmured, raising his flask. "Let us pray for a swift conclusion."

The curtains parted. Two men in identical white suits with red carnations tucked into the lapels stood side by side. Henry Chance wore garish paint around his eyes (black) and mouth (red). He was a few inches shorter than Lee, but stockier in build. He tipped his hat at the audience and nudged Lee in the ribs.

Merriweather's skin was chalk-white, his lips bluish, like a freshly unearthed corpse. In life, without makeup, both men were pleasant-looking, but under the blazing spotlights they resembled a pair of grinning ghouls.

Freddie choked on his whiskey. Calindra's hands tightened on her folded gloves as Lee took a low bow. Merriweather's eyes roamed across the audience, then moved up to the boxes. He spotted Calindra and his smile widened.

"Merriweather's got some cheek," Freddie said tightly.

"That's one way of putting it," Ava said. She stared at Lee with loathing.

Sebastian rubbed his forehead, wishing he were anywhere else.

"Welcome to the Duel of the Linguists!" Chance declared, spreading his arms. "I'm Doctor Deathless and this is my partner, the Grim Creeper. Can you say hello?"

The kids in the audience gave a gleeful shout.

"We have a little wager about who's the best linguist," Henry continued. "And we're going to settle it tonight, right on this stage. But we need your help. Are you ready?"

A roar, louder than the last.

"Wonderful!" Henry beamed. "What I need you to do is cheer at the top of your lungs! You'll be the judges about who performs the best tricks. And now . . . our illustrious assistants!"

Three phantoms scampered out. They wore red devil costumes with horns and pitchforks. The phantoms leered at the audience, their faces stretching like taffy. The children erupted in screams of laughter. Henry whispered something and the trio's heads turned toward Lee. They rushed at him with pitchforks extended. Merriweather threw out a hand, growling words in a phantom tongue. The sharp tines halted inches away from skewering him.

"This is ludicrous," Calindra muttered, her jaw tight.

A chair floated out from the wings. It began to jitter against the stage, legs tapping a fast rhythm. The chair tilted and flew towards Henry feet first. He gasped and flung his arms out, whispering fervently. The chair skidded to a halt and resumed its feverish jig.

"Why, that was a low blow!" Henry declared, balling his

fists. He looked out at the audience. "Should I let him get away with that?"

"Noooooo!"

A second chair shot out, hitting Lee at the backs of his knees. He sat down heavily, his hat falling off. Henry brandished his cane like a conductor. The chair rose up, sending Lee spinning like a top. Merriweather's long arms flapped. He barked a command and the chair floated down to earth. "Time for dessert!" he yelled.

Suddenly, Lee held a cream pie. He hurled it at Henry Chance, who gamely took the pie dead in the face.

"What time is it?" Hardin whispered to Freddie.

"It's only been ten minutes," Freddie replied glumly. "I'd say we have another thirty before there's any hope of a reprieve."

The silly act went on and on. The haints conjured volleys of flaming arrows and dropped heavy weights from the rafters above the stage, all of which were deflected by the intended victim at the last moment. It was more comical than frightening. The "duels" were punctuated with dance numbers, performed to lively tunes from the orchestra.

Every time one of the men managed to get the upper hand, he would gesture at the audience to cheer. Hardin's temples pounded by the time Henry Chance ordered the haints to douse Lee with a washtub full of soapy water.

The children loved it, pointing and clapping with glee. Lee shook himself off with a scowl. His hair was plastered down against his skull. Water dripped from his chin. He shot an angry glare at Henry, who grinned at the audience and shrugged.

Something must have gone wrong with the air conditioning because the temperature had been steadily rising. Freddie produced a handkerchief and mopped his forehead. His green eyes looked glassy. Hardin suspected he'd polished off the whole flask. Calindra looked wan and ill.

Enough, Sebastian thought. *To hell with intermission*. He was about to lean over and suggest they step into the lobby for some air when the lights cut out. It only lasted for a few seconds. The kids were starting to hoot and holler when they came back on. Lee pointed his cane at Henry and growled something. The tallest phantom glided over, its bare feet dragging along the stage.

Chance held his palms out. He looked terrified. The audience laughed louder. The phantom extended a pale hand. Henry was trembling, shaking his head in a mute plea. The grim appeared to reach *into* his chest. It pulled out something red and shiny.

Hardin blinked. *That* was different. Much darker than the first part of the act. He knew it had to be an illusion, but by God, it looked real.

The phantom tossed the red thing at Merriweather's feet. The box was just above the stage and Hardin could clearly see what looked like a lump of muscle. Ragged veins trailed from the edge.

Henry Chance's mouth sagged. His knees gave out and he collapsed on the stage. The phantom turned to the audience. It bowed with a flourish. For a long moment, no one made a sound. They just stared.

Merriweather started laughing. "Oops," he said.

Long seconds passed. The audience waited for Henry to get up.

He didn't.

A young child in the second row started crying. His mother stood, squaring her shoulders indignantly. "This is entirely inappropriate," she declared, taking the child by the hand and dragging him towards the aisle.

People were muttering now, twisting in their seats.

"What the hell was *that?*" Freddie whispered. "What the *hell*. Did Merriweather just . . . ?"

Considering the gaping hole in Henry's Chance's chest,

there was a surprisingly small amount of blood. Hardin realized that this was because he no longer had a heart to pump
it out.

"Yes," Sebastian said faintly. "I . . . I think he did."

On stage, Lee pointed his cane at the woman. "Sit down,"
he ordered.

Her knees buckled and she obediently collapsed into the
lap of a portly gentleman in the aisle seat, her mouth a perfect
O of surprise. He yelped with indignation.

"The show isn't over yet," Lee said. "It's rude to walk out
in the middle, don't you think?"

His voice sounded strange, Hardin thought. Different
somehow. Nothing he could quite put his finger on—

Lee growled a command. A phantom flew down. It seized
the woman's hair and yanked. For an instant, Hardin couldn't
grasp what he was seeing. Half of her simply disappeared, as
if she'd been sliced in two with a cleaver. Her mouth opened
and closed. Her eyes bugged out. Then she was simply gone.

Full-blown panic erupted. People pushed and shoved to
reach the aisles. Children howled. Phantoms swooped over the
milling mass, pulling at hair and neckties.

Sebastian shot to his feet. "Everybody out," he snapped.
"Now!"

He reached for Calindra's arm, but she pushed him away
with a glare. "I'm not an invalid," she muttered. "I can walk
perfectly fine."

Her voice had steel in it, as always, but her gaze was
riveted to the stage where Lee paced up and down, gesturing
with the cane. Jagged syllables poured from his mouth. The
crowd stampeded for the twin exits, jamming them up. Lee
pointed his finger at a red-faced man in a cowboy hat near the
back. Two phantoms materialized on either side of him, each
taking an arm. An instant later, the man was gone.

And an instant after that . . . .

A red rain pattered down from above, thick and viscous.

Those unlucky enough to be standing beneath it were drenched in crimson. They slipped in the mess, crying out in horror and revulsion. Hardin watched open-mouthed as more people started vanishing. They did not go gently. A violent yank and it was as if they'd never existed. Few had time to scream.

Sucked into the ether.

A shout from the next box broke Sebastian's paralysis. Pedro Braga was on his feet, his deep baritone slicing through the cacophony. The words were unintelligible, but he was obviously trying to bring the phantoms under control.

The haints ignored him. And more had come into the theater, streaming straight through the walls. The screams reached a higher pitch as the floor began to vibrate. A chandelier fell with a crash. Plaster dust choked the air. Lee Merriweather stood in the spotlight, looking out at his handiwork with grim satisfaction.

"Get down," Hardin hissed, pulling Calindra to the floor. Ava and Freddie were already crouched behind their seats. They crawled to the exit as two dozen Gorras with rifles filled the other boxes.

"It's about damned time," Freddie said shakily.

Sebastian heard a fusillade of gunfire. It went on and on. Merriweather stood in a *spotlight*. There was no way they could miss — and not even the savant could stop a bullet. But when he glanced over his shoulder, Lee still stood there on the stage, a smile on his face.

In the narrow corridor that ran behind the box seats, four members of Braga's personal security huddled around him.

"Evacuate the Reina del Sur," Braga was saying in rapid Spanish. "Alvarez has the command."

"What about the transports?"

"We can't use them. They're all phantom-powered. Take people out on foot. Get them to the football stadium."

"And if it spreads, sir?"

"Then we go to Code Red. Start the protocols now, just in case."

"What's Code Red?" Sebastian asked.

Braga turned to him with a haunted look. "Citywide evacuation. Let's hope it doesn't come to that."

"How could this happen, Pedro?" Calindra demanded.

Sebastian detected guilt in her voice. *We should have warned him. It's our fault as much as his.*

"I have no idea," Braga grated. "Henry vouched for Merriweather personally. The boy's gone mad. And Henry . . . ." Braga's face crumpled and he looked lost. Then his jaw firmed. He turned to the guards. "Escort my guests to safety. I'll stay and deal with it."

"But sir—"

"I said I'll stay. Take the back stairs." He strode into the box without waiting for a response. Braga shouted at Lee. The two men locked eyes. Shadows thickened around Merriweather. Braga stood his ground. Sebastian admired his courage, but there was nothing more he could do and his own duty was to Calindra and her grandchildren.

They hurried to a flight of carpeted steps leading down, two of the guards in front, the other two taking up the rear. Their guns were drawn, though Sebastian doubted weapons would do any good. Calindra stared straight ahead. She'd allowed him to take her arm, and she leaned against him, her breath coming shallowly. More rifle fire erupted behind, followed by screams, but it didn't sound like Lee.

It sounded like the Gorras.

And what will we do if the grims come for us?

Sebastian had always taken the phantoms' obedience for granted. They were supposed to *like* people. Ask them nicely, and they listened.

He thought of Carnarvon City and the thousands of haints Calindra had attracted with the clocktowers. If the revolt spread beyond Aguadulce . . . .

Sebastian suppressed a shudder.

The lead Gorras avoided the chaos in the theater lobby, steering the group through a private door that opened straight into the casino. The chandeliers flickered on and off. Hardin caught a glimpse of red and white chips littering the carpet. The Gorras spread out in a line, scanning the shadows. In a flash of light, Hardin saw two dealers crouched under one of the roulette tables, but the place was otherwise deserted.

"Are the elevators working?" he asked one of the guards in a soft voice.

"I'm not sure," the man whispered back. "Better to get you out the front, sir."

Sebastian hesitated. Only an airship could run without phantoms. They were propelled with great clockwork screws. If all the grims had gone mad, it would be the only way out of the city.

"Ava," he said. "You're a qualified pilot, aren't you?"

She gave a terse nod.

"Then we're going up," he said.

The guard frowned. "I don't think that's a good idea. Mr. Braga said—"

He cut off with a surprised grunt. A shadow loomed behind him. The lights flickered. Hardin grabbed the guard's hand, but some force had hold of him. The fingers started slipping through Hardin's grasp. The man screamed, clinging on with a death grip.

"Jesus," Hardin snarled. "Help me!"

The other three rushed over just as their comrade's mouth went slack. He was somehow yanked *sideways* — even later, when Hardin recalled that moment with perfect clarity, he couldn't quite comprehend it — and Sebastian was left holding a hand no longer attached to anyone, the wrist severed as cleanly as if it had been cut with an axe. He dropped it with a strangled cry.

"Sebastian!" Ava hissed, pointing.

More shadows were coming.

They ran.

Toward the main lobby of the Reina del Sur, where a knot of harassed red jackets tried to funnel a hysterical mob through the glass doors. Hardin was eyeing the crush of people when a phantom materialized, one of the starvelings that made him uneasy at the best of times. It reached for Ava, who seemed rooted to the spot.

Calindra made a guttural sound deep in her throat. Sebastian feared she was having a stroke, but then the phantom's bug-eyed gaze shifted away from Ava and he realized Calindra was speaking a tongue. She lowered her head in submission, palms upraised. The hair on Sebastian's arms stirred. He understood the sentiment, if not the words. It was a plea for mercy.

The creature hesitated, then vanished into the ether. Calindra sagged against him. She grasped Ava's hand and squeezed it.

"It . . . it listened to you," Ava stammered in surprise.

"This time," Calindra murmured. Her eyes were glassy with shock. Her voice trembled. "How could they do this to us, Sebastian? How could we have been so wrong about them?"

"It's Merriweather," he growled. "He's a savant. He turned them somehow."

"Even still—"

"Later," he said firmly. "We'll worry about what it means later. But right now we have to keep moving."

He pulled Calindra out of the way as four men in tuxedos barreled past, hugging pillowcases that bulged suspiciously. One of them tripped over the severed hand. With a squeaky "Jesus Christ!" he dropped his sack. Silver dollars spilled out. He gulped and ran to catch up with his fellow looters. The three guards looked at each other.

"Hey, that's casino property!"

"Just head out the front doors, sir," one of them shouted to Hardin over his shoulder, as they took off in pursuit.

Someone fired a gun in the air, which did nothing but add to the general chaos at the lobby doors. People started screaming and shoving even harder to get out.

"We'll head for the north elevator bank," Hardin said. "Follow me."

They turned away from the sweating crush of bodies and made for the arcade, a long gallery of boutiques and snack shops. This part of the hotel seemed largely untouched.

"How many phantoms do you think are in Aguadulce on a normal day?" he whispered to Calindra as they slunk along in the shadows.

"I don't know. Hundreds. Possibly thousands."

"If they'd all turned, everyone would already be dead. That means it's a few bad apples."

Freddie barked a laugh. "*Bad apples*. More like sharks in a goldfish bowl."

"It means we might actually make it to the roof," Hardin snapped. "Just stay close."

He finally spotted the elevator bank, but the way was blocked by four capering haints. They had one of the maids' carts and were taking it for joyrides. Sebastian pulled everyone back around the corner before they were seen.

"Over there," Sebastian said, pointing to a restaurant with a flickering neon sign advertising the Longhorn Steakhouse. "There must be a back way out through the kitchens. We'll take a service elevator to the roof."

Ava and Freddie gave tight nods. They stepped inside. Black and white landscape photographs of the vast Braga ranches hung crookedly on the walls. Gravy and mashed potatoes were ground into the rug, along with chunks of meat that Sebastian dearly hoped was sirloin. A single ladies' slipper, dark blue velvet with a gold buckle, rested on one of the tables. What looked like a hank of human hair was tucked inside.

Ava shuddered. "I think we should take the stairs. I don't want to be stuck in a glass box if phantoms come."

"Now there's a happy thought," Freddie murmured.

They both looked at Sebastian. He gave a reluctant nod.

"Can you make it, grandmother?" Ava asked.

"Of course I can," Calindra replied tartly, but sweat beaded her face. The temperature was rising. Freddie's copper hair stuck to his brow in damp curls. The stench of spoiled food, with undertones of something worse, made Sebastian's stomach roll.

I'll carry her if I have to, he thought grimly. It's only thirty flights.

He'd started for the swinging doors to the kitchen when Freddie grabbed his coat sleeve. Hardin followed his gaze to the floor-to-ceiling window on one side. It faced a wide veranda with a swimming pool beyond. The dark waters reflected a strange orange glow, which is what had caught Freddie's attention.

In the skies above, an airship was burning. It seemed to fall in slow motion, trailing banners of flame. The nose of the ship pointed down, but the gondola was intact. Sebastian could see light through the portholes. All those people . . . .

He stood transfixed as it crashed in a fiery explosion somewhere in the city below.

"Mother of God," Freddie breathed.

The distant wail of sirens shattered the silence.

"Change of plans," Hardin snapped. "We'll take the train. It's parked three levels down."

Ava nodded. She seemed surprisingly composed. "How do we get there?"

The kitchen's service door led to a labyrinth of corridors hotel guests never saw. Hardin managed to snag a harried red jacket long enough to get directions to the stairwell that led down to the platforms. Twice they met phantoms. Calindra spoke to them in a pleading tone and the haints drifted away.

She leaned heavily on his arm by the time they reached a large waiting room with wooden benches and a four-sided clock above the central ticket booth. Boards on the wall announced arrivals and departures. Half a dozen slot machines were sandwiched between the men's bathroom and a shoeshine stand. There were a few pieces of abandoned luggage, some with the contents spilling out, but no signs of violence.

The place was deserted. Sebastian relaxed a little. He'd come down to the train several times to check in with Ned Carver and Elzy Mack. It was parked on a private track adjacent to the elegant waiting room Braga reserved for his personal guests.

Hardin hustled the Carnarvons inside. Calindra sank down on a burgundy couch. She looked ashen, though she sat with a straight back, hands folded in her lap. Ava sat next to her. Freddie made directly for the bar and knocked back a shot of whiskey.

"The ice is melted," he said glumly, peering into a bucket.

"I don't care," Calindra said. "A glass of water first, please, Freddie."

Her grandson obliged. Hardin shook his head when Freddie held up the bottle, but the women both had a stiff belt of whiskey.

"I never realized Lee was so . . . so *angry*," Calindra said. She looked at Sebastian with hollow eyes. "Why would he punish those people? Perfect strangers. It makes no sense."

"I'm not surprised," Ava declared. "I always said he was dangerous."

"Grandmother's right. I don't understand why he let us live," Freddie said. "We were sitting ducks in that theater. But he let us go."

"Maybe he had something worse in mind," Ava said. "I hope to God they shot him."

Calindra gave a brittle laugh. "Lee was the only savant of his generation. I used to regret that. Now I'm thankful."

Freddie drained his glass and set it on the bar. "Well, I suggest we leave before the truth comes out. Only problem is we'll need phantoms to run the train."

Hardin nodded. "I have an idea about that. There's one I can be reasonably sure hasn't turned. Doc."

"The one in Cortez's gun?" Freddie hazarded.

"Sebastian is right," Calindra said. "Lee was never able to influence him." Her face darkened. "I couldn't either."

Hardin turned to Freddie. "Will you go see if the engineer's aboard? It's parked on Track Four. I'll head back up. We can't leave Cortez and Tanaka. They're both in the infirmary."

Ava stared at him. "Do we have time for that, Sebastian?"

"Doc doesn't listen to anyone but Ruth. And I'm not abandoning them. It'll take me ten minutes at the most."

Ava looked ready to argue, but Hardin's stubborn expression seemed to make her think twice. "Fine," she said coldly. "Ten minutes."

Hardin caught Freddie's eye. "Let's go."

They left the women in the private waiting room. It was eerily quiet in the main station.

"Sure you don't want me to come with you?" Freddie asked. "I'm a linguist. Maybe I can be of help if you run into trouble."

Sebastian shook his head. "I want everything ready to go as soon as we're back. If the train's sustained any damage, better you discover it now."

Freddie shot him a doubtful look. "I'll try."

Hardin peeled off to the elevator bank. He jabbed the button, wondering if he should take the stairs. The lights were still flickering, though the complex hadn't lost power. Not yet.

Phantoms ran the turbines, but Braga's engineers had built huge underground copper-zinc storage batteries that would hold for a while. If it cut out while he was in one of the lifts . . . .

But the infirmary was on the sixteenth floor. It would take forever to climb the stairs and he'd promised Ava to be back in ten minutes.

Maybe the Gorras had put a bullet between Merriweather's eyes. But maybe they hadn't. Maybe he was looking for the Carnarvons right now.

Hardin stabbed the button again. A car finally arrived — mercifully with no phantoms. He stepped inside and pressed the button for sixteen. A corona of light shimmered in the corner of his right eye, though there was no pain yet. He prayed the migraine would hold off long enough for him to get everyone safely out of Aguadulce.

The floors crawled past. Finally, the doors opened on the infirmary. Sebastian stepped out of the car. The first thing he noticed was a splatter of fresh blood on the floor. It had fallen in droplets, almost straight down. Not a bullet wound. No, this looked more like a nosebleed. It led to one of the elevators and disappeared.

He ran down the corridor. Tanaka's bed was empty. So was Ruth's. Someone had set her loose.

"Well, thank God," Sebastian muttered. "Now where the hell did they go?"

22

"COME BACK!"

Tanaka's voice faded as I yanked the stairwell door open and barreled into a hallway on the fourteenth floor. It looked like the regular part of the hotel. Room numbers flashed past as I ran to the bank of elevators. I slammed my hand down on the button. When I looked back, three of the red-jacketed guards were running my way. Tanaka hobbled behind.

"Cortez!" she called. "Just hold up!"

I was about to run again when the bell dinged. The ornate bronze doors opened. I leapt inside the car without looking — and crashed straight into two Gorras.

Each grabbed one of my arms. The doors slid shut. The car descended. I twisted and writhed, but they were both big men and they held me fast.

"Just relax, now," one of them said with a fixed smile. "Don't make it harder than it needs to be."

I didn't much care for their eyes. They reminded me of the nurse. I quit struggling and peered down through the glass wall. I could hear distant shouts below, though we were too high to see much.

"What's going on?" I asked. "What's happening in the lobby?"

They didn't answer.

I went limp and made a retching sound. "I think I'm going to be sick. They gave me something. Oh, boy…."

Their grip didn't slacken, but the Gorra to my right shifted his weight just enough for me to slam a knee between his legs. His breath burst out in a whoosh. From the corner of my eye I saw a gun coming up. I awkwardly knocked it away. Glass shattered. Hot wind blew into the car. The one I'd kneed was curled in a ball on the floor, gagging. But the other gave me a hard shove. I stumbled back and hit the waist-high handrail. Air blew up through the back of my gown. The Gorra hooked a foot behind my ankle, trying to flip me out through the broken glass.

Terror made me claw at his face. He jerked back, bleeding and cursing. I dropped to grab his partner's gun just as he lunged forward. Momentum carried the Gorra straight over the rail. He fell silently down to the lobby below. He didn't even scream.

I scrabbled away from the edge, heart beating so fast I thought it might burst. The other Gorra was up on hands and knees. I yanked the gun from his holster and pointed it at him, but I didn't shoot. I couldn't do it. He was just a pawn.

"Stay away from me," I panted. "Or I'll kill you, I swear it."

He stared at me with blank eyes. Then he banged his fist down on a red button. The elevator jerked to a stop. The lights dimmed and went out.

"Dammit," I muttered. "What'd you do?"

I tried all the buttons. The panel was dead.

Dammit, dammit, dammit. That gun would've come in handy if I found Roger, but I'd need both hands to escape and madwomen apparently didn't get gowns with pockets. I opened the cylinder and shook the bullets into my palm. I threw them out of the hole in the glass. The gun went next.

It wasn't pitch dark. I could see the Gorra, sitting against the wall. He watched with that same dead stare as I forced my fingers into the crack and pried at the door. It inched open. I finally got it wide enough to wedge my back to one side and used my legs to push all the way.

I nearly sobbed when I saw the second door above. We were halfway below another floor. My fingers were bruised, the nails ragged and torn, but I could reach it. With a furious burst of energy, I forced it open six inches. Then ten. Light poured in. I was hauling myself up when a hand closed on my ankle. I kicked out blindly and heard a grunt. Arms trembling, I hoisted myself the rest of the way.

I rolled to my back, panting. The lights flickered. I heard a strange slithering, rattling sound in the shaft, followed by a thunk on the roof of the car. A second later, I realized it was the cable snapping.

This time, the Gorra screamed on the way down.

LEE'S EYES OPENED. Planks of rough, unfinished wood stretched six feet above him. His head hurt. He touched an ear and felt dried blood.

Somehow, he'd ended up on his back underneath the gallows. Lee crawled out to the wings. He spotted the towel Henry had used to wipe cream pie from his face and used a clean corner of it to scrub the white greasepaint off. For some reason he couldn't explain, it felt important to do this right away.

I don't want to be the Grim Creeper, he thought foggily. What I want is a glass of water. Ice water, so cold it beads the glass.

The red carnation in his lapel was crushed. He absently

slid it out from the buttonhole. Lee couldn't remember anything after Henry dumped the washtub over his head, but his clothes were soaking wet so he couldn't have been knocked out for long. He dimly recalled the lights going out. A flash of pain in his skull . . . .

When he saw the theater, his mouth went even drier.

Something had happened. Something bad.

Wallpaper dangled in strips like flayed skin. Broken glass littered the red and gold carpet. A chandelier had smashed down across the center seats, but he saw no bodies.

There was blood, though. Plenty of that.

The theater was deserted.

Lee walked in a daze down the stairs and out to the lobby. The doors stood wide open. Shoes and bits of clothing littered the ground. He stopped, lightheaded. The phantoms must have gone crazy. But Henry said he'd worked with them for years. What could have provoked them? And who had dragged Lee under the gallows?

He raised a shaking hand to his forehead. Henry, maybe. *He was trying to protect me. Oh God, don't let him be dead.*

Lee stepped through into the casino. Even in the middle of the night, there were always people gambling. He'd come down a few times when he couldn't sleep. The tables never closed. But the casino was equally deserted.

Whatever had happened, it spilled over into the hotel. Slot machines tipped on their sides, spewing tokens. He saw more blood, though not as much as inside the theater. Playing cards were strewn everywhere. It looked like a whirlwind had blown through.

The X. Had to be.

Time to run, he thought, adrenaline starting to pump. *Far and fast.*

Lee paused at a whimper from behind one of the slots. He cautiously approached. A woman and small boy cowered in the narrow space between two machines. She had her hand clamped over the child's mouth. They both looked terrified. Lee crouched down.

"Hey," he said softly. "I won't hurt you. But you can't stay here."

She hesitated, then took his hand. Lee hoisted her up. He lifted the boy and set him on his feet. The child stared at him, hiccuping. His mouth was smeared with chocolate.

"What happened?" Lee asked. "Something hit me on the head."

"Phantoms," she whispered, eyes darting around. "We'd just bought ice cream. They started tearing the place apart." Her voice caught. "Hurting people. I saw . . . ." She glanced at the boy. "It was horrible."

He frowned. "Phantoms? Like more than one?"

She nodded.

"Any idea why?"

"None. We were on our way to play ninepins when it started." She tucked a strand of sweat-damp black hair behind her ear. "We almost went to the show, but Manny wanted ice cream instead. Thank God we didn't. I think it started in the theater." She shuddered. "I heard people screaming in there."

"We'd best get you out of here," Lee said. "Come on. I speak a few tongues."

"You're a linguist?" she asked hopefully.

Lee nodded. "I'll keep you safe, I promise."

They made their way to the main lobby. A small crowd filed out the exit doors under the watchful eyes of the Guardia Territorial. Lee looked around for Henry, but didn't see him. They joined the queue.

"Where were you when it happened?" the woman asked.

Lee opened his mouth to reply when he heard a shout. A man was pointing.

"Oh my God, it's him!"

Heads turned. Most people looked confused, but a few stared at him in shocked recognition. Lee stood there, dumbfounded, as the Gorras dove behind the reception desk. More stood outside, beckoning frantically for the line to move. The crowd at the lobby doors surged to get away from him. A potted palm tipped over with a crash. The woman he'd escorted out of the casino snatched up her child. She stared at Lee, a sick expression on her face, then darted into the milling crowd.

Lee held his hands out. "Listen! You've got it wrong. I didn't—"

The Gorras behind the desk started firing.

Lee ran. Bullets droned past his head. One nearly parted his hair. He threw himself around the corner of the gallery leading to the shopping arcade, heart pounding.

"What the hell?" he muttered.

A chill ran down his spine.

They think I did it.

Wild scenarios ran through his mind. Maybe it wasn't the X at all. Would Calindra go so far to destroy him? She'd been in the audience. So was Pedro Braga, though Lee dismissed him immediately. Braga had no earthly reason to trash his own hotel and murder his own guests. Lee lingered on Calindra, though. Maybe she'd started something that got out of hand.

Of course, there were actually *three* savants in the theater, besides Lee. They were Henry's phantoms, after all. But what could he possibly have to gain? And Lee still didn't see why anyone thought it was *him*. He'd been unconscious for most of it.

Lee peeked around the corner. The guards were regrouping, shouting to each other. He circled around, back toward the casino, broken glass crunching underfoot. If he found a phantom, maybe he could make it talk.

Or maybe it would just kill him.

Lee decided not to risk it. He found one of the mirrored doors leading into the service corridors and used his key to open it. He needed to get out of Aguadulce. The only question was, airship or train? Lee had watched Mr. Beach at the controls. He thought he could fly a zeppelin himself. But if he got caught on the roof . . . .

Lee headed down.

If he couldn't steal a train, at least he could get out through the tunnels. He pelted through the corridors and found a stairwell. There were no sounds of pursuit.

At least Mr. Beach was already gone. Lee tried to stay calm, not to give in to the panic that clawed at his chest. But the terror went deeper than just being blamed for all those deaths. Phantoms were all he had. In truth, Lee felt more comfortable in the company of haints than he did with people. He'd been talking to them since the cradle. In all those lonely years at the academy, it was the phantoms who'd kept him company. For Calindra, being a savant was about the power it gave her. But for Lee, it meant he had friends.

Friends who always came when he called. Who never treated him like a freak of nature.

If they'd turned on him, what was left?

Maybe it's not all of them, he thought desperately. It *can't* be all of them. I just have to get away. Far away.

He burst into the main train station. The clock in the center of the waiting room had stopped at six minutes after eight. Lee stood beneath it, catching his breath. He looked at the archways leading out to the platforms, each with a different track number. Did it matter which one he chose? They all went somewhere. Lee had just decided on lucky seven when he heard the patrician voice of Calindra Carnarvon.

It was faint and coming through a half-open door. Lee knew he should keep going. Hardin might be in there, too. But he had to know.

Did she do this to me?

He crept up to the door and peeked though the crack. Ava

Carnarvon was pacing up and down. Calindra sat on a couch, a glass cradled in her hands. To Lee's relief, they were alone.

"He said he'd be back in ten minutes," Ava said angrily. "It's been twenty!"

"I'm sure he'll be here soon," Calindra replied. "I'm more concerned about your brother. I just hope he didn't do something foolish."

"You're too hard on Freddie," Ava said. "You always have been."

"Freddie makes his own choices," Calindra replied icily. "He's a grown man, even if he rarely behaves as one."

"That's not fair. You treat him like a child. You treat all of us like children! If you only gave us more responsibilities within the company—"

"Responsibility is *earned*. Look at Richard. Look at all he's accomplished despite his infirmity."

"If you'd ever given Freddie a single word of encouragement, he might have turned out more to your liking," Ava said bitterly. "But at least he's loyal to the family."

Lee rolled his eyes. As much as he wouldn't mind confronting Calindra right there, it seemed like a stupid idea. If Hardin was coming back, he intended to be long gone. He started to turn away, but Ava's next words froze him in his tracks.

"You invested everything in Merriweather and look what he did! You created a *monster*. We should have killed him when we had the chance."

"Ava." The tone was sharp. "That's enough."

"I always knew Lee was trouble. It's why I—" She cut off abruptly.

There was a fraught silence.

"Why you what?" her grandmother asked softly.

"Nothing." Lee detected a panicky edge to Ava's voice.

"Why you *what?*"

Lee flinched at the compelling tone. He'd endured it

plenty of times himself. When the younger woman spoke again, her voice was a dull monotone, the words coming slowly as if dragged from her lips. "Why I took matters into my own hands. Someone had to."

Calindra rose and stalked toward Ava. She towered over the younger woman by several inches. "Clarify," she snapped.

Ava looked up at her defiantly. "I hired someone to find him. In case Sebastian failed."

"*Who?*"

Ava gripped her skirts. Her mouth worked, fighting to stay shut.

"Who? Speak, girl!"

"The Reverend Jolly," Ava burst out. "He came to me right after Lee ran away. He said he'd catch him for a bounty. I told him about the bunker under the city. He was supposed to bring Lee there."

Calindra's green eyes blazed. "And then what?"

"Then we'd make him cooperate." Tears shone in Ava's eyes. "Lee was supposed to protect us. That was his job. And he abandoned us!"

"Does Freddie know?"

Ava stared at her grandmother without replying.

"I'll take that as a yes," Calindra said coldly. "My God. Did you know Jolly murdered all those people in New Jerusalem?"

"Of course not! But it doesn't change anything."

"You stupid, stupid child." Calindra's voice was a whip crack. "You could have destroyed everything I hold dear. Everything I've built—"

"I've protected it!" Ava cried. "Can't you see that? It was never Merriweather we had to worry about. I realize that now. It was the Class X! But it's ours now. It will protect us from the others. Keep the phantoms in line."

Calindra recoiled. "What are you talking about?"

"I've spoken to it." Spots of color burned in Ava's cheeks.

"Why do you think it let us go tonight? Spared us? That was the new bargain! Give it Lee, and we gain control of Aguadulce and the rest of the Southern Territory."

"You spoke to it?" Calindra stared at Ava in astonishment.

"Grandmother, please." Ava laid a hand on her grandmother's arm. "Hear me out. What's done is done. Lee will take the blame for everything that happened here. But he doesn't matter anymore. We have an X! We can do whatever we want. It promised me—"

"*Promised* you?" Calindra said scornfully, shaking her hand off. "You're an even bigger fool than your brother if you think you can control that thing. People died tonight! Does that mean nothing to you?"

"Every war has its casualties. *You're* the one who taught me that, grandmother."

For the first time, Calindra looked old. Lines of disappointment creased her mouth. "What about Richard?"

Ava scoffed. "He's too busy in his laboratory to see the bigger picture. He hasn't a clue."

"Well, thank God for that. At least I have one heir left."

"What?"

Calindra turned away. "You're dead to me, girl. You and your brother both."

Ava stiffened. "You can't—"

"Watch me. As soon as we're back in the city, I expect you to leave the tower. I don't care where you go."

"But I . . . ." Ava shook her head in denial. "Please, don't do this. It was a mistake. I promise you, I'll never—"

"And you'll take nothing but the clothes on your back. Be grateful it isn't worse. When Sebastian learns what you've done, he'll want to arrest you. I'll wait to tell him until after you're both gone. The man has a temper."

Ava stared at her grandmother's back with loathing. She looked wildly around the room. Her gaze fell on a heavy cut-glass ashtray. Ava snatched it up.

Time seemed to slow. She raised it high and stepped toward Calindra.

"Hey!" Lee yelled before he could think too hard. He rushed into the room. The ashtray crashed down on the back of Calindra's head. Lee caught her as she crumpled. Ava dropped the weapon and backed away. She was breathing hard. Lee watched with growing panic as Calindra's pupils dilated and fixed on the ceiling. Her fingers spasmed, then relaxed and lay still.

"*You son of a bitch.*"

The voice was low and tight with rage.

Lee turned. Sebastian Hardin stood in the doorway.

"He killed grandmother," Ava screamed. "Oh my God!"

Lee raised his hands.

They were covered in Calindra's blood.

23

I TOOK the stairs down to the casino. Tokens spewed from the slot machines, but no one stopped to pick them up because the place was empty.

Whatever Roger had planned, it was already happening.

I felt sorry about the two Gorras. It wasn't their fault. The poor men were just carrying out orders they couldn't refuse. To my relief, I didn't meet any more security on the way. I didn't want to hurt anybody else if I could help it.

I passed the posters for Doctor Deathless and made my way into the theater. It was like walking through a nightmare, the kind where awful things are happening and you can't do anything about it, but you can't wake up, either.

And you know the worst is still to come.

My mouth was dry with fear as I stepped through the doors. I hadn't a clue how to stop him. But I somehow knew he'd be waiting.

Roger sat cross-legged on the stage. The red greasepaint around his mouth was smeared, making his grin even more ghoulish. His eyes shone like a cat's in the blackened sockets.

"Ruth! You made it." He glanced at the bloodied aisles.

"Well, you missed the opening act," he amended. "But you're just in time for the grand finale."

I stood there, swaying on my bare feet. Wishing I had my own diabolical plan. But I was fresh out of ideas.

"What'd you do?" I swallowed. "Is everybody . . . ?"

"Dead? Not yet. And I didn't do a thing. It was all Merriweather." He chuckled. "At least it sure looked that way to the audience."

"What did you *do*, Roger?" I demanded again.

"Why, we put on a show. It just wasn't the one they expected."

"Where's Lee?"

"He skedaddled. Just left a minute ago. You might have caught him if you'd been a tad quicker." Roger sighed. "I'll admit, I'm disappointed. Most of the cast ran off when it started. No loyalty. But enough stuck around to get the ball rolling." He winked. "I told you I had some twists and turns in store. See, Aguadulce is a big sandcastle and I'm the incoming tide."

"Like Hazardville," I said.

"Sure, except it won't be fire. The Gorras are mobilizing in their garrison." The phantom stared at the far wall and my skin crawled. He was looking through it to the city beyond. "New Jerusalem was a test, Ruth. To see what I could make people do."

"I thought you said that was all the reverend."

"He's a good soldier," Roger replied absently. "But he has other work to do now. I'm letting the Gorras round up everybody in the stadium. Then I'll stop by and give the order to finish it off. By the time the Gorras are done, there won't be a soul alive. Then they'll turn the guns on each other." He chuckled. "All down but nine. Well, two. You and Lee. I'm counting on you to spread the word, Ruth."

I felt a wave of despair. "Where's Doc?"

"Right here." He opened his jacket and drew the Collier.

"Safe as houses. He won't be coming out to play though. Not anytime soon." Roger's face brightened. "I have an idea. How about a game while we're waiting?"

That sounded dire. "Can I ask you something first?"

He aimed the flintlock at me and mimed shooting. "Fire away."

"Did you kill Henry Chance? Or did he never exist at all?"

Roger smoothed his blonde hair. "Henry's a figment of my imagination. See, I came here not long before you did. It was easy to talk my way to Mr. Braga. By the time I was done with him, he thought he'd known me for years."

"Then why are you doing all this? You could have whatever you want just by asking."

Roger covered a yawn. "I thought you understood me, Ruth. I wanted a challenge. But enough about that. *I want to play a game.*" There was a new, whiny edge to his voice.

"What is it?" I asked wearily.

"Ever heard of Phantom Roulette?" He flipped open the barrel of the flintlock and nodded to himself. "See, there's only one bullet inside. And this is a six-shooter." He spun the barrel and snapped it shut with a flick of his wrist. "Is the bullet in the chamber?" He chuckled. "Well, who knows?" He held the gun out. "Come on up here, Ruth. Join me!"

I stared at him.

Roger laughed. "Come on. It's not a trick, I promise."

I climbed the stairs to the stage and walked over to him, skirting a puddle of pink goo that looked a bit like bubble gum.

"Go on," he urged. "Take it."

I reached down and took the gun. Then I pointed it at his head and thumbed the hammer back. If he was here in the flesh, maybe I could do some damage.

"Aw, come on," Roger drawled, holding his hands up. "You're not really going to shoot me, are you, Ruth?"

I pulled the trigger. The hammer fell on an empty chamber.

Roger hooted. "Now we're talking! Your turn."

I lowered the gun.

"You're supposed to put it to your head now. Fair's fair." He studied me. "Come on, Ruth. Doc won't let you get shot. Give it a go."

"No."

If Doc was in there, if he had any control, he would have made sure the bullet was in the chamber when I shot Roger. I knew that for a fact.

Roger's smile vanished. "Then I'll torture him."

He crooked a finger and a black shadow oozed from the gun. Roger gathered it into a ball and squeezed his fist. Doc screamed. It was a weak, pitiful version of the scream I'd heard in the infirmary, but it still cut me like a knife.

"Stop!" I begged. "Please stop. I'll do it."

"Good." Roger opened his hand. The shadow puddled on the ground. Cowering.

I cocked the gun and pressed the muzzle to my right temple. Before good sense could prevail, I pulled the trigger.

Click.

"Told you," Roger said. "Try it again."

"Your turn," I said, my voice shaking with hatred as I aimed the gun at his face.

Click.

"Well, that's three," Roger remarked. "It's getting exciting now." He laid a finger along his nose. "You know what I'm picturing, Ruth?" The phantom spread his arms wide. "Nine horsemen. The meanest sons of bitches you ever met. I'm talking the absolute dregs of the Northern Territory."

His eyes had a misty, faraway look. "Jolly and Mr. Cage riding in the van. The sun setting behind them. And they will cover the earth in ashes, starting with Lucky Boy since it's on the way to Carnarvon City. How does that strike you for a third act?"

"You're crazy."

He shook his head as if waking from a daydream. "Where were we? Oh yes, it's your turn."

I raised the gun to my temple. My hand was trembling. Roger watched with a merry light in his mad eyes.

"Two bullets left," he said. "Fifty-fifty chance."

I cocked the hammer. I thought of Marshal Hodges. The red ruin of his face.

"I'm rooting for you, Ruth." Roger's teeth shone white against the crimson paint. "Come on, this is more fun than Old Maid, you have to admit."

He knew I'd played cards on the train.

How?

Because he was watching from the ether.

Sweat trickled down my face. He knew everything about me. All that talk about sparing me . . . . I could see it in his eyes. This was just part of his game.

But he wasn't in the ether now. He was here. In the flesh.

I swung the barrel around. Roger's eyes widened. Before he could react, I pulled the trigger.

Click.

The gun tore from my hand. It flew across the theater. Without seeming to move, Roger stood in front of me.

"That's cheating," he said softly.

He stared at my chest, his gaze intent. A crawling sensation came over me.

"I can see your heart beating, Ruth," he said with revulsion. "It's disgusting."

"Don't," I whispered. "Just hold on minute."

"It was *YOUR TURN*," he roared. "If there's one thing I detest, it's a cheater."

I backed away. Roger followed. "I'm disappointed in you, Ruth," he snarled. "Sorely disappointed."

Something hard pressed into my back. The shadow of a crossbeam with a noose stretched long across the floor. The platform for the gallows.

"*Pitter patter, pitter patter,*" he said in a childish, sing-song voice. "Do you want to see your own heart? I'll show it to you."

Roger reached out a slug-pale hand. Then he staggered as something crashed into him from the side. It was the little phantom girl from the train, the one with the white streak in her hair. Roger grabbed her by the scruff of the neck, shaking her like a terrier with a rat. She kicked and spat. He growled something in a phantom tongue and she growled back.

"Leave her alone!" I yelled.

"Shut your mouth," he snarled.

My lips clamped together. His hand sank into her stomach like he was reaching through water. The girl's form wavered. I saw a flash of something else behind it, something strange and alien. She made a grunting sound. Roger squeezed his fist and I heard a wet *pop*. The little phantom clawed at him. A coat button flew off. Beneath Roger's jacket, he wore a leather sheathe at his belt.

My sheathe.

And in that sheathe was *my* Bowie knife.

I still couldn't utter a syllable. But he'd made a mistake. He should have told me to *stay*.

I threw myself forward and yanked the knife free. Roger spun around, face twisted in rage. Before he could move, I drove the six-inch blade into his foot with all my strength. It went straight through, sinking deep into the floorboards. I'd expected to hit bone, but the knife pierced him easily. Like cutting through gelatin.

Roger screamed. Red-hot needles jabbed my skull. It sounded like a grizzly being stung by a swarm of wasps. I hung on for dear life while Roger thrashed and gibbered. The bit I'd pinned to the stage wasn't a foot anymore. It was a chunk of throbbing pink flesh with weird purple strings running through it.

"Ruth!" Doc hollered, his voice tight with pain.

I looked around wildly.

"The gun's over here!"

A shadow capered against the wall under the box seats. I let go of the knife and half-fell off the stage, the revolting carpet squishing under my toes as I rushed over to Doc. Behind me, Roger howled in fury. One arm had sprouted tentacles and they were wrapped around the knife, trying to pry it loose from the boards. His flesh bulged around the blade, oozing that pink goo. I fell to hands and knees, groping frantically under the seats. My fingertips brushed a walnut grip. The flintlock.

I grabbed it and thumbed the hammer back.

Roger looked up at me, lips pulled back in a red snarl. His tentacles flexed. The knife came free just as I took aim and fired the last bullet. It hit him dead between the eyes. Roger shimmered like a heat mirage. For an instant, I thought I saw something behind him, a whirling twister of pure darkness. The ground lurched under my feet. A wave of vertigo hit me. The next thing I knew, my cheek was pressed against the carpet.

"Get up, Ruth!" Doc's shadow stretched across me. "Shake a leg!"

"Quit yelling in my ear," I groaned. "You okay?"

"No, I am not. Roger gave me a real licking. I hurt all over."

"Me, too." I sat up. The room spun like a carnie teacup ride, then righted itself. The stage was empty. "Did I kill him?"

"Probably not, but he's gone for now. We have to get to the train, Ruth. I'll fire up the engine, just run!"

"I have to find Hardin." I crawled over to the Collier, which had slid down the aisle. "And what about Lee?"

"Never mind Lee. He wasn't harmed." Doc hesitated.

"And I don't think you want to be with him when he's caught,
Ruth. Roger set him up to take the fall for everything. Just get
moving!"

"What about that little haint? She saved my life——"

"She's gone, Ruth! If she's alive, she'll hide from him."
Doc's voice rose to a screeching pitch that hurt my ears. "But
you need to run, unless you want to wait for him to come back
and finish you!"

"Okay, okay." I wished I had some more bullets. "What's
the quickest way to the train?"

I DIDN'T PARTICULARLY CARE to ride in an elevator again, but
Doc insisted it was the fastest way down and he'd make sure it
didn't break down or fall. I found the closest lift, which was
out in the casino by the slots, and hit the button for
sublevel F.

"What *was* he, Doc?" I demanded, bouncing on the balls
of my feet. "What are *you*?"

I glanced at his reflection in the glass. He looked terrible,
pale and dazed, but when he spoke, his voice was all silky.

"You know, Ruth, maybe we should take the zeppelin
instead. There seems to be an altercation below. It would be
wiser not to get involved——"

"What altercation?" If he'd had a body, I would have
grabbed him by the necktie. "What's happening? Haints?"

"Not haints."

"What then?"

Doc winced. "Lee's down there. And Hardin."

The doors slid open to a large waiting room. Archways
with track numbers led off on both sides.

"Wait!" Doc cried as I stepped off the elevator.

"For what?' I snapped.

"Don't get involved. I can promise you, it won't end well."

I wearily squared my shoulders. "That's what I'm worried about. Where are they?"

"Ruth—"

"Look, Merriweather's an idiot, but he ain't responsible for this mess. I need to explain who is."

Doc's reflection glared at me from the glass ticket window. "Hardin's not going to listen."

"Yes, he will. I'll make him."

"You don't know— Dammit, Ruth!"

The place was deserted, but muffled sounds came through an open door. I ran over, gown flapping around my bare legs. It was some kind of private waiting area. Ava stood in the corner. She had a tiny, satisfied smile on her face. Just a few feet away, her grandmother lay in a spreading pool of blood. Ava didn't seem to notice. Her eyes were locked on Hardin, who was beating Lee like a dusty rug.

"Stop it!" I yelled.

Ava's head turned. She saw me and the smile wiped right off her face. She donned an expression of horror but it was too late. I'd seen her. And Ava knew it.

Lee groaned as Hardin delivered a knee to the ribs and followed it with a roundhouse that sent him spinning like a top. Lee crashed into the wall. Hardin grabbed his coat and popped him again. Lee's head snapped back. Blood gushed from his mouth.

I doubted Merriweather had ever been in a fistfight in his life, but it wouldn't have saved him even if he'd been a heavyweight champion. Hardin's self-control was gone. He didn't acknowledge my shout. I'm not sure he even heard it. He was completely focused on Merriweather.

Only one thing would drive him off the deep end. He thought Lee had killed Calindra. If I hadn't seen Ava, I might have wondered, but I knew the truth.

And I knew that if someone didn't stop him, Hardin would beat Lee to death right in front of us.

They were on the ground now, Hardin sitting astride Lee while Lee tried to shield his face. I launched myself at Hardin's back and tried to pull him away. He shook me off like a flea. His knuckles were bloody, but he showed no sign of slowing down.

I cocked my gun. The sound finally got his attention.

Hardin slowly lowered his fist. He was panting hard. He looked up at me and I recoiled at the expression on his face. Like a wild beast.

The barrel wavered as I aimed it at Hardin's chest. I gripped the butt with both hands to steady it.

"He's a murderer," Hardin growled.

"Just let him up," I said, trying to keep my tone calm even though my own heart was racing.

We stared at each other for a long minute. Hardin rose to his feet, his eyes locked on mine. I saw anger and hurt and a terrible grief. Merriweather rolled over and spat out a tooth.

"Lower the gun, Ruth," Hardin said tightly. "You have no idea what you're doing."

"Run, Lee," I said, putting some snap in my voice.

Lee didn't even look at me. He pushed to hands and knees. Then he crawled to a couch and used it to stand. He was swaying on his feet. I feared he'd collapse right there, but I didn't have any bullets left and I wouldn't have shot Hardin even if the marshal called my bluff.

From the way Hardin eyed Merriweather, that wasn't far off.

"RUN!" I shouted, giving Lee a shove toward the door.

His long legs started hobbling. Hardin took a step after him and I got between them, my gun pointed at his chest. He swore, but didn't try to follow. Lee vanished around the corner, leaving a bloody handprint on the door jamb.

"She only had a few months left!" Hardin raged. "Merri-weather stole that from her. She was going to let that little bastard walk free and he killed her—"

"What?" Ava interrupted, her face white. "What do you mean, a few months left?"

"Calindra was dying," he said brokenly. "She didn't want you to know."

Ava tilted her head. Her eyes lost focus, then sharpened again. "Oh my God," she sobbed. "I can't believe it!"

"Don't pretend you care," I said coldly. "You wanted him to kill Lee, didn't you? Tie up the loose ends—"

Ava rounded on me, pure rage on her face. "She's unstable, Sebastian. Arrest her."

I stared at her with disgust. Her chin raised defiantly. "Well, it's true," she said. "Look at you."

My wrists were raw from the restraints. Blood spattered my gown, which, judging by the breeze up my backside, had fallen open in the back. I lowered the gun.

"I'm more sane than you are," I said. "You're going to prison for the rest of your life, Ava. I bet Lee saw you do it. When he's done testifying, you won't see a penny of your grandmother's fortune."

She shook her head in wonder. "How dare you speak to me like that? My family *built* your town. You're nothing but a hayseed with a tin badge—"

I stepped forward and punched her in the face. Ava dropped like a stone. She fell across the couch and didn't move. Hardin stared at me like I was a stranger. He seemed to have aged ten years.

"Get out," he snarled. "Just go. You have a ten-minute head start. I'll give you that, Ruth."

"Listen to me. It was all Roger—"

"Enough! Not another word." He looked down at Calindra. Then he knuckled his right eye. He was crying, but it was more than grief. He was in the grip of a migraine.

Everything I needed to tell him stuck in my throat. Doc was right. He wouldn't hear a word of it. Not in this state.

"Come with me," I pleaded, holding out a hand. "Before she wakes up. You have to trust me on this. *Please*."

I saw a brief struggle on his face. Then duty won out, as I expected it would.

"I can't do that," he said grimly.

"Hardin—"

"I made a promise to Calindra and I mean to keep it." His face set. "Lee killed her. And *you* let him go."

"No, Ava killed her," I said, getting angry myself.

"That makes no sense at all," he snapped. "You weren't even here. Lee was the one who . . . ." He bit off the words. "Just get out." His blue eyes burned. "Go! Or I *will* arrest you!"

I stood there for a moment, tears pricking at the back of my own eyes. Then I walked away.

When I turned back at the door to the platform, Hardin was kneeling next to Calindra, cradling her body in his arms.

24

I RAN DOWN THE PLATFORM. I felt like a load of bricks was poised over my head, but I wouldn't let it come tumbling down. Not until I was far from here.

The train sat parked at the end. Freddie stood on the steps of the observation car smoking a cigarette. He looked up as I came near.

"I couldn't find the engineer," he said ruefully. "Mr. Mack must have taken off. I figured I'd wait around in case he came back. Glad Hardin found *you*, though. We can't leave without a phantom to run it." He grinned. "Not that we'd have deserted you. I mean, my sister wanted to, but Hardin wouldn't have it."

"Get off the train, Freddie," I said.

He looked me up and down, taking in my disheveled state. "What?"

I aimed the gun at him. "Get off the train. And get your hands up."

Freddie took a pull on his cigarette. He squinted at me through the smoke. "Have you lost your mind?"

I laughed, and it must have sounded totally unhinged

because he jammed the cigarette in his mouth and raised his hands.

"I'm jacking this train," I said, gesturing with the revolver. "And you're in my way."

Freddie came down the stairs, eyeing me warily the whole way. When he reached the bottom, he tried out a grin. "This is some kind of joke, right?" he asked out of the corner of his mouth.

"Nope. Your sister just killed Calindra and she'll order Hardin to kill me if I don't go," I said. "So I'm going."

Freddie stared at me, his face draining of color. The cigarette fell from his lips. Then he turned and ran down the platform for the waiting room.

I climbed up the ladder and fell into the driver's seat.

"Doc," I said wearily. "I know you're rough around the edges, but I need your help now. We have about two minutes left before they come for us, if Hardin keeps his word."

It was quiet and I feared Doc had gone too far into the ether to hear me. But then a weak reflection appeared in the side window. For once, his face was solemn. Sympathetic, even. He didn't even say *I told you so.*

"Where to?" he asked.

"North," I said. "Just take us north."

Water hissed in the boiler. Steam piped through the cylinders and up into the firebox. The pistons started cranking. Doc tooted the horn and we rolled out of the station, gathering speed in the tunnel.

I stared through the cab windscreen, too numb and heartbroken to thank him. It wan't fair to blame Hardin, but I did anyway. He should've given me a chance.

The law meant nothing, I realized bitterly. Not when the people in charge were evil. And Ava Carnarvon was evil. Hardin wasn't, but he worked for *her* now.

That was the moment I lost my faith. I didn't trust anyone but Doc. And even he had lied to me.

We rounded a tight curve and I saw a pale figure in the beam of the headlight, staggering along the tracks not thirty yards ahead. It startled me out of my wallowing.

"Stop the train!" I yelled, bracing my palms on the control panel.

Metal squealed on metal as Doc hit the brake lever. Sparks flew through the darkness. Lee Merriweather crouched in the beam, his arms around his head. The wheels locked up but the train was still skidding forward on the track. Lee stumbled backwards. The cowcatcher stopped a foot short of him.

I stuck my head out the window. "Merriweather," I called in a shaky voice. "You okay?"

Lee let his arms fall, blinking in the light of the beam. His face was a mess, both eyes swollen nearly shut, but he grinned at me through busted lips.

"Where'd you get the train, Ruth?"

"Found it lying around." I climbed down the ladder, which ended right over the front left wheel. It was a tight squeeze, but I made it around onto the track.

"Uh-huh." Lee bobbed his head. "Well, you sure are a sight for sore—" The rest was cut off as I hauled back and punched him in the face. Not as hard as I'd hit Ava, but hard enough. Lee landed on his bottom. He stared up at me in disbelief, cupping his nose.

"That's for being a complete—" And here I said some words I'd never said out loud before. Every single one I knew, just strung together. It shocked him into silence. I stood over him, breathing hard. I would have given him a worse licking if Hardin hadn't already done it for me.

"Just get on," I snarled, turning my back and climbing back up the ladder.

After a minute, Lee scrambled to his feet and followed, muttering beneath his breath. The train started rolling again. I strode back to the observation car and sat down on a couch. Lee followed, keeping a safe distance.

"What was that for?" he demanded, gingerly touching his nose. "I didn't kill her. It was Ava. I didn't hurt anybody!"

"Maybe not," I said. "But if you'd just left like I told you to, none of it would have happened. Not like that, at any rate. When are you gonna learn, Lee? Everything you do just turns to . . . to pig manure!"

He hunched his shoulders. He looked like a stork with a broken wing. I felt a small stab of pity.

"There's water in the kitchen," I said. "Go clean your face."

Lee shot me a glare, but he stood and limped toward the back of the train.

"That was a nice left hook," Doc said approvingly. "I think you found the one spot Hardin missed."

I could see him reflected in the window, brown hair springing up like a jack-in-the-box. His saucy grin slowly died as I stared at him, unblinking.

"Why don't you come on over here in the flesh?" I suggested. "Maybe I'll test out my right hook."

"Well now, if I could appear in the flesh, I wouldn't be in this predicament, Ruth," he replied sourly. "But that's what the binding does to a soul. I'm afraid a reflection is the best you'll get."

"Too bad. Since you lied to me and—"

A shout from the galley sent me running to the dining car. Lee was standing there with a frying pan. Ned Carver pressed against the far wall, blinking in confusion.

"Deputy Cortez?" he whispered. "What's going on?"

"I figured you went back to Carnarvon City," I exclaimed.

Ned shook his head. "Mr. Hardin told me to wait on the train. I was sleeping in my compartment until we started moving." He looked at me and then Merriweather. "Who's this? You two been fighting?"

Lee lowered the frying pan. "She punched me in the face," he said. "For no earthly reason."

I stared at Ned. "You must be a pretty heavy sleeper."

He shrugged. "Where's everybody else? Where's Mr. Hardin?"

Just hearing his name brought that weight an inch closer to crushing me. I still wasn't sure if I'd betrayed him, or he'd betrayed me. A little of both, maybe.

"A lot's happened, Mr. Carver," I said. "But first . . . meet Lee Merriweather."

Ned's face froze. He made a strangled sound.

"Let's all go sit down," I said. "It's a long story."

"BY GOD," Ned said when I was done, my throat hoarse from talking. Lee had told his piece, too. Everything tallied with what Roger had said, and what I'd suspected. Darkened desert flashed past the windows, though I could still see the faint glow of Aguadulce behind us.

All my clothes were back at the hotel, but Ned had lent me a clean shirt and pair of trousers. He did the same for Lee, though Merriweather was a lot taller and I had to look at four inches of hairy ankles sticking out of the cuffs. Now we sat in the dining car, cupping mugs of hot coffee.

"I can't believe I slept through all that," Ned said. "Poor Mrs. Carnarvon. Are you sure Miss Carnarvon . . . ?"

"I was standing right there," Lee said flatly. He looked ill at the memory.

"Dang. And Mr. Hardin thought it was you?"

"I can't really blame him," Lee said in a grudging tone. "Guess I would have thought the same thing. I had her blood all over me."

Ned looked nervous. "What if they think I helped you? I mean, I feel terrible for the mess you're in, but I don't want to hang."

"Don't worry, we'll let you off somewhere," I said. "They

can't blame you for being aboard. Just say we tied you up." A sudden thought made me turn to Lee. "What about Mr. Beach? I clean forgot about him."

"He left town before the show. With luck, he's already far away."

"Well, I'm glad for that," I said. "I always liked the professor."

"Hey, you want a steak for that eye?" Ned asked Lee. "They gave us a whole bunch on ice."

"Sure," Lee said gratefully. "I'll take some of the ice, too."

"Comin' up," Ned said, bounding to his feet. He looked glad to get away from us for a minute. Lee shot me a sidelong look.

"What happened after I left?" he asked cautiously. "I'm surprised Hardin let you go."

I stared into the dregs of my coffee. "Don't want to talk about it."

"Would you really have shot him?"

"'Course not."

Lee looked a little disappointed.

"I didn't have any bullets left, anyhow," I said.

"Why didn't you just tell him about Roger?"

"He wasn't gonna listen."

"Yeah, maybe not." Lee leaned back. "How'd you know I didn't kill her, Ruth?"

I looked at him. "I just knew."

"How?"

I sighed. "Because you're not a murderer. And I saw Ava's face, before she saw me. She wasn't upset at all. She was enjoying it."

Lee frowned. "Why are you smiling?"

"I punched her in the face. Boy, it felt good."

He rubbed his jaw. "Anyone you *haven't* punched today, Ruth?"

I flexed my fingers. They were still sore. "Doc," I replied

after some consideration. "But only because it's physically impossible."

"I'm right here," a voice muttered from the ether.

"Good," I said tartly. "Hey, if you're here, who's running the train?"

"I found some haints."

"What?" I sat up. "How can you trust 'em after what happened?"

"Relax, Ruth. These are ones that ran away. They're just as scared of Roger as I am. They won't hurt anybody. They didn't even want to come. I had to beg." He sounded put out.

"I still don't like it," I said.

"Well, you're free to have an opinion. But I'm tired. The time I spent with Roger was not pleasant."

"What about the little girl?" I asked. "The one that saved me. You know what happened to her?"

"Afraid not."

Lee frowned. "Did she happen to have a white streak in her hair?"

I stared at him. "That's the one. How did you know?"

"She came to me, too. Tried to get me to leave before the show." Merriweather sighed. "I should have listened."

Cool night air blew through the window. I pulled my leather jacket tighter. I'd found it right where I left it when Hardin and I headed into New Jerusalem, hanging over the back of one of the chairs. It looked wrong without the copper star, though even if I still had it, I didn't deserve to wear it anymore. I was a lawbreaker now. There'd be no going back, not ever.

But I knew one thing that was going to happen before I finally went to my compartment and fell into bed.

The Class X phantom called Doc was going to tell me everything, even if it killed the both of us.

25

NED CARVER CAME BACK with a steak for Lee's eye and some ice wrapped in a dishcloth. Lee slapped the steak on the left side of his face, the ice on the right. He propped his elbows on the table to hold them in place.

"You all hungry?" Ned asked. "I could whip up some bacon and eggs."

"In a minute," I said. "But you're welcome to stay for the interrogation. You have as much a right to know as we do."

Ned tipped his hat back, eyebrows quirking. "Interrogation?"

"Well, Mr. Carver, this phantom is about to reveal the greatest mystery of our lives. You want to hear it?"

"Sure." Ned sank into a chair.

"What," Doc said in a low tone, "is the meaning of this?"

"I want the truth," I said. "All of it. Time's past for prevarication, Doc."

"Well, well. Aren't you fancy?"

"I'm serious. Show yourself."

His reflection appeared in the window, lounging at the table across the aisle. "You won't like it."

"I didn't expect to," I said. "Let's start with this. *What are you?*"

"A Class X." He sighed. "There, I said it. Go ahead and crucify me."

The blood pounded in my ears. I picked the gun up and held it next to the open window. Doc's eyes narrowed.

"I didn't ask what we named you. That's just a . . . a made-up phrase! It means nothing at all. I asked what you really *are*."

"Your brain can't fathom it," he said sullenly.

I dangled the gun out the window. "Should I drop it?" I snarled. "Should I drop it right now?"

"Dammit," Doc exploded. "Fine! I'll try."

Lee and I leaned forward in our seats. Ned watched with interest. I wouldn't have thrown the Collier away, but Doc seemed to believe I might.

"Go on," I prompted. "Spill the beans."

My money was on ghosts, but I was ready for anything.

Doc steepled his fingers. "Where to begin? Okay, let's start with the ether. It's just space, but it's a higher level of space."

I wasn't about to admit that he'd already lost me.

"Uh-huh." I waved the gun. "Keep going."

"Remember how I said it was like a picture show? Well, that's what you look like to us. Flat." He riffled the deck of cards. "Like these."

Lee frowned. "I read a paper once about higher planes. Is that what you mean?"

"Bingo." Doc sounded surprised. "By any chance, was this paper written by Gael Lopez?"

Lee nodded slowly. "Yeah, I think it was. I didn't understand most of it, but I got that far."

Doc gave me a smarmy smile. "He's Ruth's father. Changed his name to Cortez when Calindra exiled him to Lucky Boy. If our Ruth here had an ounce of curiosity, she might have read one of them herself. But she'd rather devour trashy dime novels—"

"They *ain't* trashy," I said through gritted teeth.

"Your father taught at the academy?" Lee asked me in astonishment.

"Yes, but I'm not getting sidetracked telling you the whole story." I stabbed a finger at Doc's reflection. "That's what he does. This, right here. He's an expert at steering conversations into the wilderness. Not this time. Let's get back to the planes."

"How many do you occupy?" Lee asked, his voice a little muffled from the steak.

"Five," Doc said. "Uno, dos, tres, cuatro, *cinco!*" With each number, he sent a playing card flying.

I leaned over to Lee. "How many do we live in?" I whispered.

"Three," he whispered back.

Doc was examining his fingernails and smirking.

"Oh, the heck with it," I exclaimed. "What are the three? Just tell me."

If Lee had been patronizing, I might have hit him again, but he nodded excitedly. "You already know, Ruth, you just take it for granted. Planes are a way of describing the space around us. You have up and down, forward and back. Left to right."

"Well, yeah," I said.

"And each one is at right angles to the other one."

"Okay." I was still following, more or less. We'd done geometry at school.

"So a fourth plane would be at right angles to every other plane. The same for the fifth."

"Yeah." I nodded. Then I shook my head. "Nope. I can't see that."

"Told you," Doc muttered.

"Of course you can't see it," Lee said. "But you can guess

at what our world might look like for his kind. Just imagine it, Ruth. If you saw a world projected on a screen, well, you could touch different parts of the screen without passing along the plane of the screen itself. Now imagine you could pick things off the screen and move them from one place to the other, because you're standing in front of it. It would look like magic to the people living in the screen, right? Objects would appear and disappear without seeming to move through space."

I frowned. "I think I can picture that." I turned to Doc. "So what do you call the other, uh, directions?"

He glanced up. "Voonwise and flenwise. Does that help?"

"No," I said.

"So the phantoms are beings from another plane," Lee said softly. "How about that." He grinned at Ned Carver. Ned shrugged and smiled back.

"*Higher* beings." Doc yawned. "I guess the hard part's out of the way. What else do you want to know?"

"How come you couldn't just tell me that?" I asked. "It's not like you're demons from Hell."

Doc rolled his eyes. "Our parents said we couldn't. That it would upset you too much. Your little brains might break."

"Give us a bit more credit," I said. "Hold up. You really are kids?"

"Most of us." A haughty note entered his voice. "Roger and I are older."

"Like teenagers? That explains a lot," I muttered. "Where are your parents?"

"Busy," Doc said vaguely.

"Doing what?"

"Just leave it," he snapped.

"Okay, okay." I wanted to keep him talking. "So all this time we've been exploiting children." I looked at Lee. "That feels wrong."

Doc started laughing. "You misunderstand, Ruth. Your

world? It's like . . . ." He cleared his throat. "Well, it's like a toy chest. We come here to play. When we run out of things to do at home."

I sat back. "You're right. I don't like that."

"Me neither," Ned said. He'd taken it all calmly up to that point. Now a frown creased his forehead.

"So we're . . . *dolls*?" Lee sputtered.

"I did not use that word," Doc said defensively. "I did *not* use that word."

"You might as well have," Ned said.

"Look, we're careful not to break you," Doc added, which didn't help. "Most of us, anyhow."

I crossed my arms. "So your friend Roger came here to play with his *dolls*, and now he's bored and ripping their heads off. Is that about the size of it?"

"More or less," Doc conceded.

We were all quiet for a minute.

"Well, that's a real kick in the teeth," I said.

"I'm sorry," Doc said. "I really am."

"You should be. How could you be friends with someone like that?"

I stared at his reflection. Doc shifted awkwardly.

"I used to be different. But like I told you before, being bound changes a person. I don't see you as . . . toys . . . anymore."

"I guess that's a start," Ned said.

"Well, how long have you been bound?" I asked.

"Twenty-three Earth years. Since the tornado leveled Three Bars."

It seemed like an awful long time. "Doesn't anyone miss you? I mean, why haven't they come looking?"

Doc was quiet for so long I regretted asking. Maybe he didn't have anyone.

"Time passes differently for us," he said at last. "Twenty

years for you is just a few weeks in my world. Roger made it look like I ran away."

"Ran away from home, you mean?"

"Not home." His reflection shifted so I couldn't see his face. "I'd rather not talk about it right now."

Doc sounded so forlorn, I relented. "Well, maybe Roger's dead," I said. "Maybe I killed him."

"Doubtful," Doc said.

"Why? I hit him in the head."

"No, you hit a teensy part of him, Ruth."

The weight came down on me then. I wondered how many people had died in Aguadulce and how many more would die when Roger came back. If Mrs. Carnarvon had been alive, I might have gone to her. Something told me she would have given me a hearing. But it was all such a mess now.

"Poor Calindra," I said, glancing at Lee. "She wasn't the nicest person, I know, but it's still awful. I wouldn't have wished that on her."

"Me, either," Lee muttered. "Ava's the one who put the bounty on me. I heard her admit it. Calindra was furious. Threatened to cut her off, her and Freddie both."

"That lying . . . ." I trailed off, fists balling.

"The twins have been in league with Jolly all along," Lee continued. "That's how he knew where the underground bunker was. Ava must have told him about it."

I remembered that day at the academy. I'd always wondered how the reverend knew to go to Mr. Beach's house. Ava must have called him when she told me she was getting security.

"But why?" I wondered.

"Roger promised her all kinds of things. And now she's in charge." Lee sighed. "Her and Freddie."

An unpleasant thought occurred to me. "I bet she'll want

Richard out of the way. And she's got the full weight of the marshals behind her. No one will believe us."

"We'd better stay away from Carnarvon City," Lee said. "Where's safe?"

"Nowhere," Doc replied glumly. "Roger's hurt, but when he's done licking his wounds, he'll be looking for us."

"I do know one thing," I said. "Where the reverend is. Roger sent him up to the Northern Territory."

"Then we'll go south," Lee said immediately.

I turned to him. "Go ahead. But Roger said they planned to stop in Lucky Boy. So I'm going home. Least I can die with my family and neighbors."

Lee's face fell. "I'm sorry, Ruth." He stared down at his hands for a minute. Then he exhaled a sigh. "I'll go with you, if you'll have me."

I stared at him in surprise. "What for?"

"I'm doomed no matter what I do," he said lightly. "Might as well be a thorn in your side for a while more."

Doc coughed. "That's awful sweet," he said. "But I have a better proposal."

"Let's hear it."

"Well, we *could* go to Lucky Boy and sit there waiting for the hammer to drop. Or we could go straight up to the N.T. and throw a wrench in Roger's plans. He's a bully and you surprised him. We might have a little time before he gets the courage to come back."

"Hunt down the reverend and Cage, you mean?" I asked slowly. The idea was not without some appeal. At least they were human. If I could bring a measure of justice to the people of New Jerusalem, I'd have accomplished something before Roger ended me. And maybe, just maybe, I could stop them before they got to Lucky Boy.

"I might just do that," I said. "You in, Merriweather?"

Lee swallowed. "I'm in."

I considered what I knew about the Northern Territory. It wasn't a whole lot.

"The N.T. is big," I said. "They could be anywhere."

"Not anywhere," Lee said. "In square miles, yes, it's vast. But most of that is unsettled wilderness. There's only a few towns of any size. The reverend will be in one of them. Especially if he's recruiting."

"It'll be winter up there."

I'd heard the stories. Snow as high as a roof. Frosts so hard the sap burst in the trees.

"Then we'll steal supplies," Lee said.

I sighed. "Doc, is there any chance we could get help from some other X's? I mean, the older kids? There must be some who don't like Roger. They could give him a licking."

Doc shook his head. "They're scared of him. Besides which, they don't come here anymore. Your world . . . well, most of us grow out of it, you know?"

I thought of a dollhouse gathering dust and shook the image off.

"Maybe you could try calling into the ether for that little girl. I want to make sure she's okay, but she also had the guts to stand up to Roger and we could use some allies."

"I can do that," Doc agreed.

I thought about her for a minute. She'd saved me twice, once on the train and again in the theater. The kid was brave. I remembered the awful popping sound I'd heard when Roger reached into her body.

"So that blobby pink stuff, it's what you're made of?" I asked.

Doc's mouth pinched. "You're made of blobby pink stuff, too," he shot back. "It's just covered by skin."

"I mean, how come you look the way you do in that reflection? Like a person?" I asked. "At the end, Roger grew tentacles. Do you have tentacles, too?"

"I have my own parts, thank you very much. And I do not refer to them as *tentacles*."

"What do you call 'em?"

"There's no point in telling you words that mean nothing," he replied in a weary tone. "You can't picture the real me and that's that. What you're seeing now is a projection." Doc tapped his forehead. "From my mind, Ruth."

"Then you *can* do magic," I said triumphantly.

Doc mumbled something. I caught the words *superstition* and *tiny brains*.

"Look, even when phantoms are here in the flesh, they're only partly here," Doc said. "The rest is in our world. In the planes you can't see. But if we allowed you to glimpse just that little bit of our true bodies, you'd run screaming. It looks like—"

"Pink blobby stuff with purple strings," I interrupted. "Yeah, I saw that already."

"And no one would want to play with *that*. So we just project a different picture. One you can comprehend."

"And children are the least threatening," Lee put in shrewdly.

"Yes," Doc admitted. "Though the little ones can never get the eyes right."

"Where's *your* body?" Lee wondered.

"Roger stuffed me inside a penteract." Doc stared at me, a smile dancing at the edges of his wide mouth. I stayed stubbornly silent. "That's a hypercube, Ruth. It has thirty-two vertices, eighty edges and eighty faces." He paused. "It's not very comfortable, but I've gotten used to it."

"Can we break you out?" Lee asked.

"It's inside the gun. But you can't just open it. Not without the key. And I don't know where he hid it." Doc's tone was light, but I felt sorry for him.

"I'll help you any way I can," I said quietly. "That sounds awful."

He gave a forced laugh. "It's not so bad. At least you found me. I'm not alone anymore."

"No, you're not," I said with feeling. Lee nodded. I patted the gun. "I'll take good care of you, Doc. Until we find the key."

Doc looked away, but I think he might have blushed if phantom mind-projections did that. "Thanks," he mumbled.

"Back to business," I said briskly. "I guess we're going up to the N.T. I don't see much choice. We're the only ones who know what's happening and we're wanted criminals now. Except you, Ned."

Ned Carver gave me a faint nod. He'd been very quiet and I could see he was chewing over all he'd heard. At least I had the advantage of knowing Doc for years. Lee was accustomed to phantoms, too. But for Ned, I imagine it was a lot to take in. I was still struggling with it myself. Especially the dollhouse part. Then he surprised me by saying something sensible.

"You still have a big problem," Ned pointed out. "All the tracks north go through Carnarvon City."

Lee smiled. "That's why we'll switch our mode of transportation."

"I'm not stealing anything else," I said firmly.

"We don't have to. The zeppelin Mr. Beach took isn't back in Aguadulce."

I stared at him.

"Well, come on. We could hardly land an airship with Carnarvon colors on the roof of one of the hotels. That would have raised too many questions. Mr. Beach set it down in the desert and we walked out. Took a bus into Aguadulce from a town called Tres Colinas. It's up ahead." He shrugged. "I was headed there when you almost ran me down."

"What about the train?" I wondered.

"I'll have a couple of the youngsters keep it going," Doc said. "Except we won't be on it."

"How much farther?" I asked Lee.

"A few hours." He stood. "Come on. I want to show you something before we get there."

"What? I'm tired."

"You'll see."

I followed him to the caboose. Lee went out to the little balcony. He started up a ladder leading to the roof.

"Where are you going?" I called after him.

He looked down, his cheeks flushed from the wind. "Come on, Ruth!"

"I ain't going up there," I said.

"Why not?"

"Because we're moving at thirty miles an hour and I don't fancy getting killed."

Lee climbed the rest of the way and stood up. Ned's shirt whipped around his thin frame. It made me dizzy to look at him. "Last chance," he said. "Unless you're scared."

I muttered under my breath and started up the ladder, clinging to the rungs with a death grip. The roof of the train was about twelve feet across and gently rounded. When I reached the top, Lee was already on his back, looking up with his hands laced behind his head. I crawled over.

"This what you do for fun?" I muttered.

"Best view in the world," he said.

I pulled the jacket tighter around me. There wasn't a single light, just the endless dark of the desert and the sky above. It was a moonless night and the stars were brighter than I'd ever seen.

Was Doc's world up there somewhere? Or did it exist alongside ours in some way I couldn't understand? I tried to picture voonwise and flenwise. Directions at right angles to every other direction. It made my head hurt.

I glanced over at Merriweather. He didn't look smug or arrogant or any of the other expressions I'd grown accustomed to. For the first time, he looked peaceful. The train chugged along, rocking gently to and fro. I slowly relaxed.

"Well," I said. "I lost my morals and you found yours. I expected you'd do another runner, Lee. Didn't take you for a hero."

He met my eye, then turned away. "I thought it would be different," he said softly. "More fun. It was, at first. I never planned for it to go so far. I just wanted to see the outside." He sounded wistful. "See how normal people lived. Eat a fancy dinner in a nice restaurant. Have some ice cream from that little place by the tower."

"Fanny's Fountain."

"That one. So I did. And I was on my way back to the academy when I passed the train station. A wild idea took me, that I could go see the Northern Territory before I went home, but the marshals followed. Guess you know the rest. One thing led to another."

"Would you take it back if you could?"

His face hardened. "No. Only trusting Henry Chance. That was stupid."

"Well, Roger's a savant," I said. "Don't blame yourself."

"Thanks, Ruth." I felt him looking at me sidelong. "So you think I'm a hero?"

"Sure," I said. "It takes courage to go after the Reverend and Mr. Cage. They scare me and I don't scare easy."

"No, you don't." He held up a bony wrist and flexed his fingers. "Wish I looked the part, though. I never liked myself much."

That surprised me. "You have a nice face," I said stoutly. "I mean, when it's not beaten to a pulp."

Lee scowled. "I don't want to be *nice*."

I laughed. "Why not?"

"I'm serious, Ruth. I always wanted to be dark and handsome like Hardin."

Hearing his name cut me to the bone. "Well," I said. "At least you're taller."

The stars blurred. To my relief, Lee let the matter drop. He might be a savant, but he knew when to shut up.

Tres Colinas was a sleepy little town about four hundred miles north of Aguadulce. We blew through the station without stopping, but a few minutes later, Lee told the phantoms running the boiler to slow the train to a crawl. He sat up in the engineer's cab, studying the scenery. We were passing through badlands like the ones around the border, with twisting canyons and hills of wind-worn rock.

Lee suddenly leaned forward and growled at the haints. We slowed to a stop.

"The airship is hidden back in that gully." He pointed to a pile of stones next to the tracks. "See the marker we left?"

"So this is it," I said, turning to Ned. "The haints will take you on to Carnarvon City."

He glanced at the shadows hovering by the boiler. "I've been thinking. And I'm not so sure it's a good idea."

"They won't hurt you," I said. "They aren't the ones that did Roger's bidding."

"It isn't that." Ned gave me a level look. "It's Miss Carnarvon. If she did kill her grandmother, wouldn't she figure you told me so? I mean, even if I say I was hijacked, she'll wonder what I know."

"He's right," Lee said. "If Ava thinks Mr. Carver's a threat, she'll get rid of him."

"Hardin wouldn't let her do anything to you," I said.

Ned Carver snorted. "No? I like Mr. Hardin, but he does what they say. That's his job."

I bit my lip. "I'm sorry about all this."

"You didn't know I was on board. Point is, I can't go back. But I do have some cousins up in Lovelock. I don't know 'em well, but they'd take me in. Maybe you can just drop me there. I'll figure things out."

"We're being hunted by a Class X," I said slowly. "I can't promise he won't show up. Lee and I are both fugitives now. Poor company for a nice fellow like you."

Ned fiddled with his hat. "Well, as to that, I know you, Miss Cortez, and I count you a friend. Think I'll take my chances."

I smiled at him. "Then we're glad to have you, Mr. Carver."

"Call me Ned."

"And you call me Ruth."

"Lee," Lee said, extending his hand with a grin.

"All right," Ned said, shaking his hand. "I'll fetch my things."

"You got a shaving mirror?" I asked him.

Ned nodded. "Sure do."

"I'd like to borrow that, if you don't mind."

Ned headed for the galley. I heard him clattering around.

"What else are you taking, Ruth?" Lee asked me.

"Just ammo. And my sunglasses. Hey, Doc?"

His shadow stretched out beside me.

"Can you ask the young 'uns to move some water and food to the airship? Just enough for a few days. Plus any extra clothes and blankets." I paused. "Maybe a couple of shotguns, too. And a crate of that Winchester double-ought."

Doc flitted off. I felt better having stolen a few hours sleep in my bunk. I'd even taken a bucket bath and found a pair of Hodges' boots that were only a size too big. The Collier sat in a holster at my hip. I'd taken it from Hardin's compartment. It had his initials burned into the leather. I felt bad stealing from him, but it was the only one I could find.

"How do I look?" I asked Lee.

He studied me for a minute. "Honestly? Like death warmed over." Merriweather had lost a canine tooth on the upper right. He probed the gap with his tongue. "What about me?"

"Like you got thrashed to an inch of your life."

He started to laugh, but it turned into a pained grimace. "A fine pair we make."

I curled my arm into his. Lee looked surprised, then pleased.

"Come on," I said. "Show me the ship."

We hiked back into the canyon. The zeppelin was waiting just where Lee said it would be, set down on a flat stretch of ground with the cables secured to wooden pegs pounded down with mallets.

"It was Mr. Beach's idea," Lee said. "Said there was no point keeping it with the Carnarvon colors and all. He wanted me to give it back."

"How?" I wondered.

"I'm not sure." Lee smiled. "Anonymous letter, maybe? We never got that far."

"I hope he's all right."

"I'm sure he is." Lee sounded like he needed to convince himself this was true. "He went to see his sister. She lives by the ocean."

I studied the zeppelin. It was one of the small, fast models. "So you really think you can fly this thing?"

Only Merriweather could manage an arrogant grin with two busted eyes and a fat lip. "Course I can, Ruth. Child's play."

When everything was stowed away, he fired up the screw that turned the propeller. We rose out of the canyon, the nose of the airship pointing north. I watched the train, emblazoned with Carnarvon Lines in blue and gold script, start chugging north again. With any luck, by the time they figured out we'd switched to the zeppelin, we'd be too far gone to catch.

It was a small ship so quarters would be tight. I put my leather jacket and ammo in a corner of the oval gondola. Ned pressed his face to the window, enjoying his first ascent in a zeppelin. Once we'd leveled out, I found the shaving mirror and propped it on a table. A second later, Doc's reflection appeared. It was the clearest I'd ever seen him.

He had hazel eyes and a dusting of freckles across his sharp nose. His hair was unruly as ever. He seemed to be wearing a pair of red flannel underwear of the kind they called a Union Suit.

"Well," I said, sliding into a seat. "Ain't this cozy?"

"You need to reload the Collier," he said crisply. "And oil it. Roger was neglectful."

"All in due time. I got some questions first."

He huffed in exasperation. "What more could you possibly ask?"

"I don't know, only about a million things. What's your real name?"

He made a sound like a goat regurgitating a tin can. Ned Carver looked over in alarm.

"How 'bout we just stick with Doc?" The haint nodded and I made a mental checkmark. "Next question: Do you have a head?"

Doc scoffed. "Obviously."

"What it's look like?"

"Like a head."

"Like my head?"

"Obviously *not*."

"How's it different?"

He paused, his expression deadpan. "I've got four noses."

"Now you're messing with me. Are you a man?"

"That's a rather personal question."

"Why?"

He heaved a sigh. "We have six different genders."

I considered that. "Do you have six you-know-whats, too?"

Doc stiffened and I chuckled.

"You are foul-minded, Ruth Cortez," he said.

"Just curious. You never answered that one, but I'll let it go for now. Do you have plants and trees and animals where you live?"

"Make her stop," Doc growled.

Lee and Ned paid him no attention. Their heads were bowed over a game of pinochle.

"Fair's fair," I said sternly. "You know all about me. You can look in my stomach and see what I ate for breakfast. I'm just trying to get a handle on things. Now, I was thinking, if you live on five planes, maybe there's creatures that live on seven or eight planes. How do you know you're not *their* toys?"

I laughed and slipped my dark glasses on. "Wouldn't *that* be a kick in the teeth?"

26

When dawn broke over Aguadulce, not a single phantom remained inside the city limits. There was no electricity. No air conditioning. No trains, buses or trams. The hotels sat dark and empty, the temperature inside a sweltering ninety-nine degrees.

Only the zeppelins were running and there weren't nearly enough to ferry everyone out. Anxious crowds stood in long lines at the football stadium under the watchful eyes of the Guardia Territorial. No one knew why the grims had stopped their rampage — or when they might come back. Every time a zeppelin touched down, it was all the Gorras could do to keep people from breaking through the barriers and swamping the landing pad.

Sebastian Hardin was in too vile a mood to spare them much thought. He waited with Freddie and Ava atop the Bella Luna as their ship was flown in from an aerodrome on the outskirts. Calindra's body lay in a glossy black coffin near the gangway. Every time Sebastian looked at it, he felt a wave of unreality. She'd always been larger than life, a brilliant, ambitious woman with a will of iron. If she was more feared than loved, that was the price of what she'd built. Sebastian was one of the few to know her softer side.

He never should have left her alone.

"You look exhausted," Ava said, laying a tentative hand on his sleeve. "How's your head?"

She wore a black dress and black hat with a veil that did little to conceal her spectacular black eye. Sebastian wondered where she'd managed to find mourning clothes in the midst of the wreckage. She'd even located a pair of black lace gloves.

He still wore the tuxedo he'd borrowed from Freddie. It was a creased, rumpled mess. His knuckles still bore traces of blood. Looking at it gave him a sick satisfaction.

"I'll live," he muttered.

Pedro Braga had already come and gone. Henry Chance was missing and presumed dead. Braga still didn't know Lee Merriweather had been trained by the Carnarvons, but he was launching an inquiry. The truth would come out and Hardin wanted to be long gone when it did.

He'd managed a few hours of fitful sleep in a darkened room, but the migraine lingered, a dull hammering in his right temple.

Freddie leaned against the wall, silently smoking a cigarette. He'd hardly spoken a word since he'd burst in and seen Calindra's body. Sebastian had feared he'd faint on the spot. Then Ava had stirred and Freddie ran over to her. He hadn't looked at his grandmother again. Ava had sobbed uncontrollably in his arms, but Freddie himself was dry-eyed and subdued. Maybe it wasn't surprising given the rocky relationship he had with Calindra.

Sebastian had barely been functional by that point. He'd thrown up in a wastebasket and collapsed on the couch in the waiting room. The pain had never been so bad. Even the slightest sound was like glass shattering inside his head. The worst had finally receded, enough for him to make it to the top of the Bella Luna. Now he just wanted to sleep for a week.

Sebastian looked up as the elevator doors opened and two Gorras appeared with a handcuffed Abel Beach. The professor looked disheveled, the sleeve of his coat torn along one seam. He glared at Hardin, who glared back.

"We found the man you asked about, Mr. Hardin," said the first — a captain, judging by the bars on his shoulder. "He was about to get on an airship. Tried to run when we pulled him off the line."

It had been a risk asking Braga's own men to look for him, but the professor knew everything. Hardin needed him in custody before Braga figured that out. So he'd made up a story. Beach was wanted in Carnarvon City for passing bad checks. A marshal had seen him in one of the casinos and recognized him. Middle-aged man with distinctive dreadlocks. Armed and dangerous. It was a long shot, but if any of the Gorras spotted him among the evacuees, Hardin would be much obliged if they delivered him into custody.

Sebastian hadn't expected Beach to turn up, but now he had at least one thread tied to Lee. Merriweather had come back for his mentor once. Maybe he'd do it again.

"Excuse us for a moment," Ava said to the captain. She dragged Hardin to the side.

"You should have consulted me first," she snapped. "*I'm* in charge now. Me and Freddie."

Sebastian felt a surge of anger. "I didn't think you'd object."

"Grandmother granted him amnesty. She told me so herself."

"He's Merriweather's accomplice. Beach might know where he went. Or even what he'd intended." Sebastian stared at her. "How can you possibly consider letting him go?"

For a moment, Ava looked as if she might do exactly that. She hurried over to Freddie and whispered in his ear. Freddie shook his head. They argued in fierce whispers. Freddie scowled and stabbed a finger at Beach. The captain waited, looking uncomfortable.

Sebastian silently stewed. The last thing he wanted was questions about Abel Beach. Finally, Ava composed herself and came back.

"Thank you for sparing the men," she told the captain with a cool smile. "I know the Gorras are hard-pressed keeping order. We'll take custody of him now."

Hardin nodded at two of the marshals who had come with the Carnarvon party the day before. They stepped forward and waited while the Gorras removed the handcuffs.

"Hold him at the gangway," Hardin instructed his marshals, praying Beach would keep his mouth shut.

The way Hardin saw it, the professor was in deep trouble either way. If he made a fuss and ended up in Braga's hands, things might go even worse for him. Abel seemed to agree, because he kept silent as the marshals escorted him away.

"Mr. Braga sends his regrets," the officer said. "He wished to see you off personally, but there is so much to attend to."

"We understand," Ava said smoothly. "Please extend our sympathy for his losses."

The captain bowed. "Most certainly. And please accept ours for your beloved *abuela*. Rest assured we will find Mr. Merriweather."

Hardin shook hands with the captain and watched him walk to the elevator. The moment the door closed, he rounded on Ava. "We need to leave. Before they start wondering what the hell *that* was about!"

Ava arched an eyebrow. Sebastian reined in his foul temper. Calindra would've had his head for speaking like that.

"Apologies, ma'am," he said stiffly.

"Accepted." She glanced out the window. "Relax, Sebastian, the ship is here."

The enormous nose cone filled the glass. It glided up to the mooring mast, which sat atop a structure resembling a lighthouse. Cables winched tight, securing the ship in place as the gangway was extended to a gap in the rigid airframe. Porters began to load the valises and steamer trunks — most of which belonged to Ava.

"What were you arguing with Freddie about?" Sebastian eyed her closely. "If you know something, I'd like to hear it."

Ava sighed. "I merely thought we should honor my grandmother's final wishes. What could Beach possibly tell us? He wasn't even there. But Freddie took your side." She tossed her head. "Honestly, I don't care. I just want to go home."

"That's all?"

"That's all." She sighed. "My God, stop looking at me like that, Sebastian. You're right. We'll lock him up and throw away the key." Ava shot a look at Freddie. "Put that cigarette out. You can't smoke on board and we're about to leave."

Her brother ground it into an ashtray. "The queen is dead," he murmured. "Long live the queen."

Ava pretended not to hear. She lifted the veil. Tears brimmed in her eyes. "It's time, Sebastian. Would you help bring Calindra's coffin aboard? I think she would have wanted that."

He nodded, his own eyes stinging. "Of course."

Sebastian joined three of the marshals. They each took a silver handle and carried the casket up the gangway, securing it in the hold. They boarded and the mooring rope was cast off. The gondola had eight large portholes set into curving wood-paneled walls. Deep carpets covered the floor. The lower level was arranged into separate sitting areas, with the sort of comfortable furnishings you might find in a library. Circular stairs led to sleeping quarters above.

Hardin took an armchair and stared out the porthole, watching Aguadulce dwindle behind them. Ava sank down across from him, tossing her hat and gloves on the table. "Thank God," she said. "What an ordeal."

Hardin glanced at her. "How soon can you spare me? I want to catch the trail while it's still warm."

"Trail?" Ava shook her head. "Oh, Sebastian. You won't be going anywhere. I need you in Carnarvon City."

He stared at her. "Merriweather killed your grandmother. How can you let that go?"

"I'm not *letting it go*. But we have other priorities. I'll need to settle the will and arrange for the funeral. I can't think beyond that yet."

"You saw what Lee did in Aguadulce. What if he comes to our city?"

The look she gave him was pitying. "And how exactly do you plan to stop him? No, cornering him is what led to this disaster. He panicked and lashed out. I won't make the same mistake."

"Merriweather's just a man. I could have killed him ten times over if I'd set my mind to it. Just give me a rifle and a clear shot—"

"Enough, Sebastian." Her gaze went flat. "You keep talking about Lee, but I wonder if that's who you really want to chase after."

He scowled. "Don't be ridiculous."

"They must be together," Ava pressed. "Ruth Cortez hijacked *our* train. At gunpoint! Maybe they planned to run away from the start."

"I doubt that," Sebastian muttered.

"You don't still have feelings for her, do you? After what she said to me? Those baseless accusations?" Ava's hand unconsciously went to her blackened eye. "She's a lunatic!"

"I'm not discussing this with you," he said, more roughly than he'd intended.

Ava twisted her gloves. "I'm sorry. Truly, I am. None of it's your fault, Sebastian. She had us all fooled. It must run in her blood. Her father was afflicted, too."

Gael Cortez taught at the academy in Carnarvon City

until he had a falling out with the Carnarvons. It was all before Ruth was born.

"Calindra told you about him?" Sebastian asked. He knew only the barest details.

Ava nodded. "Gael harbored bizarre ideas about the phantoms. They only grew worse with time. It's why she sent him to the frontier."

"What ideas?"

She laughed. "The sort of nonsense you'd expect to see at a midnight matinee. Pure science fiction."

Hardin stared glumly out the window. Before everything fell apart, he'd thought about taking Ruth to the nickelodeon theater on Ash Street. He'd walked past it almost every day for the last four years and never once gone inside. Ironically enough, the current double feature was *I Married a Phantom* and *It Came From Planet X*.

"My point," Ava continued, "is that madness often runs in families. In fact, there's a condition called dementia praecox. The onset is usually late teens or early twenties. One of the students at the academy suffered from the illness. He ended up in a hospital. It's characterized by exactly the sort of hallucinations and erratic behavior Ruth displayed." Ava sighed. "I feel sorry for the girl, but there's nothing we can do for her now."

Sebastian doubted Ava felt sorry for anyone but herself. "I'm not done talking about Merriweather," he said. "You can't order me to sit on my hands and do nothing."

The false concern slid away. "I think I can. With all due respect, you work for me now. Me and Freddie. Don't you, Sebastian?" She gazed at him anxiously. "Or do you plan to leave us?"

Promise me, Sebastian.

"Of course not," he said.

"Then I expect the same loyalty you gave my grandmother. I know you didn't always agree with her decisions, but you respected them."

Yes, I did. And If Lee had bashed *your* head in, Calindra would see him hang before she gave a thought to anything else.

Sebastian did not say this aloud, but Ava seemed to read the thought in his eyes. She reached across the table and laid a hand over his. Her fingers were icy.

"I swear to you, once things are settled, I'll see her killer is brought to justice." Ava glanced at her brother, who slouched in an armchair, staring out the opposite porthole. "Right, Freddie?"

Freddie turned to her. He stared at Ava for a long moment, his face expressionless. "Right," he said.

The tension between the twins was palpable. Hardin assumed it was because Ava had taken charge and was treating Freddie in the same condescending, perfunctory way their grandmother had. Maybe Richard would be a counterbalance. Sebastian certainly hoped so. He didn't relish the thought of appeasing three warring factions.

Sebastian looked up as Marshal Tanaka walked over. She wore a fresh bandage, but she was back in uniform and he was glad to see she wasn't limping anymore. "Miss Carnarvon," she said respectfully, nodding at Ava. "I'm sorry for your loss."

"Thank you, marshal."

Tanaka looked at Hardin. "Word with you, sir?"

"Sure." He rose, grateful to get away. He felt Ava watching as they climbed the spiral stairs to the small galley on the upper level.

Tanaka poured two cups of coffee. "Feeling better, sir?"

"It was just a headache," Hardin snapped. "Why does everyone keep asking me that?"

He knew he sounded defensive, but he'd managed to conceal the migraines for years before Ruth came along. Her mother got them too, and she'd recognized the signs.

"No offense meant," Tanaka said mildly.

"No," he muttered. "I'm sorry. Truth is, I've been meaning to talk to you. But I haven't had the chance."

She blew on her coffee. "I thought you'd want to hear what happened with Cortez last night. Because a few things are troubling me."

"Me, too," Sebastian admitted. "I went looking for you both. You weren't in the infirmary."

Tanaka nodded. "It wasn't long after you left. Maybe an hour or so. I was reading and I heard a scream. It was . . . eerie, sir. Never heard anything like it. So I went to check it out."

"Ruth was awake?"

"Yeah. She said it was her phantom, that he was in trouble. I felt bad for her, sir. Tied up like that." Tanaka looked a mite guilty.

"You let her go," Hardin said.

"I did, sir. She begged me to."

Dementia praecox. Madness runs in families . . . .

"Did she seem crazy to you?"

"No. Just upset." Tanaka paused. "I would have been, too, if they'd restrained me like that. And I'm telling you, I heard a scream. It wasn't Cortez." Her voice lowered. "I reckon it wasn't *human.*"

"Then what?"

"The nurse tried to stop us from leaving. Cortez knocked her flat. She seemed real wound up. She said something bad was going to happen and she needed to warn you." Tanaka frowned. "Here's the thing, sir. She turned out to be right. When I got down to the lobby, all hell had broken loose. But before that scream, it was quiet up in the infirmary. My door was open. I'd swear nobody came down the hall. Cortez didn't have any visitors. So how could she have known?"

Sebastian shook his head. "I don't know. Did she mention Merriweather?"

"No, but she did talk about a Class X."

The night before was a blur. He remembered seeing the aura — that always came first — and then the pain hit. By the time he'd walked in on Lee, the migraine had him in a vise. But he did vaguely recall refusing to hear a word of explanation from Ruth.

He'd never been so angry in his life.

I'm not wrong, he thought, a bit desperately. I *can't* be wrong. It isn't possible.

"I saw Lee order a phantom to kill Henry Chance," Sebastian said. "I saw him do all of it. Saw it with my own eyes! There was no Class X. They're pretty damned hard to miss." He scrubbed a palm over the day-old stubble on his jaw. "What happened after you two left the infirmary?"

"We ran into security. Cortez insisted we couldn't trust them. She took off and jumped into an elevator. That's the last I saw of her. It was chaos in the lobby. I evacuated with the rest. I hoped she'd gotten out, too."

"I don't suppose you know what time it was?"

Tanaka shook her head. "No, but I can tell you that what went down in the theater was already over. I ran past the doors. They were open and no one was inside."

Sebastian worked through it for a minute, trying to piece together a coherent picture. It didn't add up. "So what was Ruth doing between the time she left you and the time she came down to the waiting room?"

Tanaka shrugged. "Dunno. You think it matters?"

"It might," Sebastian muttered. "I spent about half an hour hunting around for you both. I finally headed back down to the train." The memory brought a fresh wave of anguish. "One minute. If I'd been there one minute earlier, I could have stopped him from killing her."

"At least you got Beach."

Hardin didn't answer. His head was pounding again.

"Don't blame yourself, sir," Tanaka said firmly. "We'll

catch Merriweather. I still can't believe Cortez helped him get away. Why would she do that?"

Sebastian couldn't bring himself to tell her the rest. That Ruth had accused Ava Carnarvon of murdering her own grandmother. He wasn't naive — he understood there was a lot of money involved — but he'd known Ava since they were teenagers. He couldn't believe it of her. And why on earth would she have chosen that particular moment?

Lee was the one with the obvious motive. He'd been covered in Calindra's blood.

Yet Sebastian knew he wouldn't be able to let it go. He had a reputation for being relentless. Sometimes he forgot to eat or sleep, if he was trying to figure something out. It's why Lee Merriweather was the only fugitive who'd ever gotten away.

And he just couldn't swallow Ava's sudden change of heart. She'd hated Merriweather even before the murder. It was totally out of character for her to give him a free pass. And when she'd seen Abel Beach in handcuffs ... . Well, for an instant, it hadn't simply been anger on her face. Sebastian could have sworn he saw a flash of fear. Like the professor knew something Ava wanted to keep quiet.

I'm not wrong, he thought again, though it was less certain now. But I can't move on until I sort this out.

He sipped his coffee, eyeing Tanaka over the rim. He'd handpicked her for the job — not just because she was a damned fine marshal, but because they'd worked together many times before. If it came down it, he thought she'd be loyal to him before Ava.

If it came down to it.

Sebastian thought again of Ruth's telephone lying off the cradle — as if she'd tried to call for help before she jumped.

"Remember how I told you something was going on?" he said quietly. "But I wasn't sure what?"

Tanaka's gaze was steady. "I remember, sir."

"Well, I still feel that way. There's pieces of this that don't make sense."

He watched her face. Tanaka was sharp. She knew what he was saying. And she knew it bordered on treason. To his relief, she only nodded.

"I agree, sir," she said evenly. "Like I said, Cortez was wound up. But she might have had a good reason to be."

"Keep an eye on Beach," Sebastian said. "Don't leave him alone with any of the other marshals. When you need to rest, come get me."

"Yes, sir."

"And keep all this to yourself, all right?"

Her eyes flicked over his shoulder. "Ma'am."

Sebastian turned. Ava stood in the door to the galley. Her skin looked bone-white against the dull black crêpe of her mourning dress. "Is there more coffee?"

Tanaka poured a cup and handed it to Ava.

"Thank you." She took a sip and smiled at Sebastian. "So, what were you two talking about?"

27

Snow gusted in powdery drifts against the platform as the train pulled into the station.

"Ruby Creek!" the conductor called out the window. "Next stop, Little Pine!"

It was near the end of the line and the train was mostly empty. A figure emerged at the top of the metal steps, swathed in a long black coat and muffler. It hunched against the frigid wind, half supporting a second figure that moved with a limp. The storm had begun the night before, burying the town in a chill white shroud. It was only October, but winter in the Northern Territory arrived early and stayed late.

Twilight painted the snowdrifts in deepening shades of purple, but cheerful lanterns shone in the windows along the main street. The pair trudged along, finally stopping at a three-story brick building with a sign that said *Hotel Xavier*. The first floor saloon was packed despite the fact that it was only marginally warmer inside than out. Two dozen men in heavy coats crowded around the tables playing cards. They all looked over, the hum of conversation ceasing abruptly, as the newcomers entered in a swirl of snow.

"Howdy, boys!" a booming voice declared. "Grand weather out there."

The hostile mood eased as the men saw a clerical collar on the older man, who was large and bearded. The reverend's companion, twenty years younger and blonde, had a thin, wasted face as if he'd suffered a long illness. He leaned heavily on a cane. But there was something in his flat green gaze that made them bury their faces in the cards again.

The Reverend Josephiah Jolly brushed snow from his collar and smiled at the barkeep.

"I'm looking for the manager of this fine establishment," he said.

The barkeep wiped a greasy glass with an even greasier rag. "That's me."

"I'll take a room for me and my son," Jolly said.

"We're full up," the manager said apologetically.

"How can that be?" Jolly frowned. "Ruby Creek ain't exactly a hotspot."

"Why, everyone's come to see the hanging tomorrow. Some folks are staying overnight on account of the weather."

The reverend glanced at his companion. "Who's meeting his Maker?" he asked.

The manager dropped his voice. "Winslow Cheever. And good riddance, I say." He looked the reverend up and down. "Ain't you here for it like the rest of them?"

The reverend nodded thoughtfully. "Sure I am. Just wanted to be certain I got the right town."

"Well, I'm afraid there's nothing for you 'cept the stable. You'll find it's the same everywhere."

Jolly leaned forward. He whispered something and the manager's eyes went blank for a moment. He swallowed hard.

"You know, now that I think of it, there might be one room left," he said. "Follow me."

"Much obliged, sir," Jolly said serenely.

He led them up the stairs to a small room on the third

floor. It had two lumpy mattresses, wall hooks to hang clothes, and a porcelain basin and washstand. Someone else's belongings were strewn around the room. The manager hastily gathered them up.

"Privy's out back," he said. "How long you staying?"

"Depends," Jolly said. "I'll let you know."

"What's your names?" he asked. "For the register."

Jolly told him. The manager withdrew. Jolly eased his companion down on one of the beds.

"How's them stitches, son?" Jolly asked.

Mr. Cage eased his shirt up. A jagged red line, sloppily sewn up with black thread, crossed his abdomen. "Holding," he said. "Hurts, though."

"You shall be avenged," Jolly said solemnly. "Legion told me so."

"I want that girl." Cage's face darkened. It was the first expression he'd shown since they entered the hotel.

"And you'll have her," Jolly promised. "As soon as we finish the task Legion set us."

He reached into his coat pocket and took out a folded piece of paper. The reverend ran a finger down the list of names and chuckled.

"Well, now, that's what I call divine timing. You just take it easy, son," he said. "I'll bring up supper in a while."

Mr. Cage stared at him for a moment, then lay back and stared at the ceiling.

Jolly hung his duster coat on the hook and went back down to the saloon, where he stood by the wood stove, rubbing his hands together. This time the men barely glanced at him. As Jolly had expected, the talk was all about Winslow Cheever.

"I heard the Prince of Hangmen himself is coming. And he's real particular about it. The rope's got to be an inch-and-a-half thick, soaked and air-dried before being tallowed or soaped to soften it up."

"What difference does it make anyhow?"

"All the difference in the world if you want a clean drop."

"Remember Dutch Charley? The noose slipped and it took him eleven minutes to go."

"That's why you need the finest hemp. With a big old knot, so the neck breaks. Otherwise you'll be kickin' your heels for a long time."

"I hope the snow stops long enough to see it proper."

"Maybe his head'll come straight off, like Black Jack Ketchum. I saw that one myself—"

"Hobble yer lip, Cal McKendry. You never did."

"Did too! I was just a boy, but I remember it well. They sold souvenirs."

The reverend listened with half an ear. At last, he turned to the fellows at the nearest table. "So what'd Cheever do?" he asked mildly.

The men chuckled. "What *didn't* he do?" one said with a wink at his companions.

"Rape?" Jolly persisted. "Murder?"

"Just name a deadly sin and Winnie's guilty of it, reverend. But what they got him for is killing a deputy who tried to arrest him for stealing a horse. What do you want with Winnie Cheever?"

The reverend scratched his beard. "Well, I've been called out to give him last rites. A chance to repent his sins."

This elicited roars of laughter.

"Winnie knows he's going straight to Hell," one said. "He'll spit in your eye as soon as ask forgiveness."

"Where do they have him now?"

"Up in the jailhouse."

"Which way's that?" Jolly asked.

"Head to the right, end of the street, you can't miss it."

The reverend fetched his coat. Mr. Cage was sleeping like a babe, one hand curled around the hilt of a hunting knife at his belt. Jolly paused for a moment, regarding the yellow-haired man with fondness. Then he raised his collar and headed out into the snowy darkness.

The jail was a small wooden building next to the courthouse. It was only one room, drafty despite the lack of windows, with a barred cell taking up the rear. Three marshals huddled around the wood stove.

"Evening, gentlemen," Jolly said with a polite smile. "I imagine you've been expecting me."

The marshals swapped glances. They were all big men and hard-looking. One of them stood, his hand falling to the Colt at his hip. He had a long mustache and light blue eyes that regarded the reverend warily. "Who are you?"

"Name's Reverend Jolly. I'm here to see if your prisoner wants to confess his sins before the Lord."

The marshal snorted, his hand relaxing. "Good luck."

He walked to the cell and banged a stick on the bars. Winslow Cheever was lying on a hard bench with his back turned. At the noise, he rolled over, scowling.

"Can't a condemned man sleep in peace?" he demanded.

"Preacher's here to see you."

Jolly stepped into the light of a lantern burning on a table next to the cell. Cheever looked him over with disdain. "Ain't interested."

The reverend examined the prisoner with a critical eye. He had a large, bulbous nose and small, devious eyes. He didn't look like much, but looks could be deceiving. Jolly leaned forward, his face intent. "You sure about that, Mr. Cheever?"

Winnie sat up. He picked a speck from the blanket and flicked it away. "Goddamn louse," he muttered.

"Can you let me in there?" Jolly asked the marshal.

"He's violent," the marshal warned. "And he don't strike me as 'specially religious. Maybe it's better if you talk from out here."

"I have faith," the reverend said serenely. "The Lord will watch over me."

The marshal hesitated.

"It's every condemned man's right to give a confession." The reverend spread his hands. "Surely you won't deny him that."

The marshal shrugged. He gestured to the two others, who stood in readiness should Cheever try anything. Then he took out a ring of iron keys and unlocked the cell.

"You behave," he said to Winnie, slapping the stick into one calloused palm. "Unless you want to be carried up to that gallows with two broken legs."

Cheever spit on the ground but said nothing, watching with beady eyes as the reverend stepped inside the cell and the marshal locked it behind him. The lawman returned to his companions at the wood stove, but they all kept a sharp eye on their prisoner.

"You got any dip?" Winnie asked, baring tobacco-stained teeth.

"I'm afraid not," the reverend said in a soft voice. "But I do have a proposition for you."

"What's that?" He sucked his lower lip. "Bare my soul and fly up to heaven with the angels? Think I'd prefer to roast with the other sinners, you damned vulture."

The reverend folded his hands. He glanced at the bench. "May I?"

Winnie sighed. "Just get it out of your system. My beauty sleep's ruined anyhow."

The reverend sat down, ignoring the lice that wriggled across Cheever's blanket. "How'd you like to do God's work?"

Winnie laughed. "No thanks, preacher."

The reverend simply stared at him until Winnie's mirth subsided.

"You don't know what God's work is yet," Jolly said.

Cheever spread his skinny arms. "Well, go ahead. Enlighten me."

Jolly leaned forward and whispered in his ear. Winnie's eyes narrowed. He laughed, but there was a mean edge to it. His fists balled.

"I think you're putting me on. You think it's funny to play tricks on a condemned man?"

"It's not a trick, Mr. Cheever."

He licked his lips. "Then get me out of here right now."

"All in proper time. I want your word you'll carry your end first."

"Who sent you here?"

"I told you. Legion sent me."

"What if I said you're crazy?"

"Then I'll leave and you'll never see me again. But I'll see you. I'll be in the crowd watching when they walk you out tomorrow morning. Better hope they tie that noose right. Else it can take a real long time to die." Jolly looked at him placidly. "I was there when they strung up Black Jack Ketchum. Know what happened? The rope was a bit too long, and Jack was a bit too fat, and he clean lost his head."

Cheever's mouth worked, but no sound came out. Jolly saw fear in his eyes. That was good.

"Of course, Jack had it easy compared to some others." He plucked a louse from his beard and pinched it between two ragged nails. "I believe the longest a man ever dangled before the doctor pronounced him was twenty-two minutes. It would have been a mercy to cut him down and shoot him like a rabid dog, but that's not how official hangings work. You'll be conscious for most of it. Hearing the screams and cheers of the crowd while your tongue swells up and—"

"That's enough!" Winnie's hands were trembling now. "I'm coming 'round."

Jolly glanced over at the marshals. They were talking

among themselves, though the one with blue eyes glanced over occasionally.

"Like I said, you're just the first. I'm gathering up a posse. It'll be elite, mind you."

Winnie frowned. "What's that mean?"

Jolly smiled. "Only the worst of the worst."

Cheever's chest puffed out a little. "Well, I like the sound of that, reverend."

"I bet you do. You'll be a rich man by the time we're done. Practically a king." He took a Bible from his pocket and opened it to a well-worn page. "The sun shall be turned to darkness, and the moon to blood." He winked. "You think you're famous now, Mr. Cheever, just wait."

Winnie eyed him doubtfully. "I'd still prefer to get this rodeo rolling right now. Why wait?"

Jolly chuckled. "Because the good people of Ruby Creek came all this way for a spectacle and I for one ain't going to deprive them of it. That just wouldn't be fair play." He closed the Bible and returned it to his pocket. "Now, those marshals will be wondering what we've been talking about all this time. You need to pretend you just found God."

Winnie frowned. "All due respect, reverend, they ain't gonna believe it." Yellow teeth flashed. "Besides which, I got a reputation to uphold."

Jolly nodded slowly. "You may have a point there, Mr. Cheever. Let's play it your way." He stood and raised his voice. "Last chance to repent, son. Hellfire's waiting."

Winnie grinned, then tightened his face into a scowl. "You can go rot, you pig-bellied scoundrel! Take yer Good Book and shove it where the sun don't shine!" He turned his back and curled onto the bench.

"Sorry about that, reverend," the marshal said, unlocking the cell door. "Only thing Winnie's fit for is the end of a rope."

"Oh, I've heard worse," Jolly replied. "Comes with the

vocation. Mayhaps he'll be singing a different tune when they tighten the noose."

"You attending?"

"I wouldn't miss it." He smiled. "See you in the morning, gentlemen."

When the reverend got back to the Hotel Xavier, he went straight up to his room and sat at the window, watching the snow fall.

Legion had not come to him since he gave Jolly the list of names and sent him north, but the reverend was untroubled. The angel would return in due time and Jolly would have progress to report.

Winnie Cheever didn't know it yet, but he was merely a tool. A tool in the hand of the Lord to cut the scales from the eyes of the unbelievers. Tools came in all shapes and sizes, but sometimes what you needed was a razor-sharp blade. Mr. Cage understood.

For years, Jolly had preached the Word, but only a few listened. Time was growing short. Clearly, more extreme measures were required. Legion had explained everything, showing him visions of the battle to come. Humanity must unite behind a single purpose. Behind their Messiah. And the quickest way to make people listen was to show them what happened when they didn't.

When Legion first found him in New Jerusalem, his life had been unremarkable. Oh, he had an obedient little flock, but Josephiah Jolly had always known he was meant for greater things. Now he understood his destiny. It took a fierce will to accept what needed to be done. Mr. Cage relished the work — perhaps a bit more than he should have, Jolly allowed — but who could fault a man for his devotion?

"All for the greater good," he murmured. "Put on the whole armor of God, that you may be able to stand against the schemes of the devil."

Josephiah Jolly grew up on stories of the old days, before

the grims were supposedly tamed. He knew their true nature. It was only a matter of time before they all turned. At first he'd balked at using the phantoms himself, but he'd come to accept the necessity. How could he turn people against them without showing them what phantoms were capable of? Besides which, the ones that Legion sent him were all baptized to the cause. They knew their place.

Even so, Jolly found it distasteful. He looked forward to working with disciples of flesh and blood. The names on the list might not be his first choice, but a tool was a tool. And they had the skills he was looking for. Not just the skills, but the stomach to do it right. The perfect thing would be a dozen Mr. Cages, but such men were rare.

Which, Jolly reflected, might not be a terrible thing.

As much as the reverend loved his adopted son, in his heart of hearts, he was a wee bit afraid of him.

New Jerusalem, for example.

He sighed. That was a real shame. He'd taken no great pleasure from how it all turned out. They'd been his flock, after all. But Legion said it was all part of the big picture, of which Jolly could only see a tiny fragment, and who was he to question the will of the Lord?

"Mysterious ways," Jolly whispered to himself, as the snow outside deepened. "Yes, indeed."

Mr. Cage had come to him like a gift, not long before he met Legion. He'd arrived on the train with no money or possessions. When he showed up at the church, Jolly had taken him for a deaf mute. Mayhaps a runaway from one of the struggling farms. But the reverend believed in Christian charity and Mr. Cage had proven to be a hard, uncomplaining worker. The day he did speak, to ask for a second helping of grits, Jolly was so startled he dropped the pot.

Turned out Mr. Cage just wasn't much for words, which was fine since the reverend liked to talk and Cage didn't seem to mind listening. When a few cats went missing and he discovered the remains hidden in the barn, Jolly realized the man had peculiar tastes, but by then he'd grown fond of him. And he had an inkling that he might have need of such a man in the future.

Boy, was he right.

"You shall be avenged, my son," he said again, savoring the sound of the words.

When they were done up north, he had big plans for Lucky Boy. Ruth Cortez had no idea who she'd messed with, but she surely would.

When the dawn broke, he laid a hand on Mr. Cage's shoulder. The yellow-haired man's eyes shot open. He sat up with a groan. The bandage around his stomach was looking a bit putrid, but Jolly felt confident he'd heal as the Lord intended. Besides which, the town doctor was probably already at the jailhouse.

"How about a nice hot breakfast?" Jolly said. "We got an exciting day ahead."

A LARGE CROWD had gathered around the gallows, which sat on a sturdy platform fifteen feet above the ground in an open yard behind the courthouse. A makeshift fence had been erected to hold people back, but the crowd surged against it as two dozen beleaguered marshals snapped at them to keep order.

Some of the more enterprising townspeople were selling cups of hot cider and other refreshments. Men sipped from flasks, stamping their feet. The women clustered together in dark bonnets and cloaks dusted white. Off to the side, a group of children in bright woolen scarves, their cheeks pink from the cold, were having a spirited snowball fight. Someone had brought a fiddle and the strains of *Sweet Holly from Hatchet* drifted above the children's screaming and general hubbub.

The yard was churned to slush by the time the Reverend Jolly arrived, Mr. Cage limping with the cane at his side.

"Well," he said, looking around. "This is quite a festive occasion, ain't it, Mr. Cage?"

Cage failed to acknowledge the remark, but the reverend was accustomed to his companion's reticence. Jolly purchased a hot bun, declining a whispered offer from a shifty-looking waif to buy Cheever's toenail clippings for two pennies. He gave the bun to Cage, who stuffed it into his mouth whole. Then he set off for the gallows, where the Prince of Hangmen stood waiting for his charge to appear.

The Prince's real name was George Murkins. He was an unassuming man, small and grey, with a thin, mournful face and wispy beard. He always wore black and rarely smiled, as befit his profession, which he took very seriously, hence the moniker. From what the reverend had gathered in the saloon the evening previous, it was deemed an honor to have Murkins attend one's hanging. His services were in high demand and he was known as a perfectionist.

Murkins' specialty was overseeing multiple hangings at the same time, which drew the largest crowds, but Winslow Cheever was apparently notorious enough to merit his fee.

Jolly pushed through a knot of reporters and approached the marshals standing guard near the base of the platform.

"How's my prisoner faring this fine morning?" he asked in a jovial tone.

They exchanged glances. "You the Reverend Jolly?"

"None other."

"I heard Winnie didn't want last rites."

"Well, he might change his mind when that dark rider comes for him. Plenty of 'em do."

"Hang on, reverend."

Jolly waited while the marshal went to confer with his superiors. The reporters seized this opportunity to elbow their way over, notepads in hand.

"How do you spell your name, sir?"

"Just like it sounds." Jolly smiled. "Will I be in the papers?"

"If you give me a good quote," the reporter quipped.

"Okay, here's one." Jolly leaned in. "Cheever gave me a full confession from his cell. He admitted to dark dealings with phantoms. Said they incited him to wickedness and abetted him in his crimes."

This statement was met with stares of frank disbelief. Jolly's smile curdled.

"Cheever, a linguist?" The reporter chortled. "The man can't spell his own name."

"You doubt me, son?" Jolly demanded.

"Aw, reverend." The reporter stifled his grin. "I think he was having you on."

Jolly stabbed a finger at the notepad. "You print what I said. Every word. I—"

He turned as the marshal walked over. "Go on up," he said, frowning at the reporters. "We won't have it said Winnie was denied last rites. Hear that, boys?"

The reporters grinned. "Come on, let us inside the fence. How are we supposed to write a proper account with all this rabble pushing and shoving?"

The marshal ignored their pleas, leading Jolly through a gap as the reporters grumbled behind him.

"No respect for the press."

"Wish I'd brought a box to stand on."

"Hey, they selling whiskey around here? I'm out and my toes went numb two hours ago . . . ."

By the time Jolly ascended the platform, Murkins had been joined by the town doctor, a plump man in spectacles who looked decidedly nervous. Sweat beaded his brow despite the cold and one foot jittered against the wooden planks. He clutched a stethoscope in his hand. A black doctor's bag sat at his shoes, which looked freshly polished.

"First time at a hanging, doc?" Jolly asked.

The doctor nodded. "I hope it goes smoothly." He swallowed. "I've heard stories."

Jolly nodded in commiseration, glancing at Murkins. "I'm sure the condemned man's in good hands."

The Prince of Hangmen stared straight ahead over the heads of the crowd, exuding an aura of infinite patience. But excitement was building, all eyes now fixed on the platform. Even the children had abandoned their snowball fight, the littlest ones perched on their fathers' shoulders for a better view.

Finally, six marshals and the sheriff of Ruby Creek escorted Winslow Cheever from the jailhouse. The crowd fell silent. He sneered and swaggered up the steps. The rope hung from a twelve-by-twelve-inch crossbeam. Murkins dropped the noose over his head, placing the knot precisely at the left side of his neck.

"Any last words?" the sheriff said. "You have the right to address the crowd if you choose."

Winnie composed himself. "Yes, sir. I do."

"Go on, then." The sheriff held up his hands and the crowd, which had started to whisper and point, fell silent again.

"I know I've done wrong," Winnie said in a loud, halting voice. "I . . . I was blind. But I've seen the light."

The Reverend Jolly gave him an encouraging nod. "You're doing well, son," he said in a soft voice. "Keep going. Remember what we talked about."

Cheever gulped. "You all will, too. For behold, I have the power to tread on snakes and scorpions!"

The sheriff shot a puzzled look at the doctor. "What's he talking about?"

The doctor shrugged distractedly. His spectacles had fogged up and he was juggling the stethoscope while trying to wipe the lenses with a sleeve.

"There's a holy war coming," Winnie said, his voice gaining strength. "The end of days!"

A flashbulb popped. The reporters in the front started to laugh.

"Well," one quipped, "it's surely the end of *your* days, Winnie!"

Cheever scowled. "You'll see," he spat. "Choose your side wisely. That's all I got to say." He nodded jerkily at Murkins. "Get on with it."

Jolly took out his Bible and intoned a prayer for the condemned man's soul. Snow fell thickly, coating the gallows in a blanket of white. Winnie was hooded for the final drop through the trapdoor. The watchers drew a collective breath as Murkins pulled the wooden lever.

The trapdoor sprang open, but Winnie didn't fall through. He stood on thin air, or so it seemed to the crowd.

There was a moment of confusion. Murkins yanked the lever again, although the trapdoor already stood wide. Then the doctor gave a high-pitched, womanly scream.

The platform was alive with snakes. Timber rattlers, to be precise. The largest of the pit vipers, each measured five and a half feet long with a sinuous diamond pattern down the back. They seemed groggy and surprised to find themselves on the gallows in broad daylight. The rattlers coiled into defensive postures. Then one of the marshals racked his shotgun and started firing. That riled the snakes. One bit the sheriff, who threw himself from the platform. It was high off the ground and he landed badly, his ankle snapping. Shotguns boomed as the marshals scrambled down the scaffold's thirteen steps.

The crowd broke and ran. Jolly pressed his palms together in a quick prayer. Vipers slithered at his feet, but they ignored him. The Prince of Hangmen wasn't so lucky. He knelt amid a rippling mass of snakes. Again and again they struck.

"They will pick up serpents with their hands," Jolly said,

seizing one of the snakes. "And these signs will accompany those who believe. In my name they will cast out demons."

The forked tongue flicked. Hostile reptilian eyes stared into his own. The rattle blurred a warning. The snake struck — and its fangs hit an invisible wall. Jolly smiled and loosed the snake, which seemed a bit stunned at the turn of events. It slithered away posthaste.

"Help!" came a muffled cry from beneath the black cloth. "Get this damned thing off!"

Jolly yanked off the hood. Cheever's face was red. The outlaw's eyes bulged when he saw the snakes. His hands were still bound behind his back, but he started kicking his legs in a macabre imitation of the gallows dance.

The reverend held out a hand. A shotgun flew up from where it had fallen on the ground. The stock slapped into his palm. He checked to make sure there was a shell in the chamber and took aim. Not at the fleeing marshals, but at the reporter who'd mocked Cheever's last words.

Mocked the gospel.

The man had been bowled over in the initial stampede. He sat up and raised his hands when he saw Jolly pointing a shotgun at him.

"Wait! Just hang on—"

The reporter's blood sprayed Mr. Cage, who leaned on his cane at the foot of the scaffold. Cage didn't even glance at the dying newsman. Scorpions and centipedes skittered around his boots, but he paid them no mind, either. He was more interested in watching the marshals, who lay twitching and panting shallowly. The venom of timber rattlers usually took a few hours to kick in, but the lawmen had been bit a dozen times each. Maybe more. Under their coats, the skin would be swelling and blackening like overripe fruit. Mr. Cage thought he'd like to see that.

His reverie was interrupted. "Come here, son," Jolly called.

Mr. Cage limped up the steps. Winslow Cheever still had the huge noose with its seven windings tight around his neck. He shivered as he looked at the rattlers crawling over the hangman's corpse.

"I don't care for snakes," Winnie said faintly.

"They won't hurt you 'less I say so," the reverend replied. "You're my apostle now. Just like Mr. Cage."

Cheever gave the big blonde man a discreet once-over. He looked rough, and not just because of the cane. Winnie resolved not to turn his back on Cage if he could help it.

"Might I get the rope off?" he asked hopefully.

"You might." The reverend's eyes glittered. "You a true believer now, Mr. Cheever?"

"I sure am," he responded quickly. "I'm your man."

"You mean the Lord's man."

Winnie bobbed his head. "Sure, that's what I meant."

"Free him, Mr. Cage."

Cheever tried not to flinch as the big man pulled a hunting knife. He cut through the heavy slipknot, then did the same with the ropes binding Winnie's hands. As soon as he was loose, Winnie stepped away from the space above the gaping trapdoor, back to the safety of the wood planks. The phantoms had kept him from falling through somehow, but he didn't like standing over fifteen feet of open air. Especially not with that noose around his neck.

When Winnie had heard the door bang down . . . . Well, despite the reverend's promises, he'd thought it was the end.

"What now?" he asked, rubbing his wrists. The snakes were gone, presumably in search of a warm, dry place to bed down, but scorpions and other stinging things with too many legs still formed a wriggling carpet beneath the gallows. They swarmed over the reporter in a solid mass. Winnie dearly hoped they'd go away before Jolly made him come down.

"Now we pull together the rest of our posse," the reverend

said. "That's where I'll need your help. You're gonna help me find them."

"I can do that," Winnie said. He spat over the edge of the platform. "Damned lawmen got what was coming to 'em." Small, mean eyes narrowed. "What about the rest? I say we burn this town like Hazardville."

Jolly shook his head. "Blood will be shed, brother, but we got other priorities at the moment." He flung his arms wide, snow swirling around him. "Pray with me, boys!"

Winnie immediately bowed his head, not daring to wait to see if Cage did the same. The yellow-haired man still hadn't uttered a single syllable. Maybe he was slow-witted.

"God bless the babies and the gentle little lambs," the reverend said, eyes squeezed shut and full-moon face turned to heaven. "God bless the wolves, too, that eat the lambs. Wolves need sustenance, don't they, Mr. Cheever?"

"Uh, amen," said Winnie. He hadn't prayed since his mama dragged him to church by the ear at the age of six. It all sounded a little . . . *irregular* . . . but who was he to judge?

"For lo," the reverend declaimed, "we walk amid the demonic shadows, but we fear not . . . ."

The sermon went on until Winnie couldn't feel his feet anymore. Jolly finally shut the Bible with a thump. His black beard was rimed with frost.

"Let's go, boys," he said. "That heavenly trumpet is sounding! Time to get in apple pie order and round up the rest of the apostles."

"Who's on that list again?" Winnie asked.

The reverend fished out a slip of paper. "Billy Easter. Moritz Le Blanc—"

"The Frog," Winnie interrupted. "I mean to say, that's what they call him. Not to his face though."

The reverend nodded thoughtfully and returned to the list. "Orville Royal Loving. His brother, Kirby Knox—"

"Half brother. And don't never call him Orville. He'll cut your ears off. Just stick with Royal."

The reverend smiled. "You see, Mr. Cheever, you're proving useful already. Juan Garcia Morales—"

"The Ghost." Winnie looked a bit shaken. "This is quite an infamous outfit you're pulling together, reverend."

"Thank you, son. Chalkey White." Jolly frowned at the name. "That for real?"

"Apparently so. His papa had a sense of humor." Winnie paused. "By all accounts, Chalkey himself does not. Who else?"

"Elmira Poole." Jolly folded the list and returned it to his pocket.

Cheever blinked. "The Black Widow?"

"Such colorful monikers. God bless the Northern Territory!" Jolly chuckled. "I guess she killed her husband?"

"Only about seven of 'em in a row. I thought they hanged her in Tip Top."

"She must have slipped the noose." The reverend winked. "It does happen, Mr. Cheever."

Shadows shrouded the three men as they trudged through the snow to the stable next to the jailhouse, where they saddled up the dead marshals' horses.

Hidden in the ether, another trio laughed and laughed at the joke they'd just played.

The big boy was right. Breaking the rules was *much* more fun.

AFTERWORD

Join Kat's newsletter at www.katrossbooks.com so you don't miss the third and final book, DEVIL OF THE NORTH. You'll also get exclusive discounts on ebooks and audiobooks, and occasional pictures of cats.

ACKNOWLEDGMENTS

I owe a special debt to the mathematician Edwin Abbott, whose book *Flatland* blew my mind as a kid and percolated over the years into the story you just read.

In the Department of Bizarre Coincidences, I also discovered (after naming my characters and coming up with the phantoms' origin) that an actress named Lee Meriweather had her debut in the 1959 sci-fi movie *4D Man*, about a scientist who discovers a formula that lets him pass through solid matter. Whaaat?

Huge thanks as always to Laura Pilli for her encouragement and suggestions, and to the wonderful team at Acorn Publishing.

ABOUT THE AUTHOR

Kat Ross worked as a journalist at the United Nations for ten years before happily falling back into what she likes best: making stuff up. She's the author of the Lingua Magika trilogy, the Fourth Element and Fourth Talisman historical fantasies, the Gaslamp Gothic mysteries, and the dystopian thriller *Some Fine Day*. She loves myths, monsters and doomsday scenarios.

www.katrossbooks.com
kat@katrossbooks.com

f facebook.com/KatRossAuthor

📷 instagram.com/katrossauthor

📌 pinterest.com/katrossauthor

ALSO BY KAT ROSS

The Fourth Element Trilogy

The Fourth Talisman Series

The Fourth Empire Series

Nightmarked Series

Lord of Everfell Series

Lingua Magika Trilogy

Gaslamp Gothic Collection

Some Fine Day (dystopian YA standalone)